Dangerous Companions

By Peter Richards

Dangerous Companions
is for Deborah for her endless listening

Copyright © 2024 by Peter Richards
All rights reserved.

No portion of this book may be reproduced in any form without written permission from the publisher or author, except as permitted by U.S. copyright law.

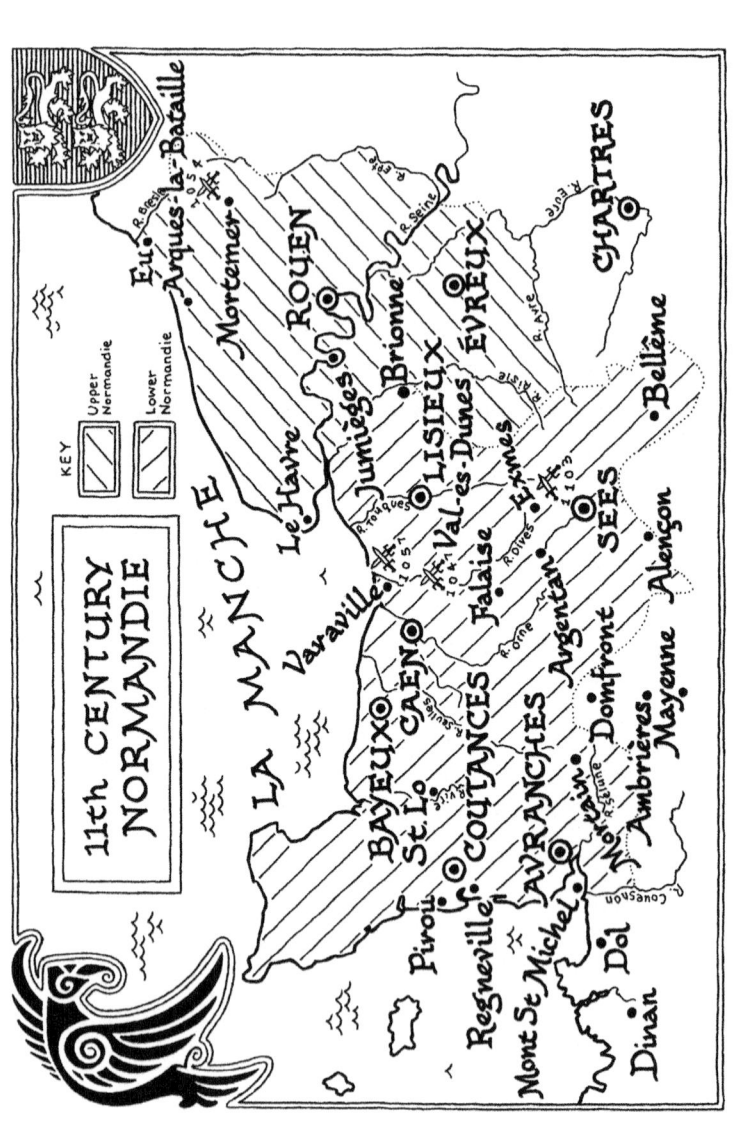

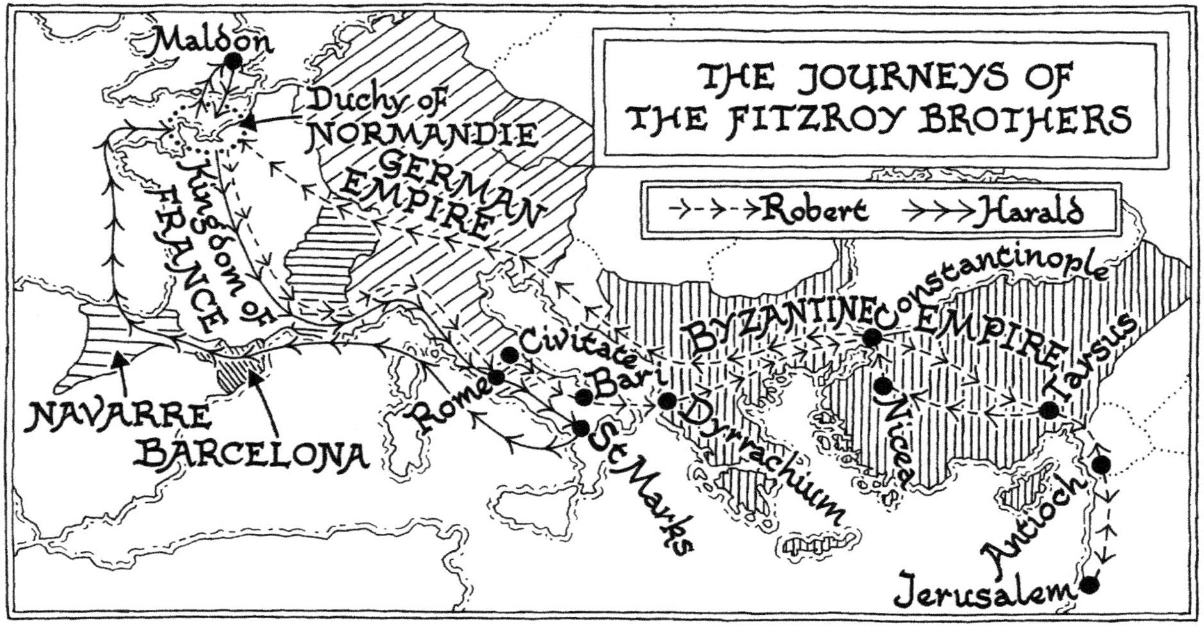
THE JOURNEYS OF
THE FITZROY BROTHERS
Robert
Harald
Maldon
Duchy of
NORMANDIE
GERMAN
EMPIRE
Kingdom of
FRANCE
NAVARRE
BARCELONA
Rome
Civitate
Bari
St Marks
Dyrrachium
BYZANTINE
Constantinople
EMPIRE
Nicea
Tarsus
Antioch
Jerusalem

Prologue

In the year 1002 Jarl Bjorn Halfdanson fled the shores of Saxon England with the remnants of his clan and his only thoughts were of their survival. He had not the slightest inclination to plant roots in medieval France and even less to develop a powerful dynasty there. Eleventh-century Normandie was a turbulent place where the Jarl and his Norse settlers thrived and assimilated with the indigenous Franks and other local people. Quickly establishing a reputation as an uncompromising warlord, Halfdanson pledged his allegiance to the Duke of Normandie. He went on to protect the Duchy's borders against invaders and earned his liege-lord's trust and reward.

As the years passed, his people thrived under his leadership and his family grew strong. The Jarl's fame as a great warrior increased as did his influence among the barons and counts of the Duchy. When Duke Robert died returning home from pilgrimage to the Holy Land, his son William was entrusted to the Jarl's care and protection. The eight-year-old Duke was taken into the sanctuary of Halfdanson's fiefdom and his grandsons, Harald and Robert Fitzroy, became the boy's companions and protectors. The three 'pages' grew to adulthood and became embroiled in the political intrigue of Normandie as William's enemies plotted his downfall. Jarl Bjorn defeated every adversary who opposed the young Duke until the great Norse warrior finally succumbed to an enemy spear as he defended his charge.

Duke William came of age and, once knighted by the King of France, raised an army and wrought bloody vengeance on all those who stood against him. With Harald and Robert at his side, he dispensed swift justice to those who opposed him until he exerted complete authority over Normandie and its belligerent warlords. The Fitzroy brothers were rewarded for their unflinching loyalty, but not in equal measure and their jealous and divisive liege-lord drove a wedge between them. Harald's childhood sweetheart, Eleanor was given to his brother Robert in marriage, together with her father's lands and fortune. During the bitter quarrel that followed, Harald's recklessness prevailed and he was forced to travel south to the Kingdom in the Sun as a fugitive and an outlaw from the Duchy. Robert was promoted to the Duke's chancellor while his brother eked out a harsh life as a soldier of fortune in the baron wilderness of Apulia in southern Italy.

Years passed and the stars of both brothers rose in their ascendency. The Norman diaspora in the south gathered beneath Harald's banners while in the north his brother became a consummate statesman and general. Normandie and the Duke were imperiled by the devious French King Henri who wanted the Duchy for himself. They were also threatened by both the censorship of the Pope and the hemorrhage of its best fighting men leaving to join the Norman adventure in Italy. The Kingdom in the Sun was in existential danger too and in 1053 its enemies mustered beneath the Papal standard, intent on driving Harald and his Norman exiles into oblivion. Storm clouds gathered above both of the brothers' fiefdoms as a host of enemies assembled their forces and prepared to challenge them.

Table of Contents

Chapter 1: The Reckoning of Civitate	1
Chapter 2: The Papal Camp	10
Chapter 3: The Fate Of The Pontiff	20
Chapter 4: A New Prince	28
Chapter 5: Changing Seasons	37
Chapter 6: From Demons To Angels	43
Chapter 7: The Widowed General	51
Chapter 8: Mortain, 1057	55
Chapter 9: The Duchy Prays For Deliverance	64
Chapter 10: The Journey South	71
Chapter 11: The Reunion On The Cliffs	80
Chapter 12: The Decision	94
Chapter 13: Caen, Spring 1056, Normandie Awaits	104
Chapter 14: The Prodigal's Return	117
Chapter 15: The King's Nemesis	124
Chapter 16: The Aftermath	131
Chapter 17: The Return To Mortain	142
Chapter 18: The Lioness Of Mortain	155
Chapter 19: A New Home	167
Chapter 20: The Return Of William's Right Hand	177
Chapter 21: The Duchy Comes Of Age	185
Chapter 22: The Voyage Of Tears	193
Chapter 23: The Court of King Edward	207
Chapter 24: Caen, 1058	216
Chapter 25: The Road To Jerusalem	223

Chapter 26: The Fading Lioness, Mortain 1058	238
Chapter 27: Return From The Shadows	251
Chapter 28: Guardians Of The Pilgrims Way	261
Chapter 29: Harald Returns To Duty	267
Chapter 30: The Duke Impresses, 1059	281
Chapter 31: The Count Of Mortain Journeys Home	293
Chapter 32: Defending Normandie's Border	308
Chapter 33: The Relief of Dol	316
Chapter 34: The Last Muster	322
Chapter 35: The Reiving of Brittany	335
Chapter 36: The Last Rebel	341
Chapter 37: A Gathering Storm	354
Chapter 38: The Reckoning Of The Fitzroy Brothers	369
Chapter 39: Robert's Other Reckoning	379
Chapter 40: Back From The Dead	387
Chapter 41: The Prison of Mortain	394
Chapter 42: Escape And Flight	398
Chapter 43: Evas Prayer Sets Sail	407
Glossary	413
Characters	415

Chapter 1: The Reckoning of Civitate

Harald found himself walking in a green meadow and looked down at his boots, wet with morning dew. He did not recognise the place and there were no landmarks from which to take bearings. The grasslands seemed to stretch away endlessly in each direction. As he walked, the two ravens he had seen flying overhead during the night swept down onto the ground before him. They hopped around in agitation flapping their wings and turned to him. The birds looked up, heads quizzically cocked to one side and thick black beaks wide open.

"I have no food to give you, brothers. I have not eaten for two days myself and I am on my way to join my warriors. We are to fight a great battle today against an army many times our size."

"You do not need food when you have the blood of the Wandering Warriors coursing through your veins," said one.

"You can talk?" exclaimed Harald.

"Of course we can; we are Odin's thought and memory," said the other bird.

"Then tell me, brothers who shall win the battle today?"

"Why, the warriors who fight with their heads and not just their hearts. But if you wish to live until the day's end just answer this riddle for me. What is the bloody-backed beast laying its body against yours and giving you shelter?" asked the first bird.

Harald struggled, trying to remember the answer to the ancient Norse riddle.

"Why, it is my shield, of course," he replied triumphantly.

"We have taught you well, Hari. Take care and do not let it drop. When the battle is done, we must take news of the victorious side to our master," said the second bird.

"Make sure you prevail," said the other. "We shall all be displeased if we see you in Valhalla later, for it is not yet your time to feast in the great hall."

Then the birds took to the air, flapping their enormous wings close enough to his face that he felt their feathers brush his skin. He tried to follow their progress but lost sight of them as they flew toward the sun. When he took down the hand shielding his eyes they were gone.

He felt urgent hands shaking him awake and looked up into the anxious face of his young squire Jeanotte.

"Lord, you were dreaming. It is time to rise."

Harald was dragged out of his dream like a man being pulled from the depths of the ocean and groggily got to his feet. He yawned, stretched his giant frame and ran a hand through an untidy mop of dirty, blonde hair before scratching a stubbled chin. Gathering his senses, he looked around. Thousands of men lay all about, still sleeping as the early morning mist began to dissipate in the growing light. Lines of war-horses tethered closely together nickered softly as if to remind their masters that they too had empty bellies. Pages poked around the dying embers of the campfires, throwing on the last of the wood to bring a little warmth into the early morning, although there was nothing to cook on them. Squires began to rouse their masters and prepare them for the slaughter that lay ahead.

Harald watched his troops slowly awake to a day which might see them perish on the plain of Civitate stretching out below them. They had all answered the call of their liege-lord, Humphrey, the count of Apulia and Calabria, to take their stand against the allied forces of Pope Leo who had vowed to eject every last Norman from Italy. Despised and feared in equal measure the adventurers from the north gathered beneath the Hauteville banners to prevail or perish in their resistance.

A thousand heavily armed horsemen waited patiently in their camp on the summit of a large hill. Their standards and *gonfanons* flapped around damp and lazily in the early morning breeze. Where once there had been a rolling expanse of green sward there was now only a brown carpet of sparse growth burnt by the fierce sun and further denuded by famished Norman horses. Men and animals were all hungry and tired from their exhausting efforts to get here and the odds were heavily stacked against them. Only last night, news had reached the camp that a Byzantine horde of ten thousand men was approaching from the south and the Normans would be crushed between two armies. Harald turned his gaze toward the plain at the foot of the hill where another enemy host spread out in an untidy mass of tents, field stables and campfires. He contemplated the events that had led him to this place where his destiny would be decided - for better or worse.

The Normans first arrived in southern Italy decades before and fought for whichever Byzantine prince paid the highest. Their success as soldiers of fortune were richly rewarded with gold and grants of land and they thrived through weight of arms. They were joined by more and more of their kin who settled and prospered in new Norman duchies but whose power soon began to be loathed by their neighbours. Avarice and greed caused fearful tremors throughout the region until insurrection against the new landlords fomented and spread its bitter contagion. Byzantine, Greek and Italian leaders approached the powerful Pope Leo in Rome who listened sympathetically to their plaintiff outpourings. It was not long before he recruited an army to rid the land of these oppressors. The Papal Alliance now massed on the field beneath Harald and his confederates.

"Fifteen thousand in front of us and another ten thousand marching toward our rear," Harald mumbled to himself. "Long odds, long odds."

He spat onto the ground and cursed his enemies before reaching inside his *gambeson* to touch the amulet. Thor's golden hammer had hung from his neck since boyhood, and he rubbed it reassuringly and uttered a silent prayer to the old Norse gods. His thoughts were interrupted by his squire, and he gratefully accepted a cup of weak ale. Behind Jeanotte came two younger boys who between them carried a full-length chain-mail *hauberk*, gleaming dully in the pale light of dawn.

"You have been busy, boys," said Harald inspecting their burden.

"We took sand from the riverbank and cleaned the mail, Lord. Here, your helm and shield have been cleaned too. And *Gunnlogi*, we have whetted the blade well and she is as keen as ever. If our General is to lead us onto the battlefield, we need him to shine brightly so that all his men might see him. He will reflect God's light so strongly into our enemy's eyes that they will throw down their arms in fear of him," replied Jeanotte passionately.

Harald stretched out the night's stiffness and looked into the expectant young faces. In that moment he felt a great wave of affection wash over him and smiled at the three, making to move forward, but his squire held up his hand.

"No, Sire. We cannot let you lead us to confront our enemies just yet. Not until we have shaved you and cut your hair."

Jeanotte nodded to one of the smaller boys who had miraculously procured a cup of hot water. They sat Harald down and went to work on him, gently shaving his face and the back of his head with a sharp knife. When they had finished, they stood back and considered their work. He studied their concentrated expressions, one after the other, and was transported to another time and place in his memory.

He and his brother had been waiting to attack a force of Breton soldiers on the borders of Normandie. Harald was twelve years old, and it was the first time he had been in combat. It was a moment he had trained for since he was six and he had shown himself able and willing to join the fight. The *conrois* of mounted warriors was commanded by his father, Torstein the Younger and all eyes were on him waiting for the order to charge. Harald's emotions were a mixture of excitement and trepidation as he sat astride the wilful stallion who snorted and pored angrily at the ground with iron-clad hooves. Then they charged, initially at a trot, so not to tire the horses or break formation. Each of the twenty-five horsemen rode knee-to-knee in a tight line with his comrades. At the last minute they galloped with couched iron-tipped lances pointed at the enemy in front of them. Harald remembered the noise of the thundering hooves and then the clash of steel as their lances hit home. He struck a Breton horseman in the chest, but his lance did not strike squarely, and the blow glanced away. As he passed, the man recovered and struck Harald's shield with an axe blow of such fury that the boy was removed from the saddle. Winded and fighting for breath he was overcome with fear and struggled to get to his feet. Harald fought to control the dread and tried to remember the lessons from his hours of daily training on the parade ground. He looked up to see his opponent looming above him, axe raised to strike the killing blow. The young boy closed his eyes and pissed himself uncontrollably. He squinted them open to see his assailant hurtling through the air as a Norman horseman rode his would-be killer down at the gallop. Harald got to his feet to see the remaining enemy warriors riding away in defeat and looked down to see the steam rising from his wet legs. Then his father was beside him with an arm around his shoulder.

"Well met, Hari. Now, back on your horse and join your comrades," he encouraged.

With trembling hands Harald took the proffered reins of his horse and remounted. His first battle had almost been his last, but he had come through unscathed except for a little dented pride. He had fought many more fights since then, but he never forgot that day and the fear that rendered him completely useless.

As Harald sat patiently waiting for his young charges to finish with him, he silently reaffirmed his long-held belief that 'boys did not belong on the field of battle'.

"Gentlemen, if you are finished with me, I should like to get on my way. You have done me a great service and must have worked all through the night. For that, I thank you. You will all be great knights one day, but alas not today. I do not want to find any of you on the battlefield. Jeanotte, I will see you later this morning when I return from our *parlais*. Have my arms ready when I come," he said.

He could see the boys were crestfallen at the news that they were to be denied their place in the ranks of the Norman cavalry.

"Do not look so dejected, boys," he added sympathetically, "you will have work enough behind the lines. You must always obey your General, you know."

Jeanotte went to fetch his war horse and Harald saw that the huge beast had also been groomed and brushed so that his coat shone. The three acolytes helped him don his equipment before he mounted the stallion and went in search of the Lord of Apulia.

Duke Humphrey was where Harald had left him the previous evening, overlooking the enemy positions. Standing next to his brother, the Guiscard, both men were in full battle armour, as were all the rest of the commanders. The sons of Amicus, Aureolanus, Hubert, Rainald Musca and Count Hugh were all there. Dressed resplendently in colourful surcoats and chainmail they stood beneath the banners atop the hill where they awaited their champion.

"Our company is complete then," called the Guiscard as Harald joined them. "I should like to know how a man can look so well-presented after a week's march on these dusty roads."

"If I make a good impression on his Holiness then perhaps, I will get my reward in heaven after all," replied Harald.

The company joined in with the joke and laughed.

"Now to business," said Humphrey, "if we cannot sue for peace today, we are more than ready for battle and tonight we shall be dining from the Papal baggage train. With that in mind let us see how our foemen are presenting themselves this morning."

All eyes looked across the plain below them where the huge camp was coming to life, battle lines taking shape. The Papal allies had set their camp on the banks of the River Staina and it stretched some distance beyond the walled town of Civitate. The Norman commanders were silent as they looked at the great, seething mass of the allied Italian, German and Lombardic troops below them. Duke Humphrey spoke again.

"I shall shortly be going, with Lord Harald into the enemy camp, bearing this banner of friendship given to me by the old Roman Emperor. I will attempt, one last time, to dissuade the Pope from fighting us. If I fail, we must attack them before they have a chance to do anything else. It is vital that we prevent them from linking up with the army of Constantinople who are closing in on our rear–for then all will be lost. If we do not emerge from their camp the advance must begin, but if we emerge with the banner still flying you must hold fast."

"And if the banner is not?" asked the Count of Aversa.

"Then you, Richard, will lead your dogs of war into their right flank and crush them."

The Count nodded his understanding.

"Aye, Lord and we shall turn their remnants into your vanguard in the centre. That is if there are any left standing."

"Then, my captains, for God, Apulia and Normandie we shall prevail by peace or through battle," declared Duke Humphrey.

There was no more discussion. Harald and the Duke mounted their horses and walked them down the path from the hill-top and across the plain toward the enemy camp. Their banner hung limply in the oppressive stillness as the two men made their way forward.

Chapter 2: The Papal Camp

Pope Leo IXth stood on the top of Civitate's battlements looking toward the hill less than a league away and to the two horsemen walking down its slope. His white robes were crisp and clean, for he insisted that they were changed regularly as soon as they showed the first signs of dishevelment. It was difficult for his retinue of servants to oblige him in this request, as they had been on the road with him during the many months that he had been recruiting an army. He was forty-one years old, neat and solemn. Beside him stood another German, his chancellor, the bull-like Frederick and between the two of them they had amassed a considerable army. They had been successful in recruiting men from Germany and Italy to the Papal colours, with the sole purpose of ejecting the troublesome Normans from Italy. Their army was camped before them in an enormous, tented town under the command of an assortment of captains. It had been a long recruitment campaign and the army marched almost the length of the country gathering pace and size as it went. They had answered the Pope's call from all over the empire and today the banners of many Italian states, including Rome itself, hung loosely, waiting for the wind. Pope Leo had been particularly pleased when a contingent of formidable Swabian warriors answered his call and they now proudly stretched out in a long, thin line in front of the camp. He was also expecting the imminent arrival of a Byzantine army of at least ten thousand coming from the south and the wait was making him anxious.

"Argyrus is late," said Leo. "I do not want to fight these Normans until the Greeks arrive."

"The Byzantines are not known for their time-keeping, your Eminence. It is small wonder their empire is on the wane. I agree, it would be a diligent move to wait until they get here but even without them, we have more than enough troops. Your doughty Swabians could probably carry the day on their own," said the dour Frederick.

"Possibly, Chancellor but let us try and stall these Normans a while longer. God encourages us all to be patient," said the Pope.

Their attention was taken by two approaching horsemen riding beneath the banner of the German emperor.

"It will do them no good flying that rag again," said Leo, "but let us hear what Humphrey has to say for himself this time. He has shown himself to be a decent man in the past, but he cannot control his people."

He signaled to a servant who scurried to prepare horses for him and his chancellor. They walked down the steps of the high battlements where a coterie of attendants awaited them. Before long they were both in the saddle and Pope Leo's horse was led out of the city gates and through the long lines of his allies to meet the visitors. They were joined on the way by numerous Italian Counts and Prince Rudolph, the leader of the Swabian contingent. Together they rode out with their leader to parlay with the Normans.

Humphrey and Harald rode nervelessly toward the ranks of their foemen. When they arrived at the outlying Italian picket lines, they did not slow their advance until they reached Pope Leo and his delegation who now numbered twenty-five bustling horsemen. When they were a few paces from the Pontiff they reined to a halt and Humphrey spoke.

"Good morning, your Eminence," he said courteously.

The Pope held out his hand and Humphrey leaned out from his saddle, took it and kissed the ring.

"Good morning, Duke Humphrey. I hope by now you have reconsidered your position and will be taking your people home."

"This is our home my Lord. I can only restate my position that we are here under the blessing of the Emperor and that the lands upon which we live have been legally given to us as payment for the fealty we have given to the Lords of Italy – including Rome. We have no wish to fight your army. May I reiterate that we are servants of the Holy Mother Church and seek only to serve her," said Humphrey in carefully modulated tones that resonated in the still morning air.

"As I have repeatedly told you, your people are not welcome anywhere in Italy. I know you to be a man of honour but your men are brigands," said Pope Leo pointing his finger at Harald, "why, even this man here, this general of yours, is known as the Cut-throat of Calabria."

Harald said nothing, but simply stared at the men surrounding the Bishop of Rome who sat fidgeting in the saddle beneath their brightly coloured banners. None of them returned his menacing gaze except one enormous German knight, who glowered back before spitting on the ground.

"Send these outlaws back to the land that whelped them, Lord," said the Swabian leader. "They are without honour and I would rather my men do not sully their blades with their tainted Norman blood."

"Please, Prince Rudolph, these men are here to seek my pardon and if they leave in peace I must consider it," said Leo irritably.

"We do not seek any Papal pardon, Holiness. I am here in the hope of avoiding bloodshed to either side," continued Humphrey as diplomatically as he was able.

"Then you must do your worst, but I give you this day to turn around and leave. If you or a single man of your command is here tomorrow, you will suffer the consequences. I give you until then," said Leo.

Humphrey said nothing but turned and nodded to Harald, who took the banner staff he carried in both hands and snapped it like a twig in front of him before throwing it to the ground. The meeting was over, and the Normans turned their horses around and casually walked them back through the enemy lines. They were still under the Pope's protection within the terms of truce but that did not prevent the hostile jeers of his army ringing in their ears as they departed. Then, they kicked their horses into a gallop and rode swiftly toward their respective companies.

They had not covered half the distance toward the Norman lines arrayed across the sloping ground of the foothills when they felt the ground shake beneath them. The *battaille* of Richard of Aversa's cavalry thundered past them on their left in a blur of movement. Over a thousand heavily armoured men and horses, each in ten lines of a hundred, swept forward, lances to the fore, toward the bulk of the Pope's Italian infantry. Harald had no time to look and see the effect of their charge, but he heard it well enough as it crashed into eight thousand startled foot-soldiers. He left Humphrey and returned to his men to make ready their assault. Harald lost sight of the Duke who disappeared from view and soon he was standing before his own men on the far right of the battlefield. He heard Robert Guiscard's voice booming out,

"Your General approaches, let us make ready to follow him," he cried out and a great cheer went up from the Normans of Calabria.

The two boys, who had brought him his armour earlier in the day, now rushed forward struggling with his shield and lance between them and he reached down and took them.

"Where is Jeanotte?" Harald demanded above the clamour. They said nothing and just cast their eyes downward.

"The men have been waiting for your address, General," said the Guiscard bowing his head deferentially.

Harald threw back his head and laughed.

"You honour me," he said before turning to his horsemen. "We have ridden far to fight for this land which we have justly earned. Today we will fight for the right to keep it. Your deeds here will be written into history and to carry this day we shall need to overturn the odds. Look for my banners and follow me to where the fighting is thickest. You will find me there with your Prince and we will sweep all those who defy us back to the lands that spat them out. God and right are on our side."

Another loud roar of approval sprang up from the ranks, which bristled with raised lances. As he waited for the roar to die down, he walked his horse along the lines of horsemen and saluted them. Harald spied a warrior in the first *conrois* who he did not immediately recognise. The man wore a full steel mask over his face, covering his features. He stopped in front of him and lent out of the saddle,

"I know it's you in there, Jeanotte, you cannot disguise yourself from me. Stay close to me today and do not stray from your comrades."

Then he turned and rode back to the Guiscard.

"We wait on your command, Hari," called his friend.

They looked out over the battlefield. On the far-left Richard Drengot's cavalry had been completely swallowed by the massed ranks they had attacked. The enemy's right flank buckled under the impact of his charge and parted at the apex of the attack giving way to more *conroi*. As they watched, the Italian and Lombard lines moved about frenetically before breaking and fleeing from the deadly collision.

The progress of Humphrey's companies in the vanguard was less certain and after they exchanged numerous fusillades of arrows with the enemy, they moved in to engage with the Swabian and Papal knights in the centre.

"We shall finish off Richard's rabble of an enemy over there and go to your brother's aid," shouted Harald to the Guiscard.

He turned to lead his men out to cut off the retreat of the Pope's main force. They rode hard and fast to intercept thousands of desperate, fleeing men trying to escape the carnage. Harald was one of the first to arrive and speared a Lombard soldier lifting the man off the ground. More of his company arrived and created havoc among the disorganised ranks. As each *conrois* punched holes in the enemy lines and left the action, they wheeled away before returning to the fight once again. This part of the battle was won, and he ordered his men to depart from the rout and follow him, leaving the remaining pursuit to Drengot's men.

Humprey's vanguard was struggling in the centre of the field. After rallying his men around him, Harald and the Guiscard led them into the flanks of the Swabian and Papal knights that were gaining the upper hand. The fighting here was of a different order to that on the left of the battlefield and the Norman foot-soldiers were forced back under the ferocity of the German counterattack. The enemy were then checked by the challenge on their flanks as Harald's *conrois* hurtled into them. However, the Swabian warriors gave good account of themselves wielding enormous double-handed swords to great effect and cleaving the bodies of men and horses as they swept the bloody field. The Guiscard's horse was eviscerated by one mighty sword strike, throwing its rider to the ground. Harald went to his friend's aid and other warriors rallied around but he lost him in the chaos. He discarded his lance which was now useless in the close quarter fighting and drew *Gunloggi* from her scabbard. It was as hard a fight as he could ever recall and his cohort cut a brutal swathe across the blood-soaked ground. They hacked, thrust and stabbed with their swords at any of the enemy who refused to submit.

Harald saw Jeanotte also lose his horse and fought to get to him. The squire was about to receive a killing sword thrust before his master rode the boy's huge assailant down and his *destrier* crushed the man's head beneath flailing hooves. Harald reached down to drag Jeanotte to his feet and as he did so he caught sight of a flashing sword blade aimed at his own head. He managed to get his shield up at the last moment and deflect the powerful blow that still knocked him from his saddle. He watched helplessly as his attacker hit the ground; felled by the Guiscard who had remounted yet again to come to his aid. It was a moment of respite that allowed him to catch his breath and get back onto his horse before re-entering the fray.

The fighting continued unabated for some time before the ground in front of the Norman line cleared as the Count of Aversa concluded his pursuit of the Italians and the Lombards. He and his men now entered the fight, drawing the attention of the Swabians who, despite the length of time they had been fighting did not appear to tire. However, the growing weight of numbers and sheer desperation of the Normans began to carry the day as they hacked and slashed at a resolute enemy who finally began to show signs of weariness. But rather than surrender, the remaining German troops fought on and, one by one they dropped from exhaustion to be finished on the ground by Norman steel until none were left alive.

The last of the remaining Papal allies died, the fight was over, and the enemy had been routed. The maelstrom of battle abated almost as quickly as it began and the sound of steel on steel ceased. The noise was replaced by men and beasts in their death throes. Harald looked around him, desperate to find the Guiscard, who had been unhorsed three times by the time the fighting had stopped. He was found with a broad smile across his bloodied face and called over to Harald.

"I think I could live to be a hundred and never fight in as bloody encounter as that."

"You are like a cat with nine lives. You must surely be on the last one by now," replied Harald.

"You seem to have had your difficulties too. We may have to get you a new shield, Hari," he said pointing to the tattered remnant of wood and leather, still strapped to his friend's arm.

They looked across the field of battle, which stretched for a league to the left and right of them and was covered with the dead and dying of both sides. Men staggered, dazed and senseless across the plain and maddened, rider-less horses galloped away to escape. Humphrey's men had carried the day but the triumph had come at a cost, although not as great as their enemies', of whom few remained still alive. It had been a close-run thing, but now not a single Swabian swordsman was left standing. It emerged later that Humphrey's line had been close to defeat before Harald's men stiffened their resolve. By the time Richard Drengot entered the fray the heat of battle was dying, and the contest was all but over.

In this pitched battle on the dusty fields of southern Italy, where no quarter was given or asked, the myth of Norman strength and indomitability became a reality. The enmity of the local population, which had brought matters to such a dramatic climax, was rendered impotent and with it, the last opportunity to eject their despised enemies. The Normans would not be going home to Northern France. The victorious warriors gathered around their captains and all eyes looked to the walls of Civitate where the Pope and his small entourage looked back at them and nervously pondered their fate.

Chapter 3: The Fate Of The Pontiff

In the aftermath of battle, the Norman wounded were tended, and the dead removed from the field, for Christian burials. The two hundred or more Italian and Lombard nobles who had surrendered were rounded up and put together under guard. They would be taken off to Capua and imprisoned while their ransoms were collected. There were at least a few hundred men-at-arms captured during the fighting, and they were put to work digging several huge pits, into which they collected and interred four thousand or more of their fallen comrades.

The allied camp of the Papal forces was empty as dusk approached, until the victorious troops arrived and began to forage in earnest for food and drink. Each one of the three thousand remaining Normans was starving and parched after some of the fiercest fighting many of them had ever known. They were not disappointed as they rifled through the tents and wagons, revealing copious supplies of food and wine. An abundance of horse fodder and wagon loads of oats were also uncovered and fed to their ravenous animals. It was not a moment too soon, for as soon as hostilities ceased the first beasts began to drop dead from hunger and exhaustion. Once they were fed and watered, the victorious army fell upon the contents of the captured camp. Many men had not eaten for two days and the discovery of the richly endowed Papal baggage train was a gift from God.

The citizens of Civitate watched from the city walls as the Norman troops rewarded themselves with newly discovered bounties. The anxious Civitatians feared the victorious Normans would invade imminently and loot the city, but today they had nothing to fear. After the simple pleasure of eating and drinking their fill in the knowledge their future was secure, Humphrey's men fell, exhausted, into the tents of their vanquished enemies. Tomorrow might be a different matter but tonight they would leave the citizens in peace. Inside the city walls was the man who imperiled their lives; Leo IX might yet prove a very costly guest to the inhabitants.

When the fighting began to wane, and the outcome of the battle was becoming obvious the Pope could not be found. He disappeared with his small entourage, retreated to his quarters and knelt before the altar of the small private chapel. He remained in this state of genuflection for several hours after the end of the battle. Pope Leo had failed to rid Italy of the Normans, he had failed his people and he had failed God. The defeated Pope feared the wrath of the triumphant army which would surely bear down on him and the town that sheltered him. There was nothing left to do except pray to God for deliverance and a merciful end.

Around midday the next day there was great activity outside the city walls. Duke Humphrey ordered that earthworks be constructed and a siege of the city begun. The Duke was not concerned with the fate of the people inside although they could be expected to suffer when the walls of Civitate were breached, and the city sacked. It was the Pope of Rome he wanted, and he had the time and men, and now captured materiel, to ensure this happened whatever the cost of human life. News that the Byzantine army had turned back home allowed the Duke to focus on the single task of capturing the Pontiff. It was still early in the summer and an effective siege of the city could be conducted at his leisure.

Inside the walls of Civitate, the city council met and decided they were unwilling to harbour a wanted man, even if he were the Pope. That evening the huge city gates were opened and the Bishop of Rome, leader of the Papal states was pushed, unceremoniously into the open ground between the walls and the Norman earthworks. All work stopped as Leo, with six of his followers, shuffled forward, preparing themselves for whatever ghastly fate awaited. Duke Humphrey quickly assembled his commanders and captains and came out to meet the frightened delegation. He approached the Pope curiously and when he was within a few paces of him, Leo raised his head and summoned the last vestiges of courage.

"Duke Humphrey, we are your prisoners. On behalf of my charges, we throw ourselves at your mercy."

There was an awkward silence before Humphrey spoke at last.

"You have nothing to fear at my hand, your Holiness. I was pushed into a fight I did not want, but at least the matter is settled now. It is true you are in my custody, but it is also my God-given duty to protect you. You are still the Vicar of Christ and we are your flock. I ask you to bless us for we are first and foremost followers of the Lord, who hopefully sees fit to forgive us our sins – great and many as they are," he said.

Then, to Pope Leo's amazement, the Duke of Apulia went down on one knee. He was followed by the Guiscard, Harald, Richard Drengot and all of the captains and men at arms. To the Pope's further astonishment, a congregation of three thousand kneeling men waited on the hard Italian ground for his blessing. Heads bowed, they did not see the Pontiff weeping as he collected himself to address the army. Then in a high, tremulous voice he started,

"Orbi et urbi," intoned Leo beginning the blessing to his battle-weary flock.

Duke Humphrey was the first to rise and held out an open palm toward the Pope who moved toward him. As he did so Harald, at Humphrey's shoulder, noticed a sudden movement from within the ranks of onlookers. Spinning around he saw one of the Italian hostages rushing toward the Pope with a huge Swabian sword raised above his head. He was no more than ten paces from his intended victim before Harald was between them. He struck the would-be assassin a killing blow across the throat with *Gunnlogi* and the man dropped like a stone, dead before he hit the ground. The Pope stared open-mouthed; his now grubby white garments spattered with the dead man's blood.

"A timely intervention, your Holiness. This 'Calabrian Cut-throat' appears to have saved your life. Now come, follow me and let me offer you some refreshment. We have much to discuss," said the Duke of Apulia, putting his arm around the captive Pope and leading him off.

The army was stood down and now the Pope was safely in Norman hands, there was no need to lay siege to Civitate. The city, while still cautious, opened its gates to Humphrey's triumphant men who wandered in to drink and carouse. In two days, the Norman captains would collect their share of the plunder and the battle group would be dismissed. They left in high spirits, considerably wealthier than when they arrived. When the ransoms were paid they would all receive their share. More importantly they had secured their future although it still required the Pope to ratify the claims on their lands. Until the Papal seal was given, officially recognising the right of the Normans to their fiefdoms, the Pontiff would remain in the care of the Duke of Apulia. It was decided that Pope Leo be imprisoned in the city of Benevento. Harald, having saved the Pope's life, was appointed to oversee his incarceration and garrison the town with five hundred men.

A few days after the battle Harald and the Guiscard sat at a table outside a wine shop in Civitate. They were about to drink their fourth jug of wine as they sat, relaxing, in the last rays of the evening light.

"I had not put you down for being such a forgiving Christian, Hari," said the Guiscard.

"Nor I," said Harald, "perhaps I should have let him die. He nearly cost you your life after all."

"I am here now and that is what matters. How are you looking forward to your life as a gaoler?"

"It is a necessary job if I am to establish you as the Prince of Calabria. I am told Benevento is a fair city and it will make a change from St. Marks while I wait on the Pontiff to agree the treaties your brother would have him sign."

"You will be richly rewarded, for it is no mean city and they will pay a great deal of gold to have their own Prince back. A hundred thousand *solidatus* is a King's ransom not a Prince's."

"Ah, yes, Prince Rudolph – I shall be delighted to see his face one more time. We have hopefully taught him a little humility."

"What will you do with yourself in Benevento? You may be there some time."

"The first thing will be to get them to open the gates and I will decide after that. I will send for Eva, if it is a stay of any length of time. Pope Leo has a reputation for stubbornness and is not to be released without agreeing to every last treaty. Your brother is a harsh task master you know,"

"...but a generous one, Hari. And after that?"

"Then I shall return to St. Marks in triumph, and we shall take our great army to Sicily to eject the Moors," said Harald, raising a cup of wine to his friend.

They drank until the early hours, two great warriors enjoying a close fraternal bond. They had lived, fought together and shared many moments of hardship that might have broken weaker men. It was five years since the arrival in Italy that forced them to scratch a living in desperate conditions. In that time, they had overcome many obstacles together and arrived at a point where they earned hard-won respect, title and not a little wealth. This was not the end of their partnership but perhaps a high-water mark of their time together. Although they had left the pagan beliefs and gods of their ancestors in the far distant past each man believed that the Norns could yet still tinker with their fates. The threads which bound them to their expected destiny could be severed, at any moment, sending them hurtling in a direction that neither of them might comprehend. For now, they could bask in the afterglow of an uncompromising victory and the certainty that they had secured a giant step forward for the Kingdom in the Sun.

Chapter 4: A New Prince

It took three days ride to arrive at the great city walls of Benevento. At the head of five hundred Norman cavalry Harald reined his horse to a stop and surveyed the scene. He watched men appear at the battlements, peering down at him and considered how they would gain access to the city. Pope Leo rode at his side. He was Harald's hostage, but he had been treated as if he were a hugely important guest of honour, which was exactly what he was.

"I have no desire for any more conflict, your Holiness, but if the city is not surrendered at once I shall have no option but to lay siege to it. I know they have only a small garrison left for we dispatched most of them at Civitate, and the rest of them fled south. Their Prince is in chains in Capua and they will die before they see him again unless they hand over the city to me," said Harald.

He looked at Pope Leo who sat dejected and tired on a dusty, piebald *palfrey*. His white robes were filthy and caked with grime from the ride and his disposition was careworn and even a little surly. He shrugged disinterestedly. Harald continued.

"I will starve every last one of them out if I have to. I will not have to risk a single man to do so and I am prepared to wait until Christmas. Your intervention will save many lives."

The Pope accepted the invitation with a sigh of resignation and kicked the mare forward until he stood before the great wooden gates to the city. An unarmed man emerged from the postern gate, approached his horse and knelt before him. He watched the Pontiff reel off a number of instructions, before the man got to his feet and returned to the castle. Moments later the huge doors swung open and Leo looked back toward Harald and his waiting men. The ancient city had been surrendered without a fight and the Normans advanced through its gates to take possession.

If Civitate had been a rich and fair town, then Benevento was truly an opulent citadel of great wonder. This was the capital of the southernmost Lombard Duchy and it was a beautiful city, which had become rich and powerful at the centre of the trade routes. It was closely allied to Rome and had been the headquarters of Pope Leo for the last year as he campaigned to build his great army. The Pope considered his abject failure as he rode disconsolately behind Harald through the cobbled streets of the great city. The people stood in silence watching the procession following a small, mounted escort of Benevento's civilian leaders. Harald had told these men that the town was now under his control and that the colours of Humphrey of Apulia were to be flown from the ramparts. He also told them that his men and horses were to be watered, fed and quartered. The law here was now Norman and any dissenters would be dealt with harshly.

His words did not fall on deaf ears and, once they overcame their reticence, the local people became good hosts and welcomed the new arrivals. Harald took the deserted palace of Prince Rudolf, a grand old Roman villa within the city, for his own quarters. Pope Leo was installed nearby, in the house that had been his home during his previous time here, and in this gilded cage he was guarded day and night.

As soon as it became clear that there would be no local resistance to the occupation, Harald sent for Eva and within days the two were together. Their reunion was joyous, and it was only when he first spied her escort coming in that he realised just how much he had missed her. He leapt down the stone steps of his villa, three at a time and launched himself onto his unsaddled horse to ride out to meet her. Then galloping toward the little column of riders he pulled his horse to an abrupt halt before sweeping Eva out of her saddle in an ardent embrace. Harald turned the huge stallion and with his prize sitting across the great beast's shoulders he carried her home leaving the escort trailing in his wake.

It was a day later, and they both sat, immersed in the warm water of a large, stone bath next to their bedchamber. Their reunion had been frantic, and when they finally emerged from their room they found servants had prepared a bath, filled with water from a nearby hot spring.

"You might notice a few differences from our home in St.Marks," said Harald.

"So I see. These Lombards are pampered folk," said Eva, her head bent back to marvel at the ornate mural on the ceiling.

"I am sure you miss our home but we will just have to put up with this as best we can," said her husband smiling before raising a cup of wine to his lips. "You may have seen the previous owner in Capua on his way to Humphrey's prisons."

"I saw many chained men coming in. You won a massive victory, Hari."

"We won a hard-fought victory," he corrected. "I have never known such intense fighting."

"Well, it is over now, my love. I gave thanks to all the gods that you should be returned to me whole. Even the Christian one. I pray that this peace will last," she said.

"There is little fight left in our enemies now. They are dead, in chains or scattered to the four winds."

"How long do you think we will stay here?" she asked.

"Until the Pope accedes to our demands and accepts us as papal vassals at the very least. He must agree to the treaties and then I will release him. After that we shall be secure from the threats of Rome and its allies."

"And what sort of man is he?" she said.

"You will find out soon enough, Eva. He might be beaten but he is a stubborn man. If we get what we need it will be worth the wait," he said before the warmth and the wine overcame him and he dozed off.

Eva was delighted to find a wardrobe full of clothes and dresses that had been found for her. She selected a plain blue silk dress which fitted her tall frame and went off, barefoot, to explore the rest of her new home. The Roman villa had changed little since its construction three hundred years previously and had been perfectly maintained. Each room was exquisitely decorated with murals and the floors were all finished with minuscule tiles in a variety of designs. She found a beautifully manicured garden at the back of the villa, and spent some time discovering a multiplicity of exotic plants and flowers that blossomed in the Italian sunshine. Alpine lilies, red poppies and sunflowers grew in carefully managed profusion beneath well-ordered peach, lemon and orange trees. She sat for a while on a marbled bench leaning forward to splash her face with the cool water coming out of the mouth of a large carved, stone fish. Eva smiled absentmindedly and considered her own changing fortunes. Three years ago she had been in the thrall of a violent Moorish slaver and now she lived in a palace with a man she loved more than anything in the world. Her damp face dried quickly in the afternoon sun and feeling the back of her neck beginning to burn, she decided to move. She went inside to find Harald lying across their bed snoring softly. She slipped her dress off and let it drop on the cool, tiled floor before lying down beside him. Then she put her head on his broad chest and tried to fight against sleep just in case it might somehow break the spell of her happiness.

When she woke in the morning she knew it was no dream, slipped off the bed and walked over to an open window. A jasmine-scented breeze wafted through the room, making the silk curtains billow. She felt the warmth of the early morning sun on her naked body and laid her hands across her belly. She knew beyond any doubt that she was carrying Hari's child. Her husband woke and called over to her.

"Eva come away from the window. The guards will see you and they need no distractions. Besides you will need to put on a few clothes if you are to meet the Pope. If I cannot persuade him to agree to our terms maybe you might have better luck," he snorted. "On second thoughts perhaps, you should go as you are – I am sure it would make him change his mind."

"I do not want to leave here, Hari. I am just beginning to get comfortable. Besides it is not every day that a merchant's daughter becomes a princess."

"Then we shall just have to behave like good Christians and sit through his mass at the cathedral before our audience with him. It will do no harm to show the local people that Normans are not the baby-killing barbarians they think we are. Now come back to bed, it is still early, and I have not yet built up an appetite for breakfast."

Later in the day they sat in front of a large congregation of Lombards and Italians listening intently to the Holy Shepherd's service. Although she feigned interest in Pope Leo's words, Eva's thoughts wandered, imagining her husband's seed taking root in her womb. She suspected her husband was also pretending to be enraptured by the papal address for she knew, that deep down, his pagan sympathies were still rooted firmly within him. She was however, impressed at his willingness to try diplomacy and win the support of both the people and the Pope.

When the service was over, Harald presented Eva to the Pontiff. She bowed and kissed the holy ring.

"I am indebted to your husband, lady. Without him I would not be here," said Pope Leo.

"Not all Normans are as bad as their reputations your Holiness," she replied.

"I have no doubt madam, but never-the-less many of your husband's countrymen have done their comrades a disservice and the sins of the few must be suffered by the many," he replied haughtily.

"I am from an altogether different bloodline," countered Eva, "so my judgement is based on my personal experience, and I can only ...."

She did not finish for Harald gripped her arm, stopping her in mid-flow.

"We must go now, Holy Father. My wife has had a long journey getting here and I would like to take her home. So, if you will excuse us," said Harald signalling, to his escort of men-at-arms that he was ready to leave.

The Pope looked quizzical and without another word turned to go back into the church. Harald bent down and whispered in his wife's ear,

"The man angers me too, Eva, and although he is our prisoner, he is still the Pope and believes he has some semblance of power. We must keep him at arm's length until he gives us what we want."

The couple mounted the horses and with their escort trailing behind them they trotted home through the streets to the villa. It was a short journey, and the streets were busy, providing the local people ample opportunity to observe the new Lord. They were soon back in their new home within its high-walled compound, which could be easily defended by the small bodyguard that Harald had installed in these early days.

The main body of his troops were garrisoned in nearby barracks recently vacated by the defeated Lombard soldiers. Should there be an uprising then his men could extinguish it quickly enough. As it was, there was little angry sentiment toward the Norman occupation and life continued as usual for the people of the city. They had their Pope living amongst them again and appeared to be content to live in peace with the Normans. For their part Harald's men made every effort to be benevolent occupiers and the Beneventians showed little distain when taking their gold and silver in the wine shops and brothels.

Chapter 5: Changing Seasons

It was not long before Eva managed to persuade her husband that she did not need a bodyguard to venture out of the compound although he insisted that she be accompanied by at least one-armed man. The recently knighted Jeanotte often volunteered to accompany her on her excursions about the city, where she delighted in its marketplaces and Roman monuments. When her belongings finally arrived from St. Marks, she set up an apothecary in the town and treated whoever called on her services, be they rich or poor. The small trickle of early visitors grew rapidly as word of the yellow-haired healer dispensing free care quickly spread throughout the city.

Harald's men continued to train diligently but there was precious little fighting for them and no call for them to mobilise. He was pleased, for it meant his wounded men and their horses were given a chance to heal in peace. He was able to spend a good deal more time with his wife and they grew closer than ever. He visited Pope Leo each and every day to ask if he had changed his mind and was ready to ratify the treaties with the Normans. The answer was always the same and the Pontiff remained as intractable as he had since the first day of their arrival.

One day, Eva decided to visit her neighbour and cut some flowers from her garden to take to the Pope. He had installed a local priest and the young man refused to allow her into the house, on the premise that his master was at prayer and could not be disturbed. Eva remonstrated with the man and Leo, hearing the sound of raised voices, came to find out what was going on. She was invited in at once and taken through to his office, a cool marble walled room to the rear of the villa.

"I am sorry, Lady Eva, my secretary did not recognise you," he said.

"I hope I am not disturbing you but thought you might appreciate these," she said proffering a basket full of flowers to him.

"You have my thanks, Lady, I do not spend as much time as I would like in my garden for I constantly feel the cold despite the summer heat."

"You are suffering, your Holiness?" asked Eva.

"It is the Roman fever that affects me with great chills even in summer. There is no cure," he said.

"Ah, yes, I am familiar with the malady. My people call it the shaking sickness. Many of them came back from Vinland afflicted, but they also came back with a remedy for their ailments," she ventured. Seeing she had caught his interest Eva continued. "It is nothing more than some tree bark and taken with water will ease your pains. I bought some from a Moorish trader in Cantanzaro only recently. Would you like me to bring you some?"

"I could not presume on such kindness," said Leo.

"Nonsense, it is no more than one neighbour does for another. I shall be back tomorrow," she said triumphantly.

Eva returned to administer her remedies to the Pope and discovered that it was not the only ailment that afflicted him. He also still suffered from the effects of the bloody flux and although he had partly recovered years ago, he was still laid low from time to time. After four weeks, and under her watchful eye, Leo professed to an improvement in his health and seemed to take on a happier countenance. She visited him regularly and he began to see her in a different light.

"You know you have a great talent, Eva," Leo confided in her one day.

"Would not the Church of Rome condemn me as a witch then?" she asked.

"Not all men of the church are as enlightened as they should be. When I return to Rome I promise to do my best to exhort the virtues of different forms of healing," he said earnestly.

"You are returning home soon then?" she enquired.

"I hope to as soon I will agree these treaties that your husband would have me sign. If you would tell him that I have some good news for him I would be grateful," Leo answered with a smile.

Eva returned to her home that day in two minds. She knew that if the Pope returned to Rome her stay in Benevento would be over. Her affection for the city and its people had grown in the ten weeks they had been here and she would miss it greatly when she left. Harald did not feel quite as passionately and hankered for the spartan existence of St. Marks. She knew she would follow her husband but, all the same, she would miss this place and the pleasant lifestyle to which she was quickly becoming accustomed. She found him at home and led him into the garden, where they sat by the fountain in the afternoon sun and she imparted her news. Harald was overjoyed to hear that the Pope had at last acquiesced.

"You have worked wonders on that stubborn fellow," he said happily. "You truly have him under your spell. If it is possible, I think I love you even more."

He got to his feet, picked her up and gently tossed her into the air and caught her as if she were a small child.

"Gently," she told him firmly, "for I have a second piece of news. Come the New Year you are to be a father."

Harald set her back on her feet once more and stood back smiling broadly.

"Before you say anything I would like to give birth here in Benevento. After that we will follow you all the way to Sicily if you desire it."

"I can refuse you nothing, Eva. We can stay here as long as you like - forever if that is what you want."

On an impulse they rode out into the countryside and watched Fulla hunt until the sun went down. The hawk, delighted to be back in the skies, returned a quick kill; a large jack hare which was spitted and roasted in their make-shift camp.

Husband and wife sat with their backs against a large rock and watched the red orb of the sun descend into the west. They watched in silence as it disappeared and shared a skin of wine. As the last vestiges of daylight shimmered and died, Eva got up and walked over to the bed she had made up from blankets by their campfire. Undoing the buttons of her dress, which dropped to the ground, she stood naked in the glow of the fire. Then, smiling she reached out both arms toward her husband,

"*Kom til meg*, Hari," she said hoarsely. Needing no second invitation he joined his wife and they lay together until their passion had run its course. She fell soundly asleep and did not feel him lean over her and kiss her.

"I am proud of you Eva, no earthly force shall ever separate us," he whispered before pulling his cloak over them both and putting a giant hand over the almost imperceptibly small bump of her belly. He pulled her closer to him and inhaled the soft scent of summer jasmine flowers she wore in her hair, before joining her in a deep, dream-filled sleep.

Chapter 6: From Demons To Angels

Harald sat opposite Pope Leo at a wooden desk, upon which lay a dozen or more parchment documents. On each document was written, in small Latin script, the name of the Norman duke, count or knight and the title of the land to which each man laid claim. Each document was related to the land in the duchies of Apulia, Calabria, and Naples and the principality of Capua. After the titles of land were written a lengthy description of Rome's recognition of these hereditary claims, and the acknowledgment that the men of Normandy residing in the south were papal vassals. A priest stood at the Pope's shoulder and presented the unsigned documents in front of the Holy Father for his signature. After each was signed it was removed and another was put in front of him, until the process was complete. When it was done the Pope looked up at Harald and smiled.

"There, it is finished. Everything that Duke Humphrey has asked of me I have agreed to. It is now up to the lords of the Kingdom in the Sun to keep the peace which has taken the lives of so many."

"Thank you, Father. I am no more than a pawn in the game, but I will play my part. The Duke is an honourable man and he will keep his warriors in order," said Harald.

"Including his brother, the Guiscard?" asked the Pope.

"We will do our best with the Guiscard," replied Harald. "My friend is headstrong and occasionally reckless, but he is no fool and he stands to lose more than he will gain through any belligerence. Besides, his sights are on ridding Sicily of the Moors, rather than making war in Italy. We are all part of your flock now."

"Then I thank God for that, for I would not wish to face your people again on the field of battle. As my captor I bear you no ill-will and without you I would not be alive today. You have been a gracious host under the circumstances, and I suspect that not all of your defeated enemies have been treated so well," said the Pope without a hint of rancour.

"You are free to leave whenever you wish, Holy Father, but my wife would rather you stay a little longer until you have recovered your strength for the journey back to Rome," said Harald.

"Your wife has watched over me with great care and I am feeling a good deal better than when I arrived. I shall take her advice and stay a little longer, but my desire is to be back in Rome before winter comes," said Leo. "Now, we should plan a service in the cathedral to recognise our new fraternity. I should very much like to see Duke Humphrey to mark the occasion here, if that is possible?"

Word was sent to Capua that the Pope had acceded to all the Norman demands and within ten days the Duke of Apulia sat with Harald and Eva at a service of thanksgiving. Dressed in a brilliant white robe and carrying an ornate mitre, Pope Leo addressed a congregation of over a thousand people at which he blessed all the Normans in the Kingdom in the Sun. He asked God to guide his people and their new Norman brothers, so that every man and woman in Southern Italy might live in peace. Then, toward the end of the service the Pope called Harald forward to receive his personal blessing. He obeyed the unexpected request and knelt before the altar. With his head bowed in genuflection Harald heard the sound of footsteps and looked up to see the altar boys holding the Papal banner and in a strong, resonant voice Leo called out.

"This man you see before you, Harald Fitzroy, is a loyal servant of the Church of Rome. I give him my banner so that none might doubt him or his affiliations. He is as loyal a vassal as any here and not only does he have my blessing but also my friendship. I give him this ring as a token of my esteem," said Leo, pressing the bauble into Harald's hands.

With that the service was finished and the congregation left the cathedral. Humphrey and Leo repaired to nearby clerical offices and the handover of the signed treaties were completed. The Pope's endowments were not the only gifts Harald received that day. Duke Humphrey presented him with a substantial fiefdom that ran south from the city of Benevento for several leagues. It was given, the Duke told him, for his outstanding service throughout the Civitate campaign and beyond.

"You have friends in high places now, Hari," said Humphrey over a cup of wine in the town a little later. "Your part in establishing us in the south deserves some recognition. By the way, the Prince of Benevento will be released soon – his family have paid the ransom. You are a wealthy man now."

"Ah, Prince Rudolph. He will be wearing a different look on his face since last we met. Will he be returning here?" asked Harald smiling broadly.

"That is your decision to make. Your word is the law here – at least for the time being. You may stay and rule yourself if it pleases you."

"I will think on it, Lord," said Harald. "My first child is due in the New Year and my wife seems to have put down roots here."

"That is your decision again, but if and when you go you must appoint a successor, for it is folly to leave a void. Now, I am keen to meet your wife. It is rumoured that she has bewitched the Pope, you know. Let us finish our wine and you can take me to this palace of yours."

The next day the Duke of Apulia returned home with his escort. He carried with him the treaty documents that attested to his people's ownership of their land. Humphrey's tenure in southern Italy could no longer be denied and the future of the Kingdom in the Sun was assured, at least for the time being. Pope Leo stayed for another sixty days, during which time Eva tended to him and tried to build up his strength for the journey back to Rome. Deep down she knew that it was a hopeless task, and that the Pontiff's ravaged body was destined for an imminent demise. When he left with his escort, she knew she would not see the Pope again. There was a genuine and heartfelt affection between the two of them when they said goodbye.

It was shortly after the Pope left Benevento that another of its citizens returned home. Since the battle of Civitate, small numbers of men began their surreptitious return like so much flotsam and jetsam on the high tide. The Norman garrison paid little attention but duly noted their arrival. These were men who had fled the field at Civitate despite outnumbering their opponents significantly and now they skulked back like hungry dogs returning to their kennels. Their leader also returned, after his release was assured by the payment of one thousand golden solidus coins which were now under guard in the Norman barracks. Harald had given leave for the Prince of Benevento to return home after the man had sworn fealty to him. It was an ignominious return and to add further insult his villa was still occupied by Eva and her husband. However, Rudolph bore his newfound status well enough after Harald suggested that one day he might return to his former seat of power when the Normans left. That prospect seemed to be a distant one as the longer Eva's term of pregnancy went on, the more she became embedded in the Beneventian lifestyle.

Christmas in the city was a joyous occasion and one of deep religious significance. The traditional rites were strictly observed, and the Feast of the Nativity was celebrated by Norman, Lombard and Byzantine alike. Eva stood proudly at her husband's side for Mass on Christmas Eve in the great cathedral. As she listened to the Christmas hymns, she felt a great warmth and belonging for the city. For their part the local people had long taken her to their hearts, for she could often be found, late into the evening, dispensing remedies to those who needed her. Her husband was seen as a man of great reputation and one who commanded respect and since he had received the Papal blessing the people saw him in a different light.

The festive season came and went and a few days before Easter Eva knew the time had come to give birth to her child. She was attended by a local midwife and several of her servants, who moved her into the bedchamber to prepare for the delivery. Eva was resolute throughout a long labour which stretched over two days. Harald became a constant visitor, nervously coming and going as the midwife assured him that all was well with his wife. A healthy child would be borne to them, they were promised. They had decided to name the child Bohemond if he were a boy and the infant cried lustily almost as soon as he entered the world. The baby was cleaned and wrapped in linen before being put to his mother's breast. It was at that moment that Harald looked into Eva's eyes and realised something was amiss. She had a look of fear that he did not recognise. He looked at the midwife and asked her what was wrong.

"She is bleeding, Lord. It will not stop," cried the woman frantically.

One of the women took the baby from his mother's breast as the rest of them worked feverishly to staunch the flow of blood which now soaked the birthing-bed. Eva reached for her husband's hand weakly but as he whispered words of encouragement, he felt her grip lose its strength and slip. He looked at her whitening face and saw only confusion.

"Do not leave me, Eva. Your place is here with me. The gods have ordained it, and we are blessed," he said, willing her back into this world.

"You will take good care of our child. Promise that you will not resent him for anything that has happened to me. I am getting cold, Hari. I need your arms around me," she said in a barely audible whisper.

Harald watched the eyes in his wife's ashen face dull. Eva's lifeblood drained from her exhausted body, and he was consumed by great fear. She breathed her last and died even as he bent down to kiss her for the final time.

Chapter 7: The Widowed General

Eva was given a Christian burial in the city's cemetery two days later. Harald did not care whether she was interred as a Christian or a Pagan. He was simply bereft at the loss of his great love. From the depths of his despair, he could scarcely be reached and neither ate nor slept from the time of Eva's death until the moment of her burial in the part of the graveyard reserved for the great and the good. The garrison turned out in martial splendour to honour her, and they stood behind their leader in silent ranks as six of their number carried the heavy lead and stone coffin to her grave. Hundreds of people from the town also filled the burial ground. She had only lived amongst them for nine months but in that time, she tended the sick and administered her remedies to many of them whatever their social standing. They also knew that Pope Leo held her in the highest regard, reinforcing their view that she had died a worthy daughter of the church which earned their further respect. Harald neither cared nor noticed anyone and stood numbly at her graveside unhearing and unseeing of anything around him.

He had lost many friends and family in his twenty-nine years in this world. Death was a constant companion in his life and it visited, uninvited to take many of those around him. They died in war and in times of peace and although the bereavement of those closest to him was keenly felt he never dwelt overly on their loss. However, Eva's sudden departure was something unfathomable and brought a level of pain that he had never known before; more so because he had been powerless to prevent anything that had happened to her. They had been together a little over two years and the great love they shared had burned intensely. At times, Harald thought, too brightly for it to last. The Norns had cut Eva's chords and sent him spinning toward the abyss.

He turned around to see the ranks of his men standing behind him and mumbled a few words to dismiss them. As they ebbed away he was left with his two young squires for company. The boys had been with him since the eve of the battle of Civitate, where their father and older brother had died. After Jeanotte had been knighted Harald took them into his service. The youngest boy Thomas, his face wet with tears stood beside his brother choking back his emotion.

"You can stop that sniveling," barked Harald. "Now saddle my horse and fetch Fulla. We shall go hunting while there is still warmth in the day."

When they returned with the horses, they saw he had not moved from his position beside the grave and was alone. He heard them approach and without a word mounted, took the hawk onto his gauntlet and spurred the horse into a canter with the boys following in his wake.

When they reached the open countryside, he slipped her jesses and Fulla flew into the evening sky. Hunting sluggishly, she finally managed to kill two rabbits and provide the hunters with an evening meal. The boys made camp and cleaned and spitted the rabbits before roasting them over the fire. Then they brought wine for their master who sat dolefully petting the bird. They sat and ate in silence before Harald, who had consumed two huge skins of wine fell fast asleep where he lay.

He was walking with Eva in a land he did not recognise and they were between two armies. They were striding toward an army of Saxons who called out to them, welcoming them into their ranks. Behind the couple stood a host of Normans and he could hear his brother Robert calling him back to their lines. Eva hesitated and did not want to go, but he took her hand and told her not to worry for there was nothing to fear. They walked closer to the Saxon warriors and the lines opened up to reveal their leader; a king wearing a golden crown. He beckoned them forward. As he did, two ravens swooped out of the sky and picked Eva up between them, carrying her off, up toward the sun. Harald looked up to see his wife disappearing into the sky while she cried a torrent of tears that fell onto his upturned face.

"Turn back, Hari, it is not safe. Turn back." He shielded his eyes to follow the flight of the ravens until he could no longer see them. When he looked away, he was still between the two armies, but they had engaged in battle and were fighting. He drew his sword and joined them, killing any who stood in his path, not knowing whether they were friend or foe.

Harald woke abruptly and brushed his wet face with his sleeve. He was drawn to the cawing of ravens but could not see from where the birds called. On the other side of the dead campfire lay Thomas and Gilbert fast asleep while at their heads slumbered Fulla perched on an old log. Harald's mouth was dry from the night's drinking and his head ached dully. He got to his feet and poured water over the back of his neck from a bucket that the boys had filled the night before. He walked out of their camp to piss and as he did so he looked around at the landscape and tried to fathom the dream that had been so vivid. After a few moments he turned and walked back to wake the boys and knew what he had to do.

Chapter 8: Mortain, 1057

Robert Fitzroy was with his wife in the *solar* of Mortain Castle. He sat in a high-backed chair watching Eleanor pluck at the metal strings of a *psaltery* held on her lap. He closed his eyes and let himself drift away to the dulcet tones of the harmonies that resonated gently through the chamber. They were alone after a servant had taken the three children to their beds. It was late in the summer and the evenings had started to draw in without becoming too cold. There were a few flickering candles yet to splutter out and the room was lit mostly by the light of the hearthfire. He opened his eyes to see Eleanor looking at him. No matter how often he looked at her he was always surprised by her beauty, which never faded despite the onset of age and children. She wore her hair long; braided in a plait that reached her waist. An expensive dress of Byzantine green silk with wide sleeves pushed back to play the psaltery revealed a closely pleated undergarment.

"You were sleeping," she gently admonished him.

"No, I was not", he said. "It is not every day a man can enjoy listening to his wife's skill on the strings. You have become an accomplished musician, I think."

"That is because I am left here alone too often and have plenty of time to practice," she replied. Robert failed to take the bait and instead chose to praise her.

"I know you have little spare time, Eleanor. Running this vast estate while I am away would keep an army of servants in work. Yet, you seem to manage it effortlessly," he said raising a cup of wine to her. "Do you think you might find enough time to add to our little brood of Norman warriors? You Werlenc women have earned a reputation as fine rearers of children."

"Despite your mother's disparaging remarks about my narrow hips not being broad enough to produce more strapping Fitzroy sons?"

"It was said in jest. Anyway, she loves you like a daughter."

Eleanor threw back her head and laughed.

"It was a good job I came with such a dowry. It certainly helped her accept me as your wife more readily," she said in a mocking tone. "Now, tell me what news you have heard from Italy on your travels. Is it true what they are saying about your little brother?"

"Ah, the 'Papal Shield'. He has certainly earned a name for himself in the south and he is a married man now, you know," he said, observing her closely and watching for a reaction.

The fact that Robert had been ordered to take Eleanor as his wife by the Duke of Normandie, with the intention of driving a wedge between the brothers, was never mentioned. Harald and Eleanor had been childhood sweethearts and had been devastated by the arranged match. The Lord and Lady of Mortain both knew it had been a great injustice, but as the years passed and their union grew stronger it was never spoken of. The betrothal and marriage had been little more than business at the time, but Robert always suspected that Eleanor still harboured some feelings for his younger brother. If so, she did not reveal it and her face remained impassive.

"Then I hope he has found happiness at last," she said. "Do you think perhaps he might bring his bride back to Normandie?"

"It is unlikely for under the law he is still an outlaw. God might forgive him, but William will not," said Robert. "I for one would be glad to see him – particularly if he came with his army at his back."

"… and carrying the Papal banner, of course, before which all men will kneel," she said mischievously. "It would certainly improve your chances of recruiting allies if he did, would it not?"

"You toy with me, Eleanor," he said resignedly before getting up and going around to the other side of the table. Then he took the *psaltery* out of her hands, put it on the table and led her to their adjacent bedchamber.

Robert lay awake long after their fond reunion and listened to Eleanor gently breathing as she slept. He thought of recent events and the last two months campaigning to the south in Maine, battling the forces of the Count of Anjou. He had rebuilt the castle in Ambrières just in time to beat off a concerted effort by Duke William's arch enemy, Geoffrey Martel. After leading a particularly brutal charge, Robert won the day and dispersed the enemy forces. But now he had grown tired of war and the continual battle to stem the ingress of Normandie's enemies across her borders. He was thirty-three years old and longed for the day when all the boundaries were secure. He knew that it would take forces far greater in number than those available to him and the Duke. Robert understood that without increasing the size of the Duchy's army they would always be under threat from one enemy or another. The ten thousand available men, including squires and peasant farmers, were not nearly enough to stave off the unwanted attentions of the King of France and his allies. They may well have given King Henri a bloody nose in the past, but defeat to Duke William only seemed to encourage the French monarch to challenge again. The cream of Norman military elite were no longer in the Duchy but now resided in southern Europe, where the opportunity for land and wealth hung like a baited wolf trap.

Duke William had designs on riches far from his immediate sphere of influence, and the jewel of the Kingdom of England was always at the forefront of his thoughts. "After all," he would often remind Robert, "it has been promised to me by the English King himself." While the Duke dreamed of kingship, Robert Fitzroy fretted on how he might continue to rebuff the King of France and his confederates. The Count of Mortain had been fighting enemies all his life and he desired only to retire his *destrier*, worship God and never raise his sword in anger again.

One day during the recent campaign, the fighting in Maine had lulled and he sat drinking wine in the town square of Domfront. He was approached by three knights returning to Normandie from Italy. They were veterans of several campaigns in the Kingdom in the Sun and had captured and ransomed many noble Byzantine prisoners. They were now rich men returning home having been discharged by their Lord, the Count of Apulia.

"So, you have news of my brother?" said Robert excitedly, offering the travellers a seat at the table.

"We do, Lord. Your brother is the most famous Norman in Italy, and I had the honour to fight by his side at Civitate. He is well and prospers in the city of

Benevento where Pope Leo is his guest," said their leader a wizened grey beard of about fifty years.

Robert felt his heart leap at the news and gave them wine and food.

"It is an age since I saw him last, so I need to know everything. Please tell me all you know of the battle," he asked before the men had a chance to sit down.

"At Civitate, he and Lord Humphrey entered the enemy camp together," said another of the men.

"We watched him from our hilltop overlooking the field and his helm and armour shone like burnished gold in the sunshine. He was like a vengeful angel descending from heaven to do battle with the devil's host," piped up their squire. "They struck fear in the enemy's heart and before they could recover, we galloped down and smashed them."

"Your brother was everywhere that day, Lord. No man could put a blade on him. He was the first man on the field and the last one to leave. His people treat him like one of the saints," continued the older man in reverential tones.

Robert questioned the men until dusk fell and then invited them back to the castle, where he insisted on hearing all the details again of what they knew of Harald. They were fulsome in both their story of his brother's achievements in Italy and of the reputation he had carved out. When they finished their tale by describing how Harald had been blessed and recognised by the Pope, Robert was filled with deep joy. He dismissed the men and went to pray until the new day started to dawn. Then, he retired exhausted, but euphoric, at the recent news of his brother. Two days later Robert left the castle in the hands of the new *castellan* together with a small garrison and returned home to Mortain and a wife and family he had not seen for some time.

Robert slept well into the next day after his long ride home. When he finally woke up he found Eleanor sitting on the bed looking down at him.

"Is it late?" he asked abruptly. Then realising he had few if any duties today, he relaxed and smiled. "I must blame you for wearing me out, Eleanor. The thought of your welcoming bed sustains me through the most tedious of campaigns."

"I am just doing a small service for the Duchy, husband. It is really not too much of a hardship you know," she replied. "Now come and eat. The kitchens have sent up breakfast for you."

She put a tray of food next to him and watched him as he wolfed down a selection of porridge, bread, cheese and beer.

"You called his name last night in your sleep," she said.

Robert looked quizzical as he continued to eat, shrugging his shoulders.

"Hari, of course," she replied to the unasked question. "Now tell me about his wife, I am curious."

"I know little of her. Only that she is a Norse woman who he freed from Moorish slavers. She was in chains and on her way to somewhere in Byzantium when he rushed in and saved her. Apparently, he had not even looked at another woman since leaving Normandie and then never looked upon another after he found her," said Robert.

She turned and walked toward the window.

"He was always a romantic soul, despite his wild ways," she said.

"Well, he has now forged the name of Fitzroy indelibly on the Kingdom in the Sun. He has the Pope's blessing, the Hauteville's backing and is a man of land and wealth. He is a man after my grandfather's heart, and I am proud of his achievements."

"Then you should tell him so. Swallow your pride and make up your differences before one or the other of you dies," said Eleanor stridently. "You Fitzroys may be great leaders of men but you are all stubborn and proud."

"Nothing would give me greater pleasure than to see him once more, but until William forgives him it is impossible."

Robert stayed in Mortain only for a few more days. He had business with the Duke that could not wait much longer and, leaving most of his weary troops behind, he continued on to Caen with a small bodyguard. He started to miss his family as soon as he led his column through the town gates and onto the road north, and prayed fervently that he would be returning to see them again before too long.

Chapter 9: The Duchy Prays For Deliverance

Two days later Robert sat in Duke William's private chamber. He had been in the service of the Duke for twenty years as his protector and companion, long before either of them could even shave. He sat opposite his Lord and delivered news which was of no great surprise.

"The King of France has made powerful allies of the Angevins and the County of Maine. He has also been courting Brittany. We can expect to see them all here come the spring. They are gathering their armies in the south, even as we speak."

"How many, Robert?" asked the Duke.

"Thirty thousand all told. Maybe more. And they will not be dividing their forces this time. We can expect a single host marching at the heart of the Duchy."

"You are convinced of the veracity of your information?" asked William.

"Straight from the mouths of several of the prisoners we took when we broke out of the siege of Ambrières. All with the same story – the Duchy of Normandie can expect a massive invasion in the spring. They will come from the south and try to sweep up everything in its path," said Robert.

"Then we shall be ready for them when they come," said William.

"We shall, Lord but this is the biggest threat to the Duchy yet."

"I am, as always, open to your counsel, Robert but until my excommunication from Rome is reversed it will be hard for us to gain friends abroad. The success of your brother in the south is doing us no favours either – men seem to flock to his banners – at a great cost to the Duchy it would seem," said William.

Robert felt his hackles rise as they always did when he heard his brother spoken of unjustly; even if it came from his master. He resisted the temptation of an angry retort and answered in his normal, well-modulated tones.

"It is no secret that Harald has been impulsive, as all young men are wont to be. His actions here were never meant to slight you in any way, Lord. He has always put you first, even when it meant his life was in danger. We must have allies for we cannot defend our borders and thirty thousand enemy soldiers heading to Caen will be many more than we can resist," Robert stated, waiting for the significance of his words to sink in before continuing. "If Harald could be persuaded to return with an army, it might save the Duchy. It might also prevent the loss of any more warriors to the Kingdom in the Sun. After all, he fights beneath the Papal banner now and if he fought once again for Normandie – there are many who would reconsider their allegiances."

Duke William shook his head in disagreement.

"You grew rich and powerful when you were given Mortain whilst your brother became an outlaw. He would surely hold this against you and take his revenge just as Cain slew Abel," countered the Duke.

They both understood the inference and there was no escaping the fact that there might still be a major rift between the two brothers. Robert considered these words and after a little thought responded.

"I cannot tell what is in his mind and many years have passed since we parted. Harald may have forgiven the injustices against him and even if he has, he still might not come. I am told he is regarded by many as a prince in the south and one who wears the Pope's ring."

"Your brother is a hot-head, Robert. He may have a following but so do the rest of the Hauteville adventurers in Italy. I too have heard of the great deeds of Harald Fitzroy on the Italian battlefields, and whilst I hear your wise words, I cannot help but think they may be tinged with some fraternal longing. If he can be persuaded to leave his Byzantine fiefdom to support us, what payment will he and his men require, and furthermore can he guarantee the support of Rome and lift my accursed excommunication?" asked the Duke.

"I do not know what is in Harald's heart, after all I have not seen him for nine years. But Normandie is in dire need of help, and I believe we must consider the matter before it is too late. May I suggest that you take counsel from Archbishop Lanfranc on this subject, Lord. You know he is highly thought of in the Vatican and may well offer a different opinion on how we might garner support from the Holy See," suggested Robert.

William considered the proposal and reluctantly nodded his head in agreement.

"Very well, I shall talk to the Archbishop. If he agrees with your views, I shall reconsider," pronounced William stiffly before changing the subject.

The Duchy was in grave danger and urgent help was needed just to survive, but the Duke's designs abroad also needed support. Without an ally in Rome, occupying the English throne would be an impossible task. Robert knew William was stubborn to the point of being immovable if he felt his pride was at stake, and it would take considerable persuasion to change his mind. He also knew that William yearned for the English crown and was prepared to do anything to get it, even if it meant forgiving his brother and welcoming him back home.

Whenever he stayed in Caen, Robert always started his day in the private Lady Chapel. Today was no different and he knelt in quiet reflection. He prayed for the delivery of Normandie from her enemies. He prayed for safety for his family and the protection of Duke William from harm. Most of all he prayed to be reunited with his brother Harald. So deep in prayer was he that Robert did not see the cloaked figure who knelt down beside him. It was only when he had finished his devotions, crossed himself and got to his feet that he noticed the man next to him.

"For such an irreligious fellow your brother has many pious friends," said Archbishop Lanfranc.

"You may have the grace of God, Father, but you have the stealth of a footpad," replied Robert. Both men turned to face each other and embraced.

"Come let us sit, at least to get some blood back into my old legs," said Lanfranc, "I have something of great importance to discuss with you."

They sat on a plain wooden bench and Lanfranc unwrapped the details of the protracted meeting he had with the Duke. William had been angry. Not with Robert, he hastened to add, but with the situation that the Duchy had found itself in after many years of successfully repelling each and every enemy who had invaded. The Duke was without friends or allies outside of Normandie, and the only man who might now be able to offer vital support and succour to him in his hour of need had once been cast out as an outlaw. The Archbishop argued Harald's case and had persuaded William to swallow his pride. Just as Rome might be induced into lifting the charge of *consanguinity* and excommunication against William, so the Duke might lift the disgrace of being outlawed against Harald. After much discourse and logic from Lanfranc, the Duke relented. Not content with this new stance, the Archbishop doggedly argued that if Harald Fitzroy could be encouraged to return home at the head of his army, he should be amply rewarded when the invaders had been repelled. Once again, the Duke relented, albeit unwillingly. Finally, it was agreed that Lanfranc should travel to Rome to petition the Pope to have the charges against Duke William dropped.

"You have done well, Father. I have never been able to get the Duke to budge when it came to letting my brother return," said Robert.

"You think he will come?" said Lanfranc.

"I do not know," replied Robert with a sigh. "There was bad blood between us, you know. When brothers fall out like that there is often no forgiveness."

"Time is a great healer and I hear he has a wife now to whom he is very close. I also believe the Pope is a great admirer of both of them," said Lanfranc. "Perhaps the woman he has been searching for since leaving Normandie? William will speak with you today and ask you to get your brother back."

Robert thought for a moment, marvelling at the Archbishop's insight into the fraternal rift that caused his brother to leave. He turned his head and smiled at his mentor.

"You must tell me one day, Father, the source of all your information."

"That might take longer than you think," said Lanfranc returning the smile. "Godspeed, Robert. I will not take any more of your time for you have a long journey ahead of you. The Lord will be with you with each step you take."

The Archbishop got to his feet and left Robert alone with his thoughts.

The meeting with Duke William a little later was short and perfunctory. In return for Harald's renewed fealty, he would be offered land and title. The land would come from captured territory taken when the conflict with King Henri was over and there would be more than enough gold and fiefdoms to satisfy an army of voracious Norman exiles. Beyond that, Robert had a free rein to negotiate with his brother to ensure he returned with as many men as he could muster.

There were eight hundred leagues of road to ride to get to the south and Robert would take an escort of twenty men with him. He decided that his younger brother Floki should accompany him on the mission and sent a rider requesting that he join him with all haste. Within a few days Floki clattered through the gates of Caen castle, and the following day the company left for the south beneath the banners of the two ravens of Regneville.

Chapter 10: The Journey South

For the second time in a decade more Fitzroys took the road toward the Kingdom in the Sun. Robert and Floki's journey was not quite so desperate as Harald's had been and they were neither challenged nor threatened in any of the regions through which they passed. They and their knights were wealthy travellers and could well afford the creature comforts on the road which their brother and his band, almost a decade before, could not. By night they stayed in the towns and burgs that lay close to the overland route to Italy. The weather was, for the most part, fair and spring-like and enabled Robert to re-acquaint himself once again with his younger brother, Floki. They had seldom ridden together other than to go to one battle or another, and the simple pleasure of spending time on a, hopefully, peaceful mission was not lost on either of them. "At least," thought Robert, "I hope it will be peaceful," for the manner in which he and Harald had parted nine years previously had been anything but.

The journey was not completely without incident, and one evening they reached the town of Nevers, close to the borders of France and Burgundy. Soon after they entered through its gates Floki was wrongly recognised, much to his delight, for his older brother Harald, who had once rid the town of an infestation of brigands. It was an understandable mistake for he was the spitting image of his sibling, albeit not quite so long in the leg nor broad in the chest. When the townsfolk discovered the provenance of the Norman visitors they were feted as honoured guests. It was all Robert could do to prise Floki away the next morning from the clutches of the local women.

Twenty-five days after leaving Normandie they reached the coastal city of Genoa, where they hired a ship to take them south to Naples. The *cog* in which they sailed arrived ten days later and their group disembarked in the busy seaport. None of the party had ever been this far south and many of the younger men stood wide-eyed on the bustling stone quay. Timber, cattle, hides, wool and honey were among the disparate cargos that were unloaded from countless ships lying tied to the quay, to the fore and aft of their vessel. The dock was a maelstrom of activity as men, horses and wagons all vied for space and produced a deafening cacophony of noise, accompanied by more than forty different foreign tongues. Although the city was firmly in Byzantine hands, Robert marvelled at the number of his countrymen they passed on their way through its streets. They searched through the labyrinth of tiny roads and passages to find the lodgings that the captain of their ship had recommended. After finding their destination late in the day they spent a comfortable night in a large pensione before getting back on the road toward Benevento.

"It seems our brother is quite famous in these parts," said Floki, as the two rode side-by-side. "If I can believe the men we met last night we should be travelling across his land as we speak."

"He has certainly made a reputation for himself here - of that there can be no doubt. I hope we will get more news of him in Benevento, where he was last seen," replied Robert as the column trotted on.

"They said they fought by his side at Civitate not more than two years ago. I never doubted Harald's courage or his valour but he has surpassed all my expectations. How will you persuade him to return to Normandie?" asked the younger man.

"I am not sure whether I can persuade him or whether he will even listen to me now. It seems like he is a prince in these parts - respected and revered. He is even known in Rome as the 'Papal Shield'. I could scarcely believe my ears when I first heard but it is true, so it would seem. Our brother - the friend and protector of the Pope of Rome? Why, I could hardly ever get him to set foot in a church in Normandie much less sit through a whole service," mused Robert.

"Well, I for one will be delighted to see him. He cannot have changed too much surely," enthused his brother.

They spent another few hours travelling along the road and passed huge fields of vines, olive groves and verdant pasture from which grazing cattle paid them scant attention. They continued on between two steep hills and as they turned sharply to the right, the city of Benevento shimmered before them in the afternoon sun. In the distance they saw two horsemen riding toward them at speed. The riders drew to a halt before the column and one of them introduced himself as Rudolph of Benevento. They were armed only with swords and neither they, nor their horses wore armour. The Prince, a giant of a man of about forty years spoke first.

"My Lords, do I have the honour of speaking with the brothers of Harald Fitzroy?

"You do, sir," Robert replied courteously. "We are searching for him. Do you know if he is well?"

"I believe he is well enough but sadly he is not here. He left the city last year to return to his comrades further south. But please, he would want me to be a hospitable host to his kin. You must let me offer you a place to rest from the road before you continue your search. My city is yours for as long as you wish to stay. I must apologise, but I heard only this morning that Harald's kinsmen were on their way to Benevento. You must take us how you find us, I am afraid. Please follow me and I will tell you all you need to know," replied the Prince.

Rudolph led the column toward the high-walled city and through its stout gates. He directed them through cobbled streets and into the compound of his elegant residence, the Roman villa which had once been the home of Harald and Eva. A team of grooms appeared from nowhere to take charge of the Norman horses. Robert's entourage were all ushered into the house and met by a steward and an army of servants, who showed each man to his quarters, a palatial room of his own. Still wearing their *hauberk*s and helms the men made noisy progress toward their lodgings.

Robert and Floki were taken into the garden by the Prince to a marble table on which sat a jug of wine and some cups. They all sat down and were served by an immaculately attired servant. Floki, could no longer contain his excitement and implored the Prince to elaborate on news of his brother. He told them everything he knew, starting with the Norman victory at Civitate and their brother's part in the battle, the capture of Pope Leo, the Prince's imprisonment in Capua and Harald's brief reign as the governor of Benevento. He also described the Pope's subsequent release, his blessing of Harald, the birth of Bohemond and the death of the infant's mother.

"When Lady Eva died your brother was bereft. He mustered his men and left after giving the city back to me," he said sadly. "He may have defeated me in the field at Civitate but I bore him no malice. I have never seen a man fight like your brother that day. He was everywhere, leading his horsemen where the fighting was thickest and making dead men of all my warriors. He is an honourable man, your brother and held in the highest regard by Rome – as was his wife."

"And what of the child, is he still here?" asked Robert.

Rudolf shook his head.

"Two days after Harald buried his wife, he gathered his men and went south. He found a wet-nurse, put them both on a wagon and took them with him. Harald said little to me other than he was going south to kill moors and that my city, wealth and rank were all restored to me – including this house. Then he left and it was as if the Normans had never been here at all. Harald still owns large tracts of land around the city, but he has not returned. They are well managed by dependable men, and we hope he may one day come back to them. Gentlemen, may I ask why you seek him? It is a long way to come even for a reunion with such a famous warrior as your brother."

Robert looked at the Prince for a moment and told him the purpose of his mission. Rudolph listened intently, nodding occasionally and when Robert had finished, he spoke.

"I hear he returned to the fortress of St. Marks where, reunited with the Guiscard they took their men to make war on the Saracens. You will know, I am sure, that they are both formidable warriors but together their partnership is one to be feared by all. I almost have a little sympathy for their ungodly foemen. I do not know your brother well enough to know if he will go home with you, but I wish you well in your quest. Men still flock to fight beneath the Papal banner even if Harald's benefactor in Rome has been succeeded," said the Prince.

"Pope Leo is dead?" asked Robert, betraying some slight alarm.

"Do not fear for Harald's support from Rome. A Papal blessing is eternal, and he wears the Pope's ring which guarantees him and his followers the Church's benevolence.

Now gentlemen, we have prepared a modest meal for you and your men this evening. You may want to go to the chambers that have been prepared for you and refresh yourself after your long journey. You and your men are my honoured guests for as long as you wish. If you are travelling on to St. Marks this might be the last place of comfort you will experience for a while," replied Prince Rudolf smiling.

The evening meal turned out to be more of a feast and many of the town's Burgundian dignitaries came to pay their respects. Prince Rudolf proved to be a generous host who lavished care and attention on his guests. In the days that followed the Fitzroy brothers toured the city, visiting the places where Harald was well-known and even celebrated. They spent the remainder of their time hunting with hawks in their brother's favourite wilderness.

"This is Fulla, your brother's beloved hawk," said Rudolf to Robert as they rode out one morning for the day's sport. "Lady Eva was devoted to the bird. But since her passing, and his leaving, the bird has pined for both of them. You would do me honour if you returned her to her master."

He reached out his arm and the saker falcon hopped effortlessly onto Robert's gauntleted wrist.

Duly refreshed and rested from the lavish hospitality heaped on them by a generous host, Robert and his knights returned to the road south three days later. It was another seven days ride before they reached the fortress of St. Marks. The Fitzroy brothers and their companions stood at the foot of the ascent at the top of which the castle's imposing sandstone walls rose at its peak. The party looked back up the hill, past the sprawling town and the untidy jumble of the garrison's barracks to the gates of the fortress lying beyond. The hawk, which had been docile and sluggish on the journey suddenly flapped her wings and strained at the jesses wrapped around

Robert's wrist. He released her and she shot up into the air, flying toward the castle at great speed before roosting in the upper battlements. Her fellow travellers continued up the hill, through the dusty streets of the town toward the castle gates. Before they reached the summit the gates opened, and the figure of a woman emerged and stood waiting for them. As they came closer Robert could make out her tall and elegant frame dressed in a long-sleeved blue dress. She was bareheaded, about thirty years old and her dark hair hung down before one shoulder in a braided plait. She was smiling broadly displaying dazzling white teeth, which stood out all the more against the dark, tanned skin of her face. Her elegant, angular visage and alert countenance exuded confidence as she walked toward them in easy, long-limbed strides before standing in front of them, hands on her hips.

"We have been expecting you, gentlemen. Have you come to take your brother home, I wonder?" said the Duchess Alberada.

Chapter 11: The Reunion On The Cliffs

Horse and rider were reunited in the waves that lapped gently up and onto the beach. He had waited patiently in knee-high water for his warhorse, Damascus ,to be coaxed down the ramp from the ship and into the sea. Harald watched nervously as the *destrier* jumped off the end. Then he took the reins from his squire and hauled himself into the saddle and smelling his master's familiar scent once more the animal was calmed.

"There you are, boy, that was nothing to concern yourself with," he said gently into the horse's ear before spurring him on through the shallows and up the beach.

Seeing their captain on the sand, waiting horsemen moved toward him. They were in no great hurry now that they were back on friendly soil and nearly home. Harald looked to his left and his right to follow the progress of the other boats of the returning raiding fleet. There were fifty-five vessels in all, beached in the shallows and disgorging their cargoes of men and horses. The ships were full to the gunwales, not only with warriors and their mounts but with all kinds of booty. Gold and silver coin, gem-encrusted candlesticks, boxes of jewellery, bolts of silk and damask, huge earthenware jars of myrrh and incense, carpets and precious religious items were all being carried up the beach and heaped in a great pile beyond the high-water mark. The wretched men who carried these burdens were regularly beaten if they slackened and they could now only be sure of one thing – a life of misery until their ransom was paid.

Harald looked with satisfaction at the fleet he had assembled with the Guiscard. They had bought or built the war galleys in ports all along the Italian coast. Nearly all the craft were Byzantine *dromons;* shallow-drafted, two-masted and each with a single bank of oars. They were fast, deadly vessels, as adept at smashing through banks of enemy oars as they were of transporting warriors onto a beachhead at great speed. Their work was now done and they lay peacefully in the shallows; soft waves breaking gently around their hulls. Behind Harald stood one of his squires carrying the Papal banner – a yellow cross on a white background that snapped and folded in the onshore breeze.

They had just returned from a successful series of raids in Sicily, during which time a combined force of fifteen hundred Norman horsemen, Neopolitan infantry men and Sicilian archers had raided the island in a series of lightning strikes. It had not been an easy campaign and once the Saracen forces had woken up to the threat of invasion, they put up a dogged resistance. Harald and the Guiscard had miscalculated the strength of the opposition that met them. They had reckoned on rolling over the scattered Islamic fiefdoms along the island's southern tip but were instead surprised by a professional *Zirid* army from North Africa. After initially making huge incursions inland the invaders were pushed all the way back to their boats. The two Norman commanders rallied their troops and crushed the defenders in a pincer attack around the town of Messina.

"That was a close-run thing," thought Harald as he looked down at the dried blood on his hands from the fighting that had only finally stopped at dusk yesterday. A final charge had won the day, allowing the Normans time to fall back to their boats and escape on the morning tide before reinforcements arrived.

"A profitable visit anyway, Hari," shouted the Guiscard to his friend, guessing his thoughts.

"Perhaps, but I think we need to get some better intelligence next time," replied Harald seriously.

"I agree we were a little fortunate and the Norns smiled upon us. I would rather not rely on divine intervention next time though," said his friend nodding at the banner flying above them.

"God favours the brave," said Harald looking up at the banner.

Truth be told, he was not a great believer in the power of the Christian God. He had, however, the utmost faith in the influence it made on other men which, at times, seemed almost supernatural. The banner caused warriors to believe, when all hope was lost, and the most faint-hearted seemed to find hidden depths of courage and resilience when the tide of battle flowed against them. He had seen the effect of this belief among the men only yesterday and although he did not put his trust in the power of Jesus Christ he could not doubt the inspiration that this 'Messiah' provided. Harald touched the Thor's Hammer amulet that hung around his neck beneath his shirt. The Guiscard smiled at his friend's involuntary gesture knowing that Harald still had faith in the old Norse gods of his ancestors.

It was still only mid-afternoon on the sandy beach of Centraro where each of their ships lay peacefully. Many of the men would camp locally to enjoy the calm after the storm of battle, and the nearby town was well stocked with wine and whores in preparation for their homecoming. Now they had reached the safety of friendly shores, they would rest in the lee of the cliffs before making the short walk into the town where the brothels and wine shops would be happy to take their coin. As soon as his men and horses were all ashore, Harald would return to the castle of St. Marks with his two squires, Thomas and Gilbert. The previous day the boys had both done well when the call to arms came. They had not let their Lord down and joined the warriors in routing the enemy as night fell. Harald was proud of them both and the two orphaned brothers were like his shadow, seldom moving far from his side. They were as different as chalk and cheese, the older, quieter one had a large, owlish face and was constantly checking and chiding his larger, rumbustious sibling for some minor infraction or another. But both were as brave as lions when it came to the fight, and they had been his constant companions ever since Eva had died.

"It looks like we have company," said the Guiscard looking up to the cliff tops and shielding his eyes with one hand while pointing with the other.

Harald looked up to where he gestured. There were several horsemen looking down at the beach. He could not make out the figures against the sun, but he could see one of them was a woman.

"Not any of ours I think and anyway they have certainly come to the wrong place if they are looking for trouble," said the Guiscard. Then he let out a cry of delight, "I do believe one of them is my wife. Let's hope she has brought some decent wine with her. I have quite a thirst."

He leapt on his horse and galloped off toward the zig-zag path leading up the face of the chalk cliff. Harald, grumbling disconsolately at his friend's undue haste, followed on close behind him. They reached the top of the cliff quickly, one behind the other on the thin, rocky path and paused to let the heavy horses get their wind back. As they did so both men looked toward the group of twenty or so riders who stood dismounted and were regarding them intently. Some carried their lances casually over one shoulder as they waited. Harald let out a stream of profanity when he saw the small dove-tailed pennons fluttering from the ends of the spears. The two black ravens of Regneville were clearly visible as the little flags fluttered and tautened in the wind. Without hesitation he drove his spurs into the horse's heavily muscled flanks and Damascus flew toward the waiting group standing no more than a hundred paces away. They looked up, surprised as horse and rider hurtled toward them.

It all happened in the matter of a few heart beats. The woman turned toward the sound of muffled hoofbeats on the green sward and raised her hand in greeting. Robert and Floki Fitzroy followed her gaze to watch the giant rider on his enormous stallion bearing down on them. Before they could react, man and beast drew to an abrupt halt in front of the group and reared up in front of them. The rider slid off its back in a single fluid movement. Almost before the horse's front legs reconnected with the ground, Harald stood before it and moved swiftly toward his older brother. Robert did not have time to utter a word before Harald was on him, emitting a loud roar, wrapping his giant arms around his brother in an unbreakable bearhug and lifting him off his feet. The grass beneath Harald's wet boots was still damp from an earlier squall and he slipped carrying both of them crashing down. The two men tumbled to the ground and Harald landed heavily on Robert, winding him. Several of his comrades drew their swords at the sight of their Lord under attack but Floki held up an outstretched hand to dissuade any intervention.

"Rendement, brother?" shouted Harald. "I have you at last," he bellowed with a huge joyous laugh, the like of which neither Alberada nor her husband had heard since his return to St. Marks.

Harald got to his feet and hauled Robert up from the damp grass and hugged him again; this time in a far less physical manner. He looked round and saw his younger brother and grabbed for him in a similar fond embrace. Then, recognising several of his former comrades-at-arms from the company he flung his arms around them too, one after the other. The Guiscard now dismounted and, also well-known to the visitors from his time with the 'Riders', made his own hearty welcome. When the handshakes and back-slapping had subsided, Alberada held up her hands, and spoke loudly, in an effort to be heard. She had, she said, prepared a reception for the home-coming warriors and the visitors from the north and if they were to get there before nightfall they should leave immediately. While the army of St. Mark's completed their disembarkation, unloading men, animals and materiel on the beach below, the little party made the short journey home.

As dusk was falling the riders passed through the gates of the castle, to be met by a small army of grooms who took the horses off to the stables. Alberada, meanwhile, sent the men to wash, change and return to her private courtyard where preparations had been made for them.

When the men from Normandie had arrived three days before they had been made welcome and given comfortable quarters. She sent servants to Harald's old house which had long been deserted ever since he left to fight at Civitate. They cleaned and repaired it and the Duchess moved the brothers into the solid stone building that lay just outside the castle walls.

"They lived here as man and wife for a year or more," she explained as she walked them to their new quarters. "They seemed blissfully happy together then. I did not know your brother before he and Eva were married but my husband said he was reborn after they met. Did you know they were cousins - distant ones - but cousins none-the-less. She told me once that she was a Norse woman - from your grandfathers' hometown. Look, the bird is looking forward to going home."

She was watching Fulla who seemed to come to life on Robert's wrist, as they approached the house.

"When she left here, Eva took that bird all the way to Capua and then onto Benevento - where you found her. I cannot tell you much of your brother's life in that city, but I understand he grew to be a man of great influence and he and his wife were happy. Had she survived childbirth I suspect that they would both have stayed there."

"And what of the child, Lady? Our nephew," asked Floki.

"Ah, Bohemond. Harald returned here with his warriors shortly after Eva died. The baby was with them, and he asked me to take him. I put the boy with my son's nurse and since that day his father has not so much looked at the child. I cannot tell what might happen, but the boy is happy enough and is quite at home with my clutch of Hautevilles."

"And our brother," asked Robert. "How has he fared?"

The Duchess shrugged.

"It is difficult to say. His mood has not changed much since his return, and he seldom talks. My husband says he is only content when he is fighting or riding to war. He said it felt as if he had lost a brother but gained a ghost. Now come, let me show you your quarters - you will be more than comfortable here," she replied sadly. "I cannot tell what reaction you will get from Harald but if you can make him laugh again, I will be quite prepared to give him back to you. It will be a price worth paying. Anyway, they are due home and as soon as their fleet is sighted, we shall go out to meet them and we can see if you can make your brother smile then."

As they walked through the doors of the house Fulla flapped her wings and struggled against her jesses to take flight. Robert released her and she flew straight to the wooden perch on the other side of the room where she settled peacefully. When the Duchess left the brothers alone Robert considered what she had told them.

"Whatever feelings the reunion stirred within Hari, laughter might not be one of them," he thought.

At the reunion feast three days later, the knights of Normandie and their hosts were seated around a large wooden table and Robert and Floki sat either side of their brother. The balmy evening air was redolent with heavy citron aromas from the lemons, oranges and bergamots that ripened in the garden. The men talked quietly, in contrast to the enervating noise of the cicadas. Alberada, sat next to her husband and when all were seated she got to her feet and raised her cup of wine to the men.

"Most of you here are well acquainted with each other and I seem to be the only foreigner," she said confidently. "I am a lone woman from Burgundy in the midst of two dozen fierce Norman warriors - but I feel I am safe and amongst friends."

"You are right on both counts, Lady, and we thank you for your hospitality," answered Robert.

"If anyone should fear anything it is our guests, they have no idea how much wine a Burgundian Princess can consume at a single sitting," interjected the Guiscard.

"Be that as it may," she retorted, "I drink to the health of my friends new and old. I drink to brothers reunited and warriors returned safely home."

Alberada raised her cup and each man stood and did the same. Then she clapped her hands and a procession of women emerged bearing trays full of food. Suckling pig, roasted boar and an assortment of baked river fowl were brought out and put on the table. They were accompanied by an abundance of local fruits, vegetables and baskets of bread. As the wine jugs were drained, so new ones were brought out, filled with the harvest of local vineyards. The wine flowed, as did the conversation until even the noisy cicadas were drowned out. Loyal toasts were made and returned. The Guiscard was called upon to provide his account of the recent campaign in Sicily, which he did with drama and great gusto, lauding all the feats of his friend Harald Fitzroy, the mighty Papal Shield. The revellers listened attentively to his sterling account of the cavalry charges and acts of individual heroism before he called to his friend.

"Come now Hari, tell us the story of Civitate and the day you saved the Pope from death." bellowed the Guiscard with one hand on Harald's shoulder, "Is there a man here who does not want to hear the tale?"

Each man banged his fist on the table demanding to hear the story. Harald shook his head coyly but to no avail. The volume increased until it became obvious that his former comrades would not take no for an answer. He lumbered to his feet to great applause and held his hands up for quiet. Alberada looked on intently, willing Hari on. She watched his younger brother Floki looking up at him admiringly and noticed how alike they were. Finally, he broke into his story telling of the long, hungry march to the battlefield, the scattering of the Byzantine horde and the crushing of the Pope's Swabian vanguard. He told of saving the Pontiff's life and the march to take Benevento. Then he stopped abruptly as if remembering something hidden deep within him and could speak no more. The Guiscard, sensing that his friend needed assistance, broke in,

"Three times I was unhorsed at Civitate, and three times Harald was there to save my life. You should all remember that this man does not reserve his favours only for Popes. He smiles on us lesser men when the mood takes him. Gentlemen, I give you my friend and deliverer, Harald Fitzroy, without who I would not be here today."

There was unbridled applause around the table and Harald smiled, even if it was a little abashed, thought Alberada. In an attempt to divert attention from her friend she raised her voice above the clamour.

"Surely it is time we heard from one of the famous Riders of Regneville. I am told they have many famous tales to tell? Count Robert, would you do us the honour of telling us the story of the Wandering Warriors? Your brother has often spoken of its magic."

"You know a man of my beliefs cannot promise magic," he said sternly in her direction. "...but I cannot say no to a lady."

Robert crashed his wine cup onto the table and in one movement he was on his feet to launch into the famous saga of his grandfathers. He was surprised how easily the words came and how much pleasure they gave him. He glanced at the faces looking up at him as he lovingly recited the well-worn phrases and stanzas that his father had taught him as a boy. When he approached the last verse, he looked down to see his brothers looking back.

Not for gold, they fought, nor Queenly favours
Not for lands, nor wealth, nor hearthfire legends
For they fought for each other, and the reputation
Of the Wandering Warriors of Haugesund

The table erupted into applause and Robert resumed his seat. When it had died down sufficiently, Alberada excused herself and bid her guests good night. Any semblance of knightly good behaviour went with her and the revellers drank long into the night. The serving women continued to dispense even more wine, but on seeing their mistress retire for the evening, many took up invitations to sit and sup with their guests. When it became obvious that the time had come to retire the men began to stagger off to their quarters.

"Hari, it is time to go to bed. Come with us, we have something to show you," said Floki. "Robert, you take one arm and I'll take the other."

They hauled their brother to his feet and the three of them wove their way across the courtyard and out through the castle gates to their quarters.

"This is my house," announced Harald quizzically when he had gathered himself enough to realise where he was. The door was opened by one of the page boys the Duchess had allocated, and he sleepily ushered them into the fire-lit room.

"There she is, Hari," said Floki, leading his brother toward the hawk, sitting motionless on her wooden perch.

"Oh, Fulla," whispered Harald in drunken recognition. "How I have missed you."

Then he stumbled to the floor before passing into unconsciousness.

Chapter 12: The Decision

Harald opened his eyes and looked up at the high wooden ceiling. It felt good to be back in his old house, back in the marital bed he shared with his beloved wife. Then he gathered his senses, remembering he was alone and had been for over a year. Before he had time to sink back into the melancholy in which he had existed since his return to St. Marks, he was interrupted by the sound of singing from the next room. He got up and found Floki seated at a large wooden table and singing 'The Song of The Riders", a refrain that the men of Regneville often took up on their long marches.

"I have not heard that tune for many a year now," he said sitting down on the opposite bench. "The last time was on the road to Val-es-Dunes, with Serlo riding by my side."

"The Riders have had one or two illustrious leaders since then you know. Perhaps, I have not had so many battle honours as Serlo yet – but my time will come. Some of the men still talk of your own feats of arms," replied Floki.

"They must have good memories then for it has been many years since I led the Riders," said Harald. "Anyway, I hear you have earned yourself a passable reputation in my stead, little brother, but you still have some way to go."

"I shall not take your bait, Hari," Floki replied good-naturedly. "Anyway, you appear to have done well enough for yourself in your own little kingdom here. News of the 'Papal Shield' floats in on many of the trading ships that dock at Regneville. Come, let us eat this food that the Duchess has sent down from the kitchens. She is a fine host, that woman and a beauty to match."

"And a good friend to me, before you say something you might regret. As well as the wife of my best friend," reprimanded Harald. "Now tell me where our brother has gone? He will miss breakfast – a night's drinking gives a man a great appetite."

"There will be plenty left for him. There is enough food here to feed half the Riders, Hari. He has gone to pray, of course. He will be on his knees right now, I believe. Tell me truthfully now – will you return home to Normandie and help us make the Duchy safe from the French? You agreed to come last night when I asked."

"I did no such thing, Floki. Anyway, I was in my cups when you tried to take advantage of me."

"Take advantage of you, Hari? Hah - that is rich. But seriously we are in trouble and need your men and arms."

Harald looked at his brother and smiled warmly before he spoke.

"I shall not come with you, brother. My place is here – and I have Saracens to kill. It does my heart good to see you both and I have missed you - more than I can say. But no, I will not come - Normandie will fight on with only two Fitzroy brothers to defend her. She shall prevail as she always does."

"Robert was not to blame for the way Duke William treated you. The Bastard has always been jealous of the regard in which Robert holds you, you know. However, he was not quite so sure of your brotherly love yesterday on the clifftops. I thought you were going to kill him," replied Floki, changing the subject.

"So did I, but what happened between us all those years ago is gone forever. I was angry when I first saw Robert but as I lay on top of him squeezing out his last breath, I could scarcely remember what we fell out about in the first place," said Harald throwing back his head and laughing. "Now, eat that quickly for I believe I promised you a tour of our fortress."

At the same time as the two younger Fitzroy siblings were climbing the stone staircase to the high battlements, their older brother sat at the front of a small private chapel. He was not alone and sat beside his namesake Robert the Guiscard. The men were well-known to each other, and their families had been friends and allies for the last two generations; they shared a mutual respect.

"I have not seen Harald in such fine form for some time," said the Guiscard. "It is good to see him laugh once more. Your brother was in need of you."

"We are here for a purpose, all the same," said the Count of Mortain.

"I am aware that you need him at home but I also need him here. Even if I could dispense with his services, the loss of his followers would cause me problems. We plan to invade Sicily in the spring, and finding another thousand men quickly would not be easy," said the Guiscard without a hint of rancour.

"What if I were able to compensate you for such a loss? Would you be able to delay your attack on the Saracens for another year?"

The Guiscard shrugged and smiled inviting Robert to continue.

"If the King of France and his allies are defeated next year, there will be a great deal of hard-won land that I expect will become part of the Duchy. The Duke will reward his allies well and your family will be duly recognised for their contribution," stated Robert unequivocally.

"I have your word?" asked the Guiscard.

"As God is my witness," came the reply.

Later that day a group of riders left the castle. The three Fitzroy brothers, two squires and three falcons made their way into the Calabrian countryside. Having refound her master, Fulla was determined not to be separated from Harald again. The two boys each had a hooded peregrine falcon sitting calmly on thick leather gauntlets.

It was mid-afternoon by the time they reached the hunting ground, a small arid plain between two densely forested hills. Fulla was the first to take to the air as soon as her hood was removed, and her jesses slipped. She flew fast and high and then rested on the thermals, gliding effortlessly in search of prey. The hunters watched her graceful and perfect descent as she spied a lone rabbit caught out in the open. She hesitated for a moment and swept into a dramatic dive, killing her quarry in an instant. One of the boys galloped out to retrieve the dead rabbit before the two other falcons were released and put through their paces. Before long, six cleaned and spitted carcasses were being roasted over an open fire. Floki went to join the boys leaving Robert and Harald sitting together on an old log, rewarding their birds with scraps of offal.

"It is many years since we have done this together, brother. It is long overdue," said Robert. "Seldom has a day passed when I have not lamented the manner of your leaving the Duchy. I bitterly regretted my part in your departure and for that I apologise."

"You have little to reproach yourself for, Robert. You did your duty to the Duke as I tried to do mine. Anyway, the journey south has given me land, title and two years with Eva which I would not swap for anything. I have no bitterness in my heart for you – we are brothers, and our bond is still strong," said Harald wrapping a meaty arm around Robert's shoulders.

"Good. That is settled then. But glad as I am to see you, know that I am here on the Duchy's business," he replied.

"I do know that, but my answer is the same as I gave to Floki, I cannot come home with you– much as I would love to – my commitments are here," said Harald stoically.

"Hear me out," said Robert raising a hand whilst retrieving a leather pouch with the other. He reached into the bag and pulled out two identical gold warrior rings. Holding one in each hand, he held them out.

"Remember when Grandfather gave us these?" he said looking intently at his brother.

Harald said nothing as he remembered the warm summer's evening in Regneville when, as a ten-year-old boy, he stood together with Robert. They had just recited the great saga of their grandfathers' journey, in front of an audience of several hundred guests at the annual feast to remember 'the voyage of tears'. The Jarl had proclaimed that the Duchy was safe in the hands of its young guardians and presented them with their gifts – two bands of gold to be worn on their arms as a sign of loyalty. The ornament had been Harald's most treasured possession as he grew into manhood. The only time he had ever parted with the ring was when he gave it to Eva before her journey to the refuge in Capua. He looked up at his brother with some surprise.

"He gave us these to remind us of our oath to him. That we should protect his *aett*, his family, with our lives. That is what we have always done even if it meant we had to follow Duke William unquestioningly. Until you were driven away, we both kept our word to support our liege-lord. I am sorry if you were betrayed but I am asking you now to return home to help me protect our homeland," said Robert.

"How did you come by my arm-ring? I gave it to Eva," asked Harald abruptly.

"She gave it to the mid-wife before she died, and the woman placed it with your son before you returned to St. Marks. Lady Alberada found it and kept it safe. She gave it to me when we arrived a few days ago," replied Robert passing one of the rings to his brother who took it, turning it over in his hands. "I cannot turn back time, Hari, and if I could share what I have with you, I would. I promise you, and whoever returns home with you, that they will be well rewarded."

Harald said nothing as he considered his brother's words, allowing him to continue.

"Do you remember the story of Maldon?

"Grandfather's estates in England?" Harald answered.

"Yes. They have been returned to us by the English King and they are now yours for you to reclaim. We want you to have them," said Robert smiling at the look of surprise on his brother's face. "They are yours whether you return home or not."

Harald was considering these words when Floki came over to join them carrying a skin of wine.

"You are coming home then, Hari?" asked the younger brother.

Before he could answer Robert interjected.

"He is thinking about it, Floki."

Harald put the skin to his lips and took a deep draught.

"Let me talk to the Guiscard first," he said finally before calling over to his squires. "Hurry boys, we have some hungry men here. We must feed them soon before they die of hunger."

The brothers sat drinking and eating as the sun dropped behind the hills and it grew dark. They talked long into the night until one by one they fell asleep in the glow of the dying campfire embers.

Five days later, Robert and Floki left St. Marks with their men and took the road north. They stopped in Rome where they had arranged to meet with Archbishop Lanfranc and escort him back to Normandie. From there they travelled by ship to Genoa and then on through the Kingdom of Germany, before crossing into southern France. An uneventful journey saw them into the Duchy of Normandie sixty days after leaving St. Marks. The party arrived safely back in Caen as the leaves were turning to gold.

Their hosts in St. Marks had been sad to see the party depart, none more so than Harald. Alberada and her husband had been delighted to see the change in the mood of their friend and the effect that the reunion with his brothers had on him. The Guiscard willingly gave his blessing for Harald's forthcoming journey home and his campaign next spring in Normandie. It would mean delaying the invasion of Sicily, but he was confident that Robert Fitzroy would make good on his promise to enrich his family in the north. His friend would never know the details of the pact that the Guiscard had made with the Duchy's chancellor, nor did he need to.

At a time of year when life in St. Marks traditionally slowed down, through the autumn and into winter, the castle became the focal point of activity. Harald worked tirelessly at the task of recruiting, training and supplying a company of a thousand men to make the journey north in the early spring. Ships, horses, arms and vittles all needed to be organised and readied for the long journey to Normandie. To maintain an element of surprise the fleet would transport them to Barcelona where they would march across Aragon to the opposite coast of Spain. Another fleet would take them onward, north along the coast of France before disembarking in Regneville and joining up with the rest of the Duke's army. It was a bold plan, and a great deal would depend on the sea winds, but Harald was certain of its success. He had no shortage of recruits for the campaign, and there were many Normans in the Duchy of Apulia who relished the opportunity to return home and relieve the King of France and his allies of the rich lands that bordered Normandie.

Harald and his men worked feverishly to prepare for their new year's undertaking. In the year or more since Eva had been torn from him, he was finally able to come to terms with her loss. He still mourned her passing painfully, but with his newfound purpose he found life more bearable. Harald also took time to acquaint himself with his son Bohemond, who he had not so much as held in his arms since they had left Buenevento. The boy was now part of Alberada's growing family and he saw her as his mother.

Several weeks after the Christmas festival, everything was in order. Harald was finally at peace with himself, ready to wreak havoc on Normandie's enemies and counting the days when he would lead his army of elite warriors home.

Chapter 13: Caen, Spring 1056, Normandie Awaits

While Harald was making good his preparations to depart, three men sitting around the huge table in the great hall of Caen Castle, huddled conspiratorially close together at one end. At the sound of a servant approaching, they stopped their conversation and waited for the man to retire before resuming.

"Your powers of diplomacy are to be congratulated, Archbishop. You are sure that the charges against us have been dropped by the Holy See?" asked Duke William.

"On the contrary, Pope Victor went to great pains to express his gratitude to the Norman people for protecting his predecessor, the Sainted Leo. Not only has the threat of excommunication been withdrawn against you and the Duchess Matilda, but you are now highly favoured in the eyes of God and the Mother Church," said Lanfranc of Pavin.

William clasped his hands together and smiled contentedly as the Archbishop continued.

"However, my part in this change of mind is but a small factor. Your brother's role in the transformation cannot be underestimated, and without him we could not be assured of the support of Rome," said Lanfranc turning toward Robert.

The smile dropped from William's lips.

"And your brother, Robert. You are convinced he can be relied upon?" asked the Duke brusquely.

Before the Count of Mortain could answer, Lanfranc interjected.

"Harald Fitzroy is held in the highest esteem by Rome. He is known as much for his loyalty as for his bravery and if he has committed to come eight hundred leagues to fight for his homeland we should take him at his word," said the Archbishop unequivocally.

"My brother will be here come the spring. He has promised a thousand men and we will pay them with gold from the ducal coffers and land from the territories we retake. That is what we have pledged," said Robert.

"That is what we have pledged," repeated Lanfranc.

Both men looked to Duke William for affirmation, who said nothing but merely nodded before continuing.

"With a thousand men from the south, we can raise another six from the Duchy and perhaps two from Flanders?" asked William.

"Perhaps even a few more," said Robert. "Now we have Rome on our side we no longer fight alone."

"We have little time to lose, gentlemen," said William. "Call a council of all my noblemen here, in Caen, in twenty days. We need to be ready to meet the threat from King Henri and his allies. They will be here, in our midst by Easter, driving through the centre of the Duchy and we must be ready for them. Now, make haste for we will need as many men as we can muster - as well as God and all his angels."

Within twenty days the barons of Normandie were assembled in the great hall of Caen castle. Noblemen from the regions of Coutances, Bayeux, Evereux, Lisieux and Rouen all answered the call. Allies from further afield in Flanders, Maine and Brittany made heavier weather of the journey in the damp spring conditions. Despite roads still sodden from winter, they all arrived.

The hall was full as Duke William addressed them, and when he was finished each man knew what was expected of him and the consequences that would befall them all if Normandie fell. When the Duke announced that Harald Fitzroy's company from the Kingdom in the Sun would be fighting with them under the Papal banner, there was great excitement in the room. The hubbub died down and each man, from the most powerful Count to the smallest viscount, stood and promised his fealty and that of his men to the ducal cause. They would all be ready to fight to eject the French invaders, hopefully for the final time

By the time the last of the guests had departed the next day, Robert estimated that an army of ten thousand was conceivable.

"Would it be possible to defeat one three times that number?" he wondered watching from the battlements as the last party of horsemen departed. He warmed his hands over the glowing coals of an open brazier and considered their chances of success. "If Hari returns, anything is possible. God's speed, brother," he said to himself. Then he closed his eyes and prayed that come late spring Normandie would be delivered.

Christmas in the Duchy had been a quiet affair that year. As always there were great religious activities undertaken, as one saint or another was celebrated, and as usual many church services were held. Against this backdrop, there was desperate activity as preparations were made for the invasion that was expected by Easter. Robert made a brief trip home to Mortain for the celebrations, which gave him ample opportunity to inspect the defences thrown up around the town. His fiefdom would not be far from the direct line of march expected by the invasion force of King Henri. As he would not be there in person and neither would the majority of his fighting men, he wanted to ensure that the town was as well prepared as possible. Eleanor and the children would remain in

Mortain Castle, and should the worst happen and the town was attacked they could escape north to the coast where a waiting boat would take them to safety.

All over the Duchy similar plans were made, walls fortified, and palisades raised. Castles were strengthened, great earthworks were thrown up, gatehouses reinforced, and moats dug out. However, it was not the castle's occupants nor the inhabitants of the towns that surrounded them who could expect the least mercy. In the open countryside the farms, hamlets and communities had the most to fear and would be the first target of the invader's rapacious appetite. The people waited and watched for the signs of impending doom and destruction that would descend on them in the New Year.

Robert's spies came and went with increasing regularity. He visited the southern borders of the Duchy as often as was feasible to glean every last piece of intelligence on the enemy's plans. He was not disappointed, and a considerable amount of activity was in evidence.

As winter turned into spring, news came that King Henri of France had set up camp in Le Mans where he waited with an army of twenty thousand cavalry and foot-soldiers. The French host was further swollen with the arrival of another of Duke William's enemies, Geoffrey of Anjou. When mercenaries from Brittany and Maine arrived the invasion force exceeded thirty thousand men in all.

The Normandie winter had been particularly harsh that year and thick snow covered the land almost until spring. When it finally melted much of the Duchy in the north became a quagmire. The roads, clogged with mud, hindered the least movement of William's men and horses marching to the rallying point at Falaise. By the time Easter came, only half of his banner-men had arrived, and news came that King Henri's army had crossed the Duchy's border and were advancing on the road to Caen. Such was the size of the invading army that its ravenous head consumed all in its path and the French foragers pillaged everything they encountered. There was not a single farm, village or town that escaped from being put to the sword and burned to the ground. As the King's ponderous column wove its way ever more slowly through Normandie, it grew fatter and richer with plunder.

Heavily outnumbered, Duke William gave the order for his camp to break up and retreat. While he fell back to Caen to await the remainder of his forces, Robert marched forward with a force of two thousand men. They needed to engage with the enemy and slow them up whilst reinforcements gathered to the north. He took his men south and within half a day's march they sighted the enemy on the move.

The French host was huge and spread out for over a half a league at its forward position; behind the enemy thick smoke-trails from burning farms and villages wreathed the grey skyline.

"I do not think I have ever encountered an army quite this size," said one of the captains riding at Robert's side.

"You were never one to shirk a challenge, Rolande," replied Robert.

At that moment there was a break in the dark, grey clouds above and a shard of sunlight shone onto their column.

"Look, God's light always shines on the righteous," he continued.

Both men crossed themselves.

"Nor shall I shirk my duty today, Lord. What are your orders?"

"The ground is too heavy to test their flanks with a charge. Deploy the *hobelars*. We will welcome our guests with a few volleys of arrows when they come into range."

The order went out and five hundred mounted archers rode forward and dismounted in front of the Norman troops, forming up in three lines, one behind the next. King Henri's army drew to a halt two thousand paces away and frenetic activity resulted in a group of cavalry forming up in a loose line before their banners. It took some time before they were ready to advance across the muddy ground separating the two adversaries, but finally a group of about a thousand horsemen started their charge toward

Robert's men. The French horsemen covered over half the distance between the two groups before they became bogged down in a sodden meadow. As they did so the first fusillade of Norman arrows rained down on the hapless cavalry, which was quickly followed by another and then another. The air was filled with the sound of trapped horses and men, wounded and dying in the mud. After several more volleys Robert ordered his archers to cease and remount before the whole column departed back the way they had come.

"They will not be quite so unprepared next time, Rolande. When we find some dryer ground, we shall start to harry their flanks. Remember I do not want any close engagement - just a few skewered Frenchmen to slow their progress for now," he said looking up at the clouds which had rolled back to bathe the day in bright, midday sunshine.

It was not long before the thrusting waves of *conroi* began to dart in and then away from the French wings causing the huge column to compact and grind to a halt. With each attack Norman speartips took a deadly toll on the invasion force.

By the time Robert's men returned to the fray, to charge a second time, the invaders had managed to improve their defence and actually chased their tormentors away with a charge of their own. Such was the speed of the Norman withdrawal that any pursuit was futile. The Lord of Mortain, satisfied that hostilities were concluded for the day, led his men eight leagues north where they settled for the night in the small town of Exmes.

The few locals that were left made their compatriots welcome and all the remaining food and wine was brought out. Robert commandeered the empty house of the local priest, a small stone building near the church at the town's centre. After he was happy that all the necessary guards had been placed around the perimeter, he dismissed his captains and retired. As he always did when campaigning he gave thanks to God for delivering his men safely, before lying down on the bed. He reminded himself that orders were to be given to burn the town when they left in the morning and quickly fell into an exhausted sleep.

It was in the early hours of the morning before dawn when he was brought out of his slumber by hands shaking him awake vigorously. He opened his eyes abruptly and squinted to see Aubin standing over him in a state of panic.

"Quickly, Lord we are under attack. The French are upon us," shouted the squire pulling his master to his feet.

Robert, had fallen asleep still wearing his mail and needed only to strap his sword belt around his waist before he was ready.

"How many?" he asked.

"Thousands, Lord. Quickly before all is lost."

The door to the room was kicked in and they both looked up abruptly. By the weak light of a candle, they saw a heavily armed Breton *serjeant*, sword raised, hurtling toward them. Aubin took the full force of the man's overhead strike, cleaving his head in two with a single blow. As the attacker struggled to retrieve his blade, Robert was on him in an instant, stabbing his dagger up to the hilt into the man's eye and killing him instantly. The squire's killer fell on top of the boy's body and Robert stepped over them both and into the little street outside, which was filled with the sound of combat.

The wooden buildings opposite him were ablaze and the flames leapt from one building to the next. Startled Normans escaping the conflagration raced into the chaos outside to escape. Men were fighting hand-to-hand, with little room to manoeuvre. Robert saw a solid phalanx of a hundred or so Norman soldiers, shields to the fore, pushing past him towards the enemy in front of them. His men, recognising their leader, opened their ranks until he stood in their midst. He heard Rolande, at their head, his voice the embodiment of calm.

"On me lads, easy now. Move forward and link up with the others. We have the Commander now," he called in the same reassuring tone that Robert had first heard as a boy.

The group moved forward with iron discipline that betrayed any individual fear from within. It moved slowly, pushing back the ranks of Frenchmen that blocked its progress, slashing and hacking at the heads and bodies before them. The Norman advance gained momentum and suddenly, like a dam breaking, the enemy line in front of them broke and fled. The dense formation of men around Robert thinned out as they sprang forward to pursue their foe. He looked up to see they were in a large open space by the town's main gates and although his group had repulsed the solid formation in front of them, they were now beset by foemen on their flanks.

New enemy troops entered the melee to oppose them. With space enough to wield his sword, Robert plunged into a group of French foot-soldiers on one side and felled a man with a blow to the neck. The enemy resistance was stiffened by a group of Angevin cavalry who entered the fray and he saw two of them racing toward him, lances lowered. The first spear missed him but the second caught him a vicious blow between chest and shoulder. It lifted him off his feet and hurled him backwards into the ranks of his own men. Robert fell to the ground, grievously wounded, his life's blood pumping out where he lay. The last thing he remembered was looking up through a sea of staggering legs towards the lightening sky.

"Harald, where are you brother? I do not want to sit at the table in Valhalla without you," he shouted as the last of his strength left in his body.

As quickly as it started, the fighting stopped. The French and Breton troops were thrown back and the Normans regrouped with their comrades camped outside the town. Together they charged their attackers and beat them back until the enemy turned and fled. The defence however, was made at a great cost. Their commander had been struck down and many men were lost during the bitter fighting.

During the previous day's retreat, they had been followed to Exmes, albeit at a distance, by a large force of French cavalry. They killed all the guards and entered the town in the hours before daybreak and had they not been discovered quickly, the slaughter would have been complete. When it was over three hundred Norman warriors lay dead and many others were badly wounded.

Rolande mustered the troops for the retreat north. They departed in haste as soon as it was light and left their dead comrades where they had fallen. Those too injured to ride stayed in the town to meet their fate at the hands of the advancing Frenchmen. Robert's stricken form was placed on a wagon and the whole depleted column made its way back to Caen to reunite with Duke William's main force. Fleeing ahead of the main French army, they made a desperate flight, during which more men died from their wounds. They marched all through the day and the next night and by dawn on the following day they limped into the valley leading to Caen.

Chapter 14: The Prodigal's Return

Floki Fitzroy stood with his father, Torstein the Younger, on the high stone walls of Regneville castle. They were watching and waiting, as they had done for the last twenty days for the arrival of Harald's fleet. The younger man shielded his eyes from the glare of the spring sunshine and looked toward the gap between the two isthmuses, which acted as the gateway to the wide estuary. Floki was first to spot the large Byzantine *dromon*, a war galley under full sail coming through the gap. It veered to port and came off the wind at some speed followed in close order by other vessels of varying shapes and sizes. He grabbed the older man and hugged him excitedly,

"There, Father, he is here. Harald has come," he shouted.

Torstein allowed himself a smile as the sails of the sleek vessel slackened and the oarsmen took over, powering it toward the nearest pontoon on the harbour front.

"I never doubted it. His timekeeping is as bad as ever but at least he is putting on a good show for us."

The rest of the fleet hove into view and Harald Fitzroy was spotted standing in the prow of the lead ship - much to the delight of two hundred local people gathered on the harbour. He stood behind a carved wooden hawk's head at the ship's prow. With his long mail coat, braided beard and hair he might well have been mistaken for one of the old Norse sea kings, thought his mother. Siegrid fought to contain her excitement at the front of the throng. One after the other the sails of each galley were dropped, and the rowers took over.

Each of the double-banked oars of *Evas Prayer* rose and fell with expert precision, as did those of the following galleys. They raced in line over the flat water of the estuary with smooth elegance. As the ships approached the jetty, the wide-bodied *chelandia* moved off down-wind to land cavalry horses nearby in the flat shallows of the long sandy beach.

Evas Prayer docked, Harald leapt onto the pontoon to be claimed by his mother; who was the first to arrive. His huge bare arms embraced her and he lifted her off her feet ahead of the arrival of the rest of the town's people who swiftly enveloped him on the crowded jetty. Behind him the rest of the galleys swept in and tied up as their crews came out to watch their commander receive a hero's welcome from his kinsfolk. He had not stepped foot here for almost a decade but clearly, no-one had forgotten him.

"He has lost none of his popularity," said Torstein watching Harald from his vantage point on the walls. His son was now completely surrounded and would have disappeared from view were he not a head and shoulders taller than those who welcomed him.

"When do you ride?" he asked Floki.

"We ride at first light, Father. The armies of France will be knocking at our door before long if they are not stopped," said his youngest son.

"Then you will need to prise him from your mother's grasp and let him get some rest. She will be loathe to let him go to war when she has just got him back," said Torstein who paused before continuing.

"Do we have any more news of your brother Robert?"

When Rolande led the company back to Caen, they were severely depleted, and Robert was barely alive. Archbishop Lanfranc and a band of monks took him to a secluded abbey that was far removed from the city. It was well hidden and out of the path of the oncoming French army, which was rapidly reducing Normandie to a wasteland. None of the monks guessed where they were taking the badly injured Lord of Mortain and only Lanfranc knew of the final destination. The Archbishop prayed fervently for his friend and realised that it would take every healing power available to save him. Perhaps only divine intervention would drag Robert back from teetering precariously on the edge of death.

A short while after the fleet docked, Harald looked up from the map spread out in front of him on the table in his father's *solar*. He had only just extricated himself from the embrace of the townsfolk to quickly repair to the castle, where Floki and his father waited for him. After the briefest of reunions, they settled down to the urgent business of the defence of the Duchy and to make the plan on which the future of Normandie depended.

Torstein Fitzroy broke the news of Robert's predicament.

"We will lick our wounds after battle, Father," Harald said stoically before turning to his mother. "Robert is strong, *Mor*. It will take more than a French spearman to remove him from this earth. Come Floki tell me all you know."

His brother moved next to him and the men clustered around the table. Floki described the arrival of the enemy host on Norman soil ten days previously, that had raped and pillaged its way from south to north. A rapacious army of thirty thousand French, Angevin and Breton soldiers advanced in search of Duke William's army and burned, looted and destroyed everything in its path. King Henri had taken Caen without a fight and the Norman army had left only hours ahead of them. The Duke refused to face the enemy directly and chose to keep moving ahead and let them pursue him. When reinforcements arrived from Regneville they would confront the enemy on two fronts.

"How many men march with the Duke?" asked Harald

"Eight thousand," said Floki.

"And we are two thousand, with your Riders, brother?" Floki said nothing but nodded.

"Then we shall pick up their trail from Caen. The French column will be fat and bloated from all the booty they will be carrying. They will be on the march to Bayeux by now and we shall catch them here and attack their rear," said Harald pointing at the map. The captains craned over to where his finger fell until one man spoke up.

"There is nothing there but marshland, Lord, and a river," he said.

".. and a bridge that goes over it. Let us trust we can reach them before they cross. We will hit them hard and fast and drive them into the river or at least over it into the arms of the Duke," said Harald looking around at the questioning faces.

"It is still thirty thousand men versus ten thousand. Long odds I warrant," said his father voicing what the others were thinking.

"But we have surprise on our side and let us not forget the Papal Banner. Surely God will not dessert us in our hour of need," answered Harald smiling broadly. "How can we even contemplate anything but victory."

He reached for a cup of wine on the table and raising it to his comrades he said,

"Gentlemen, we shall deliver King Henri a boot up the arse such as he has never felt before."

Each man raised a cup of wine and returned his salute. "Tomorrow, we ride for victory," he added knocking his cup against the others held up in front of him.

The next day the combined column rode out of Regneville heading east. Such was the early hour that few saw them leave and by the time the *prime* bells were rung from the church tower, two thousand riders had already left. At their head rode Harald and Floki Fitzroy beneath the green and yellow Papal banner. Many of the men who had returned in the ships were from the Cotentin and keen to be reunited with families they had not seen for years. Any homecoming celebrations would have to be held after the battle and each returning warrior knew that if they failed, all would be lost.

At first, they made good speed, but as they travelled east the roads filled with refugees coming in the opposite direction. The skies began to darken with black smoke from the ruins of Caen and as night fell, the flames from the fires raging in the city illuminated the countryside for ten leagues. Harald's company made their camp on the east side of the city and as he and his men stopped for the night, they were met by riders coming west. They were scouts sent by Duke William and brought news. The Norman army was encamped on a small hill overlooking the town of Varaville and were in sight of the French host, which had stopped for the night on one side of the River Dives, no more than seven leagues from Harald's camp. He questioned the scouts thoroughly on the enemy's strength and the local terrain before sending them back with a message to the Duke. They would engage with the French in the morning and would strike hard at the enemy rear.

Chapter 15: The King's Nemesis

It was mid-morning when they came within sight of the enormous French camp. Harald's army crested a rise and came in view of the enemy host spread out for about a thousand paces; an untidy jumble of thousands of tents pitched in front of a vast area of wetland. All around there were carts and wagons, piled high with plunder taken during King Henri's march through the Duchy. The camp was breaking up, albeit slowly and rank after rank of horsemen and infantry waited patiently to take the stone road through the marshland and over the bridge across the River Dives. The King had already made the brief journey over the river with his bodyguard and a company of elite troops. He waited for the rest of his men to join him, hoping to finally confront the Norman army that had eluded him for the last ten days. Soon, he believed, he would finally crush 'the Bastard' and return the Duchy of Normandie to the Kingdom of France. When the rest of his army were ready, they would inexorably roll over William's inferior numbers; the day and the Duchy would be won.

The French monarch sat astride his horse idly chatting to his ally, Geoffrey of Anjou, when he heard the sound of horns bellowing across the open ground to the rear of his camp. He stood up in the stirrups to try and get a better view of what was happening across the river and as he did so he could make out a commotion in the ranks of his army.

The first wave of Norman cavalry galloped through the rear lines of the enemy camp and caused panic. Tightly grouped *conrois* of riders, each of fifty men, couched lances held rigidly in front of them, hit their unprepared foemen with venom. After the first spear-tips struck home, dispatching their hapless victims, the next wave of warriors followed, then the next and the next. Soon there were at least a thousand warriors driving their lances into the backs of the fleeing Frenchmen and their allies. Offered little in the way of resistance, the Normans struck down their enemy like the reaping of so much wheat. Many of their victims fled headlong toward the river and into the marshes where they quickly became trapped in boggy ground. Some made it through to the morass of waiting comrades at the stone bridge that could take no more than ten men abreast and pushed in panic to escape the carnage at their backs. The more they shoved, the more they added to the chaos in front of them as men were driven off the bridge into the fast-flowing river. Maddened horses reared up and their flailing hooves accounted for more lives as they ran amok in the bottleneck. King Henri watched in horror at the carnage taking place in his army's ranks and gave hasty orders for the men who had already made it across the river to return to the rear. They were to give aid to their comrades who were being slaughtered by the Norman cavalry.

Harald had committed half his men to this one-sided melee and unable to use their lances in the close combat zone, they discarded them in favour of swords, axes and maces. The rest stood in reserve with Floki awaiting the order to join the fight.

Meanwhile, from the far side of the river, Duke William, gave orders to join battle and his men moved forward in close order down the slope of the hill. They had waited impassively, watching their comrades drive the French invaders across the treacherous marshland toward the dubious sanctuary of the river. Frenchmen who made it through the mud and into the river's chilly embrace sank swiftly under the weight of their armour and drowned. The Duke's men ignored King Henri's isolated cohort and swept past them into the disorganised enemy ranks that had already crossed the river, determined to exact a terrible revenge.

Despite their appalling losses, the French rallied and there was bitter and sustained hand-to-hand combat all along the line. The King's army still had a vastly superior numerical advantage and gradually, as the battle wore on, it began to count. His cavalry, unable to fight in the confined space, were now on foot and formed a long shield wall behind which, more and more of their fighters formed up. They presented a stiff line of resistance against the Duke's army who began to falter and lose ground.

On the other side of the river Harald watched the tide of battle change and ordered the horns to recall his horsemen. They had done all that was asked of them and had accounted for thousands of dead foemen but despite the vigour of their repeated charges many of the enemy had escaped them. The invaders' shield wall on the opposite side of the bridge held firm and advanced steadily toward Duke William's vanguard.

Harald ordered his reserves to march forward on foot, where the enemy had formed up to guard their rear. In a well-practiced manoeuvre five hundred men advanced in a tightly packed wedge; locked shields bristling with spears. The wedge drove straight at the bridge, splintering all resistance and Harald at its apex unleashed a flurry of hacking and thrusting with a short stabbing sword. His frenzied movements were repeated by those behind him and slowly, their phalanx drove toward the enemy's heart.

Harald was in his element. He felt no fear, only rage for those who had wronged him. He felt anger to those who had outlawed him from Normandie nearly a decade before. He felt anger for his wounded brother and the bitter wrath for the loss of his beloved Eva would be delivered in full.

The Frenchmen on the bridge resisted, but the wedge drove into them, splintering all resistance. To his men it appeared that Harald was imbued with a supernatural strength which he shared with his brothers-in-arms, making them invulnerable to any pain and suffering. He was Thor made flesh and returned from *Asgard*. As he exhorted them to unleash ever greater feats of slaughter upon the heads of their enemies, they felt neither fear nor exhaustion. The Norman phalanx reached the far side of the bridge and beneath their feet the flagstones were wet and slippery, covered with the blood, gore and filth of those who fell beneath their collective fury.

The battle was far from over and they plunged on and into the vulnerable rear of the stiffened French shield wall, who turned to meet them. The company met with more resistance, but Harald would not be denied. Driven by his iron will, they splintered the massed ranks in front of them, dividing the enemy into two groups. Harald looked over the top of his shield and saw a widening gap in the French lines. In the distance in front of him he watched the ranks of Duke William's army regroup and charge again at their foemen. Harald's flying wedge that had been so dominant started to falter and unravel, but their work was done and the breakthrough had been made. Behind them, through a narrow gap, came the rest of their mounted reserve. The men on foot stood aside and watched Floki lead the charge and continue their bloody work from horseback.

By midday it was finally over. Split asunder by Harald's advance over the bridge the two groups of the huge invasion army were in complete disarray, pursued by one or the other of the victorious companies. To the left and right of the riverbank there were thousands of dead or dying men. Those lucky enough to escape the vengeful Normans threw down their weapons and armour to flee. Some of the remaining French cavalry managed to reach safety but those on foot were less fortunate and easily dispatched by a lance or a sword in the back.

King Henri and Geoffrey of Anjou surveyed the scene beneath them from on top of their hill. They saw the remnants of their army lying in tatters below them. They saw their once proud banners trodden into the mud of the battlefield. They saw the river clogged with dead men as far as the eye could see downstream. As the activity on the battlefield slowed to a deathly stop only a few riderless horses still charged about, looking to escape the madness. The French monarch quietly departed and vowed to himself never to return again to Norman soil.

Harald and Floki looked over the battlefield in silence. Like a summer squall the fighting had blown itself out leaving behind utter chaos. Their gaze moved to the peak of the hill, to the enemy commander being led away disconsolately by one of his men. A harsh voice distracted them.

"Let him go, Hari. I think King Henri has finally seen enough of Normandie. In any regard, your men seem to have taken more noble hostages than they know what to do with," called William, Duke of Normandie, to the man he had exiled nearly ten years previously.

Chapter 16: The Aftermath

Harald had wondered many times what the reunion with Duke William was going to be like. He had promised himself that he would remain calm and controlled when he met the Bastard again. The Duke had caused him huge unhappiness. He had not only lost his inheritance, his woman and his liberty, but it had also caused a deep rift between him and his brother Robert. The man who had inflicted such pain was before him, looking down from the saddle of his horse.

"Duke William, I am your servant," said Harald formally and bowed his head deferentially.

In a swift movement for such a broad man, the Duke cocked his leg over his horse's neck and jumped down. Before Harald could react, William wrapped his arms around him in a powerful embrace.

"You are not my servant, you are my brother, Hari. You could not be more welcome than you are now. For an awful moment there I thought we might not prevail, and that God had deserted us. But seeing you carving a path through the enemy ranks I knew we could not lose. It is good to see you again," enthused the Duke.

Harald was taken aback by the warmth of the welcome.

"It was like seeing your grandfather in his pomp, smiting the enemy like Samson among the Philistines."

"You gave good account of yourself also, Lord. Your *conrois* delivered a little sting themselves," returned Harald recovering from William's bonhomie.

"Please Hari, when did you ever call me 'Lord' between the two of us?" volunteered the Duke gesturing to one of his men to pass him a skin of wine. "Come, let us drink to our great victory. I do not think we shall be seeing King Henri in the near future."

William spat out one of his guttural laughs, which had annoyed Harald so much as a boy.

"It is good to see you too, William," he said and took a huge draft from the wine skin.

The two men stood and talked together as they shared the wine. The ice between them appeared to have been broken, thought Harald. The conversation was amiable enough, like two old friends meeting one another again after so many years. Harald responded as warmly as he was able but still suspected that beneath William's veneer of affability the Bastard plotted and schemed as of old.

"You will be visiting Robert?" William asked.

"As soon as I find out where he is being tended," answered Harald.

"He is not far and is being well cared for. I must warn you though, he was badly injured when I saw him last but if anyone can save him it is Lanfranc's monks. I will send one of them to guide you to him. Robert is in good hands, Hari, I pray for him every day and if the Lord hears me he will be saved," said William crossing himself. "Then come back to me in Falaise. We have much to discuss."

With his first meeting with the Duke over, Harald returned to his men who were in the abandoned French camp with its heavily laden wagons filled with all manner of plunder. Their losses had been relatively light compared to the devastation inflicted on the French and their allies. Two hundred and forty Normans had fallen in battle, but they had taken over five hundred noble hostages who would be ransomed back to their families.

"What shall we do with the pillage?" asked Floki of his brother later as they sat in the warmth of a huge fire, around which their men were sitting and drinking.

"It is ours, of course. We shall return any valuables to the Church but the rest is ours. Fair payment, I think, for deciding the battle's outcome. Don't you? In the morning I want you to take our men and the prisoners back to Regneville. You, brother, are now a rich man," answered Harald.

"You will not be coming?"

"No, I must find Robert first and then return to Falaise to meet with the Duke. My men have been promised land and silver and if the bargain is kept, we shall all be happy."

"The Duke is an honourable man, Hari. You will see," said Floki.

"I hope so, brother, for all our sakes," said Hari. "Now let's see if we can liven the evening up a little. This is a victory celebration after all."

Harald got to his feet, called for quiet among the troops and began to sing. The strains of "The Ship's Return" echoed hauntingly across the field of battle.

> *My mother wants a price paid*
> *To purchase my proud long ship*
> *Standing in the stern*
> *I'll scour the ocean for plunder*
> *My stout Norse steersman*
> *Of this sleek vessel*
> *Will come home to harbour*
> *After hewing our foemen*

The song was taken up by his comrades throughout the camp and before long the flat lands on each side of the river resonated to the ancient words.

The next morning a monk arrived in the camp riding an old roan *sumpter*. He announced himself as Archbishop Lanfranc's man and told Harald he would take him to where his brother Robert was being cared for. Taking ten men as an escort, he left immediately, and they headed toward the sea. When they reached the coast, they turned west.

Just before dusk they reached the hamlet of Rye and travelled the short distance through some dense woodland where a secluded abbey stood in a small clearing. One of their party rang the bell above a strong studded oak door which creaked open and they were met by Lanfranc of Pavin. He was pleased to see Harald and although the two men had never met he exuded a familiar warmth in his welcome.

"You can be none other than Harald Fitzroy," he said with arms outstretched and smiling broadly. "Your brother has been anxious for news of you. Let me take you to him. There is food for your men in the refectory and there are quarters here for you all for as long as you wish. Please follow me."

They walked through a labyrinth of small passages and stopped before a cell door.

"He is in here but is still very weak. When I brought him to the abbey, I doubted we could save him. His wound turned septic and festered but we prayed hard and the monks kept him alive long enough to fight the infection. God answered our prayers and gave him back to us. He has often spoken to me of you, Hari, and is proud to have you as his brother. You should know he blamed himself for you leaving the Duchy."

"That is all forgotten now, Archbishop. Anyway, he has nothing to reproach himself for. My journey since leaving Normandie has been one I would not change," Harald replied.

"Welcome home, all the same, Harald. You answered the call and God shall reward you and your men," said Lanfranc before adding conspiratorially, "and so shall the Duke, be in no doubt."

He led them through the door of the small cell. It was sparse but clean and on a small cot lay Robert whose short, shallow breathing made the only sound. The monk, keeping a vigil next to him stood up and left the room without saying a word.

"I will leave the two of you here. There is another cot if you wish to sleep," said Lanfranc before following the monk from the room.

Harald went over to look down at the wan face of his brother. Despite the severity of his wound, from which blood still seeped through a heavy dressing, Robert looked peaceful. As his brother loomed over him he opened his eyes and inhaled sharply in recognition.

"Hari? You have come."

"I have, Robert. Do not fear, you are alive and have not entered Valhalla just yet."

The two men smiled at each other, and Harald continued.

"The battle is won, brother and we are victorious. Have you strength to hear the whole story?"

Robert nodded and Harald told of his journey back to the Duchy and how their voyage had been beset by wind and storms delaying their arrival. He went on to tell of the rout of the invaders and his reunion with Duke William.

"And he was pleased to see you?" asked Robert weakly.

"He seemed so," said Harald, "perhaps even a Norman leopard may change his spots?"

"Then I am pleased, Hari," declared Robert as he searched his brother's face for anything disingenuous. "Now, there is something more you must do for me. I want you to go to Mortain and tell Eleanor that I am safe and will join her when I am well enough to travel. You must insist that I do not want her travelling here."

He watched as he saw the look on Harald's face change and his head shake in denial of the request. "You must meet her sooner or later if you are returned to Normandie. Please Hari, do this for me."

Harald shrugged resignedly in acquiescence.

"Good, that is settled then. Tell me one more time of your charge over the bridge again. It sounds like a tale from the Wandering Warriors."

Before he had finished retelling the story of the decisive charge, Robert had fallen asleep and was snoring gently. His brother lay down on the cot opposite and before long he too was fast asleep.

The next morning started with a bustle of monks in the little room. They entered without warning and flung open the wooden shutters to let in the daylight. Then they moved toward their patient and dressed and cleaned his wounds. Harald watched in fascination as the three brown-robed figures moved silently about their tasks. He looked over the shoulder of one man who was removing first the bandages and then the packing from a large hole between Robert's chest and left shoulder. Another man repacked the wound with moss and lichen before a poultice was applied and the new bandages wrapped around his chest.

"It is like being a baby all over again," quipped Harald at his brother's obvious discomfort.

One of the monks turned around and snapped at him.

"You will find breakfast in the refectory, Lord. Or, if you wish to pray the chapel is at the end of this corridor. "

"I will return shortly," said Harald to his brother. "You are clearly in good hands."

Robert returned his smile and motioned with his hand to the door.

After a little searching, Harald found the refectory, where fifty or so monks sat eating as they listened to a brother reading a liturgy in Latin from a lectern at the head of a long wooden table. A young novice brought him a bowl of porridge, some black bread and a cup of weak beer. He had finished eating when he felt a hand on his shoulder and another man beckoned him to follow. Archbishop Lanfranc was waiting for him outside.

"You are well rested, my Lord and ready to greet the day," he said energetically. "Would you care to join us in prayer?"

"Perhaps a little later, Father," answered Harald. "I must check on my men first."

"You will find them well cared for. Let us take a walk in this spring sunshine then," said Lanfranc, taking him by the arm and leading him into a small, sunlit quadrangle. The tiled square was empty save for two elderly monks sweeping the floor clear of some leaves. "I thought he would die before we got him here," he continued, "but your brother refused to go beyond the pale. I think it was his faith that kept him alive."

"Robert has always been a pious man, never more so than now I think," replied Harald stoically.

The Archbishop gave a gentle laugh.

"It was his faith in you that I am referring to, Harald. In the years I have known him I never saw him more certain of our success than when he was sure you were coming home. He often said that if you returned the Duchy would be safe. And so it has proven, you are blessed by God and the Church of Rome," said Lanfranc.

Harald laughed gently and held up his hands, palms outward, in denial.

"I am no man of God, Father. Quite the opposite. God has deserted me enough times to know that I am not his chosen one. But I gave my word to protect Normandie for as long as I am here. I have always been a loyal bannerman of Duke William although he might not always have appreciated it."

"Your roots are here, Harald. You might think your destiny lies elsewhere but I think that this is where you belong. You must stay; God has a plan for you in Normandie. Anyway, I understand that you are about to be given a great deal of land – enough for you and your men to settle on and prosper."

"Perhaps," said Harald. "I am undecided, although I am expected back in Calabria next year."

"We need you more than the Guiscard does. He can take Sicily back without you," said Lanfranc with a wry smile.

Harald laughed again.

"Is there anything that escapes you, Father?"

"Very little," confided the Archbishop. "Now when do you leave for Mortain? Lady Eleanor will be desperate for news of her husband. You may tell her that Robert will make a full recovery from his wounds. Do not stay too long for you have urgent business in Falaise to conclude, I believe."

That evening Robert was strong enough to leave his bed for a while and sat with his brother at the small table in the cell. Harald was delighted to see the recovery and in two days he was on the road to Mortain, pondering on what sort of welcome he might receive there.

Chapter 17: The Return To Mortain

Despite the defeat of King Henri and his allies, the road from Rye to Mortain was still perilous. The flow of refugees escaping his plundering army had largely stopped. The people fleeing their burning homes, charred fields and slaughtered livestock had been replaced by desperate bands of enemy soldiers trying to reach the safe havens of Paris, Anjou or Brittany. They were hungry, despairing and reckless men and made the road south dangerous for all but heavily armed troops. Harald rode imperiously at the head of his ten-man column under the banner of the Two Ravens. They were not confronted during the hours of daylight, but their camp was attacked in the dead of night and one of his men, standing guard, was shot through with arrows before the alarm was raised. The attack was successfully repulsed, and half a dozen ragged assailants lay dead by the time the column took the road again.

Harald was in a pensive mood as they neared Mortain. He was unconcerned by the prospect of further attack and far more troubled by his impending reunion with Lady Eleanor. The two had last met over ten years ago in one of their regular lovers' trysts. She had been sixteen years old, and they had spent their last night in a clandestine meeting with only her maid and his squire guarding their secret.

They had first met as children on his grandfather's estate and although she had only been five years old and he was ten, a friendship began. When he later became a page and then a squire, in the service of her father, they saw much more of each other. Eleanor was smitten from an early age with the dashing young giant of Regneville. She had to wait until she was fifteen before Harald reciprocated with his own heartfelt feelings and their bond was sealed. The two met as often as they could and although their friendship was no secret, they kept the intensity of their feelings for each other out of the public glare. That had been an age ago, when she had been taken from him and given to his brother Robert in marriage.

Harald began to think of everything that had happened to him in the intervening period, starting with the fateful night that ended in his banishment from Normandie. He remembered the desolate plight of his departure from the Duchy, when he threw himself into warring and adventure with the Guiscard. He thought of Eva and his redemption at her hands after she raised him up from a pit of bitter despair. He remembered the happiness he found with her before she was snatched away from him. He thought of his son, Bohemond, growing up eight hundred leagues away in Calabria and wondered, with more than a tinge of regret, whether he would ever see him again. He was suddenly brought back to the present by the sound of raised voices. Harald looked up and saw the road ahead blocked by the fallen trunk of a tree, behind which stood a number of spearmen. One of them, a grizzled old veteran, stood out in the road and when they were close enough to hear he called out, holding up a hand.

"Halt, the road to Mortain is closed to all but our own men. You gentlemen will surely know that we must be vigilant until the King of France has been completely ejected from the Duchy."

Harald called his column to a halt looking intently at the thick, green vegetation that grew on either side of the road for any sign of an ambush. Seeing none, he walked his horse up to the old man who stood unmoving in front of him.

"Do not come any closer," shouted the grey beard drawing his sword.

"The French army has been defeated and the King's men lie dead in their thousands on the battlefield of Varaville. If you do not want to join them, my friend you will give us safe passage along this road for I have urgent business with the Lady of Mortain," returned Harald before pointing his thumb over his shoulder to where the banner of the Two Ravens was held aloft. "Do you not recognise my sigal?"

There was movement from behind the log and another armed man appeared, engaging the first in whispered conversation. The older man turned back to Harald and bowed his head.

"My apologies, Lord Harald, I did not recognise you. These are strange times and we are wary of visitors. I will send a rider ahead of you to alert the Lady of your arrival. You are but three leagues from her castle," he said respectfully.

"Thank you, friend, but I am familiar with this road. Please have your rider tell the Lady not to be alarmed and there is nothing to fear. We bring good news of Lord Robert who lives and is recovering from his wounds."

Harald and his column were waved around the barricade to the loud cheering from the thirty or so men who guarded it.

By midday they arrived at the outskirts of Mortain. The town had been seemingly untouched by the fate suffered by the rest of Normandie. It also seemed, from the absence of men of a fighting age, that their soldiers had yet to return. Curious townspeople came out of their houses to gawk at these strangers in their midst, trotting purposefully through the streets toward the steep ascent to the castle. When Harald's men arrived at the summit, the gates to the fortress were already open and the visitors passed through the imposing stone towers and into the large, cobbled courtyard before the main keep. A small army of page boys greeted the visitors and readied to stable their tired horses. As Harald dismounted, two figures walked briskly toward them. It was only when they were nearly upon him that that he saw one of them was a woman. She was dressed like a man and wore a long mail shirt over leather breeches and black *gambeson*. Around her waist was a light sword and dagger and her long auburn hair was pulled back into a single waist-length plait that swung from side to side as she marched toward them.

"Eleanor?" enquired Harald.

"Do not think I have forgiven you yet for the manner in which you left Normandie," she scolded him fiercely.

Harald, for once, stumbled awkwardly for a reply.

"I am ..." he started before she interrupted.

"Come on, out with it. Has the cat taken your tongue?"

All of the men turned their heads toward the pair expectantly. Eleanor stared coolly at Harald, no more than five paces away from her. There was silence, except for the sound of hooves on the cobbles as the horses were led away. She stood, arms folded, glaring up at him. Then, unable to restrain herself any longer she burst out laughing and Harald exhaled deeply before his face broke into a huge smile.

"Come, this is no way to greet an old friend," she said beckoning him with her arms outstretched.

He dismounted and covered the short distance between them and reached down to embrace her. Before he could say anything more, she asked quickly,

"You have news of Robert. Tell me how he is? I must know."

"Your husband was badly injured, but he will live and will be back to you as soon as he is able. He is in good hands and wants for nothing," said Harald.

He watched Eleanor breathe a huge sigh of relief, noticing a single tear roll down her face.

"Except, of course, to have his wife by his side," he added.

She wiped her face with the back of her hand and recovered her composure. Harald spent some time answering a fusillade of questions until she was satisfied that her husband was safe.

"That is excellent news and I thank you and your men for bringing it to me. Now, I insist that you stay until at least the garrison returns. If we come under attack, I cannot hold the castle with just a handful of old men and women."

Harald began to protest that he had business back in Falaise with Duke William, but he knew that she would not take 'no' for an answer. He sent his men away to their quarters before dutifully following Eleanor into the keep and up to the family's *solar*. She gave instructions to a servant to show him his rooms then turning to her guest she said,

"I will see you later, Hari. Rest a little and refresh yourself. There are some people here who are excited by your arrival, and you will need to be at your best."

Harald thought no more of this last remark and followed the servant to his quarters. He smiled when he was shown the room, a large chamber with a huge bed. He last stayed here over twelve years ago when he had visited with his brother and Duke William when they came looking for Eleanor's father to confront him for suspected treachery. All they found was her mother, Lady Phillipa, who had quickly disarmed the young Duke with an inspired display of charm that sent him away empty-handed and besotted. Harald on the other hand, had been secretly delighted to get another excuse to see Eleanor; he smiled at the memory

On the bed he found an array of clothes laid out for him. They were Robert's and probably too small for him, but he decided to choose something for himself later. At the moment he was as tired and weary as he could remember and wanted only to close his eyes. Ignoring the food and wine that had been laid out, he managed to strip off his *hauberk* and a few of his clothes before falling into a deep sleep.

Harald woke to knocking on the door. He grunted and the servant, a woman called Agnes, who had first shown him to his room, let herself in. He watched her enter and pick up his clothes which were strewn all over the floor. She was followed by a gaggle of younger women who brought in a wooden bathtub which they filled with buckets of hot water. He rose from the bed and absent-mindedly began to strip off the last of his small clothes, which had not been changed since he had left Regneville eight days ago. He looked up at the women, all watching him surreptitiously. Agnes wrinkled her nose disdainfully while the four younger women giggled as he continued to undress in front of them before getting into the bath.

"Will that be all, Lord," asked Agnes.

Harald grunted again.

"When you are ready, Lady Eleanor, is expecting you for dinner in her *solar*," she concluded leading the others out.

He finally felt clean and with the water the colour of pitch and getting cold he got out and dried himself. He groomed his hair and beard with combs that he found on the table and selected something to wear. Harald was surprised to find some of the clothes fitted him and when he was dressed he sauntered out in search of his host.

He heard the sound of young children and decided to follow it. Rounding the end of the corridor he walked into the family *solar*, a brightly lit room which was dominated by a long oaken table, set for dinner. At the end of the room, in front of a large hearth, Harald saw Eleanor bent over a small girl who he guessed was no more than two years old. Close by, two older boys were tumbling energetically around an old hunting dog who, fast asleep, was oblivious to their rumbustiousness. He was half-way across the room when Eleanor looked up and smiled radiantly at him. She straightened and the children retreated into her skirts as they warily watched the giant stranger striding toward them.

"Children, this gentleman is …." she began.

"Papa," interrupted the young girl.

"No, he is not your father, Turid, but he is your Uncle and he has sailed across the great ocean to save us all. Richard and William, come out from behind my skirts and meet Lord Harald Fitzroy, who has come a great distance to fight for the Duchy," said Eleanor. "If you introduce yourselves to him politely you may yet be asked to dine with us."

The eldest child, a boy of seven stepped forward and thrust his hand out toward Harald.

"Welcome to Mortain, Lord Harald. My name is Richard and I have heard many great things about you. Father said you conquered Italy and would come back to rid the world of the King of France."

The other boy, William, younger and smaller, stood closely behind his sibling.

"Mother says you are a great warrior, like our great-grandfather and while you live, Normandie will always be safe," he squeaked. "She is also a great warrior and any Frenchman who enters her castle will die at the point of her sword."

Turid, determined not to be ignored, pushed her way in front of her brothers and held out a posy of flowers for their guest. Harald knelt down before her and took them.

"Children, thank you for your welcome. I have been on the road for longer than I care to remember and have forgotten how it feels to be with family. It is my great pleasure to be your guest tonight," he said.

Eleanor clapped her hands, and two servants came into the *solar* to seat the children at the table. They all sat around one end. Turid was placed on a highchair next to her mother, while the two boys sat opposite on either side of their honoured guest.

He watched Eleanor settle the children, gently bringing them to order before food was served. She wore a plain green, silk dress which had been well-cut and accentuated her athletic frame. Her long-plaited hair had been wound into a braided bun which sat at the nape of an elegant neck around which she wore a simple gold cross that rested on her breast. Harald tried, unsuccessfully, to resist the temptation of stealing glances as Eleanor tended to Turid and was caught staring. After the third time she asked,

"Well, Hari, have I changed that much? Tell me truthfully now, for I know the demands of motherhood may have taken their toll."

He laughed, slightly embarrassed.

"In truth you have changed little, Eleanor. But you have definitely inherited the look of your mother and I seem to remember she was a woman of rare beauty."

"Hari, you have not lost that silver tongue after all. I take that as a great compliment. You were one of her favourites you know."

They laughed together and the conversation started to flow between the two old friends.

The last of the sunshine faded, leaving the room bathed in the light of the hearthfire and the dozens of candles that hung from suspended lamps. When the meal was over the children persuaded Harald to tell them a story. He entertained them with tales of his adventures in Italy, full of dashing knights and beautiful Byzantine princesses. He spoke softly to his enraptured audience as Eleanor played on a psaltery. The notes floated to the high ceiling, providing a melodious backdrop to Harald's story. One by one the children fell asleep, and their nurse took them off to bed leaving the two adults alone. They sat across the table from each other, both at ease in the comfortable silence existing between them. She continued to absent-mindedly pluck at the instrument that rested in her lap before looking up and catching Harald's eye,

"Now I want to hear the real story of Harald Fitzroy and do not leave anything out. Remember, I always knew when you were making something up," she said wagging her finger in mock solemnity.

"As you wish, my Lady. I shall not omit a thing if that is your desire," said Harald and started to tell his second tale of the evening.

He began with the day of his banishment from the Duchy, when he was forced to leave as an outlaw. He told of the years of hardship when he arrived, miserable and penniless, in Calabria. He told of his first meeting with Eva and of their brief life together. He told her of his wife's death during the birth of their son and how he rode, bereft and full of anger, in search of enemies to kill in order to slake his thirst for atonement. He spoke of his joy at the reunification with Robert and of his redemption when finally setting foot back in his beloved Normandie once more. Harald could not swear to it, but he was convinced he saw Eleanor's cheeks damp with tears in the firelight as he continued his saga. Finally, when he had finished, she spoke,

"That is a fine story and one that deserves a happy ending. Will you find it here in the Duchy or will your wanderings take you away from us again?"

'That I cannot tell you, but I do know it is good to be home for the time being. I have work to do here but I also have business back in the south," he said.

"Well, you cannot leave Mortain until my husband returns. You promised," she said, fixing him with a fierce look.

"I did no such thing," he remonstrated, "but I will stay until your troops return. The Bastard has kept me away for too long. He can wait a little longer to settle our business together. It is on one condition and that is that you tell me your story."

This time it was Eleanor's turn to scoff.

"There is little to tell, Hari. Certainly, nothing to rival your tale. I will tell you in time, but not tonight, for it is not seemly for a married woman to be alone with a bachelor knight at this late hour - even if he is her brother-in-law."

She pushed her chair back and stood up before walking round to his side of the table. Eleanor bent down and gave him a chaste kiss on the cheek.

"Good night, Hari. It is good to have you back," she said, turned briskly and left the *solar*.

Harald was left alone with his thoughts and the scent of ambergris and lavender that lingered on the air, reminding him of different, long-gone times.

Chapter 18: The Lioness Of Mortain

When Phillipa, the Countess of Mortain compelled the sixteen-year-old Eleanor to comply with Duke William's wishes and accept Robert Fitzroy's marriage proposal, her daughter had been inconsolable. Eleanor allowed this period of unhappiness to last only a short while, for she knew that as a high-born noblewoman she had important duties to fulfil. Her new husband was the Duke's right-hand and much was expected of them both. Ultimately, she followed her mother's advice and knuckled down to the considerable task in hand, raising a family, making a home and supporting her husband. It could have been worse, her mother reasoned; Robert was a handsome man from a prominent family who would treat her well and pay her the respect she deserved. He was not one of those vulgar, decrepit old barons who would consign her to a life of marital servitude, producing babies year after year like some brood mare. Brood mares, reminded her mother, eventually met the butcher's knife when their fertility was exhausted.

Lady Phillipa had been right, Robert turned out to be an attentive and respectful husband who valued his wife's opinion. They had three children in a ten-year period of marriage and although he would have preferred more, she would be happy for it to stop there. Eleanor remained feisty and independent but always returned Robert's love with a genuine affection of her own.

Growing up she was the eldest of five children and the apple of her father's eye. Count William Werlenc was a devious man, but he cared deeply for his family and provided a comfortable life for all of them. He was also a rich man with land and property and were it not for him backing the wrong side, he would surely have continued to prosper. He ensured that Eleanor was schooled from an early age by the nuns from a nearby abbey; an unusual event in itself when only boys received any form of scholarly learning. He also made sure that she was trained to ride and fight from a young age. At ten years old she could hold her own on horseback or on foot fighting the pages in the household. She wielded a sword and dagger as well as any of the boys of her own age, but as she grew older her mother tried to wean her off martial training into the gentler pursuits befitting a Norman lady. Eleanor was not easily dissuaded, and she continued to train, away from the watchful eyes of her mother.

After she married and bore children, she found less time to hone her fighting skills. It mattered little for she was already an accomplished swordsman who could ride and fight if ever the need arose. When Robert was away, which was often, it was not uncommon for her to accompany her soldiers to disputes and conflicts. She had little fear of strapping on her sword and *hauberk* and riding toward danger, which earned her something of an intrepid reputation among her people.

When she settled down to marriage and motherhood, she became an asset to her husband wherever he was. Eleanor provided him with support and an astute opinion whenever it was called for. Robert was frequently away on the Duchy's business and spent a great deal of time in Caen, Falaise or wherever he was called. Duke William demanded much of her husband's time, and she was left to run the affairs of the county on her own. Eleanor did not mind overly; at first, she was a little jealous, but she had her children and her duties as the Lady of Mortain to occupy her and this took up all of her time. If she had to share Robert with the Duke, and lately her husband's passion for the church, she was not unduly concerned. She grew indifferent to being left alone so often, but she always ensured that Robert was met with an ardent welcome when he returned home.

It was a chilly spring morning and the training yard echoed to the sound of blade on blade as two combatants fought with long swords. They both wore thick leather gauntlets and padded *gambeson*s. The smaller, more aggressive figure, thrust at and parried her larger opponent, who showed great dexterity as he was forced to continually move to evade the shower of striking blows. Eleanor went through her considerable repertoire of manoeuvres provoking an agile response from Harald, who stepped nimbly backwards or to the side each time she came forward. She was breathing hard, and beads of sweat began to trickle down her face as she relentlessly attacked, but try as she might his defence was impenetrable. They each carried their heavy, steel swords high but as their duel wore on, he noticed her beginning to tire. She thrust forward once more, and he evaded the point of her weapon trapping her sword arm under his armpit. She struggled to release it but was held tight and the contest became an uneven one. He used his weight to pull her off-balance and she tripped landing heavily on the flags, her sword clattering on the stones as she released it. Harald lowered his own sword, holding a hand out to his opponent to help her back on her feet. She glared back up at him before accepting his offer and reached up with her left hand. In a blurring movement Eleanor whipped out the dagger from its sheath at the small of her back and before he knew it she held it pointing up toward his groin.

"Rendement?" she blurted out in between gulping breaths of air.

Harald smiled benevolently down at her.

"Of course, I surrender, Eleanor," he said grasping her hand and hauling her to her feet, "but only if you give me another chance to redeem myself and you stop using such underhand tactics."

She nodded, panting hard as they assumed their positions once more, but were interrupted by one of her servants running toward them. The boy was agitated and called out that a village some twenty leagues to the east of Mortain had been attacked in the night by armed men, who had killed two people before looting the houses and taking several women captive. Eleanor grimaced at the news knowing she had few enough men to guard the town let alone go in pursuit of an unknown number of desperate soldiers.

"I will get my men ready. These renegades have obviously not learned their lesson yet," said Harald, breaking the silence.

"You will go nowhere without me, Hari," said Eleanor firmly. "We shall go together."

Harald mustered his troops at the castle gates. They were joined by Eleanor and a handful of her squires before the whole troop rode east.

Around midday they saw the smoke rising from the village and rode swiftly along the road toward its source. When they arrived, it became obvious that the place had suffered a serious attack. Several of the wooden houses were burned to the ground while two corpses lay together in the main thoroughfare.

"What happened here?" demanded Eleanor from the saddle to a local man who stood dazed and bloodied before her.

"They came in the night, Lady. Wild Bretons on foot. They took everything they could find and carry, including the women. Then, they burned everything else and left. They took my daughter with them," said the man disconsolately.

"How many and which way?" asked Harald butting in.

"There were many, Lord. Perhaps double or thrice your number and all on foot. They left that way," he answered pointing toward a road leading south through a densely wooded forest.

Harald looked down the road considering the options but before he could say more, he was interrupted.

"Quickly, Hari. We must not delay, and we can catch them all before they get much further," said Eleanor.

"As you wish," he replied but before he could order his men to close up and pursue, she raced off with the four boys from Mortain, leaving a cloud of dust in her wake.

Harald caught up with her and they were several leagues down the road before it narrowed and wove up through dense forest. At dusk they came across the place where the outlaws had made camp the previous night and beside the still smoking cooking fire they found the bodies of the five women that had been taken. They had all been stripped of their clothing and the bruises, welts and burn marks on their naked flesh suggested that they had been badly abused before they died. Eleanor looked down at the tangled pile of bodies, shaking her head and cursing under her breath. There was little light left in the day and Harald ordered the column to halt and camp before night fell. The dead were buried without ceremony while the living settled down to eat and rest.

At first light they continued down the road in search of the miscreants, and by mid-morning they caught sight of their quarry - thirty-five ragged soldiers weighed down by plunder taken from the unfortunate villagers. Harald ordered his men into a tightly packed *conrois* and it was only when the Bretons heard the sound of the horses' hooves did they realise the imminent danger. Couched lances to the fore, Harald and his men charged at the bedraggled ranks. He had asked Eleanor to keep behind his men before they galloped in, but her blood was up and she ignored the request. With little regard for her own safety and, long sword in hand, she raced ahead on her nimble *palfry*. She scythed through the neck of the first man she reached and kept going. Seeing her isolated and unprotected, Harald broke from the ranks of the *conrois* and plunged after her. By the time he caught up she was in the thick of it, slashing down at the backs of more fleeing men. He joined her in the slaughter, throwing down his lance and drawing his own sword. He snatched a moment and looked back to his own men and saw with grim satisfaction the result of their deadly charge. When he turned back to Eleanor, he saw that she had been pulled from her horse and was beset by an assailant standing over her with sword raised and about to strike. Before the man could move further Harald unsheathed *Gunloggi* and the famous old blade took the Breton's head clean off his shoulders. Eleanor sprang to her feet and retrieved her own blade. She looked around wildly for more foemen to dispatch but the storm of killing was almost over. The last enemy soldiers scattered and tried to make good their escape, but realising it was hopeless threw down their arms pleading for mercy. Eleven prisoners were taken and herded together, where they knelt abjectly and waited for their fate. One of Harald's men approached him and asked what was to be done with the prisoners. He looked over to Eleanor,

"Hang them all," she said in a voice devoid of any emotion.

He looked at her and noticed that her hands were trembling, and before any of the men saw he led her off out of sight. She started to shake uncontrollably, and he took off his cloak and wrapped it around her shoulders. Then, he put both arms around her and pulled her close until she stopped shuddering. They stayed like this for a while before she took a deep breath and looked up at him. Her face was streaked with dirt and tears; dried blood matting her hair and covering her hands.

"These are nothing more than tears of rage. What we do to each other is beyond God's understanding, but I am calm now, Hari. Let us return to Mortain," she said releasing herself and gently pushing away from him.

The column mounted their horses and left the scene. All was quiet, except for the creaking of the ropes as the executed men swung in the light breeze from the boughs of an ancient oak tree. There was little talk amoung the riders and they headed back the way they had come. Even the young squires were strangely muted after their earlier excitement. They too had been shocked by the savagery committed on the five women from the village, which had driven their overwhelming desire for vengeance. They had seen their Lady lead the charge and recklessly pitch into the enemy, looking for retribution. As quickly as it had come, the storm passed and now they 'fell in' obediently behind her.

The company reached Mortain as it was getting dark. The town was lit up and bustling with activity. The local men who fought at Varaville had returned and the townspeople turned out 'en masse' to welcome them home. Harald and Eleanor slipped in through the gates unnoticed by all but the stable boys who came to take their horses. She had said nothing throughout the whole of the return journey then she turned to Harald and said quietly,

"I must go and see the children before they go to bed. Turid frets if I do not kiss her goodnight."

She started to walk off toward the keep but then stopped and walked back to him. Taking both of his hands in hers she spoke again,

"It is good to have you home, Hari. Please don't go away again so suddenly."

He watched her walk away and became lost in his thoughts until he was interrupted by a familiar voice.

"You do not seem to be able to go anywhere without causing trouble," shouted Rolande of Coutances, before slapping his friend heartily on the back.

"I hear you have been busy once again. Follow me, there are many old friends waiting to see you again," said the knight and taking his old comrade by the arm, he led him off to the town to drink the night away.

In the aftermath of the battle of Varaville, Rolande told him as they sat drinking, the scattered and defeated army were pursued out of the Duchy and beyond.

"Your part in the victory will live long in the memory," he emoted with his arm around the younger man. "It was like something out of the Saga of the Wandering Warriors, that charge of yours over the bridge. Where on earth did you conceive of such a plan"?

"Old habits die hard, Rolande. But it was effective. At least Duke William seemed satisfied with his victory."

"He is a difficult man to satisfy that one, Hari. But he knows that without you he would have lost the battle. It is good to have you back and no longer an outlaw. Fit to sit at table with all the Norman nobles once again," said Rolande, slapping his friend hard on the thigh.

"As long as the Duke keeps his promises and rewards my men we shall all be happy," said Harald raising his cup to those around him. "To old friends and fallen comrades. May we be bound by spilt blood forever."

The dozen or so grizzled knights sitting at the table returned the toast.

"Now I hear you have made yourself busy these last few days. Has the Lady Eleanor forgiven you completely yet?" asked Rolande conspiratorially.

Harald looked at his friend as he thought about the question.

"We were different people then, Rolande. Ten years is a long time. She was no more than a child and I was a headstrong fool. It is all ancient history now."

"Well said, my friend, but I for one am glad you were here to aid her. I just wish your brother came home a little more often - but such are the demands of state and church. Sometimes even the strongest woman needs another's sword arm," replied Rolande. "Now tell us all the story of when you saved the life of Pope Leo," he continued, changing the subject. "I feel that a word in the right ear might help me get into heaven yet."

"And your charge at Civitate," cried another knight opposite.

"Leave nothing out. We need to hear everything from the lips of the Prodigal Son himself," called Rolande.

"Well, my friends….," said Harald and began to tell his tale for the second time in the last few days.

Chapter 19: A New Home

It was late the next morning when Harald led his men out of the gates of Mortain Castle to Falaise. He rode down the hill and through the town before looking back toward the castle to see the single figure of Eleanor high on the battlements. She raised her hand when he caught sight of her, and he returned the gesture before turning back to the road leading west. In the five days spent in Mortain he had been reminded of all the many things that had attracted him to her when she was a girl. The forthrightness and determination that he had once found so compelling were still there, in abundant quantities. The small flashes of passion and temper had shown through on more than one occasion, and he smiled at the memory.

He had searched for her that morning to tell her he was going, but found only her maid who told him that her mistress was busy and could not be disturbed. Harald had been puzzled but left a message that he was needed in Falaise and would be leaving that day.

It had been good to meet so many old friends again the night before, swapping stories and lifting drinking cups to all his comrades, fallen or otherwise. He decided during the night that it would be his last in Mortain, and told his men to relax and drink but be ready to depart by mid-morning. Despite a few thick heads they were all ready to leave promptly as he had ordered.

Night had fallen by the time they reached Falaise and as soon as the sentries recognised the hero of the battle of Varaville they waived him through. Despite the lateness of the hour, grooms rushed out of the stables to take charge of the horses and even the doughty *castellan* came from his bedchamber to show Harald and his men to their quarters.

The next morning a servant knocked at the door of Harald's small chamber in the barracks with an invitation for him to meet with Duke William a little later in the day. When he and the Duke had met briefly on the battlefield William had apparently been happy to see him, and Hari had been gracious despite the gnawing feelings of resentment. He reasoned to himself, as he skipped up the steps, that perhaps it was time to let bygones be bygones, for providing the Duke kept his word, honour would be satisfied on both sides. Hari's continued fealty meant that he had kept the old family oaths and that was all that really counted, he reminded himself

"A Fitzroy, always keeps his word," he muttered, taking the steps two at a time.

Harald was smartly saluted by all the armed men he passed on the way to the Duke's chambers. He was shown into a large room where seated at the table were William and much to his surprise, Archbishop Lanfranc. Both men looked up to see Harald striding confidently through the door toward them. To his astonishment they both rose, and William came around the table to meet him, embracing him warmly.

"It is good to see you again, Hari. Come, sit down and refresh yourself. The garrison refectory is not known for the quality of its food and wine," insisted the Duke before releasing him for Lanfranc to shake his hand.

When the pleasantries were over, Harald sat down, taking a proffered goblet of wine. There was an awkward silence, eventually broken by the Archbishop.

"How was your trip to Mortain? Was your news of Robert's recovery well received?" he asked.

"It was, Father. Robert's family are all in good health and will benefit from his safe arrival home."

"As will he," said Lanfranc. "His wounds could easily have been mortal and there will be a long period of convalescence I think."

"Nonsense," blustered the Duke. "Robert is a Fitzroy and it is hard to put one down. I should know, Father, I have lived as one of them myself since boyhood. No, I need Robert back at my side as soon as he is well enough."

"Well, you have his famous brother back now, my Lord," said Lanfranc, "and Normandie will be a safer place for that - provided of course we can persuade him to stay. Let us give thanks, for we have all been redeemed in one way or another."

He looked at Duke William for a moment, who returned his gaze before turning and speaking directly to his other guest.

"I regret the circumstances of our parting years ago, Harald," he began, choosing his words carefully. "You and Robert were like brothers to me then as you are still. I am glad you are back home where you belong. Let us put all that behind us for your future is here with your people. We are in your debt."

Harald smiled good-naturedly, quite taken aback by William's demonstration of bonhomie and the Duke ploughed on.

"Now, you will not know this but our forces pursued the remnants of King Henri's army the length of Normandie and beyond. We chased them far into Maine and Brittany before letting the lucky ones go. What we have we hold, and the Duchy is considerably bigger than when you arrived. I should like to give these new fiefdoms to you as a fitting reward for your services. See here on the map."

All three looked down at a large map on the table and William pointed out the new acquisitions which extended the southern borders of Normandie by five to ten leagues.

"Enough to comfortably house twelve hundred men and their families," suggested Lanfranc.

"But, there will be conditions that need to be met," said William dropping any hint of his previous conciliatory tone.

"Of course, Lord," said Harald sucking in his breath and calculating the area of the new territories. "It is, after all, a very generous reward."

Harald was quite stunned by the offer but gave nothing away and remained impassive throughout the lengthy meeting that followed. William required his continued fealty and the pledge that he would secure the southern borders by commanding a standing army comprised of at least twelve hundred men. There would be six castles built in the new lands to deter invaders and Harald would garrison and maintain them. There followed lively discussions on where the funds would come from to pay for the building, and William was vehement that the recaptured plunder and hostage ransoms from Varaville should be used. Harald respectfully refused on the grounds that he had incurred his own costs by bringing his army home. The possibility of a stalemate was negated by the Archbishop's timely intercession, and the Duke graciously gave way. By the end of the meeting each man had what he needed and with honour satisfied on both sides, Harald reaffirmed his allegiance and during the briefest of ceremonies Duke William dubbed him 'Count Harald of Ambrières'. His own concession was to promise that he would not return to Italy, at least for the imminent future. He felt a brief pang of regret as he spoke these final words; the Guiscard would have to conquer Sicily on his own to begin with. Harald's lands in the south would take care of themselves for the time being. But he reasoned as he left the chamber, they were managed by trustworthy men of his own appointment and there was little cause for concern.

Early the next day Harald took his small company west to Regneville, where his army awaited him. By evening they were met on the road by his brother Floki and a small group of riders. He was eager to hear news of Robert and when he heard of his recovery a smile spread over his face.

"Our mother shall be complete, Hari," he said. "Two sons have returned safely from the wars and the other has returned from the dead. I think you should expect a small celebration. Do not think you can slip home unnoticed. I hope you are not expecting a quiet night?"

"Not a bit of it," Harald replied. "These men have not returned home but for a few moments before I hauled them off to war once again. We all have much to celebrate."

He turned in the saddle toward the column.

"Will you fellows be too tired to raise a cup of wine for your homecoming?"

There was some good-hearted jeering and he turned back and spurred his horse forward. All but two of his men had been in the original group that travelled south with him and the Guiscard ten years ago. Many of those still had family in Regneville and had barely had time to greet their kin before they left for Varaville.

They crested a rise and saw their hometown a short distance away. It was getting dark, but the road leading into the town was lined with people carrying torches. The column trotted briskly across the open ground and when they were spotted a cry went up. More people joined the cheering and before long there was a mighty sound erupting from the midst of the townsfolk which reverberated across the open ground. Huge bonfires had been lit around the town lighting up the darkness to reveal tables and benches set out for a feast. The townspeople came out to meet the column and enveloped each dismounting horseman before carrying them off to begin the celebrations.

As it was, the feasting lasted for many days. The proceedings started calmly enough with a priest giving thanks to God for the safe deliverance of the Fitzroy sons and their troops. The family and local nobles from nearby counties sat at a long table in front of a huge throng of people. After Torstein the Younger gave a small congratulatory speech to the guests, the festivities began in earnest.

Harald, for the time being at least, sat next to his mother and craned his neck to listen patiently to her constant stream of questions.

"And Robert was in good spirits when you left him?" asked Sigrid Fitzroy.

"He was mother, and will soon be back in Mortain with his family although I doubt he will stay for long," he replied.

"And Eleanor she is well? She received you with good grace?"

"She is as forthright as she was when I last saw her, mother. And to answer your next question she bears me no malice for our parting. She was but a child then anyway and we remain the best of friends."

"That is good news," said his mother, "I should hate for anything to come between you and Robert now that you have settled your differences. I hear you have a son in Calabria. News that I am a grandmother once more came from a complete stranger. I do not want my grandchildren deserted in a heathen place like Italy. You must send for him and bring him home."

"Ah, Bohemond," said Harald, "then I must start at the beginning and leave nothing out."

By the time he had finished his tale, the feasting was well underway, and he had to shout to make himself heard above the hubbub. Jugglers, minstrels, jongleurs and mummers performed in front of the revelers and servants scurried about, bringing an endless supply of food and drink to the tables. Copious amounts of wine were supplied from many different sources, including the recently captured baggage train of the King of France, and ensured that the celebrations were loud and uproarious. As the night wore on men and women staggered home or back to camp to sleep, only to return to the festivities when they awoke.

It took three days for the revelry to come to a halt, and on the following day Harald mustered his forces and prepared to move out to the newly acquired territories. Of the twelve hundred men who had journeyed back with him from Italy there were nine hundred and fifty left. They had given a good account of themselves on the field of battle and would be richly rewarded. With the ransomed noblemen, captured plunder and new fiefdoms, it had been a lucrative return to Normandie for his men. Each would be given a parcel of land, according to his rank, and warriors who arrived with nothing became landowners and men of property overnight. After bidding a fond farewell to his family and promising his mother that he would return home soon he rejoined his men. Beneath the Papal banner they marched south to their new homeland.

They reached Bellême castle in two days and relieved the garrison of its duties. Harald replaced its commander with one of his young captains, Jeanotte,, who brimmed with pride at the honour. The pattern was repeated at Alencon, Mayenne and Dol before finally reaching his new home in Ambrières five days later. The castle would be his headquarters from where he would watch and secure the borders of the Duchy. The hostile alliances of King Henri had been broken at Varaville but Count Harald knew that complacency was folly. He continued his vigilance and was ever watchful for signs of invasion. There were none and the borders were not threatened, allowing him time to fortify the castles on the new border to deter all those with thoughts of dominion and conquest. It did not, however, stop him from looking south and wondering when he would journey that way again.

Chapter 20: The Return Of William's Right Hand

Robert looked up at the early evening sky. It was clear of clouds and the striations of colour had turned from light blue to pink as dusk fell. He lay on his back in a wagon drawn by a team of oxen, making their laborious journey from the abbey at Rye to Mortain. One more day and he would be home, he thought. It seemed like a lifetime since he had last visited and although he loved to see his family, he always became restless after a few days and was quick to return to his duties in Caen. That, he had been told, would be many days and weeks away, for although the wound was now healing well he had been damaged, almost beyond repair. Caen would need rebuilding, he thought, after the depredations and destruction wrought by the French army and he should be there to organise its rebirth.

Lanfranc himself had come to Rye to finally give orders that Lord Robert might be released from the care of the monks and taken home to Mortain. He ordered that under no circumstances was Robert to ride a horse as his wounds might re-open on the road.

"Rest and the love of God and your family are all you need," he had ordered, as the monks carried his litter to the flat-bed wagon. "If God wills that it takes until Christmas for you to heal then you must accept it. The Duke and the Duchy need you fit and strong, so be patient and I shall pray for your continued recovery."

The monks had made him comfortable and covered him with furs for the journey. He was no longer in great pain and although able to walk a little he could not yet ride. His left arm was still weak, and he could not raise it but it was his pride that hurt most now. A company of riders was sent from Mortain to accompany him, and he gave them orders that when they arrived home the column should not enter the town in the hours of daylight, when the people might see and pity him. One of the riders was a squire from the castle and the boy rode in the wagon for most of the journey, providing his master with news from home including all the details of Harald's recent visit and the destruction of the French renegades.

"He is a mighty warrior, your brother," said the squire, a boy of fourteen who had been in Robert's service since the age of seven. "I have seldom seen a man so deadly with lance or sword."

"My brother is a force of nature, Gerard. I do hope that you did your duty and kept the Lady Eleanor safe during your brush with these outlaws."

"We tried my Lord, but Lady Eleanor dashed out before we knew it," emoted Gerard. "But your brother was there in a heartbeat, Lord. No harm would come to her while he was beside her."

Robert sighed, Eleanor was an impulsive woman who sometimes forgot her duties as a wife and mother. She could not expect to flagrantly mete out justice with no thought for her own safety. He gave a silent prayer and thanked God for Eleanor's deliverance, but it did not help him with the small twinge of envy he felt of Harald.

By the end of the next day's march Robert was back in the castle. He lay exhausted in his bedchamber as Eleanor fussed about giving orders to a small army of servants. The fire was built up, more blankets and furs brought in and trays of food deposited. Then she dismissed all the servants and sat on the edge of the bed looking down at her husband.

"You look better than I thought you would," she said. "I was half expecting a permanent invalide after I had heard how your wounds had afflicted you."

"Nonsense," he remonstrated, "I shall be back on my feet in no time."

He had insisted on walking from the wagon to meet her and making his way up several flights of stone stairs up to their *solar*. The effort left him exhausted and forced him to ask her for assistance for the last part of his journey.

"It will be a while before you will come hunting with me, I think," she said.

"Boar or Frenchmen?" he asked her.

"You have heard of our little spat then?" she said.

"It sounded like more than a little spat if one member of your retinue can be believed," said Robert reprovingly.

"Ah, Gerard can get a bit over-excited. You should not believe everything the boy says," she said.

"It was a good job that I sent my brother to look out for you," he said. "I wish you would not take such risks. From the sound of things these were desperate men."

"No matter, husband. I am here - alive and well," said Eleanor before swiftly changing the subject. "When you feel you can best me on the training square I will consider you well enough to resume your duties. Now let's start with eating properly again, shall we? The diet of a monk is not fit fare for the Lord of Mortain."

She reached for a bowl of soup that had been brought up from the kitchens and began to feed him. He complained that he was not an infant, but she would brook no argument and continued to proffer him food until he capitulated.

It was ten days before Robert could walk any distance and twenty before he could ride again. Ten more days after that, he picked up his sword and took some light exercise with one of the squires. It was many more days before he was fit enough to wield a blade with any potency, but gradually, he recovered from his injuries under the ever-watchful eyes of Eleanor.

Robert was eventually strong enough to ride and hunt with her and although he did not accept her challenge to fight with weapons to prove himself, she accepted that he was healthy enough to resume his duties. At first this was no more than travelling the county of Mortain to check on his lands and property, but eventually he was able to take part in some more robust training with his men.

While his brother was in the south of the Duchy, building castles and fortifications all along the borders, Robert continued to regain his physical strength. He had always been a pious man and the fortitude shown throughout the period of healing was no surprise to anyone who knew him well. He started each day in prayer and since his brush with death, he found himself spending more and more time in his private chapel. He prayed and meditated for long hours and gave thanks to God daily for his deliverance at the end of a Breton spear. Robert's children were delighted to have their father at home and he had never before spent so much time with them. Although Eleanor was also pleased to have him home, she knew that he was only thinking of returning to his duties in Caen where Duke William waited impatiently.

It was early summer when Robert departed. After bidding his wife and children goodbye he left with a column of riders. He found Caen much changed when he arrived and in the ninety days since King Henri's men had torched the houses and shops there had been a good deal of rebuilding. The cathedral and abbey had been left undamaged, despite the serious looting of its valuables. The high sandstone walls on the castle were still in pristine condition, he noticed, as if the French had only been concerned with stealing what they could and burning the surrounding dwellings before moving on. He had lingered in Mortain to please his wife, but now he was back he wanted only to immerse himself in the affairs of the Duchy and the church, which would welcome him back with open arms.

The next day he sat in the Duke's private chamber. William was obviously pleased to have his senior advisor back in office and there was much that he wished to impart. Since his ignominious departure from the field of battle, King Henri of France had fallen ill with a great malady that had taken him to his sick bed. A similar affliction had also taken his great ally, Geoffrey of Anjou and it was rumoured that the two of them would both be dead by the end of the year. The Duchy was finally at peace for the first time since Duke William had succeeded his father at the tender age of eight years old. The Pope had rescinded the Papal edict of excommunication and the exodus of Norman fighting men to Italy had been checked.

"Our enemies are falling by the wayside, Robert. Let us pray that God continues to bring his wrath down on all of them," said William with uncharacteristically good humour. "Talking of which your brother seems to have lost none of his abilities in dispatching our foemen. You did well bringing him home in time."

"We are all pleased to have Harald home, William," replied Robert, "and I am delighted his actions proved so decisive."

"Well, let us hope his skills of diplomacy have improved. He has been richly rewarded for those actions, as you know, but he has a great deal of work to do enforcing the peace in the south," said the Duke.

"He will not let the Duchy down and I would trust him with all our lives," replied Robert.

"I never had any issues with his loyalty, Robert, it was just his behaviour that was somehow questionable. Anyway, once we get him married off I am sure he will settle down. Now, we have other business to discuss. We need you to take personal charge of rebuilding our churches and abbeys to begin with.

We also need even more support from Rome if we are to take the English throne unopposed. The army will have to be rebuilt too, to dissuade any more unwanted visitors. Then there are our allies to the

East to consider; Flanders, the Vexin and Champagne must all be courted," said William. "Now, where do you intend to start?"

As was his nature Robert threw himself back into his work with gusto. Churchmen, barons, ambassadors and commanders needed to be consulted and briefed as the repair and consolidation of Normandie took place. After the Duke, Robert was now the most important man in the Duchy and he took his responsibilities very seriously. With his brothers defending the southern and western borders of the Duchy, he knew they were secure and with such reliable and stalwart defenders in place he no longer needed to take such an active military role. In reality, leading men into battle would be beyond him at present and no-one knew that his injuries still caused him great pain.

Robert confided only in God and Bishop Lanfranc and his great faith drove him forward and through the barriers of pain and exhaustion. Without even realising, his visits home grew even fewer as the devotion to the Church and the Duchy became his single driving passion.

Chapter 21: The Duchy Comes Of Age

While Robert devoted himself to religious and political servitude, Harald assumed his new role as the Marchis of Normandie's southern borders. He was now a powerful Norman baron who took orders only from the Duke himself. His delight with his new existence in the castle of Ambrières was tempered in part by a slight yearning for his old life in the Kingdom in the Sun. Harald still mourned Eva, but no longer publicly and he embraced his new life with a passion which he could barely remember. His life was full and his people adored him as much as his enemies feared him. His first act on receiving the huge grant of land from Duke William was to give smaller fiefdoms to his captains, who in turn carved out parcels of land for their men. They were ordered not to evict the local people, who lived and farmed the land, but simply replaced their old masters. The Marchis encouraged the new landlords to be generous with their charges, and they were rewarded with timely rents and honestly declared yields. Unsurprisingly, Harald found himself the subject of the attentions of many local women, both high and low-born and was seldom short of female company. On the few days when he was not riding out to range over the Duchy for one reason or another, he trained with his men or visited the castles being rebuilt. The simple wooden fortresses were each transformed to redoubtable motte and bailey constructions of Normandie sandstone creating a maelstrom of activity all along the new border. With each passing day his fiefdom grew stronger.

The flying columns led by the flaxen-haired giant became a familiar sight on the roads all over Normandie. Where once it had been Robert's task to gather intelligence for the Duke, Harald now became his eyes and ears and maintained a network of spies far and wide. The two Fitzroy brothers saw one another regularly, either seated around the Duke's council table or at meeting places across the Duchy.

After a dramatic year, winter fell once more, and the pace of life slowed to a standstill. As Christmas approached, the Duke and Duchess invited several important guests to Caen to celebrate the festival. The cathedral was packed for Mass on Christmas Eve and Harald followed a young priest who showed him to his seat alongside the Duke's most important guests. He took his place on the wooden bench with several of Normandie's barons on either side of him. Already seated in front of him were Duke William and his family and beside them sat Robert and Eleanor. He noticed his brother, who turned and smiled broadly in greeting. Harald grinned back before Eleanor caught his eye and flashed him a dazzling smile of her own. Any conversation was cut short by the start of the service as the priest began the liturgy. Then all eyes moved towards the Archbishop of Caen who addressed them from the pulpit. All except Harald, who sat directly behind Eleanor, and found himself looking at the back of her head and nape of her slender neck. He stared in fascination at the ornate construction of the twists and coils of her hair before catching the familiar scent of her ambergris and lavender perfume.

When the service was finally over, the nobleman and women of Normandie attended a Christmas feast in the great hall of Caen Castle. The top table, seating Duke William's closest advisors, was on a raised dais in front of all the other guests. With the other notable visitors, Harald took his place between the Countess of Mortain and the young daughter of the Count of Blois. The Archbishop concluded the blessing and a stream of servants filled the hall bringing out an endless supply of food and wine for the hungry guests.

"She would make you a fine match," said Eleanor, nodding subtly to the pretty young woman seated on the other side of him. Harald stole a glance at Agnes of Blois who was in earnest conversation with Lanfranc.

"I have other fish to fry," replied Harald nonchalantly, "and besides, I have no need of a wife. Particularly not one quite so pious."

"I hear rumours of other women, all the same," she said.

"Is that a question or an admonishment? In truth I am far too busy to spend time searching for a mate," he replied with a grin. "Now tell me your news of Mortain? Your husband appears to have responded well to your powers of healing. The time spent at home with you seems to have bought him back to good health."

"Alas, his recovery has little to do with his family and no sooner could he ride again than he was back to his duties in Caen," she said a little wearily.

"He is a driven man, my brother," replied Harald, "I think that sometimes he heeds only the Duke and the church."

"Well, he is very proud of you, Hari. He would not stop talking of your heroic deeds when he returned home. I can only hope the Duke has rewarded you fittingly."

"That he has. Now I am no longer an outlaw in my own country I might even find time to enjoy my new status."

"Well, perhaps the Marchis will find time to visit his nieces and nephews in the spring. Now that they have found you they seldom stop talking about you. Turid is always asking after you."

"Then tell them all I will see them soon," he said raising his cup. "I drink to the honour of Mortain and all its beautiful daughters."

Although the feast lasted for hours, the time passed quickly as the two of them immersed themselves in conversation. It had been a relatively quiet evening but when the Duke took his wife off to bed, many of the other guests left and retired for the night. Robert and his wife also took their leave and they both embraced Harald warmly before leaving. With the formalities over he sought out Rolande of Coutances, and joined him and a table of bachelor knights of old acquaintance.

"I thought you were ignoring us, flanked as you were by beautiful women," said the old knight before leaning over and whispering in Harald's ear. "I noticed you seemed quite engrossed in one particular conversation."

"You know as well as I do that Lady Eleanor and I are just friends," Harald whispered seriously.

"Quite so, Hari, but then how did you know I was referring to the Lady of Mortain?"

Rolande pulled away and looked his friend in the face, watching him bluster for an answer. None came and he quickly changed the subject, declaring to his seated comrades,

"The hero of Varaville is more than welcome at our table. Now, come sit down and tell us your news."

They spent the rest of the dark winter night drinking and it was long after the cock crowed before the last one had retired.

Harald stayed in Caen for another four days, attending several council meetings with the Duke and his barons. He was asked to report on the state of the refortification of the border, which, he confirmed was progressing well. He had also led a few raids into Anjou, before winter to test the defences of their ancient enemies and the audience listened avidly to the briefing. The Angevins, although badly beaten earlier in the year, were not ready to concede their land and he had taken five hundred riders to attack some of the towns that were within a day's ride of his castle. They struck hard and fast but experienced several spirited counter attacks proving that there was still resistance to be encountered by their old enemy.

Robert also gave an account of his activities; new cathedrals were being built in Coutances and Bayeux, an alliance had been made with the the Duke of Burgundy and his spies in the north-west reported a great deal of activity. When he mentioned events over the narrow sea in England William became animated.

"You have new information from your spies?" he demanded.

"Not much, Lord. You are aware that King Edward has forgiven Earl Godwinson and allowed him to return to England where his lands have been restored," said Robert, to which William nodded. "Well, the Earl is now dead and has been succeeded by his son Harold."

"Should we be concerned?" asked the Duke.

"Only in that young Godwinson's sister is married to the King of England, but I do not see that affects your claim to the English crown."

"King Edward himself has promised me the English throne," William stated purposefully. "You were there when he did."

"And I believe your cousin to be an honest man, Lord," replied Robert.

"These Saxons cannot be trusted, Lord," interjected Harald who had kept his silence on the matter until then. The Duke looked up and invited him to continue.

"The Godwinsons hold more land than any other Saxon family in England. They have their King's ear, while we have no representation at the English court. When the King dies without an heir, which he surely will, there will be those who may oppose your succession and take the opportunity to put an Englishman on the English throne," suggested Harald.

"My brother speaks wisely, Lord. King Edward may very well be of sound mind and body today, but should he die when we are so far away the crown could be snatched away from you by a usurper," interjected Robert.

"Then we need eyes and ears in the English court," ordered the Duke.

"Yes, Lord, I believe we do," agreed Robert.

The meeting went on for the best part of the day and it was getting dark again as the brothers walked outside into the cold winter air.

"You should visit grandfather's estates in England, it is a good time to reclaim what is yours," said Robert as they warmed their hands over a brazier on top of the castle walls.

"I agree, brother and I fully intend to. I have the very man to send ahead of me in the New Year.

Chapter 22: The Voyage Of Tears

It was well into the New Year when the snows began to melt and the winter storms in the narrow sea died down enough to make the voyage to England possible. Jeanotte, once Harald's squire but now one of his most trusted captains, was tasked with the trip to King Edward's court. He was given a letter of introduction from Duke William and was to present himself to the English court to formalise the redemption of the lost lands of Maldon. The lands had originally been gifted to Harald's grandfather but were taken from him after the second battle of Maldon before being restored once more, first by King Cnut and then by his successor King Edward. Jeanotte was to take two comrades and travel to London where he would explain, as a courtesy to the King, that Lord Harald was to 'settle' the town and lands of Maldon with his people. Jeanotte was also to ask for official ratification of the claim and to put himself at the King's disposal.

"When you have gained Edward's favour send one of your comrades back here with a message of confirmation and I will be in England by the summer. You will be my eyes and ears until then," said Harald.

"Very good, Lord. I will not let you down," replied Jeanotte.

By early summer, one of the young men of Jeanotte's group returned to Normandie with news. The party had been graciously received by King Edward, who was very keen to hear of events in his former home and the successes of his cousin, the Duke. Harald's request to resettle the Fitzroy's land and property was granted and the Norman community in Maldon was given a royal blessing. The King's generosity was further evidenced when he provided an escort for Harald's young knight so that he might enter his master's lands without 'unnecessary hindrance'. There was none but when they got to the town they found most of the buildings in a state of dilapidation and occupied only by wandering sheep and cattle. Jeanotte was declared the steward of Maldon and set about making preparations for his Lord's arrival with a will.

Harald began to make his own plans to travel to England and soon he stood on the quay in Regneville with Robert, who came to see him off. His brother brought with him a gift for the English King, a breeding pair of matched Percheron horses and letters from Duke William. The Byzantine *dromon*, *Evas Prayer*, stood waiting with its crew of forty men when Harald stepped aboard and took his position at the tiller. They cast-off and rowed across the estuary and into the open sea, followed the coastline up to the northerly most point of the Duchy before picking up some brisk north-westerly winds. The sails, bearing the Papal standard, were unfurled and Harald looked up to admire them before turning his ship across the wind to head for England.

It had been fifty-five years since Bjorn Halfdanson had taken his people in the opposite direction to the safety of the Duchy. The women, children and defeated remnants of his group of warriors arrived in the sanctuary of Normandie, where they put down roots and thrived. Harald thought of Jarl Bjorn constantly as he sailed back to reclaim their old home, a place just as foreign to him as Calabria had once been. Although his grandfather had seldom spoken of the 'Voyage of Tears', as it became known, his grandmother was far more generous with the details of their retreat. It was a bitter journey, she said, during which the people mourned the loss of a great many husbands and fathers, who died during the rearguard action, allowing the women and children to escape to the boats. Harald's other grandfather, Torstein, had perished during the action and died holding back the Saxon warriors who had come to kill them all. Exhausted and defeated, Jarl Bjorn lashed himself to the tiller of his ship, the *Drakes Head* and led the little flotilla of longships to the safety of Normandie.

It was a story that had been indelibly rooted in Harald's imagination as a young boy and he had often wondered what Maldon might be like. Now he had two days before he found out, for on the third day of their voyage, the jutting white cliffs of the English coastline loomed up out of dense sea fog. Harald turned the solid *dromon* away from the wind once more and followed the course of the English shoreline. Later that day they crossed the mouth of the Thames and then found what they were looking for, the River Blackwater, where they dropped anchor for the night.

They left at first light and arrived in Maldon by mid-morning. Two men stood waiting patiently on an ancient wooden dock as their ship hove into view. When *Evas Prayer* came to rest and her mooring ropes were thrown down to the waiting men, her pristine condition stood out in stark contrast beside the old, weathered jetty. With her crisp, white furled sails, black pine hull and decks of oriental plane she appeared an incongruous spectacle tied up on the creaking quay; a splendid queen on a decrepit throne.

Harald had been unsure of what he would find when he retraced 'the Voyage of Tears' but it was surely not this. The town had been burned down by the fleeing Norsemen and been rebuilt, but only partially. The great wooden palisade that had surrounded the town to the height of three men was no more. Huge gaps in the once powerful defensive wall stuck out like a mouthful of rotten teeth and sheep grazed on the pasture that had grown over once busy streets. The large hulk of the wooden church stood blackened and decayed in the town square; ivy grew at its base and covered its charred remains in greenery. A few less dilapidated buildings could be seen still standing but others looked only half-built before they too had been deserted. Although there were a few houses remaining, the majority of the town was in ruins, looking for all the world like an angry giant had visited in a violent, drunken rage.

Harald jumped down from the gunwales of the ship and was greeted warmly by Jeanotte.

"Welcome to your new fiefdom, Lord. I only got wind of your arrival last night, I am afraid the town will need a little more work before we have it restored to its former glory," he said.

"No matter, Jeanotte. As long as we have food and shelter, we can make do," said Harald good-naturedly. "Just show us to our quarters and we will make ourselves comfortable."

"As you wish, Lord," said the young knight. "They have been prepared. Please follow me."

With their ship secured, others followed, and Jeanotte led them all into the ruins of the deserted town until they stood in front of a large, new building; a sturdy oblong stone hall with a freshly thatched roof.

"This will be our home. At least until we have rebuilt some of these houses," said Jeanotte to his master. "It has been built on the site of your grandfather's great hall - all but cinders when we first arrived. The Saxons work slowly but I think they have made a decent fist of it."

Harald said nothing, at first but, nodded approvingly and he looked at the new hall.

"I think the old man would give it his blessing. Now tell me what happened here. I thought the town was taken back and reoccupied after he fled."

"It was, Lord. But there followed years of pestilence and then came the attacks from the Norsemen. During a final raid they razed it to the ground again and every single person was killed; over two hundred people according to an old shepherd we found here," he said waving to an ancient hut in the distance. "Since then, he and his sheep have been the only living souls to have returned. The Saxons believe this place to be cursed and at night the town is haunted by a giant Norseman who strikes down anyone he finds here."

"Sounds like one of my grandmother's stories but I am glad to be here all the same. Now, what news from King Edward's court?" said Harald laughing.

"Please, Lord, rest and refresh yourself first. We have plenty of time and I have much to tell you. I paid local people with silver to return and feed us all," replied Jeanotte gesturing to a large trestle table laden with food and wine in front of the newly built hall.

Jeanotte's audience with King Edward had been easily granted when he arrived in London with his two comrades. The young men had been respectfully treated at the royal court by an army of scriveners and monks. When they were finally ushered into the great hall they stood before the English monarch, who received them as ambassadors of the Duke of Normandie. The knight stated his case - that he was here, on behalf of Lord Harald of Ambrières, who sought permission to resettle his family land. The King, a kindly old gentleman according to Jeanotte, had been full of praise for the Duchy and all its representatives and offered his support to the venture. It had been a short meeting during which Edward expressed his desire to meet with the 'Papal Shield' on his arrival in the country. However, it was on the ride back to Maldon that Jeanotte learned most. The captain of the Saxon company that escorted them, a garrulous fellow named Wilfred, was about the same age as the Norman knight and the two of them struck up something of a rapport during the journey. The man had recently been overlooked for promotion in the King's personal bodyguard in favour of a member of one of the noble families and had become distinctly embittered. Wilfred told him that the family in question, the Godwinsons, had the King's confidence which allowed members of their powerful clan to exert undue influence throughout the kingdom. Clearly irked, Wilfred did not need much encouragement to share his feelings, albeit with a total stranger.

Earl Godwin had once been exiled for bringing England to the brink of civil war. Such was their power in the land that the Earl and his sons and daughters were soon invited home and reinstated. Their triumphant return meant that all those who had opposed them were soon out of favour and replaced by the Godwin's lapdogs, who now held sway at court. Edward's wife, Edith Godwin, had been released from her exile in Wherwell nunnery and was 'back in the King's bed'. According to Wilfred, she was excused marital duties as the King had no interest in her, or any other woman, and was far more intent on strengthening the church than creating heirs. The subsequent death of the patriarchal Earl Godwin did little to stem the family's rise, which if anything was enhanced by his four sons gaining ever increasing prominence. Jeanotte listened patiently to the captain's gossip, learning more in two days than he had any right to expect. The Saxon believed he had found a kindred spirit in his Norman counterpart and by the time he took his men back to London he had unwittingly revealed a great deal of intelligence.

During his visit to London Jeanotte recruited a team of builders, carpenters, stonemasons and serving women, who began their work as soon as they reached Maldon. They cleared the derelict site of the old hall and built a new one, replete with stables close by.

"I must commend you, Jeanotte. You are turning into something of a consummate politician," said Harald as they shared wine that evening in front of a huge bonfire in front of the new hall.

"Thank you, Lord. I am glad to have repaid your confidence. When will you visit King Edward yourself? He asked that you might visit him as soon as you are settled here."

"We will take our rest in this fine new hall and leave in a day or so. I should first like to spend some time looking over the land I have inherited," replied Harald.

"In that I might also be of assistance, Lord," ventured Jeanotte. "When I first arrived, I discovered an old monk not far from here. He lived in Maldon as a boy during the time of Jarl Bjorn and visits once a year to pray for the spirits of the dead. He is quite mad and very ancient, but I managed to get some sense out of him. For a small donation to his order, I am sure we can coax him to return."

"Is there no stone you have left unturned?" said Harald before raising a cup of wine to the knight.

"Thank you, Lord, but I too have a duty to remember our fallen comrades without whose sacrifice I might not be sitting here drinking with you now. Let us toast them," said Jeanotte, before standing up and exhorting those seated all around them to raise their cups in memory.

The next morning began slowly, and Harald slept late. He was one of the first to wake and most of the company of forty or so men still lay asleep around him. He got up and went outside where the early summer sun was breaking through the morning fog. He sat down at the table where he had been the night before and a woman servant brought him a breakfast of porridge and beer. Alone in his thoughts, he was distracted by two figures on horseback approaching the town. As they drew closer, he recognised one as Jeanotte riding beside a smaller figure, a monk dressed in an old, brown habit with the hood pulled up over his head. They stopped in front of him and the younger man helped the older one down from his horse.

"This is Brother Dominic, Lord," said Jeanotte leading the old man gently forward. The monk pulled back his hood revealing a white-haired, tonsured head crowning a wizened, brown face whose milky eyes looked out uncertainly.

"Come brother, sit down with me," said Harald, "are you hungry?"

The old man nodded his head.

"You knew my grandfather? Bjorn Halfdanson?" said Harald, tearing off a piece of bread from a loaf and placing it in the monk's hands.

"I did, Lord. A great man indeed and his cousin the mighty Torstein," said the monk with a half-smile. "I was a small boy when my father stood with them on a hill not far from here. Two hundred warriors defying two thousand of King Aethelred's warriors, marching here to take the town. You are familiar with the story?" asked the old man, his face and gestures becoming animated at the memory.

"I am, brother. My grandmother, Turid told me the story often," replied Harald.

"Your grandmother was 'The Shieldmaiden'? She was an even fiercer warrior - and deadly with her axes," the monk opened his toothless mouth and laughed out loud. "Why, she dispatched two of the men who had come to kill us. One axe for each of them," he laughed again before taking on a serious countenance. "That was a very sad day for me and my family. My mother was killed by the treacherous townsfolk, and my father died later that day defending the causeway - and I was left an orphan. Taken captive with my sister by the new Lord of Maldon. Can you imagine that - a Saxon enslaving Saxon children? But he got what was coming to him - died of the bloody flux the following year. Him and most of his warriors. God is just and vengeful."

"Your father died at the causeway?" asked Harald to which the old man nodded.

"He did - a loyal Saxon fighting in the shield wall beside his Norse brothers. I saw many of them fall that day and I will take you there if you wish. My eyes are no longer good but my mind is sharp and I know the way there. Come, take my hand and I will guide you. The memories are as if the fight happened only yesterday."

They helped the old man back onto his horse and Brother Dominic described the old road to the causeway leading to Northey Island. He led them along the riverbank to the wilderness of the marshland; along the path where the people had fled through the twisting gullys, spiraling rivulets and dark pools of the salt marshes. They followed the dry, gravel path where Harald imagined the desperate flight of his people, retreating through the panorama of mud and water, yellowing marsh grass and cushions of fecund mosses. They stopped and the old man took a deep breath, wiping away salty tears rolling down his face before describing the retreat from Maldon and the fierce battle for the causeway over fifty years ago.

Dominic was eight years old then and watched the drama unfold as he lay hidden in a nearby copse with his sister. He described how the Norsemen of the shield wall held and fought on at the crossing. He watched them fall one by one until the last of the living escaped before the rising tide covered the causeway. He told of how Torstein the Warrior Skald returned to the fray to prevent their foemen following them onto the island until, at last, he sunk beneath the water taking two of the enemy with him. Dominic paused for a moment in his story and fought to compose himself.

"Take your time, brother," encouraged Harald.

"The tide came in quickly and prevented the pursuit and the last of the people escaped. It was then that Lady Turid stopped and turned back and called to Thoren's men on the opposite side of the bank. She cursed them and they fell silent. I remember the defiant tone in her voice and my heart leapt with hope. She cursed her enemies and their children for an age to come. She promised their destruction and for years this place has been barren, and all living things here have been destroyed," said Dominic with a final sigh.

"Thank you, brother. I am in your debt," Harald said pressing gold coins into the monk's hand. "Jeanotte, please can you see our friend gets home safely. I would stay here a while longer."

Soon Harald stood alone in the bleak empty spaces of the marshes. It was low tide and he walked across the slippery stones of the causeway toward the other side. He stopped in the middle, some twenty paces from the other bank and in his mind's eye conjured up an image of Torstein Rolloson to whom he apparently bore a striking resemblance. He imagined him plunging into the enemy ranks with his great battle-axe, cleaving the heads of those who opposed him and he saw his grandfather fall beneath the swirling waters taking a brace of Saxon warriors with him. Harald took careful note of everything he observed, and had been told and promised himself that he would relay each and every detail to his brother Robert when next he saw him.

He was brought back from his musings by the sound of birds and looked up to see two ravens circling high above. Their harsh caw-cawing carried on the wind, blocking out the sound of all other birds and he looked up at them as they to and fro-ed across the face of the red, setting sun.

"You are a long way from home, my friends," he called to them.

They seemed to call back their greetings and turned to fly north. Harald watched them go and shivered, feeling the hairs go up on the back of his neck. Then he too turned away and started back to Maldon.

Chapter 23: The Court of King Edward

Harald and his contingent of twelve knights rode from Maldon, entering the city of London from the east by the Ald Gate. They were met and escorted by a company of the Kings Guard, redoubtable *huscarls* bearing equally impressive single-bladed axes; the weapons measuring as tall as a man. The Normans drew the attention of a sizeable crowd as they walked their horses over the cobblestones through the city beneath their Papal banner. When they reached the palace, an ornate Roman Villa, Harald went inside to be met by the King's steward, a thin, grey-haired man wearing his gold chain of office over a black, knee length woollen surcoat.

"The King has been expecting you, Lord Harald. May I ask you for your weapons please, they are forbidden in the Royal Hall," said the steward.

Harald unbuckled *Gunnlogi* and his seax and handed them to a servant before following the steward into a large hall.

The London court of the English King was a busy place. It was full of noblemen and women, priests and scribes, all arranged according to rank and importance. They stood in two lines on each side of Edward, who sat in an ornate chair where he had been receiving a variety of petitioners and guests throughout the morning. Harald approached the throne and bowed low, then drew himself up to his full height and waited for the King to address him. Edward jumped to his feet and opened his arms wide in greeting, before walking down the steps of the raised dais and reaching up to put his hands on Harald's shoulders. The King wore a robe of red velvet that reached the floor, and his thinning gray hair was crowned with a simple gold band. He beamed at his guest with undisguised affection.

"Lord Harald Fitzroy, defender of the faith and scourge of the French - I salute you. I trust you have found Maldon to your liking," he said in a loud, reedy voice that echoed around the high wooden ceilings and walls of the room.

"Indeed, I have, Sire. It has been illuminating to visit the place that I have only heard about in stories," replied Harald.

"You are here with my blessing, Lord Harald. I am delighted to see its lands and property back in the hands of the rightful owners once again," said the King before ordering his steward to dismiss the court for the day.

He turned back to his guest again.

"Come, I am sure you are in need of refreshment. Let us walk together."

With his arm on Harald's shoulder the King guided him back down the hall and out into a smaller chamber that had been prepared for a meal. They sat down facing one another across the table and a servant brought food and wine.

"I am always glad to see friendly faces from Normandie," confided the King, "although you will know that there are many in my court who do not share my affinity with the Duchy. The affairs of court are tedious in the extreme, when I would much rather be attending to building my abbey in West Minster. I must show it to you while you are with us."

"Not everyone knows we Normans as well as you, Lord," replied Harald. "Even the wisest of rulers must suffer a few dissenters. As for your abbey I should be delighted to see it."

"And so we shall, young man. Now tell me of my young cousin William. I daresay he has given much thought as to how he will rule my kingdom when I am passed," said Edward good-naturedly.

"He is in fine health, my Lord and sends his deepest regards. The Duke prays that it will be many years before you relinquish your kingdom to him. But when that happens, he will be ready," said Harald handing Edward a sheaf of letters from Duke William.

The smile dropped from the King's face, and he leaned forward conspiratorially.

"Might I ask that we keep these sentiments between us, for there are those here at court who covet my kingdom and would not thank me for giving it to another so easily. The thought that a Norman will rule this Saxon kingdom might well be abhorred in some quarters."

"I am the Duke's confidante, my Lord and I swear that I will not breathe a word of our conversation to anyone but he," said Harald earnestly.

"You are a man to be trusted, Harald Fitzroy. Your reputation precedes you."

"Thank you, my Lord. Now as well as a pair of fine breeding horses sent by Duke William, I have a gift of my own."

Harald placed a small, gilded box on the table and pushed it reverently toward his host.

"What is it?" he asked, examining the tiny shard of wood inside.

"It is a gift that the late Pope Leo bestowed upon me. It is the holiest of relics - a sliver of wood from the True Cross."

The King's rheumy old eyes opened wide with delight, and he shook his head in disbelief before his face broke into a beaming smile.

It was getting dark by the time it came to leave the King, who suddenly grew tired. The meeting had gone well, and Harald had been at his diplomatic best. It was not a skill which came easily to him but under Robert's tutelage he had been well prepared for this meeting. King Edward was unbridled in his support in rebuilding Maldon and offered every assistance. He had also offered an invitation to return back to court in the future to meet his noblemen, a thought far from Harald's mind as he crossed the courtyard to rejoin his men. Jeanotte was tasked with finding a tavern in the city where they could sample a little Saxon hospitality before returning to the harsher conditions of Maldon, and he looked around in the hopes of seeing his captain close by. An angry voice from behind him interrupted his thoughts.

"The land is not yours, Norman. It was stolen from my people, and it will be returned."

Harald wheeled round and was confronted by a tall, well-dressed Saxon who he recognised from the court earlier on. The man was about the same age as him with shoulder-length, fair hair and broad, bushy moustaches of the same colour.

"Maldon is mine, friend. It was given to my family by one of your kings and then given back to us again by another. Should you doubt my word I am sure King Edward will enlighten you," said Harald smiling at the enraged stranger.

"I see right through you, Fitzroy. I am no respecter of reputations and no good will come of your courting of our King," said the stranger angrily.

Harald fingered the hilt of his seax but said nothing and returned the man's stare in the half-light. They were interrupted by Jeanotte.

"Lord, I have found a suitable tavern for the evening. The men are there now," he said tugging at his master's arm.

The young knight recognised the look in Harald's eyes, which had not left the Saxon's.

"Sir, the men are waiting," he insisted.

"Very good, Jeanotte, lead me there. I have developed quite a thirst," replied Harald, before looking back to the stranger and bidding him a polite "good night".

They did not have to walk too far to navigate the labyrinth of winding streets before entering one of the many taverns surrounding West Minster. The place was packed with an assortment of soldiers, whores and tradesmen, who crowded around wooden benches and chairs in the smokey interior. Harald and Jeanotte took their seats at the table with their comrades and a small number of *huscarls* bearing the royal crest of King Edward on their surcoats. Harald took a bag of silver from his pocket and bought ale for the table, Norman and Saxon alike. The sight of so much coin immediately attracted the women who jostled for the attention of the men at the table.

"Control yourself, ladies. We are here for the evening," shouted Harald before ordering more drinks.

The *huscarls* raised their cups to him and he returned their toast.

"Here's to you, Norman," called their captain, a fair-haired Norwegian from Trondheim, "We are all Norsemen under the skin, brother. Skal."

The evening passed good-naturedly with songs sung and stories swapped. The local whores earned well from the evening and a great deal of ale was consumed. Harald learned that the man who had accosted him earlier in the evening was a Saxon Lord by the name of Harold Godwinson, who had recently succeeded his father as the leader of a large and powerful family with land all over England.

"Watch that one, Lord. He is a troublemaker who will stop at nothing to gain the English throne," said the captain quietly, his tongue loosened by Harald's generosity.

"We have no quarrel with any Saxon in this city. We are just here to pay our respects," came the reply.

"From what you have told me, Lord, he may well have a quarrel with you. He has no love for the Normans, so I advise you all to watch your backs," said the *huscarl,* "the Godwins are a law unto themselves at times."

"Thank you, brother. Your advice is well taken," replied Harald before ordering more ale for all those seated.

The evening drew to its conclusion and the Normans bid farewell to their newfound comrades before heading off to their quarters.

The next day proved a busy one. During the previous evening Harald had declared that the town of

Maldon would be completely rebuilt. No expense would be spared in its renovation he said, and the day was spent scouring London for craftsmen, labourers and servants to fulfil the task.

"We cannot have any Saxon, noble or not, trying to scare us off what is rightfully ours," said Harald to Jeanotte as the two rode side-by-side at the head of the column of men and wagons rolling back to Maldon.

"You think Lady Turid's curse has lifted," asked Jeanotte.

"It has gone from the town but whether my grandmother, wherever she might be, will free all the Saxons from its grip will remain to be seen," he said, grinning at the knight. "Now, I want you to stay here in England to oversee the rebuilding and to keep me abreast of events at the English court."

He watched the young man's face drop as he tried hard to hide his disappointment.

"As you wish, Lord."

"Do not fret, Jeanotte. I will not leave you here for long. You shall be back in Normandie soon enough when the work is done. You know you are among my most trusted knights."

"Thank you, Lord. I will not let you down."

Harald stayed until the end of the summer and watched the town's rebuilding. He did not interfere and let Jeanotte take charge of the programme, which saw the church, houses and streets take shape. People slowly started to return, first a farmer, then a blacksmith and finally a priest was sent. At King Edward's invitation Harald became a regular visitor to the royal court in London, where he was never short of companionship. Noblemen and women were always keen to engage with him and hear of Normandie and the Kingdom in the Sun. During those times he never once spoke again with Harold Godwinson and the two kept their distance. When the leaves started to turn from green to gold he decided it was time for him to return to Normandie. Leaving Jeanotte with a large bag of silver and half the original crew, he prepared *Evas Prayer* for the brief voyage home and left on the morning tide.

Chapter 24: Caen, 1058

There were sixteen guests seated at the table in Duke William's council chamber. As well as Robert and Harald Fitzroy, sitting either side of Archbishop Pavin, all the powerful barons belonging to Normandie's ruling elite sat around the large oblong table.

"Gentlemen, I have momentous news. King Henri of France is dead, as is his ally Geoffrey of Anjou. It seemed they have both succumbed to a single malady which has removed two of our most persistent enemies," announced the Duke, evoking a ripple of surprised conversation around the room.

William smiled slyly and held a hand up before the room quietened.

"We must drive home this gift from God and strike Anjou and Maine to ensure that their successors do not have any designs on the Duchy. I want two columns to advance deep into both regions to make our presence felt. The Lords of the Hiemois and Ambrières will lead their forces south to press home our advantage and destroy their remaining power base," he said looking at Roger de Montgomery and Harald Fitzroy. "Lord Robert here will ensure the expeditions are well-equipped. Our borders are currently secure, and I want to ensure we do not have to look over our shoulders if we are to expand into foreign lands," he concluded.

"Will your cousin King Edward name you as his successor soon?" asked Richard Goz, the Viscount of Avranches.

"He will name me when the time is right, and we have his trust and support."

"Will your claim be unopposed, Lord?" continued Goz.

"I am informed there will be murmurings of discontent, which is only to be expected but once the King names me there is no power in Europe that can dispute my claim," declared Duke William.

"All the same,. Lord," interjected Lanfranc of Pavin, "I believe a visit to the Pontif in Rome would strengthen our cause should we need it. We could advise the Holy See of the completion of the abbey and nunnery here in Caen, as well as many other projects you have sponsored - all to the glory of God. A little enlightenment in Rome of your dedication to the church can only strengthen our existing ties," he nodded toward Harald.

"A worthy thought," mused William. "But who shall go?"

"Why Robert Fitzroy is the obvious choice," proffered Lanfranc.

"…and not his brother, the 'Papal Shield," said William at which Harald shook his head immediately.

"I believe my duties lie elsewhere, Lord. Robert is the obvious choice," said Harald quickly.

There were a few moments of silence as the Duke pondered his options.

"Very well, it is settled then, Lord Robert we shall have to make do without your services once again," sighed William resignedly.

When the business of the day was concluded, the Fitzroy brothers sat alone in Robert's stark chambers close to the Duke's rooms in Caen castle. His brother had only returned from England the previous day and he was keen to hear all the details of his visit. Harald explained at length, from his first day to his last, the events and people he had met. He spent a good while describing Maldon and his visit to the causeway to Northey Island.

"They still fear Mormor's curse in those parts. The town has been blighted ever since," Harald said.

"No more than the Saxons deserve - even if it is a bit of ancient superstition," Robert retorted with a little too much Christian fervour for his brothers liking. "I am glad you have an affinity with the place all the same. The land has been delivered back to its rightful owner for which I have long prayed. Now tell me what you think of King Edward - truthfully!"

"He is a kindly old man, I believe. He is well disposed to the thought of a Norman on the English throne, and it makes sense. I have also heard that his Queen is still a virgin and that it is no wonder he has no natural successor. His first love is for the church and then for his people."

"You think the Saxons will allow a Norman to rule them?" asked Robert.

His brother thought hard before answering.

"They are not unlike us in so many ways. They are independent and warlike, but I have to believe that despite the wishes of their King there will be resistance. Perhaps even from outside the Kingdom - the land is very rich and fertile. Now tell me, brother, how do you feel about returning to Rome - it seems like you only just came back.

"Lanfranc's influence is strong, is it not? And there is more that has not yet been spoken of. I may be going a little further afield," suggested Robert.

Harald looked at him quizzically before he understood completely.

"The pilgrimage to Jerusalem? I knew it would only be a matter of time," declared Harald triumphantly. "I am delighted for you, brother - it has been your dream for some time, I believe. I drink to your safe journey," said Harald loudly.

"Let us keep it between ourselves, Hari. The Duke knows nothing of this yet. It will need to be broached by the Archbishop first."

"Your secret is safe with me, Robert. Have you shared this news with your family?"

His brother shook his head.

"Provided Eleanor has her horses and her children she will be able to make do without me for a while longer. Now tell me, when do you plan to return to England once more," asked Robert, quickly changing the subject.

The brothers talked long into the night. During their ten years of separation, they had both missed the closeness of this fraternal companionship, which had been a part of their lives since early boyhood. They learned from an early age that there was little to compare with 'blood-on-blood' comradeship. The wine and the hour eventually took its toll and each of them succumbed to the soporific combination and fell asleep at the table.

There was a hunt organised for the next day and William's guests gathered in the courtyard before the castle keep. Over forty horsemen, led by the Duke, left through the gateway. The great procession of noblemen, squires and servants clattered over the flagstones and through the streets of the town. They were pursued by an assorted pack of *lymers*, sight hounds and deerhounds, which careered after their masters, their baying and barking waking anyone still asleep. A league along the valley of Caen, the hounds picked up the scent of a hart and by midday the unfortunate animal was run to ground. The dogs were held back as the hugely antlered stag was finally held at bay on the banks of the river Orne and turned to face his tormentors. Duke William leapt from his saddle and approached the exhausted animal, driving a spear deep into its chest. It collapsed in front of the hunters, breathed its last breath and died. During the deer's unmaking the dogs were fed on its offal and the butchered carcass was loaded onto a wagon and taken back to Caen.

William was in good spirits as the procession made its way home to the feast he had arranged. Deer and boar were served as well as a vast selection of the Duke's finest wines. He toasted his guests and heaped praise on the achievements of many of his nobleman who had served him so well. He was especially generous in expressing his gratitude to the Fitzroy brothers, and his particular delight in the recent return of Harald "whose decisive entry into the fray at Varaville was so telling". Toasts were made and the Duke held up his hands to quieten the raucous gathering,

"I have one last announcement to make. My dear friend, the Count of Mortain, will be leaving us for a while on a diplomatic mission. He will first visit Rome and then journey on to Jerusalem to seek redemption for all of us. When he kneels at Christ's tomb he will be doing so on behalf of all the Norman people and as my father did before him, will ask for God's blessing," declared William triumphantly. "We are as strong as we have ever been and with God's grace we shall aspire to even greater accomplishments. Gentlemen, let us drink a loyal toast to our beloved Duchy."

Lanfranc, seated next to the Duke put an arm around Robert in a gesture of congratulation. On the other side of the table Harald applauded louder and longer than any man in the room and his brother beamed back at him joyfully.

Chapter 25: The Road To Jerusalem

As Harald prepared his men for the invasion of Anjou, Robert set about planning and preparing for his own adventure. It was a hazardous journey of almost two thousand leagues, a dangerous sea voyage and travel through many hostile regions. Jerusalem and the land of Palestine fell under the aegis of the fierce Fatimid Caliphate, whose army of Berber warriors had conquered the region. All Christian pilgrims travelled at great risk.

None of this worried Robert unduly as he assembled his party that would first visit Rome and then travel onto Jerusalem. The journey, he estimated, would take anything up to a year during, which time his absence from the affairs of the Duchy would be deeply felt. He had assured Duke William that he would appoint an able deputy and Rolande of Coutances was named. He informed the knight of his new role during the visit when he went home to tell Eleanor that he would be absent for some time. She received the news of his journey and his imminent departure dispassionately and wished him well. She knew she had lost her husband to the Duchy and the Church many years previously. His sustained absence from home was unimportant to her and she no longer cared. She ran the affairs of Mortain well enough on her own and had grown accustomed to long periods of living alone. The county was prosperous and well-defended, and she was content with her busy life at home.

Lanfranc had spoken to the Duke before he feasted his barons, on the benefits of a pilgrimage to Jerusalem by Robert. Not wishing to lose his chancellor's council for a year, William had prevaricated. When the Archbishop reminded him that his own father, the old Duke, had made the same journey, albeit dying on the way home, William started to be convinced.

"Rome must continue to see us as their pious and God-fearing supplicants. What more proof is there than to send your chancellor, the Count of Mortain, to the Holy Land to seek penance for us all?" asked the Archbishop.

"There is virtue in your proposal, Father," said William. "But do you think we might spare him for a whole year?"

"We shall doubtless miss his good works, Lord, but in years to come we shall thank him for his sacrifice."

Robert was jubilant when he heard the news. A pilgrimage to Jerusalem had been something he had dreamed of for years and before long, he would be on the road to the Holy Land. His wounds had only partially healed and they still caused him pain, but he was convinced that the pilgrimage would make him whole once more.

"Come back well again, Robert," Lanfranc had said. "God and the Duchy need you fit and able."

He chose six of his most zealous knights to accompany him. They were all pious men of Mortain who he had known for many years. Each took with him a squire who, it was stipulated, had to be at least fourteen years of age in order to withstand the rigours of the journey. The boys would be in charge of the pack animals and all the equipment belonging to their masters.

One bright spring morning, the party of men and boys assembled by the newly built cathedral of Caen to be blessed by the Archbishop. In front of the people of the city the Duke embraced the knights, and his wife, Matilda gave small wooden crosses to each member of the party. Harald Fitzroy stood at the front of the throng and stepped forward to place the green and gold Papal banner in his brother's hands. With the ceremony over, Robert's party mounted their horses and he led them away from the town and along the valley until they were out of sight of all the well-wishers.

It was almost two years since Robert had gone in search of his brother in Italy and he followed the same path as far as Rome. They travelled south-east across France until they reached the Kingdom of Germany, before turning south and through the city states of Italy. It was high summer when they reached the green and fertile estates surrounding Rome and before long they stood in front of the mighty gates to the city. They found comfortable quarters before sending a messenger to the Vatican requesting an audience with the Holy Father. Early the next day they were visited by a priest, with a message that the Pope would be pleased to see the Duke's Chancellor at "his pleasure". A few hours later Robert was in the Apostolic palace of Pope Benedict X.

    He was ushered into a large ornate room where the Pontiff sat alone at one end in a heavily cushioned chair. The Pope was an old man with piercing blue eyes set in a hawk-like face, completed by a grey, wispy beard. He wore a red velvet cap and a stole over a white linen alb which reached the floor. The skin of his hands which clutched his bible were paper-thin, Robert noticed, as he knelt, taking the proffered hand and kissing the Papal ring.

    "You have come a long way for an audience with us, Robert of Mortain," said Pope Benedict in a kindly tone that belied his fierce features. "It is not your first time in Rome I think?"

    "I have been here once before to escort the Archbishop of Caen safely home."

"Ah, yes, Lanfranc of Pavin is an exceedingly learned fellow, is he not? Duke William is fortunate to have that man among his clergy," replied the Pope, visibly animated at the sound of the Archbishop's name. "Now tell us of your brother, Lord Harald - he is a very famous Norman warrior we believe."

"Lord Harald prospers, your Holiness, and he defends us in the name of God beneath the Papal banner," replied Robert.

"We are always pleased to see pious Normans in Rome but tell me, what is the purpose of your onward pilgrimage to Jerusalem?" asked the old man.

"I travel, in the name of the Duchy, that God might forgive us our sins when I ask for absolution in the most holiest of places," replied Robert.

Pope Benedict smiled and bent forward as if not to miss a word.

"Why, yes, the Church of the Holy Sepulchre is where that might take place. It is, after all, the narrowest point between heaven and earth and if God wills it, the sins of all the Duchy can be absolved," said the Pope fervently. "You are devout, and your penitence will be complete, my son. Your faith will move mountains and when you stand before your foes their hearts will fail them."

The conversation flowed freely and the Pontiff, enthused by the Norman mission, became effusive in his praise of the Duchy and Duke William's leadership. Robert explained the building of the many churches, cathedrals and monasteries throughout Normandie and the promotion of a great many new clergy under Lanfranc's guidance. Pope Benedict was clearly delighted at the news, and he asked Robert to explain the progress to some of his Cardinals during his stay in Rome.

The pilgrims, for their part, were all pious men and they spent much of their time in prayer and devotion. On the Sunday before they left, the Pope personally gave them communion and blessed each one of them. For the next few days Robert was feted with several visits from senior members of the Vatican staff. When the time came to leave for the Holy Land, Normandie had many new supporters. The party gained another member before they travelled south; a priest called David was sent to Robert to act as his guide. The young man was a native of Jerusalem and the Pope felt he would be more than able to guide the pilgrims when they got to the Holy Land. At first, Robert turned David down, but persistency won through, and he finally acquiesced, letting him join the company. The priest was a distant nephew of the old Pope and Robert thought it might be seen as churlish to refuse such a genuine offer of help.

Their party, now fifteen in number, left the gates of Rome six days after they arrived and travelled south to Benevento, where Robert made himself known to Prince Rudolph once more. The Prince, a hospitable man, insisted they stay in his huge house for a few days during which time Robert learned a good deal more about his brother's time as governor of the city. The Prince was generous with his hospitality and afforded the pilgrims every luxury during their stay.

They journeyed on to Harald's fiefdom in the south, a vast estate of vineyards, olive groves and farms given to him by a grateful Duke Humphrey after the Norman victory at Civitate. They had been directed to seek out the steward, an old Calabrian knight named Alphonso, who had once ridden with Harald. The man was delighted to hear news of his master and was keen to know when he would be returning. He went to great pains describing how well-run and efficient the estate was so that Robert might inform his brother that it was in safe hands.

"It seems as if Lord Harald is a famous man in these parts," suggested the priest as the steward called for more food and wine to be brought to the table.

"I gave up being surprised by my brother's reputation some time ago," said Robert.

"You are also an important man, Lord. You have a great reputation for your good works for the church," replied David, fearing he might have caused offence. "And also, on the field of battle, I have heard your companions tell." Robert smiled at the young priest and put a hand on his shoulder.

"Once upon a time when my sword arm was stronger, perhaps. But my brother is the warrior to whom all men look to on the field of battle now. He has an indomitable spirit and I have never known him bested."

"He is a holy warrior like you, Lord?" asked David.

Robert smiled again and nodded, amused at the description of his brother who he knew had a closer association with the old Norse gods than to Jesus Christ.

They spent the remainder of their time preparing for their voyage to the Holy Land. The squires became busier than ever. The horses needed re-shoeing, equipment needed mending, mail needed cleaning and blades needed honing. The company also had to be resupplied for the sea journey, which would be a long one with few stops. All told there were thirty-five *palfreys* and *rounceys* and each of these horses needed to be groomed, fed and conditioned to ensure they were fit and healthy for the long journey. For the pilgrim knights the long days followed a set pattern, starting and ending with prayer in the local church and interspersed with constant martial training.

Suitably refreshed and resupplied the party left for the seaport of Bari, where they procured the services of a stout Byzantine *chelandion* to take them east. Flying the Papal Standard from the main mast, their priest asked God to bless their venture and they put to sea. They travelled in the company of two other ships, both sailing to Palestine and carrying pilgrims from Germany and England. After four days the little fleet had reached the edge of the Byzantine Empire and a brisk north-westerly breeze blew them toward the harbour of Dyrrhachium. For nearly all the Norman pilgrims this was the first time they had ever voyaged so far east, and they crowded along the gunwales to catch sight of the ancient city.

The ship docked the next morning onto a teeming jetty. Although early, it was already hot as men and animals bustled about. There were at least fifteen other ships disgorging their burdens and in the maelstrom of heat, dust and noise Robert gathered his company about him and left the chaotic waterfront. They departed from the city without delay and were on the road to Constantinople before midday.

The pilgrims reached the Byzantine capital fourteen days later before turning south across Anatolia and then up, over the Taurus Mountains to Antioch, a Syrian seaport where they took respite. The priest, David became ever-more animated as they got closer to the Holy Land and his religious exhortations to the pilgrims grew in their intensity. His urgings were unnecessary and the party, although tired, did not slacken their pace along the road on to Jerusalem.

They moved down the eastern coast of the Mediterranean, through western Syria on to Palestine, where the land grew dusty and arid. It was hot, thirsty work for both men and horses and their daily routine never changed. Bands of horsemen shadowed their progress at a distance as they passed, but never ventured too close to the heavily armed Normans. Onlooking bandits preferred to pick off less able pilgrims further down the road. The way to Jerusalem was a dangerous one and the remains of several unlucky travellers were much in evidence, left for the carrion to pick their bones clean.

One day Robert stopped to give aid to a dying woman they found on the road. The ground around her was strewn with the corpses of other pilgrims, who had been stripped of everything they owned. David gave her 'absolution' as she breathed her last. The bodies had all been savagely mutilated and were bloating in the heat of the day.

"Who did this?" Robert asked the priest angrily.

"Brigands. Moors. They have no love for Christian folk here, Lord. They might despise and loathe us, but they are cowards and will not attack holy warriors without an army at their back. The road through the Holy Land is fraught with danger but Christ will protect the penitent."

Robert grimaced at the smell of rotting flesh and made the sign of the cross.

"How far is it to the Lake, Father? It will do us good to get out of this place of death."

"Two days and we shall be at the place of miracles," answered the priest confidently.

They travelled away from the dusty coastal road and started to climb through a fertile, mountainous landscape before crossing into the high passes. Finally, they saw the vast inland Sea of Galilee beneath them stretching up through a green and verdant valley. The company had reached the first way point of their pilgrimage, and they arrived on the lake's western shore to make camp beneath a group of palm trees. The horses were unburdened and watered, tents were erected, and a large fire built before the party joined together in prayer. Men and boys disrobed and waded into the cold, clear water to refresh their bodies and souls. As evening faded into night Robert sat in quiet contemplation away from the main group. The light was dying as he looked over the still, flat water which Jesus once walked upon. He looked along the shore and up toward the steep hills and felt a glow within him as he remembered the stories of Christ's life. The Count finally felt at peace, a feeling he did not recognise at first. He fell to his knees and thanked God for the deep longing that had brought him to this time and place.

They stayed for two days in their camp and local traders came to sell them fresh food. Saint Peters' fish, dates and goats cheese made a welcome change from their diet of dried meat and hard bread and the Normans left the camp in high spirits. They sang hymns as they struck out on the road to Nazareth and stopped later in the day to pay homage at the Basilica of the Annunciation. After making their devotions, David led them back to the banks of the River Jordan and they headed south. Five more days passed before Robert Fitzroy and his group of warrior pilgrims stood before the most holy of Christian places, the Church of the Holy Sepulchre in Jerusalem. It had taken one hundred and sixty-five days to reach this place and they knelt in quiet prayer, each giving thanks for their deliverance.

The next day the Lord of Mortain lay face down, prostrate on the church flagstones and felt the coolness of the smooth stone on his face and hands. He was alone before the high stone of Edicule, housing the tomb of Christ. The church had been emptied of priests and pilgrims in deference to the visit of the famous Norman nobleman and he now lay still and silent, arms outstretched, making the sign of the cross with his body.

Robert prayed in this position for some time.

He prayed for the future of the Duchy, he prayed for his family, and he prayed for Duke

William. He prayed that the sins of his people be forgiven, and he prayed for the deliverance of Normandie from all its enemies.

"We have broken your laws, Lord. We have killed and stolen to protect ourselves and acted jealously and covetously towards our neighbours. I am here to do penance on behalf of my people and pray that you will still give us your blessing."

Robert could hear nothing except the sound of his own voice which echoed around the empty church. He lifted his head and looked up toward a stained-glass window depicting Christ's crucifixion and death at the hands of a Roman soldier driving a spear into his side. The sun streamed through the coloured glass and projected an image of the depicted scene, lighting up the tiles in front of him. Robert closed his eyes and lowered his head once more in supplication and it was then that it began to happen.

He felt his body shake, trembling at first then building up into a crescendo of movement making his arms and legs spasm uncontrollably. He closed his eyes tightly and a number of violent visions came to him in quick succession. He saw Harald standing in a shield wall beside hundreds of Norsemen, being beaten backwards. He saw Eleanor in chains in a dark prison. He saw the Riders of Regneville driven into the ground by giant axe-men and he saw Duke William trampled beneath their feet as they retreated. Then he saw Jesus of Nazareth walking on the waters of Lake Galilee, beckoning him and pointing to a mighty host galloping across the water toward them. Robert was leading his holy warriors onto the surface of the water, and they charged across toward the enemy lines. They shattered them like glass and watched the broken bodies of their foemen sink beneath the surface and disappear. Robert looked back and saw that Jesus was ascending into the heavens, he called to him asking him to stay and bless his men after their great victory. The Messiah made the sign of the cross and smiled at him.

"You already have my blessing, Robert Fitzroy. Fight for me and never forsake me. You and your people shall have their salvation, but I need your sword and your strength to deliver my word. Promise me that and the earth shall be yours."

"I promise, Lord", shouted Robert and Jesus disappeared into the clouds.

He woke up on the floor of the church, stiff from lying for so long on the cold, stone floor. David, the priest, kneeled over him shaking his master gently.

"Lord Robert, wake up," said the priest. "Your men are waiting for you outside."

"All is in readiness?"

David nodded and helped him to his feet, leading Robert on unsteady legs to the main door of the church. Outside they crossed the street and into the old quarter of the city. By the time they reached the Lion's Gate he had recovered his senses and walked toward the knot of men waiting for him. They saw their commander approach and turned to meet him.

"I am ready," said Robert and two of the squires carrying a large wooden cross struggled toward him. Laying their burden gently over his shoulder they stood back and watched him move off up the hill. Then the whole company, which included several local priests, each carrying a leather flail, fell in behind him. Robert led them along the Via Dolorosa to the site of Christ's crucifixion and the scourging began.

Chapter 26: The Fading Lioness, Mortain 1058

Mid-autumn in Normandie brought a riot of colour as the leaves on the trees turned from green to brown. The woods and forests of the Duchy displayed varying hues of gold and amber as the season progressed. It was still some way from winter, but there was a nip in the morning air when the Marchis of Ambrières led a party of huntsmen in search of wild boar. They were on the main road heading west toward an expanse of dense forest a few leagues from the fortress. Since returning from the punitive raid to Anjou there had been little activity, except to count the captured booty and prepare for winter. Harald's castles had been strengthened and there was no one foolhardy or brave enough to attempt to attack him from the south.

The raids into Anjou and Brittany had taken the enemy completely by surprise. Both his and Roger de Montgomery's flying columns had barrelled into leaderless and dispirited forces who retreated without much of a fight, leaving large areas of countryside defenceless. The victorious commanders had attempted to be magnanimous in victory, but the spoils of war proved too much to resist, and their columns returned home burdened with booty. Duke William had been delighted when Harald delivered the news of the crushing victory, declaring that with God and the Fitzroy brothers behind him Normandie was now unassailable.

It was in high spirits that Harald rode out that morning at the head of a baying pack of dogs and excited huntsmen. Just as they were about to leave the road and ride into open country, he was alerted to horses approaching. He saw two riders coming toward them and called his company to a halt. He soon recognised them both, one was Beatrice, the maid of Lady Eleanor, the other a knight in the service of Rolande of Coutances. Beatrice, muddied and dishevelled, was breathless as she struggled to get her words out. When finally she was able to talk, she blurted out that her Lady was in great danger. Eleanor had fallen from her horse two days ago and struck her head on a tree stump, rendering her unconscious. She was carried back to the castle but had not opened her eyes since. Harald listened to Beatrice gravely as the words tumbled out in a torrent. With Lord Robert away in the Holy Land and Rolande of Coutances travelling on the Duchy's business, Beatrice came in search of aid for her mistress.

"The children have been asking for you, Lord, and with their father so far away I felt sure you would come to our assistance," said the maid.

"Indeed, I shall. You did well Beatrice. The roads between here and Mortain are not for the faint-hearted," said Harald. "Thomas, you and I shall return to the castle," he said looking at his squire. "You will prepare us for the short trip. The rest of you will proceed to hunt boar and I shall be disappointed if I return and discover you have been unsuccessful. Now come, we have little time."

He turned his *courser* and spurred the horse back down the road to Ambrières.

When they arrived at the castle, Beatrice and the soldier were sent to the kitchens while Thomas prepared for the trip. The young squire had been Lady Eva's student during her time at Benevento and she had schooled him in the basic use of herbal medicines. For a twelve-year-old boy he had been an eager learner and absorbed her teachings with a passion. After her death, he had packed up all the remedies from her apothecary and taken as many of them as he could carry with him on the road. In his spare time, he often persuaded his older brother to accompany him into the countryside, where they gathered herbs and flowers that he knew could be used to cure the sick. Thomas prepared for the short journey and packed his master's spare clothes and equipment, as well as a bag of remedies in their saddlebags. It was not long before the squire stood in the courtyard with four fresh *palfreys*, awaiting his master. Harald came bounding down the stairs of the keep, barking the last of his orders to his steward, and when the group of four were back in the saddle he led them off on the twenty-five-league journey to Mortain.

By dusk, the next day, their destination was in sight. Harald had pushed his companions all day and riders and horses were exhausted. The road was passable but pitted and muddy and they were all filthy by the time they arrived. They entered the town and passing through the castle gates, stopped for the first time since leaving Ambrières. Servants and grooms greeted their arrival in the courtyard with great activity. Beatrice beckoned Harald to follow her without delay, into the great hall and up several flights of stairs to the family's *solar*. They were met by another of Eleanor's maids coming down the stairs as Harald raced up.

"The mistress, has she woken?" he asked.

"She has not," said the woman, "the children are in with her now."

Harald pushed past her before realising that he did not know where Eleanor's chamber was. Beatrice just pointed ahead with an outstretched finger.

He headed toward the door at the end of the corridor and found the three children sitting silently around the bed. Turid, Richard and William looked up in surprise as their uncle burst into the room and rushed over to where their mother lay motionless. He looked down with a sense of dread on Eleanor's deathly white face. Her breathing was shallow, and the fragile movement of her chest barely stirred the blankets that covered her. The fire burned fiercely in the hearth, giving off tremendous heat but Eleanor's skin was cold to the touch. From the pallor of her face Harald sensed a woman closer to death than life. He felt a tug at his leg and looked down to see his youngest nephew William had wrapped his arms around it and clung to him.

"Uncle Hari, I knew you would come to save Mama. Promise that you won't let her die," he squeaked.

Harald put a hand on the boy's head, but before he could say anything Beatrice interrupted.

"It is time you were all in bed, children. Your poor mother needs to rest," she said as another woman came forward and began to sweep them up in her meaty arms.

They all turned and looked at their uncle.

"I will see you in the morning. Now go and do as you are told. Your mother can still hear everything, you know. If she is to get well, she needs to be left in peace."

They were shepherded off to bed, leaving Beatrice and Harald alone.

"She has no broken bones, no bleeding?" he asked.

"No Lord. The physician could find nothing - not even broken skin where she struck her head," said Beatrice ruefully. "We must trust in God to deliver her back to us."

"You can do no good here. I will watch her tonight and send for you if I have need of you," he said dismissing the exhausted woman.

Another servant arrived carrying food and drink, and the man was sent to bring back water for Harald to wash himself.

"It will not do for her to see me looking like this," he thought looking down at his filthy clothes, caked with mud from the journey.

He drew a chair forward and sat by the side of the bed and watched for any sign of movement from Eleanor. There was none, not a twitch nor any sound and he fell asleep.

He was not sure how long he slept but when he awoke there was light streaming through one of the windows. Harald was stiff from the previous day's ride and from sleeping upright in the hard wooden seat, and he stood and stretched his limbs. He looked down at Eleanor, only to see that she had not moved at all during the night and that the blankets that covered her remained undisturbed. He was filled with great sadness, looking at her features which had barely changed since the time of their secret, youthful courting. There were the tiniest signs of crow's feet at the corners of her eyes but apart from that, the passage of time and the burden of childbearing had not taken a great toll on her. She was still very beautiful, he thought, even in her distressed state.

"Wake up, Eleanor," he said softly. "Your people need you. Your children need you. I need you."

He continued to talk to her, unsure of whether she could hear him until the door to the chamber opened and Beatrice and two other women entered.

"Good morning, my Lord," she said. "A room has been prepared for you. It is not far away, and I will come to you the moment she wakes. We must wash and change her clothes now if you might give her a little privacy?"

Harald nodded and took his leave. Outside the chamber he heard the voices of children and followed its source. He found his niece and nephews eating breakfast around a large wooden table.

"She has woken?" asked the oldest boy looking up from feeding his little sister.

"Not yet, William. But I will not leave this castle until she does."

"Father Albèrt says we must pray for her," blurted out Richard. "He says God will hear us if we pray hard enough."

"That seems like good advice," said Harald. "But today I would like you two boys to take my squire out riding. He is a fine swordsman and might even be persuaded to test your sword arms. You could show him how the men of Mortain fight."

The boys nodded obediently.

"You will not come with us?" asked William.

"I must pray for your mother today, and besides, I should not be far from here when she wakes."

Harald ate breakfast with them before going in search of Thomas and found the boy in the refectory, outside the keep, where the men of the garrison were fed. His squire asked about Lady Eleanor.

"Her condition is grave, Thomas. She sleeps and makes no sound nor movement. It is as if she has left her body completely. Now, come boy, I can tell when you have something to say - out with it."

The fourteen-year-old squire stumbled around, hunting for the right words.

"You might remember, Lord, when we were in Benevento, and I served the Lady Eva in her apothecary."

"I do," said Harald smiling at the memory. "We had many a lively discussion on the subject when I felt you should be better used in training at arms. She had great faith in you, Thomas, and assured me you could serve us both."

"Well, sir, Lady Eva taught me a great deal about healing and how to administer her remedies. I was a willing student and saw her heal many sick people. I believe I could help the Countess if you will allow me."

Thomas put three small glass vials on the table between them. He pointed at each one in turn and gave a detailed explanation of where the medicines came from and what they did. Harald considered the boy's words carefully before replying.

"They will bring her out of her malady?"

"That I cannot say, Lord. But I saw your late wife revive a man with a similar affliction. They are made from plants and flowers and will do her no harm."

"Then we should at least try, we have nothing to lose," said Harald and got up to go in search of Beatrice with Thomas trailing close behind him.

Under the squire's instruction Beatrice was shown how to administer the remedies to her mistress throughout the day. She was reluctant, at first, but at Harald's insistence she relented. Later in the day Thomas took the boys riding, and while he did so Harald visited a place he had last been over twenty years ago.

He watched the boys leave through the castle gates before mounting his own horse and turned in the opposite direction. On the way he stopped in the marketplace and bought a small pig. The animal was tied and carried away unceremoniously over the saddle pommel, despite its noisy protestations. Harald rode out of the town into the open countryside and followed the course of the river Cance upstream for two leagues before he found what he was looking for.

The spring still bubbled away in a clearing in the forest, water gushing out into a stream that ran into the slow moving Cance. It stood in the shadow of an ancient ash tree that towered over the clearing, its huge boughs stretching out like the limbs of a giant, dwarfing the smaller trees around it. Harald first discovered the site as a young boy on a fishing trip with his brother. They had found the spring after getting lost on their way back to Mortain and the eight-year-old Harald had been entranced by their discovery. It had been early summer and the ground around the spring was a riot of daisies, dandelions and orchids. Dragon flies, butterflies and wild bees filled the air as the boys stopped to water their horses. For Harald it became a place of magic. When he later learned that it was a *vé*, a sacred pagan enclosure where the early Norse settlers had worshipped their gods, his infatuation with the place became complete. During a visit home to Regneville he told his grandmother of his discovery. She was delighted and took the boy into her confidence, sharing the secrets of the ancient religion and their gods. Christianity had long since replaced paganism but there were still a few old Norse folk that believed in the power of the ancient deities. 'Mormor' Turid was one of their number and whenever possible she encouraged her young grandson with stories of *Thor, Frey* and *Njord*.

Today, he stood in the clearing again standing by the old spring that still bubbled away relentlessly. It was autumn and the great ash tree had shed most of its leaves, carpeting the ground in a thick blanket of yellow and brown. Harald took a deep breath and inhaled the dominant, earthy smells of the season. He tethered his horse and laid the squealing pig on the ground between the tree and the spring. Then he knelt down and laying his hands on the animal, prayed to the gods and the spirits of his dead grandparents.

"*Freya*, hear my prayers," he called. "You have one in your thrall who needs to be returned to *Midgard*. She is dear to me and the Norns have cut her chords. If you return her to us I will dedicate each battle victory to you and will never let your name be forgotten."

Then he took out a knife and cut the pig's throat in a sacrifice to the Goddess. Harald closed his eyes in contemplation and heard nothing but the wind rustling the fallen leaves. He opened his eyes to the caw-cawing of two jet-black ravens looking down at him from the branches of the tree.

The next day was Sunday and the people of Mortain packed the church to the rafters where Father Albèrt led the prayers for Lady Eleanor. Harald sat with her children in the front row of the church and psalms and prayers were recited with great fervour. After the service he took them back to the castle, each of them hoping to see Eleanor open her eyes. They were disappointed for every time they returned to her chamber, she showed no sign of consciousness.

Daily, her maids came in to wash her, change her nightclothes and administer the salves and medicines that Thomas had brought but there was no improvement. Harald kept his lonely vigil long after the household had retired and talked endlessly to her hoping for any kind of response. The second Sunday after Eleanor's accident saw the congregation fill the church again in support of their matriarch. The priest and his flock implored God again and again and beseeched him to save their Lady, but he was deaf to their pleadings.

The following day Harald woke up in the chair in Eleanor's chamber and rose stiffly. He stretched and looked down on her, shaking his head. The huge dark rings under her eyes appeared larger than normal and her once beautiful, oval face seemed gaunt and wasted.

"Come back, Eleanor," he whispered in her ear, "come back to those who love you."

He looked into her face once again and saw nothing but blankness. Then he moved to the one glass window in the chamber and flung it open to get some respite from the stultifying heat of the hearthfire. He looked out and absent-mindedly noticed the first frost of early winter had arrived. A light dusting of snow covering the land added to his feeling of desolation.

"Close the window unless you wish me to die of cold," said a small voice from behind him.

Spinning around he raced to the bed; Eleanor's eyes were half-open, and she smiled weakly at him. Harald felt his heart leap and he found himself lost for words but managed to beam a smile back at her. He took her hand, which she had managed to get free of the heavy blankets and furs, and kissed it.

"You came back to us, Eleanor," he muttered.

"From a long way away, Hari. I am exhausted from the journey.

"We have been waiting for you," he said.

"I know. I listened to your voice every single day I was away."

"What do you remember?" he asked gently.

"A land of fire and ice. I was lost and a tall, young woman found me and brought me home. It was a long journey and I thought I would never get here."

Then she closed her eyes and fell asleep.

Chapter 27: Return From The Shadows

The next day Eleanor was sitting up in bed with her children around her. She had taken nourishment and was beginning to show signs of recovery. She clutched little Turid to her breast and her boys clung to her. Beatrice fussed about her mistress, bringing extra items of clothing and constantly building up the fire. It did not take long before she was worn out again and the children were marshalled out of the room to allow her to sleep. Harald came back to see her in the afternoon and was pleased to see the rapid progress Eleanor was making in her recovery.

"There you are Hari, I have been bathed, fed and my clothes have been changed. I shall soon be allowed to walk out of here on my own," she said with a hint of annoyance.

"Eleanor," he said earnestly, "I thought I would not see you again in this lifetime. I have never seen a woman so ill and yet recover, but you need to take your time. I will not be the one to tell your husband that his wife died under my care."

"So, I have been under your care, then?" she asked.

"You have, but I must now hand you over into the care of those who will return you to full health," he continued.

"Well, I am grateful for that," she said before pausing. "I know you watched me every day. I know you spoke to me when you were here. Your words helped me return."

"I thought it was the tall woman who brought you back."

"She did and she pulled me through a hostile land that I did not recognise, but it was your words that I clung onto. You gave me the strength to fight. You will stay until I am back on my feet?"

"Alas, I should get back to Ambrières before winter sets in. It has come early this year and much as I enjoy the company of so many women and children, my duties lie elsewhere," he said half-heartedly.

"That is a great shame, Hari and we will miss you, but in the meantime, we shall have to make the most of you while you are here. Now come closer and tell me of the glories of Byzantium once more."

He did as she asked, but no sooner had he started his tale than she dozed off to sleep again. Harald looked down upon her once more and was pleased to see the roses coming back to her cheeks, where once there had only been dark shadows. He had spent far longer in Eleanor's company than he had ever done, despite her being dead to the world for most of it. The Marchis knew that the time had come for him to leave, for he had no wish to become any more attached to his brother's wife than he could help.

He was not sure whether it was divine intervention or even Thomas's remedies that had made their timely introduction, but he only knew that he was elated by her return from beyond the dark pale. He clutched the amulet of Thor's Hammer from beneath his *gambeson* and thanked the old gods. Then he left Eleanor's chamber and walked down the three flights of spiralling stairs to the main hall where Thomas waited for him.

"Lady Eleanor continues to recover?" asked the squire.

"She does, Thomas," replied his master, "and with no small thanks to you and your skills."

He slapped a hand on the boy's shoulder.

"Come, let us take a turn along the battlements and see if we can conjure up an appetite. You will need a little sustenance if you are to take the road home."

"When do we leave, Lord?"

"Tomorrow, if the roads are clear. We will leave at first light."

It was dark when they reached the top of the castle walls. The two looked down on the houses of Mortain on a starless, moonless night. The cobbled streets below were silent as people and animals sheltered in houses and stables from the snow. It began with a few swirling flakes before turning into a blizzard and created a vast white blanket, making the two hundred houses below as blind as moles. Harald cursed his luck and knew they would not be leaving Mortain until well after tomorrow.

Harald's niece and nephews were delighted that he and Thomas were snowed in at the castle. Whilst he visited their mother every day to watch her continued recovery, he made every effort to limit his time in her chamber to a minimum without seeming offish. The more he tried to make himself scarce the more the children sought him out and begged for his time. Eleanor even asked him if he had grown tired of her and her family and gently chided him for the brevity of his visits. In five days she was back on her feet and she found him on his own in the great hall.

"You need time with your family," he said defensively, "they have missed you more than you know."

"Hari, you are part of our family too. Is this not more comfortable than that draughty hall you call home?" she retorted.

He tried to change the subject.

"Have you news of Robert? Even he must have grown tired of spending so much time on his knees."

He noticed her face harden for a moment.

"Nothing - no word has come. I know he reached Rome safely enough before heading for Jerusalem, but beyond that I am in the dark," she said and paused changing the subject. "You will dine with us tonight, I hope. The boys want to recite 'The Wandering Warriors' to you. They have been practicing for days."

"It is always a pleasure to spend time with them, but you must warn them I am a hard task master," he remonstrated.

That night William and Richard stood before their uncle reciting the famous saga. They were giving a fair rendition and were a good way through it, when they began to forget their lines. Never-the-less, Harald applauded vigorously.

"A good effort, boys, but the verses about the battle of Maldon and the Voyage of Tears are an important part of our family's history. You know, I met a man in England this year who knew both of your great-grandparents and stood beside them in battle."

The boys' eyes opened wide with delight.

"Would you like to hear what he said?"

They nodded excitedly and Harald began his story. By the time he had finished they were asleep, as was their sister lying in her mother's arms. Eleanor called for the nurse who took them off to bed and poured more wine for Harald. They drank in silence by the light of the hearthfire until Eleanor spoke,

"Do you ever wonder what might have been?" she said.

Her question surprised him, but he knew exactly what she wanted to know, and he took his time to answer.

"There was a time that question tormented me every waking hour I thought of little else. Even on the long road to Italy I was maddened by the thought of you with another man. I hated Robert for taking you, even though I knew it was not his fault. It was at least a year before I even spoke to another woman, and then I met Eva and moved on."

There was silence between them again.

"Do you want to know how I felt?" she asked him plaintively.

He shook his head.

"Even if I knew it would change nothing. It was a lifetime ago and now you are my brother's wife. Perhaps some things are better left unsaid."

"I am making you feel uncomfortable, Hari. It is wrong of me, I know. Our friendship is just brother and sister now, is it not?"

He looked directly into her eyes which twinkled with the reflection of the flames, and she gave him a dazzling smile.

"Quite so, sister. Now hand me your cup, this wine is too good to drink alone."

The next hours passed quickly between them, and they spoke of many things; their lives, their children and friends past and present. Then, without warning, she announced she was tired and got to her feet unsteadily. Harald caught her arm to steady her and as he got out of his seat, he put his hand to her waist. She smiled and blamed the wine. Then, reaching up and standing on tiptoe, put her hand around the back of his neck and pulled his face to hers. She kissed him on the mouth warmly and drew away.

"Good night, Hari," she said and left for her bedchamber.

He watched her leave the room and made his way to bed. The nearby chamber was, as always, cold and uninviting. The hearthfire, made up earlier, had died down and all that remained was a few glowing embers. He cursed the servants for neglecting it and put on a few logs from the neatly stacked pile beside it, hoping they would catch and burn. Then he removed his boots and top clothes and lay on the bed thinking about what had or had not passed between them earlier. He dozed off and was woken by the sound of a door opening gently and footsteps approaching the bed. Harald stirred quietly, reaching for the dagger he kept beneath his pillow until he recognised the familiar scent of ambergris and lavender. He felt her get into bed next to him and turned over and wrapped his arms around her. He touched the soft skin of her back and she trembled.

"I am cold, Hari," said Eleanor. "I have been alone for too long."

Their reunion was frantic, and they had lost themselves in what Harald's ancestors called *matkir munr*, the great passion.

Afterward they lay entwined, and she buried her head in his chest and fell asleep. She rose before daylight and dressed without a word. He watched her pull on her dress, admiring the lithe, athletic form, that he had once thought about so often as a much younger man, before falling asleep again.

It was mid-morning when Harald finally left his bed. He looked out of the window on a bright sunny day and turned his head to the courtyard, which had been swept clear of snow. He saw Eleanor below with one of her squires training with long-swords and the clash of steel on steel resonated loudly within the castle's walls. She looked up and called up to him,

"I have waited too long for you to wake-up, Marchis Fitzroy, and have chosen a younger opponent. You can come down and take your chances if you do not mind getting cold."

Harald turned back and began to dress hurriedly but checked himself. Although he was happy, happier than he had been since Eva had died, he was conflicted. He had been well aware that his brother had ceased being a husband to Eleanor some time ago, but that was scant reason for lying with her last night, he told himself. He also knew that he could not resist her and try as he might to put distance between them, it would not prevent him from desiring her.

"Perhaps the goddess read my thoughts when I made the sacrifice to Freya before the *vé,*" he thought before dismissing the notion as fanciful. "Perhaps the Norns have cut Eleanor's chords once again and sent her hurtling toward me? No, I cannot change what the gods have decided," he muttered under his breath.

He pulled on his boots and hurried down the stairs to see her again.

Although it was no longer bitterly cold it was ten days before the road back to Ambrières was clear of snow drifts. During the days, Harald busied himself around the town of Mortain, renewing old acquaintances or spending time with his young nephews in sword play or horsemanship. During the night Eleanor visited him in his chamber and when the force of their ardor was spent they talked in low whispers before she left him in the early hours. She had been lonely for years, she told him, and seeing him for the first time when he returned from Italy rekindled a passion which had lain dormant for more than a decade. She had decided to keep a respectable distance from him, but fate had thrown them together and a physical reunion had become unavoidable. Eleanor told him not to reproach himself for taking advantage of the situation during her husband's absence. Their marriage was based only on mutual respect, and she had, up until now, been a dutiful and faithful wife. She had borne him three fine children, offered him wise council and ran his estates efficiently and profitably. Besides, she added, Robert's love was for the Church and the Duchy and like many arranged marriages theirs was a loveless if temperate union.

Ten days later Harald left Mortain, but not before they agreed to see one another before winter had passed into spring.

Chapter 28: Guardians Of The Pilgrims Way

The priest stooped over Robert's cot and bathed and dressed the wounds on his back. During the walk to Golgotha, the Lord of Mortain had insisted that the priests in their party flay him as the Romans had done to Christ before reaching his place of crucifixion. It had been a long, painful walk of a half a league during which time neither his faith nor his step faltered. When they reached their destination, he led the men in prayer before they returned to their lodgings in the city. Once inside his quarters he collapsed from pain and exhaustion and, after sleeping for two days, finally woke up.

"God will see your sacrifices, Lord. He has seen your heart and will forgive all the Norman people. The task is complete," said David.

"Our mission is not yet over," replied Robert. "We must remain in the Holy Land until Easter, protecting Christian pilgrims on their way to Jerusalem. Then we can return home."

"Oh," said David "then there is more to be done?"

"You sound disappointed," said Robert through clenched teeth as a salve was applied to the welts on his back.

"Not I, Lord. God's work is never done," said David.

"Good. We leave for Antioch in the morning."

Two days later, the group of fifteen stood beneath the papal banner on the busy dock watching a large *cog* discharge its cargo. Forty-five men and women stepped gingerly down a set of wooden planks to get onto the quay. Their leader, a stout German merchant approached the Normans and asked where the road to Jerusalem lay.

"To the south, friend," answered Robert, "but the road is dangerous for a group of unarmed pilgrims."

"So I have heard, Lord. But we must trust in God to protect us," answered the man.

"Well spoken, pilgrim, but we will escort you and see you safely there. Brigands lie in wait for unsuspecting travellers, who will only be too keen to relieve you of your gold and women," replied Robert.

The man looked unsure and hesitated.

"You have nothing to fear from us, pilgrim. We are sent by God to protect all Christian folk on their journey through the Holy Land."

"Then we shall be very glad to accept your protection. What is your price?"

"We ask for nothing in return. Meet us by the city's southern gate at sunrise tomorrow and we shall take you to Jerusalem."

The next day, the German group mustered at the city gate. Word had spread to other parties from other boats and Robert was amazed to find over two hundred and fifty people, packed and waiting for him. Not all were wealthy, there were many impoverished, ill and exhausted pilgrims who simply joined up with the company and sat in the cool of the early morning waiting to leave. Robert ordered his men to share what food they had with these people and their squires distributed it. He had ordered that their kite shields be adorned with a crimson cross on a white background, so that Saracens and brigands might see from afar that these pilgrims travelled under the protection of holy warriors. The Normans were heavily armed, and their weapons and armour displayed for all to see. Robert noticed with interest that David the priest had found a sword which was now strapped to his waist. At their Lord's request the riders dismounted and there was quiet throughout the company as they knelt as one in prayer. After receiving a blessing for the arduous journey which lay ahead of them, the horsemen mounted and led their charges off. They would stop only at the holy places and shrines that were scattered throughout the route. Robert knew that once outside the city walls, such a large group of pilgrims would be prey to Saracen robbers throughout their journey and he ordered his men to be vigilant in their defence. Each pilgrim hoped to reach Jerusalem without conflict but the sites they were to visit were spread out and it would be a long and for some, fateful journey.

At first, the sight of Norman knights deterred attacks, but such was the temptation of a large group of pilgrims, that there were several night raids. During these incursions women and booty were carried off into the dark before Robert and his men were alerted. However, they repulsed numerous nocturnal incursions and even a few in daylight before their journey was complete. Thirty days later they arrived in Jerusalem and took leave of the travellers, many of whom bid them a tearful farewell. The company had lost fifteen pilgrims during the journey, through Saracen depredations, although it would have been a great deal more without Robert's protection. During numerous sallies against rapacious attackers, they lost only one warrior, a fourteen-year-old squire who died from an arrow wound. After two days' rest in Jerusalem replacing their supplies, tending to the horses and sharpening their weapons, they turned north and back to Antioch to offer their swords and shields to more travellers from Europe.

By the time they reached Antioch they were greeted by a group of people far larger than the first company of pilgrims. This time they left on the road to Jerusalem with over five hundred people who, encouraged by whispers of safe passage had waited patiently for the Norman Lord and his holy warriors before setting out. They were also joined by new groups of knights, asking if they too might join the company, offering their arms to defend and protect the weak. Now with sixty warriors, bearing the sign of the cross on their shields they left Antioch at the head of a column of pilgrims. It was a hard march and even with a larger group of warriors the journey was not without risk. They were still attacked, and pilgrims were killed, if not quite so frequently. However, with each attack that was repulsed, the *espirit de corps* within Robert's warriors grew as did the collective belief in their mission.

By the time Easter came they had escorted over two thousand pilgrims safely along the road south. Robert returned to Antioch for the fifth and final time after which he would take his leave of the company that now numbered over a hundred mounted warriors.

Of the fourteen knights and squires who had left Normandie the previous year, half of them asked for his permission to stay and continue their work protecting the pilgrims. On Robert's final night with his men they prayed together under the guidance of their warrior priest, David, who had also decided to stay. Then Robert feasted his men in a fine manner with the last of his gold before leaving them in the morning. He was returning home a changed man, having fulfilled his promise to Duke William and the favour of Rome had been ensured. He had answered the call from Christ, received during his vision on the Via Delorosa and brought thousands of pilgrims safely to Jerusalem.

"God will surely forgive and bless the Norman people now," he thought flexing his right arm once more which had recovered its full strength for the first time since leaving Normandie.

He spurred his horse forward and with his seven companions took the road north toward home.

Chapter 29: Harald Returns To Duty

It seemed like an age that Harald had been away from Ambrières, but on his return to the castle little had changed. They rode home in silence as, deep in thought, he pondered the events of the last twenty-five days. He and Thomas had taken advantage of the break in the early winter weather and, finding the road from Mortain clear, they soon reached their castle's grey walls.

Life carried on as normal and as was customary at this time of year the garrison was stood down from duty. There would be no campaigning until next year and no need to maintain a battle-ready company until spring. With little threat from the south, the main body of fighting men were paid off, with orders to report back for duty in the cold short, days of the New Year. Manned by a group of fifty men and assorted servants, martial activities in the fortress came to a halt as Christmas approached. The town's people celebrated with the usual Christian fervour and Harald was generous in his contributions to the festival, providing a great feast on Christmas day. He had little interest in celebrating the birth of Jesus but he knew that it was necessary, as the Marchis, to be benevolent during the celebrations. He took the time visiting the other strongholds along his borders, and finding them in good order, he left the commanders to their own devices.

Harald hated these quiet times when he spent many days confined to his own castle. He was, however, not without visitors. There were several old comrades returning from the south, civil disputes to judge or nobles trying to off-load their daughters on him in marriage. The Marchis found himself thinking of Eleanor often and when he would next see her again. He did not have long to wait and ten days after Christmas a rider came to Ambrières with a message for him. She had sent one of her trusted knights to tell her lover that she would be staying at a small farmstead outside the hamlet of Ceaucé in five days' time. Harald smiled at the memory of the place where he and Eleanor had met so often many years ago.

Their clandestine meetings at Ceaucé became frequent and they spent time together whenever they could. They were careful to be discrete and tried to keep these meetings secret, each of them riding out alone to the familiar rendezvous. By the time spring arrived and the Duchy began to stir into life the frequency of these meetings had not lessened. Both of them knew the importance of vigilance and tried hard to keep their trysts a secret and away from prying eyes.

Harald also recalled Jeanotte from England in the spring. He kept his promise to his captain that he would send for him and duly dispatched *Evas*

Prayer with another of his trusted men to replace him in Maldon. The young knight, delighted to be back in Normandie, was brimming with information on the current state of the English royal court. Harald learned that King Edward was in good health and that the Godwins' power had been held in check.

"It is good to be back, Lord," said Jeanotte, draining another cup of wine as the two sat alone in the castle's great hall.

"It is good to have you back," said Harald. "Now tell me of your rebuilding programme in Maldon."

"Successful, I believe, Lord. All has gone as we planned. There has been a good deal of work and the wall around the town has been completed."

"And have you found yourself a beautiful Saxon wife?" Harald teased.

"Not yet, for in truth the Saxon women are a wild breed and difficult to handle."

"I am sure your good manners were not lost on them. Now tell me, is King Edward still well-disposed to having a Norman on the English throne?"

"He is, Lord and he took time when I was last in London to express those sentiments. He will be sending an emissary to Duke William before the summer to reinforce his wishes."

"You have done well, Jeanotte, and discharged your duties to me and the Duchy perfectly. The Duke will be delighted with your news. Now, take some more wine and refresh yourself because tomorrow we will leave for Caen."

The next day Harald and Jeanotte took the road to Caen. Since returning to the Duchy from Italy he had never been completely comfortable in the Duke's company. Despite his misgivings William had been as good as his word and rewarded him richly for his service. Harald for his part was faithful and obedient to his liege-lord, but he suspected that there was still some hidden enmity between them. He knew that his position of rank was only due to his usefulness to Duke William and felt the need to watch his back, particularly with Robert abroad.

Two days later he was in the Duke's chambers sharing some wine.

"Do you know who King Edward will send?" quizzed William.

"The King did not say. Only that he would be sending a high-ranking nobleman as his ambassador and that his sentiments toward you and the Duchy were as 'warm as ever'," replied Harald.

"Do you expect my cousin to keep his promises?"

"I do, Lord, but the Saxon nobles will not all be happy for you to sit on the English throne. King Edward is an old man and his power is on the wane."

"And what is your council, Marchis?" asked the Duke formally.

"To be vigilante and wary of treating with anyone other than the King. England is a precious jewel that many covert," replied Harald.

William steepled his fingers and considered the response before speaking again.

"It would be a costly operation to reinforce our position with might, would it not?" said William.

This time Harald chose his words carefully before answering.

"Indeed, it would, Lord, but not impossible. We have many more allies than once we did and with the support of Rome we can get many more."

"Ah, yes," said William, with a note of triumph. "You will be pleased to learn that by late summertime we hope to be able to welcome your brother Robert home. Apparently, he has been protecting pilgrims on the road to Jerusalem and has built quite a reputation for himself, I hear. He is very much the 'Holy Warrior' by all accounts. "

"He is well?" asked Harald.

"If the reports are true - he is in good health. He has left the Holy Land and is on his way home," pronounced the Duke.

"That is good news. We shall all be glad to have him home," said Harald.

"Including his family, I expect. I understand Lady Eleanor was struck down by some malady," said William.

"She has recovered well enough now," Harald answered.

"Then Robert is fortunate to have a brother like you, Hari," said William looking intently at Harald as if trying to read his face.

Seeing no reaction, the Bastard changed the subject.

"Now, how many men might we need to secure the English throne, if we had to use force? Ten thousand, twenty?" he continued.

"Five thousand cavalry and the same number of foot soldiers could carry the day, but it would require a huge number of ships. The Saxons might muster fifteen to twenty thousand men, all told."

"Then let us pray that King Edward keeps his word," mused William before focusing once more. "Now to the business of our borders. Are the counties of Maine and Anjou still at peace."

"They are Lord, all resistance in the new lands has been dealt with."

"Then you must come with me to visit our allies. They need to be reminded of why their support of the Duchy is required. We shall leave in two days' time."

Duke William was at his most affable during their mission. He was not a natural diplomat and what he lacked in charm, his physical presence more than made up for. Their mission was to strengthen ties with the other duchies to the north and east, and they visited the dukes, counts and marchis in Flanders, Champagne and the Vexin. The Duke's message was a simple one.

"Normandie's influence is growing, and with the support of Rome and the return of her warriors from the south, her power will continue to grow," he would tell his audiences in a loud rasping voice.

He spoke of the Lord of Mortain's pilgrimage to the Holy Land and his protection of fellow pilgrims with great pride, and all those who listened were impressed. Harald said little in any of these meetings and there was no real need, for his reputation and feats were well known through all of France and beyond. After sixty days and numerous visits during which they were well-received and celebrated, they returned to Caen where Harald took his leave. He was barely back on the road to Ambrières with his retinue before he was overtaken by a rider, one of the Duke's squires, who drew his perspiring *palfrey* to a halt in front of them.

"Lord," shouted the boy, clearly out of breath, "Duke William asks that you return to Caen with all haste."

"What is it? Is the Duke in danger?" asked Harald.

"No, Lord. Nothing like that. He received a visitor, a Saxon nobleman recently arrived from England. His comrades are in trouble and need your help. He will explain all when you return.

"Very well, lead on, boy," said Harald, signalling to his troop to turn around and before long they had all returned to their starting point at Caen castle.

Harald found the Duke in his council chamber. Sitting opposite him was a Saxon nobleman. The man was still muddy from the road and his long unkempt hair and moustaches contributed to his general state of dishevelment. They both looked up as Harald strode through the hall toward the long table at which they sat.

"Lord Fitzroy, welcome back," said the Duke. "I trust you had not ridden too far down the road."

"No, Lord. We had barely left Caen when the message arrived," replied Harald looking over at the Saxon who looked decidedly tired and worn.

"This gentleman is Cuthbert of Andover, and he is our honoured guest. He comes to us in the company of other Saxon noblemen. His comrades have been captured by our vassal Guy de Pontieu, who seems to think it is acceptable to take our guests hostage and then demand ransom for their release," said the Duke wearily to Harald. "I should like you to take your company to the Count's castle and have them released immediately. Then, I would like you to escort them to Rouen where we will show them some proper Norman hospitality." Harald bowed low.

"Of course, Lord. We shall leave today," he said.

"Lord Cuthbert shall accompany you and will share the details of his mission. Now please, finish your refreshment and while you do, I will spend a few moments with the Marchis before you depart," said William cordially to his guest before walking toward Harald.

The two Normans walked down the large hall leaving the Saxon to a tray full of wine and food.

"This is an outrage, Hari, which I would like you to deal with harshly - use force if you feel it is required," hissed William venomously. "Do what you need to do but get these men released and brought to Rouen safely. My reputation is at stake here and I do not want the English to feel their future king is nothing more than a brigand himself who cannot even control his own vassals. You will deal with Guy as you see fit."

'Then I will have them all in Rouen as soon as I can. We are ready to leave the moment your guest is able," said Harald, before leaving the hall and returning to his company of horseman.

Cuthbert joined them soon afterward and, provided with a new mount, they set off on the road east.

It took the company three days to reach Beaurain castle. Cuthbert had left England in the company of several Saxon lords to travel to Normandie in search of Duke William. They had been sent by King Edward to reiterate his message to the Duke that he was the heir to the English throne, and to invite him to England and the royal court later in the year. The Saxons set sail for Normandie but a storm had blown them off course and landed them near Pontieu. They anchored in the estuary of the River Somme and began to disembark in the shallows when they were approached by a large group of horsemen. The party of twenty-five Englishmen had been apprehended by the forces of Count Guy, and the noblemen amongst them taken away and imprisoned in his castle. The Saxons now languished in captivity and would only be released on the payment of a large ransom. Cuthbert, who had not been taken, had slipped overboard and concealed himself before stealing a horse and escaping.

Harald called his troop of twelve horsemen to a halt before the heavy wooden door of Beaurain Castle. It was midday and a light drizzle blew rain into his face as he looked up to the top of the stone walls, where armed guards looked down. They carried no sigils or gorfannons making it impossible for the men on the battlements to identify them. Their captain called down asking what they wanted.

"I am here on the Duke of Normandie's business and demand to see your Lord. You may tell him that Harald Fitzroy has come to escort the Duke's guests back to Rouen," he shouted.

There was silence from above before the Count himself appeared on the battlements a few moments later. Guy's weaselly features stared down, taking in the situation before he spoke.

"Ah, Harald of Regneville," called down Guy jovially, "or is it Ambrières or all of southern Italy now? It has been a while since we have been visited by such a famous warrior."

"Just let me in Guy - I do not wish to parlais with you at such a distance."

There was silence from above and after a brief pause the castle gates swung open. Harald led his men through into a large courtyard where they were met by the Count and thirty or so of his men. He regarded the man in front of him for a moment or two.

"The man has changed little since I released him - a scrawny man of little courage who lacks any real fight," Harald thought to himself.

During the battle of Larraville, the Count of Pontieu had fought on the losing side and was captured and imprisoned for over a year before his ransom was paid. The conditions of his release also demanded that he swore fealty to the Duke of Normandie and submit to becoming his vassal.

"You are holding some of Duke William's honoured guests," said Harald, without preamble. "I am here to escort them on the remainder of their journey."

"I have no knowledge of such matters," said Guy defiantly. Harald turned around in the saddle and asked Cuthbert.

"Do you see the man who took your comrades?" he asked the Saxon.

"I do, and he stands before you."

Harald turned back to Guy.

"Then I ask you again to release these men to me, and if I find they have been mistreated there will be consequences," he said.

"These men are my justifiable prisoners," replied the Count defiantly. "Under the Laws of Wreck any ship-wrecked mariner on my shores will find himself sold into slavery, imprisoned and ransomed."

Harald, dismounted with surprising speed for a man of his size and strode over to the Count. There was a sound of men nocking and drawing arrows from the tops of the battlements, but Guy raised his hand to prevent his men from taking any action.

"I care little for these ancient laws that allow dishonest men to grow wealthy. May I remind you that Duke William is your liege lord, and he commands you to release these men into my charge," said Harald calmly.

Guy did his utmost to return Harald's intimidating glare but looking up at this enormous, menacing presence he knew that he was bested.

"Very well, my Lord, but let us first break bread - you will be hungry and thirsty after your ride I am sure. Your men will be looked after well. Come, we are brothers-in-arms, are we not? Both in the service of the same liege lord?

Harald broke into a broad smile and he and Cuthbert followed Guy into his hall to take some food and wine while they waited for the five Saxon lords to be brought out.

The Count of Ponthieu tried to make nervous but polite conversation with his guests as they ate and drank. He ordered the return of all the confiscated goods, weapons and valuables as well as the release of the stranded ship and its crew. Harald even persuaded the reluctant Count to part with five horses for the journey south. They were interrupted by the sound of a door opening at the far end of the hall.

"Here are your guests,"said Guy convivially. Harald stood up to meet them as they trudged forward toward him.

"It is good to meet you once more," he said to Earl Godwinson who looked at him open-mouthed in astonishment. "I hope your stay has not been too unsettling."

Chapter 30: The Duke Impresses, 1059

It was a little past midday when Earl Godwinson and his companions were ready and mounted, and the company swept out of Ponthieu castle heading west. The Saxons had not been badly treated during their ten-day incarceration and were in good spirits, despite their ordeal. It had been two years since the Earl had accosted Harald in London and although both remembered the event, neither acknowledged the meeting until later that day. The rest of the Saxons were delighted to be free and keen to express their gratitude, but their leader was less effusive. It was only when they camped for the night in a small glade that the Earl approached Harald.

"My Lord, we are in your debt," he said, "I also owe you an apology from our first meeting. I was less than gracious and take back my words which were said in haste."

"You agree that Maldon is mine, then?" replied Harald quickly.

"That is the subject for another conversation, I think. But let us agree that I acknowledge your right to the claim. Who am I to go against my King?"

"We shall drink to a better onward journey then," replied Harald taking wine from his squire, Thomas. "If it is not too painful, I would be glad to hear of your journey here."

The two men sat on the trunk of a fallen tree and the Earl told his story. They had been sent, by King Edward, to visit Normandie. Their mission was to confirm Duke William's right of succession to the English throne on the King's death. The Saxons, all high-ranking nobles, were to put themselves at the Duke's service so that he might learn more about the kingdom he was to inherit. The party gathered at the Earl's estate in southern England before leaving on a well-equipped ship for Normandie. During the voyage the winds had turned and they were blown east up the coast, where, seeking safe harbour, they were captured. When the Count of Ponthieu realised his captives were Saxon nobles in the service of the English King, his eyes lit up with delight and was about to send an enormous ransom demand for the party. Harald's timely intervention had prevented not only disaster but also saved the Earl from considerable embarrassment at home.

They talked long into the evening and Harald slowly warmed to his namesake who had once been so hostile. He found the Earl's honesty and forthrightness appealing, compared with some of the half-truths he had to endure in many of Duke William's council meetings. During the next two days of their journey he learned more about the complex nature of the Saxons and their ruling class than he had in the half year spent in England.

Harold Godwinson was the son of the most powerful nobleman in England. His father had many other sons and daughters who were united in their distrust of the Normans, who they felt had poisoned the mind of their King with their 'sanctimonious piety'. During the family's recent exile, brought about by King Edward's desire to break their iron grip on much of the Kingdom, they were scattered to the winds. However, they succeeded in making some strong alliances through marriage and eventually the family returned to England, when Edward relented and allowed them to resume their positions of influence. Great swathes of land were held by the Godwinsons and together with Harold's brothers, Tostig and Svein, England felt their power once more. The Saxons, like the Normans, had strong ties to the Norse people who provided much of the military might behind the nobility. The *huscarls*, an elite body of Norse warriors, were the power behind the English throne and King Edward kept a standing army of three thousand loyal mercenaries close at hand. Every powerful Saxon Earl maintained a smaller force of these fierce, axe-wielding warriors.

The Godwinson's rancour toward the Normans was a commonly held sentiment by many in England, the Earl pointed out. His duty, he insisted, was to King Edward alone and any aspirations of kingship by greedy noblemen were beneath him. Harald smiled to himself when he heard these protestations for he knew only too well the hearts of men when it came to seizing power. Much as he liked the Earl's forthrightness, he sensed the man would not be above taking the English throne for himself should the opportunity present itself.

The party of Saxons were, to a man, fascinated by Harald's own story and that of his famous ancestors. He delighted in retelling the tales and was seldom able to resist a request to describe his role at Civitate or his grandfathers' part in both of the battles for Maldon. The journey passed quickly, and on the evening of the third day smoke from a thousand evening fires could be seen on the horizon. They had almost arrived at the beautiful city of Rouen.

Of all the large towns and cities of Normandie, Rouen was the glittering jewel. It was divided by the River Seine where large numbers of ships were tied up on wooden jetties on each bank. Surrounding both parts of the city there were massive stone walls, from which flew hundreds of flags, each bearing the images of the two leopards of Normandie. As they drew closer Harald noticed large numbers of spearmen standing guard on the high walls. They were all dressed in full armour and stood to attention as the horsemen approached the massive gates to the city. They were met by a single rider, a captain of the city guard named Clovis. He too was immaculately turned out, his burnished helm and *hauberk* reflecting the last red glimmer of the setting sun.

"Welcome, Marchis," he said bowing his head. "The Duke awaits you in his palace. Please follow me."

Clovis turned his *palfrey* around and led them through the gates and onto the cobbled streets of the city. The streets were still full of people, despite the hour, who turned and watched the famous Marchis of Ambrières and his strangely attired guests ride past them. Smartly dressed soldiers in Duke William's livery stood at regular intervals along the streets on the way to the palace, each of them carrying a spear and shield.

"It looks like you are expecting royalty, Captain. The city is looking its best," said Harald as they rode.

"The Duke's orders, Lord," replied Clovis as quietly as he could. "The garrison has been ordered to put on a show."

"You shame us," laughed Harald. "I have three days of road dust on me."

"You need no finery, Lord. Your deeds speak for themselves, but I can tell you that you and your guests will receive a memorable welcome. The Duke's kitchens have been busy for days."

Clovis led them through a labyrinth of streets, closely packed with shops and houses that overhung their route, until they reached a large, enclosed courtyard. A cohort of stable boys rushed out of nowhere and took the horses off to be fed and stabled as soon as the riders dismounted. The party was met by another of the Duke's staff, the grandly attired *Seneschal* of Rouen, who walked down the steps of the palace toward the party. The Count of Jumieges bowed low.

"Good evening, Marchis," he said to Harald before turning to the Saxons.

"Good evening, Earl Godwinson, welcome to the city of Rouen. You and your comrades are our honoured guests. If you are not too tired, we have prepared some refreshments for you all. I am at your disposal."

The man turned and guided them up the stairs and into a large, airy anteroom, leading into a huge chamber hung with banners and ornate decorations. There were the sigils of the present and previous Dukes, captured battle standards of vanquished armies, tapestries and all manner of religious iconography. An evening breeze blew gently through a dozen open windows high in the room, causing hundreds of lighted bees-wax candles to flicker. At the far end of the hall there was a huge crucifix attached to the wall from which a gigantic Christ-figure hung. In the centre of the room a massive circular table, bedecked with gold and silver plates, drinking cups and candlesticks, was festooned with jugs of wine, baskets of bread and summer flowers.

From his seat at the far side of the table, Duke William stood and came forward to meet his guests. He wore a long, flowing gown of purple silk over an intricately embroidered tunic, a high-necked linen shirt, woollen trousers and silk hose. On his head he wore a plain coronet of heavy gold.

"He looks more like a Byzantine prince than the Duke of Normandie," thought Harald.

"Earl Godwinson, welcome to Rouen," bellowed William, arms outstretched in greeting. "You have had an interesting arrival in our Duchy I hear? Come, sit with me, we have much to talk about. You and your comrades are our honoured guests."

"Thank you, Lord. It has been a little testing, but the Marchis has been good company and we are in his debt," replied the Earl, accepting William's proffered hand and bowing his head

"I am indeed fortunate to have Lord Harald as my strong right hand," affirmed the Duke. "Now, please allow me to present these fine folk to you." he turned around to introduce several of the noblemen and their wives standing behind him.

When the introductions were over and everyone was seated, the Archbishop of Rouen was invited to say grace before wine was brought. The Earl sat between William and his wife Mathilda and an endless supply of food was brought out by busy teams of servants. Plates of roasted mutton, wild boar and oxen were served in regal succession. There were trays of lamprey pies, grilled river fish and seasonal fruits and nuts. It was a lengthy meal at which jugglers, jongleurs and minstrels entertained their audience. The Saxons, clearly appreciating the lavish hospitality, became animated and talkative until finally the Duke and Duchess took leave of their guests. Before they left he announced a stag-hunt was organised for his guests the next day.

"Your Lord is a generous host, Harald," said the Earl, watching the Duke and his wife depart. "I had no idea that Norman feasts were quite so extravagant. He has entertained us royally."

"I am sure he wishes to make amends for your abrupt welcome in Ponthieu," the Marchis replied. "Let us see how you get on with the Norman stags tomorrow - they will give us good chase."

Harald raised his silver drinking cup and toasted Earl Godwinson before draining it, and the Earl did the same in reply.

The next day, a large hunting party gathered before the Duke's keep, accompanied by an even bigger pack of sighthounds, deerhounds and mastiffs. William was one of the first men to be ready and he and Harald waited for the others to arrive.

"What do you make of Godwinson?" he asked.

"He gives little away, Lord. It appears that he is in his King's thrall, but he has a reputation in England for being a man of ambition and one of great wealth," replied Harald.

"Then we should be on our guard. I shall invite him to stay with us for the remainder of the year and we can judge his metal. We must beware of any nobleman, Saxon or otherwise, who might rob us of our destiny."

"Do you wish me to stay here in Rouen?" said Harald.

"Not for the moment. I need you to go to Avranches after the hunt. Count Conan's Bretons have been up to their old tricks again. As soon as we relax our hold on them they turn and bite us. Geoffrey de Montgomery returned home to the Hiemois in the spring, and since then the Bretons send raiding parties, burn and loot a few towns and disappear. It may well need your iron fist but do not pursue Conan's men back into Britanny. Come back here and report what you find," said William. "The Saxons will be in good hands although the Earl seems to have taken you into his confidence."

"He is certainly a little less frosty since our first meeting," said Harald, "but let's see how he hunts before we judge him?"

"… and perhaps how he fights in the field?" replied William with a grin.

Their conversation was interrupted by the sound of guests arriving. As soon as the Saxon and Norman lords, squires, servants and dogs were all assembled, the whole entourage made a noisy departure out of the palace courtyard, through the streets of the town and into the open countryside.

The Saxon party were in a state of excitement at the prospect of the hunt. They had brought their own hounds from England and together with the Norman dogs they formed a sizeable pack.

"I wonder," shouted William to the Earl, "whether the Count of Pontieu was going to ransom these animals along with you?"

"They would have fetched a pretty price. They may have earned him more than we would; Mercian deerhounds are worth their weight in silver. Let's hope we can find a stag that can match their skills," came the retort.

Both men laughed at the joke before William led the party off to the north and along the banks of the Seine.

Before long the pastures and meadows turned into woodland and the group, losing none of its earlier momentum, entered a forest. The hounds soon picked up the scent of a stag and the hunt was on. They tracked a large hart out from the trees and back to the river. When their quarry turned at bay to face his pursuers, the hunters paused to admire the huge beast, which raised a magnificent antlered head and bellowed its defiance. The hunters waited for Duke William to dismount and dispatch the animal, but he merely looked toward Earl Godwinson.

"Your honour, my Lord," said the Duke, nodding to his squire who proffered a stout hunting spear to the Saxon leader.

The Earl nodded in deference and dismounted. He took the spear without a word and walked quickly to confront the doomed stag. Despite its exhaustion, there was still some fight left in the animal who lowered its head and charged forward. The Earl's speed belied his size, and he moved nimbly aside thrusting the long pole arm behind the animal's foreleg and into the heart. It crumpled from the fatal blow, its knees buckling before slumping forward and died in front of the hunters. The dark blood from its wound soaked the surrounding grass as it gushed out. No sooner had it finished its death throes, than the servants and squires moved in to dress the carcass. The dogs were rewarded for their labours with offal while the rest of its immense remains were butchered where it lay. A wagon was loaded with the fresh meat while servants moved quickly around the hunters serving them wine and food.

Duke William raised a full cup of wine to his Saxon guests.

"Gentlemen, I drink to your health and to the courage of Earl Godwinson, for I have seldom seen such a swift dispatch of such a magnificent beast," he called.

"A fine morning's hunt," replied the Earl with a massive grin across his huge mustachioed features. "Let us all praise the spirit of our departed friend, the stag, and thank him for his sacrifice."

Replete with more wine and food, the party mounted up and returned to Rouen at a sedate pace. The servants and squires were dismissed for the day and William led his guests off to his chambers where the only talk was of the hunt.

Harald excused himself early into the evening and retired.

He rose early and slipped out of the town at daybreak.

Chapter 31: The Count Of Mortain Journeys Home

Robert left Antioch with seven comrades the day after Easter Monday. He had one final task to complete on his journey home. When Duke William had agreed to release him from service to make the pilgrimage to the Holy Land, it was on the condition that he would retrieve his father's remains on the return journey. Twenty years previously, Robert the Magnificent left his eight-year-old son, William, in Normandie, to make his own pilgrimage to Jerusalem. He contracted a fever just after arriving and his men had borne him home on a litter. They reached the town of Nicaea, not far from Constantinople, where the old Duke had died, and his body had been interred in a local church. William had often spoken of his desire to bring his father's bones home and Robert promised him that he would endeavour to do so. Before leaving on his own pilgrimage, he had sought out the last of the dead Duke's companions and the old knight provided the details of the route, the location of the church and where the remains might be found.

Robert travelled on the coastal road north before veering overland and up through the desolate Taurus mountains before descending onto the arid plains of Isauria. There were few towns and villages *en route* and those they passed through were languid, sleepy places whose people were wary of the heavily armed travellers. They slept in the open or sheltered in caves at night, rising at dawn to travel until the sun took its toll on both men and horses. As they drew closer to Constantinople the number of settlements grew and the land became more fertile, where the pilgrims could find food and rest.

The company arrived at the little church of Nicaea some twenty days after they left Antioch. They found the tomb of Duke William's father inside in the old stone crypt beneath the building. After protracted negotiations with the local priest, who pocketed a significant proportion of Robert's remaining silver, a deal was struck. The bones were removed, placed in a wooden box and after a small ceremony, handed over.

A day later they stood in front of the mighty city walls of Constantinople, to stay a while before starting on the great journey that lay ahead of them. They entered the city that evening just as the main gates were being closed and slipped through the streets, almost unnoticed, to find board and lodging. Robert and his men were bone-weary and dishevelled and welcomed the prospect of a bed and a hot meal, however humble their lodgings. Their battered kite-shields hung from the dusty flanks of their horses and still bore the sign of the red cross against a faded white background, marking them out as holy warriors of Christ.

The next morning, refreshed after the first part of their journey home, they went in search of a church where they might pray and give thanks for their safe arrival in Constantinople. The city boasted hundreds of places of Christian worship, and the pilgrims went into the first one they found. Each man knelt solemnly before the altar of the little stone building in silent worship. They stayed there for some time in quiet retreat, unaware of the sound of the outside door opening. Robert got to his feet and turned to walk out with the rest of his men following behind him. He looked to the back of the church and saw a young woman sitting alone watching him walk up the aisle. She wore a bejewelled scarf over her head and an expensive silk dress of gold and red. Behind her stood a Norseman in the uniform of the Varangian Guard, who leant nonchalantly on a huge double-bladed axe.

"Lord," she called to Robert as he walked past her. "Please, a few moments of your time?"

He stopped and looked at her. She looked to be sixteen or seventeen years of age and met his gaze confidently.

"Do men of God come to church so heavily armed?" she enquired.

He looked down and then back at his men. They were all dressed in full-length mail and each man had a sword buckled to his waist.

"Not always, Lady. We have travelled far through hostile lands and even in Christian cities my people have not always been well received," he replied cautiously.

"You have nothing to fear in Constantinople, if you are truly men of God," she said with the hint of a smile. "May I ask your name, Lord?"

"I am Count Robert of Mortain and we are on our way home to Normandie," he replied, "and yours, lady?"

"My name is Anna, and I am a princess of this city. But tell me, Lord are you the same Norman warrior that rode at the head of God's army guarding thousands of pilgrims on their way to Jerusalem?" she asked pointedly.

"We did no more than God's will," said Robert earnestly "and now we wish to rest and pray before continuing our journey."

"Then, Lord Robert, you must allow me to help you on your way home. It seems you have earned a little assistance," she said. "But first I need something in return. Please sit with me and I will explain."

Princess Anna was the favourite daughter of the Byzantine Emperor Alexis Comnenos, who doted on her above all his other children. She grew from being an overindulged child into a strong-willed young woman, who channelled all her considerable energies into learning and writing. Her parents provided her with excellent tutors to satisfy a rapacious appetite for knowledge and she was diligent in her studies. One of her tutors had brought word to her of a noble pilgrim who had travelled to the Holy Land to gain absolution for his people. The Norman lord, it was said, had been told by God that his penance for forgiveness was to protect fellow pilgrims on the road to Jerusalem. He had, she was told, raised an army who painted crosses with the 'blood of Christ' on their shields so that Moorish brigands would know and fear them.

They talked for a while and Anna invited Robert and his men to the imperial palace as her father's guests, where they might gather their strength for the long journey north. They would be the Emperor's honoured guests for as long as they cared to accept his hospitality. All the princess required was to learn Robert's story and the history of the Duchy's warriors who, she said, were feared and respected throughout the Eastern Empire and beyond. He was reluctant to accept her offer at first, but after considering the general state of the company's health he acceded to Anna's request. The Princess left Robert with some of her servants to guide them to the palace and they went to collect their things. She rejoined her waiting retinue outside to be borne home in a litter.

Robert and his men returned to their lodgings to retrieve their meagre belongings and the two sick comrades who had been unable to leave the single room where they all slept. Battle wounds, sickness and hunger had started to take an inexorable toll on the company and Anna Comnena's unexpected invitation had not come a moment too soon for the weary warriors.

Her servants led the Normans out of the city, and they followed the road to the Blachernae Palace. They found it on top of a low hill overlooking the sea and as they approached the upper gates they were met by the Royal family's *major domo*. The tall man bowed low and welcomed Robert's party before leading them through massive stone walls and into an immaculate, cobbled square with gleaming white marble buildings on each of its sides. There was a huge church at one corner and stables at another, from which streamed an army of grooms. They waited in line for the horsemen to dismount before taking the animals off to the stables.

Robert and his men were led to the far end of the square where the Emperor's magnificent palace lay glinting in the midday sun. Its columns and walls were overlaid with golden and silver decorations and there were bronzed and marbled statues of many different hues standing outside. His men followed Robert up the steps to the massive teak doors of the building, but before they reached the top Anna emerged and beamed an enormous smile at her guests. She clapped her hands, and more servants came to take their few belongings and help the sick up the remainder of the steps. Beside the Princess stood a young man, who shared Anna's sharp facial features, slight stature and brown eyes.

"Welcome, my honoured guests," she called to them. "This is my younger brother John. Our father is away on a military campaign fighting the Pechenecs in the east, but we shall endeavour to be as generous hosts as he would wish us."

The boy bowed his head courteously to the new arrivals. Robert suddenly became aware of his own appearance. The eight Normans had been away from Normandie for almost a year and had practically lived in the saddle. Their clothes were dusty and threadbare, and their armour tarnished and patched. They had attempted to tidy themselves up before they left their lodgings, but against the opulent and pristine conditions of the palace and its inhabitants they felt like beggars.

"Thank you, Lady. It is we who are honoured to be here in your father's house. Please forgive our appearance but we have been on the road for too long and …."

"Nonsense," she interjected. "You are Holy Warriors are you not? God does not judge you by your clothes and neither shall we. As for clothing, we have organised some suitable replacements while yours are cleaned and repaired. I cannot promise you anything in the Norman style, but we may yet have you looking like a Greek prince." Anna laughed at her own joke. "Now, you will be shown to your rooms and when you are rested and refreshed, we shall meet again."

Each of the men were led off to his quarters.

Robert was taken to a beautiful sunlit chamber overlooking the sea. It was huge by any standards and comprised a large, comfortable bed chamber and sitting room which led out onto a verandah. Another servant waited by a table that was heavily laden with bread, olives, dried meats and summer wine. The man bowed low and gestured to an adjoining room where a bath had been prepared, "should it be required". Robert peeled off his dusty clothes, which were taken away to be cleaned and repaired. Then, he found the bath, full of hot water, strewn with rose petals and immersed himself. He caught a waft of burning incense and inhaled deeply. Feeling desperately tired and world-weary he closed his eyes and whispered a prayer of thanks, before nodding off to sleep in the warm water.

As dusk was approaching, Robert went in search of Anna and found her in an ornate, walled garden. She sat at a small table reading a book and looked up at his approach. The garden was a well-ordered profusion of colour - orchids, anemones, roses, cyclamen and opium flowered on each of its small terraces. A tiny waterfall cascaded into a pool filled with golden carp to one side of her, while on the other a solitary peacock strutted about displaying his plumage. Weeping willow, linden, cherry and peach trees broke up the symmetry of the carefully manicured lawns to each side. The Princess put down her book and her face broke into a smile.

"Ah, Lord Robert. You are refreshed, I hope? Come and sit with me. Your rooms are to your liking?" she enquired.

"They are, indeed, Lady. Thank you, again for your kindness and thank you for these clothes - I am a changed man," he said.

She regarded him with her head cocked to one side. He wore a long white silk shirt over a loose pair of blue linen trousers and soft brown deerskin riding boots.

"My brother John chose them for you himself. He will be pleased you like them." she said. "Now, your men have been suitably quartered and attired and I have ordered the physician to attend to your sick comrades. He told me they will be well again before long."

"Thank you again, Lady. Your kindness does you great credit," he replied.

"Do not thank me yet for there is a price to pay. I need to know your story and that of your family. I am a writer of history, you know, and not all your countrymen are well known to us. Although, your family name is quite a famous one," she said.

"Ah yes, my brother Harald made quite a reputation to the west of here," replied Robert.

"Harald Fitzroy? The Papal Shield?" exclaimed Anna delightedly clapping her hands. "I will need to know everything, but I warn you I will be harsh."

"It is a small price to pay. Where would you like me to start?" he said.

"I should like you to start at the beginning, but not now for I have arranged a small dinner for you and your men. I am told that the diet of the Holy Land can be a little sparse."

That evening Robert and his men sat around a long marble table in the Princess's private dining rooms. She sat at one end and her brother sat at the other. The 'small dinner' that Anna had organised turned out to be a veritable feast, consisting of numerous courses of food from all over the Byzantine empire. There was a huge assortment of freshly baked bread, and different wines were served in large glass goblets. Bone handled knives and, unfamiliar looking forks, were laid at the place of each guest on a white linen tablecloth and folded, embroidered napkins were provided for each guest. Seeing the consternation on the Norman faces as they started to eat, Anna gave a brief lesson on Byzantine eating etiquette and habits, and the feast began. There were local truffles, and sturgeon caviar from the Black Sea, as well as a variety of fish and seafood from the waters around the Golden Horn. Partridges, pigeons and blackbirds, as well as enormous herb-stuffed geese were brought out and consumed with gusto. Wine flowed copiously and the glasses were refilled directly from small amperes by a busy company of attentive servants. The meal was concluded with figs, apples and quinces cooked in honey and a variety of nuts from around the empire. Conversation throughout the dinner was polite and well-mannered in spite of the amount of wine consumed. Satisfied that they had been worthy hosts, the Princess and her brother bid their guests 'good night' before servants showed them back to their quarters.

The following morning Robert visited the church next to the palace before the sun rose. After his devotions he went to meet with Anna in her private gardens as they had agreed. She arranged for a scribe to be in attendance, and the dour-looking man sat at the table in front of a sheaf of paper, inkpots and quills. He was introduced as Constantine and he remained silent throughout the discourse, diligently scratching away with pen and ink as Robert told his story. He found Anna a determined inquisitor who questioned him thoroughly about one detail or another as his story unfolded. He began by telling the saga of his grandfathers and their lives as the Wandering

Warriors and the journey that took them from Scandinavia to the Baltic states and on to England. He spoke of their family's arrival in Normandie and growing up as a companion of Duke William. He spoke at great length of his family and of the feats of Harald Fitzroy and his subsequent exile in Italy. At this point Anna stopped him.

"He is like you?" she asked. "A man of great faith?"

"Not quite like me," he answered, "and I sometimes wonder whether he is a Christian at all. Harald worships different gods, I believe."

"And you wronged him for that?" she admonished.

"No, certainly not. But I did take the woman he loved for my wife."

"He has forgiven you for this slight?"

"I hope so. It seems he bears me no ill-will now."

"And your wife. She has forgotten him?"

Robert did not answer, as he pondered the question, until Anna broke the silence.

"Constantine, you may put down your quill. I have quizzed Lord Robert too much on his first day. I am forgetting my duties as a hostess," she announced. "It is time I showed our guest the rest of our home."

For the remainder of the day, they toured the royal palace that had been designed by Anna's father.

It was undoubtably the most opulent place he had ever visited. The huge compound was built on one of seven surrounding hills that overlooked the city and afforded spectacular views of the sea and surrounding countryside. The Emperor had built a council room, where a throne of solid gold, inset with precious stones, sat under a golden crown suspended from the high ceiling. The royal seat caught the rays of sunlight and reflected about the room. At night, she said, the jewels caught the light of a thousand candles like a meteor storm. Tribute from all parts of the empire were brought here to the palace, Anna told him. The strongholds beneath their feet were filled with all manner of treasure including garments of silk, jewels and vast chests of gold.

"The rents of the city alone amount to over twenty thousand gold pieces a year," she said earnestly.

"Enough to command a fine dowry for a good suitor?" suggested Robert.

"My father has a list of suitors for me, but I am in no great hurry to marry until he finds one that really interests me," she said. "But perhaps your brother Harald might be a good match?"

Robert laughed.

"You would certainly find him interesting, Princess, but whether it would be a good match I cannot say."

The next days followed the same structure. In the morning they met after prayer and talked, while Constantine recorded the details of Robert's story. In the afternoon Anna showed him more of the palace or took him around the city. Robert could not remember when he had last spent so much time in the company of a woman. He liked Anna and enjoyed her combative nature; spending time with her was a welcome change from the companionship of his men. He looked forward to their daily meetings and the more she asked him of his life the more he thought of home. For the first time in a long time he wondered how his family in Mortain were faring. He considered his growing children and their mother, who had all been so far from his thoughts during his absence from home. Such was the religious fervour which had consumed him these past few years, he knew he had paid scant attention to either Eleanor or their offspring. The more he thought about life at home the more his conscience pricked him. As his thoughts turned toward the Duchy they were tinged with regret and what he might have thrown away through his single-minded devotion to the Church and the Duke.

After ten days their time in Constantinople was at an end. It was early summer; his men had recovered their strength and it was time to leave. The Emperor Alexius was still away fighting in the east and Robert decided he could no longer wait to thank him personally for the hospitality. He bid a fond farewell to Anna and her brother and thanked them for all they had done for his company of pilgrims. She gave each man a bejeweled Byzantine cross and arranged a church service where their journey was blessed by the Archbishop of Constantinople. Their horses were brought out and she stood on the palace steps and waved them off. Mounting sleek and fattened *palfreys* and with saddle bags full of provisions, the company set off on the road north, back to their homes and families.

Robert led the little column out of the ancient city gates, growing ever more reflective as he contemplated not what lay ahead, on the road home, but by what awaited him when he finally got there.

Chapter 32: Defending Normandie's Border

Harald Fitzroy and his horsemen reached Ambrières in two days. He was keen to be back on the road to Avranches as soon as possible and had decided to take a force of fifty horsemen with him. The Marchis was glad to be away from Rouen and the interminable political intrigue which Duke William created whenever he had the opportunity. Throughout the time spent with Earl Godwinson he had developed a respect for the man and despite his earlier misgivings he admitted to Jeanotte that, under different circumstances, they might even become friends.

"High praise, Lord," said the young knight. "Who would have thought that a Fitzroy would ever take wine with an Earl of Wessex without so much as a dagger drawn."

"The Earl is no lickspittle, Jeanotte. It is good to see a man make the Duke earn his respect," replied Harald as the outline of his castle loomed large on the horizon. "Let us hope he continues in this vein and does not feel the need for courtly good manners."

"Earl Godwinson seems like a man after your own heart, Lord. I thought he would be nothing but a thorn in our flesh when we reclaimed Maldon," said Jeanotte.

"We have reached an agreement and he will not dispute our claim to the land. He would rather have my trust than my enmity," said Harald. "Now, let us gallop to the gates and see if your early promise as a horseman was not misplaced."

They dug in their spurs and raced their horses over the league to the castle while their men trailed along behind them. Once inside the gates, Harald dismissed the troop and made his way to the *solar* high in the keep. He was met coming the other way by his *seneschal*, Martin, who told him that he had a visitor. The lady of Mortain's servant, Beatrice, had arrived last night with a message for him, and Martin put her in the servant's quarters for the night. Harald had her sent up to him.

"Lady Eleanor will be at the farmstead at Ceaucé in ten days' time," said the servant. "Do you have a reply for her?"

"You know my reply, Beatrice." said Harald and the woman looked down trying to hide her smile. "Tell her I will be there and that an army of Norsemen could not keep us apart. But tell her also to be patient if I am not waiting at the door - I shall not let her down but I have some business in the west to see to first."

"My mistress is not one to be kept waiting, Lord," Beatrice prompted.

"I know that only too well. Just tell her I will be there," he replied.

The woman curtseyed and left.

At first light the next morning a column of fifty horsemen swept out of the castle and headed west towards Avranches. They arrived before dusk and the tell-tale signs of smoke could still be seen on the distant horizon. These were not farmers' fires burning stubble after the harvest and the thick, black smoke from nearby villages could only have been caused by raiders. Harald rode up the steep hill toward the imposing castle and looked west, counting several smoking ruins of the communities between Avranches and the Breton border.

"These Breton's do not stay down for long," said Jeanotte to his master who grunted his agreement.

"Lord Geoffrey should have put Brittany to the torch when we had the chance," said Harald. "It will take a far bigger campaign now and we will need to reach deep into the heart of Brittany to strike Count Conan. But perhaps we can give him a bloody nose all the same with the men we have.

"Forgive me, Lord, but did the Duke tell us not to pursue the Count back into Brittany?"

"Quite so, Jeanotte but the Fitzroys have been doing his bidding for a lifetime now and sometimes a little independent action yields quicker results. Let us see how many men this fortress can provide us with."

After a long uphill climb, they went through the gates and were met by the captain of the garrison, a young knight named Darri. He told them that the number of attacks on the villages and small towns by raiders from Brittany had been increasing. Darri had responded and sent a troop of riders out but found no sign of the attackers; only the burning remains of towns and villages.

The garrison of Avranches comprised seventy-five men and Harald told the captain to have fifty of them ready in the morning to ride out. They would cross the border and head toward the large Breton town of Dol and attack it.

"They will not be expecting us, Captain," he explained, "we shall give them something to remind them of us. Not enough to put an end to these raids but enough to draw Count Conan out perhaps and to encourage him to be a little bolder. If we can see the enemy, we have a chance of destroying him."

"And shall we hold the town, Lord?" he replied.

"Perhaps, but that might be a little too much to expect," said Harald. "Let us cause a little chaos at least, so they know what they can expect for their rebellion."

"Very well, Lord, we shall be ready to march in the morning," said the Captain.

"Have your men ready Darri. We leave at first light."

It was getting dark when they reached a small, secluded valley three leagues from Dol. Returning scouts reported that they had met no-one on the roads but had been able to spy on the town from a nearby wood. The scouts estimated that the garrison of the town contained between fifty and sixty men who were nearly all camped outside the castle walls. Harald ordered a night march, and in the early hours of the following day he split his forces in two and positioned them on either side of the Breton camp.

As dawn broke the battle-horn sounded and the Norman attack began. The first of two *conroi* of calvary charged the unsuspecting Breton camp one after the other, causing complete panic. The startled men who managed to escape ran straight into the second force of Normans and those who were not killed immediately threw down their arms. Three Breton horseman escaped the slaughter and decided to head for Dol castle, turning their horses and galloping towards its open gates. Jeanotte saw them trying to escape and followed in close pursuit with twenty men of his own. They chased them into the fortress and caught their quarry inside. After the briefest of struggles the men were quickly dispatched by Norman lances, but the commotion brought the castle's defenders into the fight. Men poured down from the walls to engage the intruders and were hacked down by Jeanotte's men, who had discarded their lances in favour of swords and axes. It was all over in moments as more and more of Harald's men entered the fray to reinforce their comrades. Shortly after sunrise the Breton *castellan* surrendered the castle; sixty-one of his men lay dead and the rest were prisoners.

Harald stood with his two captains surveying the scenes of carnage and congratulated the men on the success of their lightning attack. He gave orders that the nearby town should be razed and looted of anything of value. The castle dungeons were emptied of all their prisoners who exchanged places with their former guards. As the freed men were brought out blinking into the light their leader, a large man in a ragged cloak, walked over to the little knot of Norman commanders. He made straight for Harald, and when he was no more than a few paces away he called to him.

"Hari, it is me, Rouallon," he said excitedly.

The Marchis squinted at the ragged man until he recognised his old comrade.

"My Lord of Dol, you have my apologies, but I could barely tell it was you," replied Harald. "What trick of fate brings you to us? I have not seen you since the killing fields of Laraville."

"An ill-wind, but we are heartily glad to see you. The fortress was taken from me back in the spring by the Count of Brittany. He said we were traitors to support the Duke and imprisoned me in my own castle," replied the man ruefully.

"Do not reproach yourself, my friend. You were only fulfilling your oath to your liege-lord. Well, now you're back do you think you might hold it once more if I give you a few good men?" asked Harald with a hint of sarcasm.

"If God grants us one more chance we shall. Or die in the attempt."

"Then the castle is yours, Rouallon, but I have a use for you. If you choose to redeem yourself, my friend?" he said clapping a huge arm around his old comrade's shoulder while handing him a skin of wine. "How long do you think you might hold out with a hundred men and enough to feed them with?"

"We could hold off a mighty army for many months. Longer if we could be sure reinforcements were coming."

"Very well," said Harald. "I shall do just that. I will leave most of my men here under your command, along with all the salt pork and mutton we can lay our hands on. Then I will return to Rouen and raise an army. Count Conan will doubtless be curious of the fate that has befallen his garrison and return. When he does you must reward him with arrows and burning pitch but do not sally forth until I return. It is important you keep him occupied until we get back. Then we shall rout him once and for all."

"Thank you, Hari. I shall not fail the Duke again."

"I know you speak true, Rouallon. For both our reputations will be in peril if you do."

Chapter 33: The Relief of Dol

Leaving Captain Darri and a hundred men under the command of the newly released Lord of Dol, Harald left Brittany to return to Rouen. He ordered Jeanotte to ride ahead of him with the remainder of the men and inform Duke William of the result of their mission. Harald would follow on shortly, but he had urgent business in the Duchy that needed his immediate attention.

"I shall be no more than a few days behind you, Jeanotte. Please tell the Duke that I will be in Rouen with a thousand men, and suggest to him that he raise the same number as soon as possible. It is important that he heeds your words and that he knows you speak for me," said Harald.

"What shall I tell him will be our mission?" asked the knight.

"Tell him we need to ride back to Dol in no longer than ten days to crush Count Conan, and that the last rebel to stand against him is about to fall."

Harald watched his protege lead the men off down the road. He was proud of the young man who had once been a callow squire in Italy and followed him faithfully back to Normandie. Jeanotte had repaid his master's faith in him and grown into a man who could be relied upon when the battle was at its peak. He had also grown into a man who could be trusted to keep his master's secrets and who gave unquestioning loyalty - all qualities that commanded Harald's respect. The Marchis sent word back to the borders for his companies to assemble and muster for the decisive campaign. Orders were sent out to meet him beneath the walls of Rouen.

He followed the same road as Jeanotte, barely a half day behind him, before veering south at Domfront to Ceaucé, where he fervently hoped that Eleanor would still be waiting for him. He did not have to wait long for the answer and was gratified to see the rising smoke from the farmstead's chimney. He approached hurriedly, dismounted and led his horse into the stables. There were two palfreys already there and he turned to take the saddle off his mount. Before he had time to uncinch the girth he felt the presence of someone behind.

"Let me do that, Lord," said the man-at-arms. "The Lady is waiting for you."

"Thank you, Bertrand," he said, "I have ridden him hard, and he will need your care. When did you arrive?"

"We came yesterday evening, Lord" he replied, removing the heavy saddle effortlessly and replacing it with a woollen blanket.

"That is good. I am not too late then?"

The man shook his large shaggy head and quietly led Harald's horse into an empty stall where oats and water had been laid out. Bertrand, Beatrice's husband, had been in the service of the noble family of

Mortain all of his life. He and his wife were devoted to Eleanor, and when she rode out to their clandestine meetings, he would always be there in the shadows to watch and protect her.

Harald strode to the door of the farmstead. Eleanor had never been far from his thoughts, and it seemed like an age since he had seen her last. After she came to his bed in Mortain, they had met over a dozen times and each time he wondered whether it would be their last. His brother was on his way home and although Harald would be glad of Robert's safe return, he could not help but wonder what would become of these liaisons with his wife. None of that mattered now and he anticipated their reunion with his normal feelings of excitement. She looked up as he walked in and smiled.

"I wondered if the affairs of the Duchy had taken you away from me completely," she said feigning impatience.

"It would take more than a few Bretons to keep me away from you," he replied, as he reduced the space between them in moments before sweeping her up in his massive embrace.

As always when they met, their reunion was passionate but, on this occasion, there was an even more frantic expectation. It was as if this were their last meeting and at daybreak, they finally fell asleep, exhausted. When Harald awoke around mid-morning, he reached out for her, but she was not lying next to him. He looked over to an open window where she sat watching him, wrapped in a woollen blanket.

"It is not many people who can say they have seen Harald Fitzroy at peace," she said.

"Come back to bed, Eleanor and I will show you how peaceful I am," he said getting up and starting toward her, but she held her hand up to stop him.

"There is a matter we must discuss, Hari. You know that things cannot remain as they are," she said.

He sighed deeply and rebuffed for the moment, sat on the edge of the bed.

"You are right, Eleanor," he replied resignedly. "We both know that Robert will soon return to Normandie and whatever has passed between us in his absence - you will still be his wife."

"I feel no shame, Hari and neither should you. We did not betray him, for our marriage was over when he chose his calling over his family. Do not reproach yourself for I would not forsake a single moment of our time together," she replied fiercely.

"I have no regrets, Eleanor but when Robert returns - you will be his wife again," he said.

"Then what would you have me do?" she asked angrily.

He thought for a moment considering his words carefully.

"I would have you come away with me. Away from Normandie and away from the ties that bind us," he said calmly and waited for her response.

She said nothing but threw back her head and laughed.

"You would give up your land and your titles for me?"

"That and more. We will leave for Italy - I have more wealth there than I can count and you and your children shall live royally. You will want for nothing."

"And turn our backs on the land and people that have raised us?" she asked.

"I will soon have fulfilled my oath and Normandie will be safe from her enemies, at least for the present. My time here will soon be at an end, and I will owe the Duke nothing?"

"And what of your men - those who have followed you here. Would you leave them?"

"For you? Yes, I would. But they are settled here and have been well rewarded for their service to me. They have land and families now and I also owe them nothing. They are free to follow me if they wish."

"Am I just another of your followers then, Hari?" she demanded.

Harald shook his head and looked into her eyes.

"You will be my queen in the Kingdom in the Sun and I will raise your children as my own. I will leave everything here in Normandie behind me - my friends, my family and my men. I will do so without a backward glance if you say you will come," came the instant retort.

"You have clearly given this much thought. Did it take the prospect of my husband's return before making your proposal?" she said, anger rising in her voice.

"I have considered it often but never thought you would come. Forgive me but the idea of losing you again was something I could not contemplate," he said, "but tell me now, will you come?"

Eleanor fell silent while she pondered the question, and turned her back on him to look out of the window. Finally, she faced him again.

"Let me think on it. I will give you my answer soon," she said.

"Very well, Lady Eleanor. But in the meantime, we have much lost time to make up for," said Harald. He stood up, walked over to her, took hold of her wrist and pulled her very gently toward their bed.

Chapter 34: The Last Muster

Two days later the Marchis was riding into the camp filled with his soldiers outside the walls of Rouen. There were over a thousand of them, veterans from conflicts in both Italy and France. They were loyal to a man and had followed him across the killing fields of several countries, where he had led them to victory many times over. During years of campaigning together they had seldom tasted defeat under the 'Papal Shield', and when the order came to muster and march to Rouen they had obeyed without question. As he came into view many of his men walked out to meet him shouting greetings.

"When do we march, Lord? I hear the Bretons will be swallowing some Norman steel soon," called one.

"Will there be booty? My new wife has squandered my last riches and told me not to return empty-handed," called another.

"Will the Papal banner bring us luck one more time, Lord?" cried a third voice.

Harald returned their salutations as he approached and dismounted. Then he saw Jeanotte in the crowd of comrades and called him forward.

"It is good to be back with these fellows again. We have not marched together since Varaville - it seems like an age.

"Not even a year has passed since then," said Jeanotte, "but it is good to be back with them all the same."

"Tell me now, how were you received by Duke William?" asked Harald when they were out of earshot of the men.

"A little frostily at first but he warmed to the news in the end. If I did not know better, I would say that he was a little jealous of your success in Dol. I think he may have preferred to lead the first action against the rebels himself."

"Well, he is not a man to have his thunder stolen. There is no time for preening in front of foreign guests when firm action is called for. Has he begun the muster?"

"He has, Lord. I was there when he gave the order. We will be ready to march in two days."

"Let us trust that there is no more posturing, then - it is time to drive these rebels into the sea," concluded the Marchis.

"Five days" thought Harald, estimating how long Rouallon could hold out in Dol. Word had reached him that the castle was now under siege from a huge army desperate to take it back. Reports were of a force of at least fifteen hundred men and their siege engines, pounding away at the walls of Dol.

He left the camp and rode into town toward William's palace, where he found him seated for dinner with several of his Lords and the Saxon nobles. All heads turned as Harald was ushered into the room and shown a place at the table. While the Duke of Normandie greeted him warmly enough it was Earl Godwinson who seemed the most pleased to see him. The Saxon left his seat to come around the table and offer his hand in welcome. Harald then sat down next to William, who asked him to explain the recent events in Dol. When the story was finished, the men assembled questioned him about the likely size of enemy forces while the Duke sat back listening to the discourse around him, politely waiting for his colleagues to have their say before responding. He then thanked the Marchis for his actions in taking the castle and releasing his ally, the Lord of Dol. He went on to announce that when they were all assembled, he would lead the army toward Brittany to rout Duke Conan and his rebels - "once and forever".

When the meal and the table were cleared, he ordered his nobles to prepare themselves for war and be ready to ride. William asked Harald to remain behind in order that they might talk. When they were alone he turned to Harald with ill-disguised anger.

"Lord Fitzroy," he began formally, "there is no doubt that you a redoubtable warrior and a fine leader of men, but when I give you an order, I expect you to obey me. I specifically forbade you to ride beyond our border and take war into Brittany, but you chose to disobey me. Then, rather than deliver your news in person you sent an underling, to instruct me how to prosecute this action. May I remind you that I am your liege lord, and my orders are not to be countermanded."

Harald felt his cheeks flush a little and fought to keep his cool. Throughout their tempestuous relationship, William had always sought to exert his authority in this overbearing manner. Although he had grown used to such outbursts over the years, they seldom failed to anger him. He had thought that since his return from Italy to deliver victory to the Duchy, William's attitude toward him might have softened. However, the rancour between them had soon returned and with Robert away and unable to intercede, old enmities soon began to rise again. As he had done so often before, Harald swallowed his pride and failed to show any hint of the fiery emotions which as a younger man had been so close to the surface.

"My apologies, Lord. I did not seek to overstep my authority. When the opportunity arose to provoke Duke Conan into the open, I did not hesitate. Was I wrong to want your last remaining enemy defeated?" asked Harald diplomatically.

William's demeanour softened as he considered the question.

"I must admit that your hasty response has given us a chance to get rid of him for good. You were never one to prevaricate," said the Duke.

Sensing the heated atmosphere beginning to cool, Harald continued in carefully measured tones.

"I am told that Duke Conan's men have besieged the castle of Dol already. What are your orders, Lord?" asked Harald, although he already knew the answer.

"Your men are already assembled?" William asked, to which Harald nodded. "We will wait for the rest of our forces and then ride hard to Dol. We shall turn Conan's siege and pursue him back to Nantes if we have to."

"Very good, Lord, then I shall go back to my camp and brief my captains. Will that be all?" asked Harald and saw the Duke hesitate and the briefest of thoughts flicker across his face.

"Nothing that won't wait until we return," said William with a hint of mischief, "we have much work ahead of us."

Two days later, on a bright sun-lit morning, the army was assembled and ready. Such was the haste of its formation that there was little in the way of a baggage train or supply wagons. There was something over two thousand mounted men, who would take what they needed from the poor, unprepared Breton farms, villages and towns they passed through on their way; woe betide anyone who resided within them. The knights, men-at-arms, archers and squires formed a long column that kicked up clouds of dust from the hard, dry mud roads. Thousands of iron clad hooves echoed on the hard ground across the open country and the jangling of bridle-bits and creaking of leather added to the sounds of their rapid advance. Sigils and banners hung limply in the still morning waiting for a little wind to fill them out. Among them the Leopards of Normandie and the Regneville Ravens were clearly visible beside the Papal banner carried by Duke William's herald.

He was in high spirits riding in a knot of Norman nobles and his coarse, deep voice boomed out as he recounted the successes of previous campaigns to his comrades. Behind this group rode Harald Fitzroy with Earl Godwinson and his small group of Saxons. In contrast to the uniformly dressed Normans they looked a little incongruous. They were all bareheaded and their long hair, full beards and luxurious moustaches set them apart. Heavily armed, the Saxons carried an assortment of double-handed axes, swords, spears and heavy circular shields emblazoned with the white fighting man on a red background.

"The Duke is in a confident mood today," said the Englishman.

"As he should be," said Harald. "There is no match for this cavalry in all of France."

"They have obviously never faced a company of Saxon *huscarls*," replied the Earl.

"Then it is a good job we are not fighting in England," said Harald good naturedly. "All the same, I doubt whether they could stand an assault by a determined *conrois* of Normans."

"Your horsemen would be far too vulnerable," scoffed the Saxon. "A solid shield wall and a hail of arrows would be enough to see most of these fellows off."

"Then let us hope we never have to find out," replied Harald, "it would be a terrible waste of men." The Earl nodded in agreement and handed him a skin of wine.

Harold Godwinson and his men had been guests of the Duke for almost half a year. They had been treated with great honour during their visit and William had lavished all manner of hospitality on the group. They were entertained with hunting and feasting and the Earl had even been invited to council meetings. His treatment had come as no surprise to Harald, who had seen the Bastard court many an ally in an effort to gain support. When the opportunity to show his guests how the men of Normandie dealt with their enemies, William was not shy in inviting them on the campaign. The Earl, for his part, had shown gratitude to his host and never tired of answering the barrage of questions, from the state of the

English army to King Edward's relationship with the Scots in the North.

It took five days for the column to cross the Duchy until they reached the citadel of Avranches where they camped for the last time on Norman soil. The next day they were in Brittany and foraging parties were sent out to harry the surrounding countryside, taking everything they found. Grain stores were emptied, cattle were taken, villages and farms were looted, and communities destroyed. The countryside ahead of them was set ablaze and the roads became full of refugees fleeing south.

Harald led a scouting party of twenty riders toward Dol and invited Earl Godwinson to join them. They rode swiftly across country and reached the town undetected, where they observed the siege from a small copse on top of a nearby hill.

The horsemen saw the fortress completely surrounded and under attack from both the front and the rear. The main body of the attacking army was waiting beyond bow range while their comrades launched a series of forays against the defences. One of the thick outer walls had already been partially destroyed by a massive bombardment from three formidable *trebuchets* placed around the fortress. They watched a party of Breton soldiers, beneath a protective carapace of shields and boiled leather, carry a large battering ram up the hill and assault the main gate. The defenders responded quickly and hurled a fusillade of stones, arrows and boiling pitch onto their attackers who turned and fled back the way they had come.

"Rouallon is making a decent fist of defending his home," Harald shouted to the Earl who was so engrossed in the drama below that he did not hear at first. "He has done far better than I expected of him, but a hundred men cannot hold out against so many."

This time Godwinson heard him and looked up shaking his head.

"This is warfare I have not witnessed before," he called back as another huge projectile destroyed part of the keep.

"The siege will be over soon unless we intercede," Harald replied and pointed down to where a construction of stone and hides had been placed to the forefront of the Breton lines. "They have started mining toward the walls. When they are underneath, they will set a fire in the tunnel, and it will collapse bringing the castle wall down with it."

The Earl continued shaking his head in disbelief at the scale of destruction below.

"Come, we must return to the Duke and hasten our attack before our comrades are completely overcome," concluded Harald.

He gave the order for the scouting party to return, but as they turned away their movement gave away their position to some sharp-eyed Bretons below. A party of a hundred or more horsemen broke away from the main host and moved across the flat ground toward the hill and galloped up one side to engage with the Normans. By the time they had reached the summit, the scouting party were at the bottom of the other side of the hill, making their escape. Not content with scaring them off, the Bretons continued a determined pursuit and plunged on after Harald's men. Mounted on lighter unarmored *palfreys* they made good their retreat, heading south to the sea before turning along the coast road to join their comrades. The Breton horsemen and their heavy *destriers* soon flagged but refused to give up the chase. Knowing they needed to rejoin their main force to plan their attack, Harald's column veered off the coastal path into the marshland in an effort to short-cut their journey and finally escape the attention of their pursuers.

It was low tide when the column left the solid dirt road and led by a local man in their ranks, they sought out the causeway leading to the small rocky island of Mont St. Michel. The estuary at low tide had drained of water revealing a drying, road of rock laid down by the monks of the island's abbey. It provided a safe route across the sandy bay, although it often claimed the lives of unwary travellers who took the wrong road. On each side of the path, which could comfortably take two riders, there were treacherous quick-sands that could suck down a man and his horse in moments.

Harald gave the order for his troop to slow down to ensure they could safely negotiate the remainder of their journey. They were now well out of range of the Bretons, who had turned back to Dol. The Normans picked their way across the sands on the ancient path taking great care to follow the footsteps of the man leading the column. One of their number, a youth of fifteen named Robert Curthose, rode at the rear of the company. He was Duke William's son and the boy had persuaded his father to allow him on the trip under the watchful eye of the Marchis. Harald had politely refused at first, knowing the trip could be perilous for such an inexperienced warrior, but the boy's father had insisted, and young Curthose got his wish.

It was when the party reached the other side of the rocky outcrop of the Mont that disaster struck. Their column, riding two abreast, was still some way from firm ground and shouts came from the rear. Harald looked back and saw a riderless horse screaming in fear, sinking quickly into the sucking sands. He looked for its rider and saw the flailing figure of Robert Curthose up to his waist in quicksand where the horse had thrown him in panic. The Duke's son was desperate, caught fast and screaming for help. Harald slipped off his horse's back and snatched up a spear, holding the shaft out to the boy who tried to grab it. It slipped through wet hands, and he was unable to take a firm grip. A man raced forward and tied a length of rope around Harald who started to wade out only to become trapped himself. By now the youth was submerged to his shoulders and was crying out for God and his mother and it was only the meaty paw of Lord Fitzroy that prevented him from going under completely. His would-be rescuer was soon in extreme difficulty himself and the weight of his enormous frame was taking him under quickly. It was then that Earl Godwinson took control. He pushed aside the men vainly trying to pull their Lord free and wrapped the end of the rope around his arm. The Saxon pulled for all he was worth and straining every sinew, managed to drag Harald and Robert out of danger. It took time and relentless toil before Harald's free arm could be caught by other members of the company, while his other arm was clamped in a vice-like grip around Robert's neck. After a desperate struggle, man and boy were finally pulled clear and lay panting with exhaustion on firm ground. The Saxon stood above the two of them laughing with relief.

"Well, this is a fine catch I have made. The great Lord Fitzroy flapping around at my feet like a harpooned whale," he said.

"I am in your debt," said Harald coughing and spluttering.

"Think nothing of it, Hari," said the Earl pulling him to his feet and clapping him on the back. "You were there once to deliver me from a bad fate, and I am only glad to return the favour."

When all had recovered from their exertions the company mounted up and gingerly resumed their departure from the bay. The tide had turned and the sand on either side of their path was soon under water. It was with great relief that they finally reached the rocky shoreline and climbed up and away from the incoming tide and back to the camp where the Duke awaited news.

Chapter 35: The Reiving of Brittany

It was a dull morning the next day and the sea fog rolled off the Baie de Mont and through the ranks of the besieging army of Duke Conan. They had made a little progress with their destruction of the fortress of Dol, a hole in the defensive wall caused by the relentless actions of the multiple *trebuchets* would soon be big enough to ingress. Despite doubling the picket line around the camp since the Norman scouts were chased away the previous day, there had been no further evidence of a relieving force. A thick blanket of mist shrouded the plain on which the Breton host waited patiently for their opportunity to storm the citadel and finish off its defenders. Inside the walls, Lord Rouallon remained steadfast and despite debilitating losses he rallied his men, and the townsfolk, onto the denuded battlements to hurl arrows and projectiles down on the heads of any attackers close enough for them to hit.

The sound of Norman battle-horns high above the hum of the siege engines caused the men of Conan's army to pause and listen. This was followed by the muffled sound of galloping horses which drew rapidly closer. They could hear charging horses but could not see them through the thick murk until it was too late. Harald Fitzroy led the first of the Norman *conrois*, each of fifty men, tightly formed, into their enemies left flank. Another group of Normans reached the rear of the fortress from the inland road, raced around the side and plunged into the army's other flank. At the same time as Harald's *conroi* claimed their first victims at the end of steel tipped lances, Duke William led the second group of horsemen into the fray. The simultaneous impact caused the Breton army to compact, pushing them tighter together. Realising salvation was at hand a great cry went up from the defenders within the fortress. Unable to react quickly to the lightning strikes from each side, Conan's lines began to buckle and take the only route open to them - back toward the sea, two leagues away. Norman spears found their targets time and again against a confounded opposition and a slow retreat gathered momentum as lines broke and men panicked.

The Bretons found their way blocked by a hefty triple-banked Norman shield wall bristling with spears. Behind this redoubtable barrier stood several hundred archers who unleashed a torrent of arrows cutting down the retreating men in great swathes. Others, who did not perish at the shield wall, swarmed around and past it and onto the coast road that headed west back into Brittany. They were relentlessly pursued for some distance by Norman cavalry who destroyed the hindmost of the fleeing foot soldiers, whilst the luckier retreating mounted men, including Count Conan, made good their escape. Over half of his men perished on the flat plain before Dol, while those who lived, were chased as far as St. Malo before turning inland to regroup at the stronghold of Dinan.

After a brief respite following the victorious rout, the Normans dismantled the captured siege weapons and loaded them aboard the wagons upon which they had been brought. The Breton baggage train was taken into the fortress for safe keeping and the next morning William led his men inland. They marched eight leagues and crossed the River Rance before setting up camp in front of the gates and thick stone walls of Dinan. The newly acquired *trebuchets*, *mangols* and siege towers were reassembled and positioned in full view of the town's defenders.

With Harald at his shoulder, Duke William approached the citadel and called on the defenders to surrender. They were given until the following morning to capitulate and open the gates. Before hostilities commenced the next day, Duke Conan emerged with his captains and trotted toward the Norman camp. When he reached William, who waited for him in front of the Norman ranks, he dismounted, bent the knee and surrendered. With this final act of the campaign the Duchy's last major opponent had been removed.

A victory celebration was ordered, and over two thousand victorious warriors were feasted for two days at the expense of the city. Dinan was emptied of all its wine and food, as well as a considerable amount of valuables, as Duke William basked in his triumph. After a service of thanksgiving the feasting began and although orders were given forbidding the sack of the city, there were some exceptions as freebooters roamed the streets and claimed their spoils of war. Before the Normans left for home, the siege weapons were burned and the wagons that brought them were filled with captured plunder. The citizens of Dinan were stripped of all their wealth and valuables, but could be grateful they were still alive having avoided the blood-letting that so often accompanied the aftermath of capitulation. The column stopped briefly at Dol to retrieve the captured baggage train before travelling east where it gradually disbanded. The companies were stood down on the way back to Rouen and warriors returned to their homes and castles.

"What next for you and your men?" Harald asked of Earl Godwinson as the two men rode side by side.

"My work as an ambassador is coming to an end here. We have played our part and my duty to King Edward is done. He has made his choice for his successor, and I must do his bidding," he replied stoically. "And what about you, Hari? Surely there is no-one left within a thousand leagues for you to defeat?"

"Not in Normandie, perhaps but I have unfinished business elsewhere that is occupying my thoughts," said Harald.

"Ah, the Kingdom in the Sun is a mistress full of promise I hear," said the Earl, fishing for a response but getting none, he continued. "Perhaps, you might consider returning to England with me. We have plenty of enemies, as you know and not enough warriors - you and your men would be richly rewarded,"

"I will bear that in mind, Harold," said Hari with a grin "but I am undecided as yet."

"Then let me try and tempt you with a beautiful Saxon woman. My sister comes with a sizeable dowry and there are many noblemen vying for her hand," said the Earl, but Harald refused to be drawn.

"I have no need of riches or women, my friend. There is more than enough of both available to me."

"Perhaps you are already spoken for then?" enquired the Earl with a side-ways glance but the Marchis did not take the bait. "I can see you do not wish to reveal your secrets and so I will press you no more. But, seriously now," he continued, leaning across and lowering his voice. "Do not let others make a match for you that you do not want. I know you are your own man, but others might think you are theirs to command for a lifetime."

They both looked ahead to where the Duke was busy entertaining some of his nobles and their laughter filled the air. Harald shrugged nonchalantly.

"Ah, but my brother will return soon and the Duke will be overjoyed to have him back in his service. Then he will have little need of me again. I have killed or imprisoned most of the Bastard's enemies - believe me my work is done here," he said.

"Do not underestimate your part in the Duke's plans. He will try and tie you into them by one means or another, said the Earl seriously. "Be careful, Hari. I counsel caution before you decide to burn your bridges."

"I am bored with all this talk of politics. Now hand me that full skin of wine that hangs from your saddle. Let us drink to our next battle - wherever it may be."

Chapter 36: The Last Rebel

Whilst the Duke's column wound its way triumphantly back to Rouen, Lord Robert Fitzroy led his remaining party of pilgrims up the valley and approached Caen. Their weary horses, sensing they were getting closer to home, fresh hay and a pail of oats, became rejuvenated and picked up the pace.

"Nearly home, men," shouted the Count of Mortain as his seven doughty companions began to whoop in celebration. They were still together despite the many trials of their return. They had travelled over eight hundred leagues from the Holy Land, and although they had suffered disease and several attacks from brigands, the company and their resolve remained steadfast.

Robert was exhausted, as were his men. He looked at his comrades and saw their gaunt, weather-beaten faces. They were as ragged and disheveled as anyone would be at the end of such a journey. Their *hauberk*s were rusty and missing links of chain and the symbols on the shields were no longer discernible. The horses were as dusty and shaggy as their riders but, to a man, the warriors still carried themselves with a rigid military bearing.

They were smiling and happy as they stood in front of the city gates with dusk falling. A guard challenged and asked them to state their business. Robert called to the man,

"Lower your guard, friend. I am the Lord of Mortain, Chancellor of the Duchy and companion to William, Duke of Normandie. We are weary pilgrims returned from the Holy Land. Tell your masters I have returned."

The man squinted into the half-light at the dishevelled party and began to panic. A speedy cognition was made, and he called down from on top of the city wall to the gatekeeper to let the riders in. They plodded through the streets on exhausted horses carrying them to the castle high on the hill. Word from the gatehouse preceded them and when they finally reached the huge courtyard outside the keep the Duke's *castellan* was waiting for them.

"Lord Robert," shouted Guillaume of Falaise, a portly middle-aged man, as he barrelled down the steps of the keep. "It is so good to see you home, Sire. You have been gone such a long time; we have all missed your presence."

"A year and a half - all told. It is good to be home, too," replied Robert. "But where is everyone. The place is almost deserted."

"The Duke moved to his palace in Rouen for the summer and is returning after a successful campaign against the Bretons. He was there with your brother's army, Lord. They chased Count Conan all the way across Brittany, where he finally surrendered," said Guillaume excitedly. "But forgive me, Lord you are tired and hungry."

The *castellan* shouted for the stable grooms who ran out and took the horses from the dismounting pilgrims.

"Follow me, gentlemen, I will make sure the kitchens do you proud."

He led them all back up the stairs to the refectory, where they were seated and fed by an attentive army of servants. There was a shout from the back of the hall.

"Robert Fitzroy, I cannot believe my eyes. You are back amongst your brothers once more," called an astonished Rolande of Coutances. He rushed over and embraced Robert fervently. "I want to know everything. Is it true you were protecting the pilgrims on the road to Jerusalem? They say you saved thousands of lives and the Pope is making a saint of you."

"Rolande, my friend," replied Robert when the older man finally released him from his embrace. "I am pleased to see you too. But I have an urgent question for you - have you managed to bankrupt the Duchy in my absence?"

"Nothing of the sort, but I am glad to see you back to relieve me of my duties and allow me to return to soldiering again. You know I missed a perfectly good campaign in Brittany because of you. That young pup of a brother took all the glory - yet again!"

said Rolande feigning insult. "Now eat and drink - you look like you need a good meal."

By the time the meal was complete, two of the squires were already asleep over the table. Robert dismissed his comrades and made his excuses to Rolande, promising to meet him in the morning. He had just about enough energy remaining to locate his old rooms high in William's keep, where he found everything as he had left it. He lay on his bed and tried to take his boots off but fell fast asleep.

Robert woke up to the *None* bells the next day that announced midday. There was a knock at the door and four women appeared with a wooden bathtub and buckets of hot water.

"Archbishop Lanfranc sent us, Lord. He said you might appreciate a hot bath. He also said that he will be in his offices in the cathedral for the rest of the day. But he insisted that you should not come until you are properly rested," said one of them, a stout country girl who was dragging the bath in on her own.

Robert thanked them all and sent them away before immersing himself in the hot water. "It is good to be back again," he thought and started to plan all the things that needed his attention now that he was home. When the water began to cool, he got out, dried himself and quickly ate the food the women had left for him. Even after last night's huge meal he found himself ravenous again, and took little time consuming the tray of cold meat and bread. Then he dressed in clean clothes, hanging much looser on him than he remembered, pulled on a fresh pair of boots and made his way to the cathedral.

He found the Archbishop in the lady chapel, kneeling in front of the small altar. Lanfranc did not look up and Robert went over quietly, knelt beside him and closed his eyes in silent prayer. After a while he felt a hand on his shoulder and heard his friend get up to sit on a nearby bench, where he waited for him. When Robert had finished his devotions and got up in turn, the Archbishop embraced him warmly and led him back to the bench, where they sat and talked. Lanfranc insisted on hearing the whole story of the pilgrimage, what they saw and who they met. He wanted to know every last detail of his meetings in Rome, and was fascinated with the story of Robert's epiphany and his scourging on the road to Golgotha. The Count continued with details of his stay in Constantinople at the Emperor's palace and Lanfranc listened intently, only interrupting occasionally to seek clarification of one point or another. It was getting dark when the story was over and this time it was the *Vespers* bell that interrupted them.

"You are truly one of God's chosen warriors, my son," said the Archbishop. "You have done the Duchy no end of good through your fine works. It is a remarkable story and I commend you."

"I shall soon be as famous as Hari," said Robert light-heartedly.

"Ah, your brother," said the Archbishop gravely. "I fear he is on another collision course with Duke William. He really has no conception of diplomacy. Where your brother is concerned, it is like a red rag to a bull when they are in the same room."

"It is well that Hari is indispensable, then," said Robert more as a question.

"Perhaps, not as indispensable as he thinks. With the rout of his last enemy the Duke might feel that he no longer needs Hari's strong-arm," said Lanfranc. "Now come to my chambers, I have arranged for supper to be served for us there and I still have much I need to know."

When finally content in the knowledge that Robert had furnished him with every last detail of his trip, the Archbishop sat back in his chair and smiled beatifically at his friend.

"I cannot believe you have accomplished so much, Robert. I am so very proud of you," he said, "as will Duke William be. But what are your plans now?"

"There is much to do, Father. For a start we must decide what to do with the remains of the Duke's father. I have looked at that box every day since Easter - we are old friends now," Robert replied with a grin.

"You leave him with me. Are you planning to return to Mortain?" asked Lanfranc.

"I am, but first I have pressing business in Rouen, I think," said Robert. "My wife will not miss me for the sake of a few more weeks."

Lanfranc sighed and reached out, putting a paternal hand on Robert's forearm.

"Sometimes your family must take precedence over the affairs of the Duchy. It is a year and a half that you have been away. From the little I know of women, absence does not always increase longing. I urge you to return home," he said earnestly.

Robert blew out his cheeks and confided in his old friend.

"I am afraid that Eleanor and I grew distant a while ago. I will admit it was my fault, I answered the call of the Duchy and the church before my family. I believe it might be too late to mend bridges that were burnt years ago," he said with some regret. "I recently learnt she might have died from her accident and yet I would have known nothing of her plight had she done so."

"She is your wife, Robert, and you have both exchanged holy vows that cannot be rescinded. A loveless marriage has no purpose other than to provide offspring, but I am sure your union has a higher purpose than that."

"Then I shall endeavour to try and make things up with her, Father," he promised.

Three days later, rested and refreshed, the Count of Mortain was back in the saddle. He had taken Lanfranc's counsel to heart, and with Rolande of Coutances at his side they were both returning to Mortain. The old knight was particularly delighted to be returning home to the place that neither man had set foot in for a long time. He had been an able replacement for Robert during his absence and had done his duty with great diligence. But Rolande was in his heart a soldier and was overjoyed to be returning to his old role as a captain of cavalry.

Robert had been concerned at first when he heard of what had befallen Eleanor. He also knew that she was the most resilient of women and although slight of stature she possessed an admirable inner strength. They had not parted on good terms when he left for the Holy Land, and he did not expect a fond welcome home. However, he was determined to do what he could, but he expected nothing more than a frosty reception.

"Still," he thought, "it is good to be back in Rolande's company once more. Whatever awaits me - I will have deserved the outcome."

It took two days to reach Mortain and as they approached the outer walls of the castle, they were greeted by the commander who rode out to meet them. The man, one of Rolande's old comrades, was overjoyed to see them both and led them through the town's streets and up to the fortress.

"I am sorry, Lord," he said, "I had no idea you were coming. The Lady Eleanor said nothing of your arrival to me."

"Alas, she will be as surprised with my arrival as you are," said Robert, wondering what lay in store for him.

Rolande left him as they approached the keep, and wishing his friend good fortune with the reunion, he took his leave. A groom came from the stables to lead his horse away and Robert looked up to the windows high in the building and caught sight of a woman turning away. Before he could give it any more thought he saw that all the domestic servants had arranged themselves on the steps to the building, where they waited for him respectfully. He stopped to talk to them before entering the keep through the main door and into the great hall. As he did so he saw Eleanor coming down the stairs at the far end. He smiled at her as she walked toward him, but she did not return the gesture. They met halfway across the room, and she looked up to meet his gaze. He had almost forgotten what a striking looking woman she was, and her beauty had not diminished in the least since his departure.

"Eleanor, it is good to see you again," he said holding his arms out to embrace her.

"You look well, Robert," she said politely, "I had word you had returned, and wondered when we might expect you."

He moved toward his wife and leant forward to kiss her, but she ignored his embrace and demurely offered him her cheek.

"You will be anxious to see your children," she continued, "they will be down to welcome you shortly."

"I have been looking forward to this day for an age," he said. "But first tell me of your own fortunes. You have recovered from your accident?"

"As you can see, I am in good health. It was nothing that a few days of bed rest could not remedy," she replied coolly.

They were interrupted by the sound of footsteps, and both looked up to see their three children approaching. Richard, William and Turid stopped behind their mother and the little girl clutched at her skirts.

"Who is this man?" asked the girl coyly.

"I am your father," Robert interjected gently and, cursing himself silently for neglecting his family for so long, he knelt down to reacquaint himself with his daughter and her siblings.

A little later in the day the family sat in the *solar* round the large dining table. They had not been together for an age and an awkward silence pervaded the atmosphere. There were stilted conversations between husband and wife during which the children interjected. The boys were polite and respectful and asked their father about his trip south. The three-year-old Turid was less diplomatic and when Robert asked her about mother's near-fatal riding accident again, the girl could not contain herself any longer.

"Mama was very poorly, you know," she exclaimed in as 'grown-up' a manner as she could manage, "if it was not for Uncle Hari she would have surely died."

"Well, we are lucky that God and my brother were here to bring her back to us," replied her father.

"I think God had little to do with it, Father - but Uncle Hari would not leave us until she was better again," stated his daughter seriously.

"Thank you, Turid. Now children, it is time for your beds, I think. You will see your father in the morning," said Eleanor brusquely.

She looked at Robert, who nodded. The children bid their parents goodnight and Beatrice came in and scooped up Turid.

The little group walked out quietly, leaving their parents alone.

"They are a credit to their mother," said Robert, to which Eleanor forced a weak smile.

There was silence between them again, but he persisted.

"I have been a poor father to them admittedly but …"

"And an even poorer husband," she remarked tersely. "You chose your duty over your family. I am pleased to see you fit and healthy, but I know full well that I am here only to manage your estates and to ensure a healthy generation of Fitzroys."

"Eleanor, please," remonstrated Robert, "I am here to apologise and ask you to forgive me for my lack of attention. If my duty came first, it was not because I did not want to be here with you."

Eleanor's mouth contorted into a sneer.

"I am tired, Robert. There is no need to apologise - we are glad you have returned safely home. Now, I must go to my bedchamber, for tomorrow I am receiving a delegation of our tenants from the west, determined to avoid paying their rents. The affairs of the county do not run themselves, you know," she said pointedly. "Your quarters have been made up and I trust that you will be comfortable. Beatrice will show you to your rooms."

She got up abruptly and left the table, made swiftly for her bedchamber and quickly locked the door behind her.

Robert was left alone to contemplate his homecoming. He had known that he would not be received warmly but he did not expect such a cold reaction from his wife and family. For all his intellect he had not realised how little they would miss him. He was determined to make every effort with them during his stay, he promised himself, but if duty called, he would have to answer before long.

The Count of Mortain stayed for another ten days. He visited the men of the castle's garrison. He took his sons hunting during the day, spent nights in the town meeting his old comrades and prayed each morning in church in the town square. He accompanied his wife when she rode out for one issue or another in the county, but during that time she failed to show him anything other than a frosty exterior. He saw little sign of any thaw in her attitude and resolved to leave. Robert packed his belongings preparing to travel to Rouen to rejoin Duke William and announced his imminent departure to his family. Eleanor continued to remain aloof but wished him well and expressed a desire that they should all be together again soon. She kissed him perfunctorily on the cheek before he mounted his horse in the courtyard to leave.

"Travel in safety, Robert and with God's blessing," she said curtly. "Be sure in the knowledge that your estates here will be well-run, as they have always been, in your absence."

Then, without a backward glance he led his small column onto the road east. His thoughts of his family were already fading, and his focus was now on what lay ahead of him at the Duke's side.

Chapter 37: A Gathering Storm

Rouen was alive with activity since the triumphant Duke had returned home from Brittany. In an effort to seal Earl Godwinson's fealty he organised an elaborate 'knighting' ceremony in the cathedral. William addressed the gathered Norman nobles, publicly thanking the Earl for his service during the Breton campaign and for saving the life of his son on the sands of Mont St. Michel. The Saxon played his part and took the knee, before he proclaimed to the listening audience his duty and obedience to the Duke of Normandie. William looked down with satisfaction as he dubbed his new knight during a service overseen by the Bishop of Rouen. To complete the initiation, the Marchis of Ambrières was called upon to deliver a stout buffet about the *'puers'* ears, which tradition demanded was the only blow he would ever receive without retaliation. Harald smiled broadly as he hit his comrade on the side of the head and the Earl manfully bore the ritual humiliation, grimacing through gritted teeth. At the end of the ceremony a new sword was belted around his waist, spurs were buckled to his feet and Harold Godwinson was proclaimed a knight of the Duchy, to the general applause of all present.

The summer was coming to an end and William felt it was important that Earl Godwinson returned to England with his party to impress upon the English monarch that the Duke was ready and able to ascend the English throne. What better way to do this, William had explained to his confidantes, than to ennoble the Saxon Lord as a loyal knight. Standing on a raised dais before the Duchy's powerful barons, Harald Fitzroy watched his friend repeat the loyal oaths of obedience in front of five hundred witnesses. The be-knighting was not the only piece of diplomatic theatre enacted in Rouen since their return. The Duke had also decided that a match between Harald Fitzroy and Aelfgyva, the Earl's sister, would be good for both the Duchy and the Fitzroy family, and insisted that the Marchis had a loyal duty to accept the betrothal without demure. Harald had been unhappy at first by the *fait accomplis* but had reluctantly accepted. The girl was only nine years old, he reasoned, and when the time came to marry her he would be thousands of leagues away in Italy with Eleanor. He did not like to accept the betrothal in bad faith but the Duke would brook no argument and would not take 'no' for an answer.

Robert Fitzroy had arrived at Rouen five days earlier and his brother had ridden out to meet him on the road to the city with a number of his cohort, including the Earl. The meeting between the siblings was as warm and fraternal as ever and Robert insisted on hearing all the news of the Duchy since he had been away. By the time they had travelled the two leagues back to the gates of Rouen, he had bombarded his brother with a barrage of questions of what had transpired in the Duchy, over the last year and a half.

As glad as he was to see Robert again, Harald found his conscience wracked with guilt about his conduct with Eleanor while her husband had been away. He felt that by riding to meet Robert in the company of others he might somehow mask any signs of betrayal. Despite her insistence that the marriage was now only one of convenience, Harald had been unable to reconcile himself to the fact that he had betrayed his brother. She had recently sent her lover word that come the spring, she and her children would leave for Italy with him. This was the news he had been waiting for and now all that remained was to tidy up his affairs in Normandie and make ready to leave the Duchy for the Kingdom in the Sun. They would leave everything behind them and sail out with whoever wished to join them. With the Duchy finally secured from its enemies, Harald had kept his oath to Duke William and would inform him of his departure nearer to the time of his leaving. He was secure in the knowledge that he had done his duty to his liege-lord, but this did little to assuage his feeling of remorse for deceiving Robert.

Duke William waited in the palace courtyard for his Chancellor. He was overjoyed at his friend's arrival in Rouen and threw his arms around Robert in a great public display of affection to welcome him home. Then he spirited him away, alone, to his private chambers to hear his story. Harald made his way to a local wine shop with Earl Godwinson and the two sat alone drinking in the dingy interior filled with the noisy chatter of soldiers, tradesmen and whores.

"The Duke was very glad to see your brother back," stated the Earl.

"He has always looked on Robert as a brother, since we were boys," replied Harald ruefully. "Sometimes I think that he does it to try and drive a wedge between us."

"Blood will always be thicker than water, Hari. Now, drink up I cannot have my brother-in law looking so disconsolate," said the Earl ordering another jug of wine.

"I am not sure I share your pleasure at the betrothal. The match was made without my knowledge, you know," said Harald to which his companion merely shrugged.

"The world will be a different place when the time comes for a marriage. When men make plans for the future, God finds a sense of humour," he said knowingly.

"You will make a fine brother-in-law, but I believe this is all a ruse to get the Duke to let you return home," said Harald.

"Do not think me so disingenuous, Hari," said the Earl. "Anyway, I shall make you a Saxon prince in England with an army of *huscarls* at your back."

"I already have an army at my back and anyway what need have I for a prince's coronet?" said Harald sullenly before the Earl changed the subject.

"Rejoice Hari, you have much to be thankful for. You return home a far richer man, your reputation is greatly enhanced, and your brother has returned from great danger - a hero of the Duchy."

"That, I admit, is good news," said Harald. "What do you think of him?"

"I exchanged only a few words before the Duke hauled him away. You and he are as different as chalk and cheese. But for all that he is a likeable fellow - a pious man perhaps but a good man all the same."

"Let us drink to his health, then," said Harald standing and raising his cup in a loud voice that everyone could hear, he called out. "Gentlemen, join me in a toast to Lord Robert Fitzroy, loyal servant of the Duke and defender of the Duchy. Normandie has no finer servant."

Five days after Robert's arrival in Rouen, a great feast of celebration had been organised to mark the milestones of his achievement. The Duke had much to celebrate. The rebellious Bretons had been broken and the papal blessings on the Duchy confirmed. His trusted friend and advisor had returned safely home, together with the remains of the old Duke, and the ascendency to the English throne seemed assured. Duke William had even managed to arrange a marriage match of great importance for one of his most troublesome commanders. He contemplated his good fortune as he waited for his wife, the Duchess Matilda, to finish her preparations before going to meet the throng of guests. He paced as he waited and turned the conundrum of Harald Fitzroy over in his mind.

Since he was eight years old, Duke William had been threatened by a host of enemies, seen and unseen. He had been protected since boyhood by the powerful Fitzroy clan whose patriarch, Jarl Bjorn, had taken him under his protection and nurtured the boy as one of his own. The family had shed their blood doing their duty to the Duke and had never shirked their responsibilities, spanning three generations. However, the thorn in Duke William's side was always Harald Fitzroy. The Marchis had completely honoured the oaths of his family, but William always felt that he had never fully respected him. He had been loyal enough and answered the Duchy's call in their time of need. However, he was disobedient at times and did not always follow William's instructions to the letter. Even after lifting Harald's banishment the Duke's orders were followed grudgingly, although his effectiveness in the field could never be denied. The Duke reminded himself that the Marchis of Ambrières had been well rewarded for his duties and should count himself lucky to have such a benevolent Lord. With Robert returned and the last of the Duchy's enemies destroyed, he would not need to rely on Harald Fitzroy's support so completely. The arranged betrothal to Earl Godwinson's sister was timely and a blessing all the same.

"Let us pray this will distract him from any more interest in other men's wives," he thought to himself as he waited.

Matilda appeared and brought his thoughts back to the present. Her servants had finished dressing her and she looked resplendent in a tunic of gold overlaying a pale-blue, full-length linen gown. Her hair was woven with autumnal flowers, and, like her husband, she wore a plain gold band around her head. The Duke nodded approvingly and complimented his wife on her appearance before taking her hand and leading her out of their chambers to where a retinue of knights would escort them to the feast.

It had been a fine summer and the crops had been successful. The fields of barley, oats and wheat had all yielded a great bounty and the cattle had grown fat. At a time of year when the harvest was traditionally celebrated, the coffers of the Duchy were also full from highly profitable campaigning. There was a general feeling of prosperity in the Duchy, enjoyed by all, from the ruling barons to the lowest villeins. Against this backdrop the people of the Duchy basked in its reflected glow of power and prosperity.

Trestle tables and benches were laid out in the enormous city square of Rouen, and over two thousand guests waited for the Duke and Duchess to take their places at the top table and for the feasting to begin. The weather was warm and late summer had extended into early autumn. When they finally sat down, William and Matilda took their places among the many bishops and barons of the Duchy who had come for the celebrations. At the Duke's right hand sat Robert Fitzroy, while his brother Harald was seated on the edge of the long table on the raised platform next to the Bishop of Coutances.

Neither Harald nor the old priest were enamored at being seated on the margins, and an early attempt at polite conversation with one another was quickly abandoned. It was midday and although it was September the weather was warm and balmy. The guests, comprising invited townspeople and many of the soldiers who had been part of Harald's vanguard during the recent campaign, sat before them. There was a hum of expectancy in the air as the guests looked forward to a day's eating, drinking and entertainment, prefaced of course by a blessing from the priest. Before the proceedings could start Duke William got to his feet to address his guests.

"Welcome friends and comrades. This is a momentous day for the Duchy," he shouted with his arms and hands outstretched. "Today Normandie is at peace. Today we welcome back my good friend and brother, Lord Robert of Mortain who has sacrificed so much for us that we might be redeemed for our sins. Today we celebrate the continued support of the Holy Father in Rome. Today we say farewell to our cousins from England with whom we have such close ties and with whom we are tied by blood. None of this could have been made possible without the support of our staunch commanders and the blessing of the mother church."

He waived an arm in recognition to his guests on the platform before continuing.

"Neither could it have been made possible without the bravery shown on the field by our warriors. Their victories on the fields of Val-es-Dunes, Mortemer and Varaville turned back those who came to destroy us. Their selfless duty has earned our fighting men the respect of all of Europe."

There was great applause at the last part of the speech and Duke William waited for it to die down before continuing. It took a while to do so, but as the enthusiastic clapping dissipated it was replaced by a different sound. It started as a low rhythmic hum and then gathered momentum as the warriors, forming the bulk of the seated guests, began to make themselves heard.

"Har-ald, Har-ald," they chanted quietly before their voices raised as one. "Har-ald, Har-ald," they continued.

Their voices grew louder, and fists pounded on tables. The Duke stood there waiting for the chant to finish but it did not, and the warriors continued to shout for their commander. William turned, looked at the Marchis of Ambrières and gestured his exasperation. Harald got to his feet and came forward to stand by the Duke who was at least a head and shoulders shorter than him. He raised his hand in a request for quiet but if anything, the chanting grew louder as the townsfolk joined in. The audience finally responded to the request to desist and quietened. Harald looked at the Duke for instruction.

"They are all your followers," hissed Duke William irritably. "Speak to them but do so quickly so we might proceed."

"As you wish, Lord," he replied before turning to the throng.

He wasted few words and saluted them heartily before concluding,

"If we are finished, my friends let the feasting begin."

Harald bowed deeply to great applause from all before resuming his seat at the end of the table.

"Well met, Lord," said Robert Fitzroy to the Duke who sat back down beside him.

"Your brother has lost none of his ability to rouse a rabble, I see," he snapped.

Robert did not reply but afforded himself a smile at his brother's irreverence. The Duke was not the only guest at the top table who found Harald Fitzroy's presence irksome. The Bishop of Coutances, an ancient man of seventy years, was growing tetchy as the sun's rays beat down on his balding pate.

"You Fitzroys have learned little in your time here," he droned in Harald's ear. "I have known three generations of you, and you are all godless men - even your brother Robert, the Pope's lickspittle, is no more Christian than you are."

Harald put a giant arm around his shoulder

"Let us not forget, priest," whispered Harald in the old man's ear, "that it was I who saved the life of your precious Pontiff. I advise you to desist from slander - at least where my brother Robert is concerned."

To reinforce his point, he squeezed the old man's shoulder and the Bishop winced in pain. Their discourse was interrupted by the arrival of food and wine. An army of cooks had been preparing the feast for days and bread and wine were brought out by continuous relays of servants. Six oxen, twenty-five pigs and sixty geese had been roasted and steaming meat-filled trays were being hurried out. The bounty of the harvest from Normandie's fields and orchards was presented in a profusion of vegetables, fruits and nuts. The River Seine had been fished remorselessly for the past few days and huge amounts of salmon, trout and carp were brought out, stewed and baked. Lamphrey and pigeon pies were piled high on trays that were carried in by perspiring servants and set before the guests.

As the afternoon wore on the politeness of the revellers evaporated as more and more wine was consumed. Jugglers and magicians entertained, and poets told stories of ancient battles fought by long dead heroes. Dusk descended and musicians and dancers appeared, tables were cleared and the music and singing began. The great promise of a bright future hung in the air and spirits were high. Duke William seemed to have overcome his earlier annoyance and was engrossed in conversation with Robert. A sudden commotion and the sound of raised voices caused them to stop and look in the direction of the hubbub.

The Bishop of Coutances had harangued Harald throughout the afternoon as the effects of the wine and sun took their toll. At first the younger man had simply ignored the other and passed it off as the ramblings of an old fool. However, the Bishop's jibes and threats seemed to increase in intensity with his intake of wine until Harald felt he could no longer endure the insults. When the tables were being cleared yet again, two young women approached the raised platform where William and his nobles sat. They both called up to the Marchis, tossing up flowers and beckoning him to join them. Harald had called back to them playfully, but his behaviour only seemed to infuriate the Bishop even further.

"Go and join your harlots, Norseman. God will judge you all and your kind. You and that whore of Mortain will both be judged and condemned," shouted the old man.

Harald could bear the man's company no longer and his temper snapped. He picked up a full jug of wine and emptied it over the Bishop's head, staining the ornately embroidered cloth of his pallium and his white, woollen robe, a deep crimson.

"And I have judged you, Bishop to be an interfering old goat with nothing better to do than cause mischief," said Harald calmly.

The Bishop began to raise his voice to an even higher pitch as he screamed invective. Picking up the ivory headed crozier resting against his chair, he struck out at his assailant. The Marchis simply raised his hand and snatched the staff of office from the Bishop's grasp, before breaking it in two and throwing it to the floor. The elderly priest toppled out of his chair as he tried to get away.

"You will need a more effective weapon to bring a Fitzroy to his knees, Father," shouted Harald before realising that the conversation on the long table had stopped.

Everyone craned their necks to see and hear what was going on at the far end.

He rose to his feet and stepped in front of the table.

"By your leave my Lord," he called, bowing to Duke William who glowered at him furiously, "but it is time I joined my men."

Then, without waiting for a reply, he jumped off the platform and into the raucous crowd. Meanwhile, the Bishop was hauled to his feet defiantly screaming that God should bring retribution on the head of his antagonist. Boiling with rage, the Duke managed to keep his temper and beside him, Robert shook his head in disbelief at his brother's actions.

"I am sorry, Lord. Harald's behaviour is unconscionable. He shames me," lamented Robert.

"Nonsense, my friend. You have nothing to berate yourself for. We shall decide what to do with Hari later. Now come, let me hear again of your stay in Constantinople - it is a tale worth hearing twice."

Later that night William and Robert Fitzroy sat alone in the council chamber of the ducal palace. The noise of the festivities could still be heard a league away. It was late and both men had drunk a little more wine than was normal. The hearthfire burned low and a dozen guttering candles shed sufficient light for William to see the deep lines in his friend's weathered face.

"I will speak with Harald in the morning. His behaviour must be checked," said Robert. "Even your most successful commander must learn how to control himself. I will make sure…."

Before he could finish the Duke held up his hand to stop him.

"Alas, there is more I must share with you, my friend," said the Duke sadly.

Robert looked up and waited expectantly as William watched him intently and hesitated before continuing.

"It pains me to tell you, but you have been cuckolded. Your wife has lain with another while you have been away on pilgrimage."

Robert looked into William's face and his mouth hung open in disbelief as he questioned the words he had just heard.

"Eleanor has betrayed me?" he asked plaintively.

William merely nodded and pushed a wine cup toward him. Robert sprang up, turned his back and fought to control his emotions. He turned again to face William and with both hands gripping the edges of the table he asked in a voice that was devoid of emotion.

"Who?"

Chapter 38: The Reckoning Of The Fitzroy Brothers

Robert Fitzroy rode into his brother's camp around midday accompanied only by a young squire carrying a bundle of long hazel stakes. He had spent a sleepless night pacing the floor of his chamber, trying to decide what action he should take against Harald and Eleanor for the great wrong perpetrated against him. The news of his wife's infidelity had struck him like a thunderbolt, but when he heard that it was his brother Harald who had betrayed him, he could not believe the words he heard. William told him a few of the facts, of their meetings in the remote farmhouse at Ceaucé, the frequency of their trysts and the length of time they had spent together. When news reached the Duke that the Lady of Mortain was riding out, alone except for the company of her servant, he had her followed and the "regrettable, if incontrovertible truths established".

After imparting the sobering news, Duke William had retired to bed, leaving Robert alone to contemplate what would surely be an imminent confrontation with his brother. He visited the private chapel and prayed for guidance. When none came, he returned to his rooms and fretted the rest of the night away before the course of action became apparent to him.

At first light Robert roused his squire, Christian. He ordered the boy to prepare eight wooden stakes of hazel. They were to be twice the length of a grown man and when he was finished, he was to return with them. He was also to fetch three round, wooden shields of the sort that were still favoured by some of the Norse mercenaries who fought for the Duchy. The boy enquired where he might obtain these items and Robert simply tossed him a bag of silver coins, telling him not to come back without them.

Christian returned by mid-morning with the wooden stakes and the shields on a mule. With the help of two servants, he had found a group of hazel saplings in a copse outside the city, and they made short work of cutting and preparing the wood. The shields were easy to find, and the boy bought them for a good price from a Fresian warrior who had lost his money at dice the previous evening. Robert praised the squire for his work and told him they would be visiting the camp of the Marchis of Ambrières. The squire asked timidly the purpose of their visit and Robert replied simply,

"If God wills it, I shall kill him, Christian."

"Will you be visiting the chapel to pray this morning, Lord?" asked the boy, who had grown used to accompanying his master in what had been their daily ritual.

"No, the time for prayer is over for now. I need you to prepare me for combat."

"Very good. It shall be done," said Christian, already making a list of everything needed for battle.

"I will need no armour. Just my sword and a fighting axe," concluded Robert, adding to the boy's confusion.

Christian had squired the Lord of Mortain for four years. He had prepared him for many battles in their time together, from northern France to the Holy Land. He had travelled thousands of leagues with his master to overcome great danger at his side. However, this was one of the strangest days of his service and the thought that his Lord was about to do combat with his brother, the redoubtable Harald Fitzroy, filled him with dread. He crossed himself and prayed silently before preparing the rest of his master's equipment. There was soon little left to do, and once Lord Robert was shaved and dressed, his sword and axe whetted and the horses readied, they were ready to leave.

There were one or two curious glances as Robert and Christian left the palace courtyard. They were in their hunting clothes and led a grey mule carrying an assortment of ash stakes and heavy wooden shields. The streets were half empty; it was Sunday, and the local people were still recovering from the effects of the previous day's feasting. The bells of Rouen cathedral echoed throughout the city as the faithful were called to prayer, and the two horsemen made their way against the thin traffic of worshippers travelling in the opposite direction.

Harald's camp stood outside the city walls on the banks of the River Seine, where the land flattened out before the huge forest of Londe-Rouvray. It comprised a hundred neatly arrayed tents laid out in lines, surrounded by a wooden picket fence that could be ingressed through gates to the north and the south. The two sentries saluted Robert lazily as he passed through the picket line. One of them provided directions to where the Marchis's tent might be found.

There was little activity in the camp save for a few whores, their labour done for the night, walking back to the town. Some of the men headed down to the river for their ablutions while others sat around campfires, waiting for others to finish cooking a late breakfast.

Robert found his brother sitting in front of a large tent, around a table with his comrades. They were playing dice and drinking, from where they had not moved since returning from feasting the previous evening. It was a bright, sunny morning and Harald squinted as he looked up toward the sound of approaching horses. He recognised his brother and held up his hand to quieten the others around the table.

"Brother," he said with a broad grin. "It is good to see you, but if you are hoping that I might join you for Mass I will have to disappoint you."

Robert did not answer and merely stared back, his face expressionless. Harald left the table and walked toward the horseman in front of him.

"This is about more than my disagreement with the Bishop last night, I feel," he continued, looking behind at the burden the mule carried.

Christian moved uneasily in the saddle behind his master. Harald nodded slowly as the realisation of the situation became apparent.

"*Holmgang*?" he asked.

His brother nodded.

"Three shields for each man," said Robert. "We will wait for you on the flat land in front of the tree line. Come when you are ready."

Then, turning his horse around he trotted out of the camp to the place of their contest.

It had been Jarl Bjorn who had introduced them to their first *holmgang* when they were small boys. There was a dispute with another Norse settlement on the borders of the Jarl's land. One of their warriors had taken game from his estate without asking and despite several warnings, the hunting had continued unchecked. Jarl Bjorn had ridden into their camp with his grandsons and a handful of warriors and demanded a reckoning by *holmgang*. A small area of flat ground was marked out and he challenged the headman to combat. The man reluctantly accepted and died soon afterwards; killed beneath the relentless attack of the Jarl's axe blows. After smashing three of his opponent's shields in quick succession, the final, fatal blow crushed the man's skull. Honour satisfied, the Fitzroys left, taking with them the dead man's cattle and possessions as payment for the stolen game. It had been a brutal lesson but one which had impressed on both grandsons the need for a rapid resolution of disputes. Without a reckoning, their grandfather had told them, conflicts turned into blood feuds that lasted for generations and beyond.

When they reached the place where the *holmgang* was to take place, Robert instructed his squire to mark out the contest square. The boy set out the shields in one corner, then they sat down and waited. They did not have to wait for long and Harald arrived shortly after midday with his captain, Jeanotte. He had changed his clothes and wore a plain white linen tunic over his hunting trousers and boots. His long, fair hair was tied back, and his chest-length beard was neatly plaited. He dismounted and walked over to his brother, his hands outstretched in supplication as Jeanotte unloaded the *rouncey* that carried the shields and weapons.

"Robert," said Harald, "you have every right to take your vengeance. I tried to stay away from her, but I was weak. This was never meant to slight you, but when all is said and done you are still my brother, I have no wish to fight you."

"It is a little late for regrets, Hari. To be cuckolded by my wife is one thing but knowing you were part of this betrayal is another," spat Robert.

"She and I are not without guilt, but you left her long before anything happened between us. You were eight hundred leagues away when she was dying and alone," countered his brother.

"That still did not give you the right to slip into her bed," said Robert. Harald shook his head.

"Come brother - take your vengeance. Satisfy your honour if it is so important to you. But whatever the outcome - remember that you are not totally blameless in this matter."

"Let us get this done, Hari. Then I will deal with your mistress. Come, take up your shield, you may have first strike."

"Until death takes one of us then, Robert?"

The protagonists stood facing one another ten paces apart. Harald took the honour of the first strike and bolted forward at his brother, hammering at his shield with the heavy single-bladed fighting axe. Robert barely had a chance to raise his shield arm to parry the blow and the force of it split the wooden shield from top to bottom. The impact shook Robert to his bones and he felt tendrils of ice burst into the old spear wound in his shoulder. Composing himself, he inhaled deeply and prepared to launch himself at Harald, who stood in front of him, breathing normally and seemingly unaffected from his exertions. The return blow was delivered with venom but did not have the power of the first strike and Harald warded it off with a deft flick of his wrist. The two closed in on each other trading blows in equal measure, but the power of the bigger man began to tell, and Robert was rocked back at each collision. Sensing his brother was tiring, Harald leapt forward knocking the other's shattered shield to the ground. He did not follow-up to finish his opponent but stepped back and allowed Robert, now blowing hard, to struggle to his feet.

They continued to circle one another and Harald, seeing fatigue writ large on his brother's face dropped his guard and held his shield and axe low. Robert spotted his opportunity and feinted left, before aiming a blow at his brother's head. It was wide of the mark but close enough to draw blood from his temple. Harald nodded in acknowledgement of the blow and moved forward again with speed, hammering his brother's upturned second shield until that too disintegrated.

"Desist brother, you cannot stand against me, and I have no wish to kill you," called the younger sibling.

Robert was breathing even harder and there was blood coming from his nose and mouth. He swung his axe defiantly again and Harald stepped away deftly.

"Third shield, one life left," he added.

Robert forced himself forward and delivered a series of blows, which his opponent absorbed on his shield before that too split and was replaced. He continued the onslaught, causing Harald to step backward, and his weapon bit into his opponent's wooden shield. Such was the power of the overarm strike that the axe embedded itself and caught fast. Harald wrenched his shield sideways, taking the axe with it and removing it from his brother's grasp.

"*Rendement*, Robert. It is over," he shouted but his brother was far from finished and he rushed forward, catching his opponent in the stomach with the point of his good shoulder and winding him deeply.

Now it was Harald's turn to breathe heavily, he sucked in the warm air and tried to recover himself. As he did so Robert drew his long sword and cut and hacked at his opponent who tried to defend himself with shield and axe. Harald recovered rapidly and pursued Robert around the area marked out by the hazel stakes. Unencumbered by the weight of the heavy shield the older sibling easily evaded any further strikes. Harald, exasperated by his quarry's evasive action, threw his own shield to the ground and drew his sword, transferring the axe to his left hand. His speed quickened and he moved forward at pace swinging mighty blows. Robert continued to resist him and summoning his last reserves of strength struck a lateral blow aimed at Harald's exposed neck. His brother saw it just in time and caught its force between his own sword and axe causing the blade to shatter.

Harald grinned at the thought of his impending victory, but the smile soon left his lips as he felt the tip of a dagger slip effortlessly between two of his ribs. He looked down in amazement and watched the crimson patch of blood spreading on his linen shirt. As he did so he dropped his own weapons, releasing his grip on Robert's broken sword. His brother seized the opportunity and reversing his ruined weapon caught him a crushing blow to the temple with his sword hilt causing the bigger man's knees to buckle.

Harald crumpled and fell onto his back. Visions of long-dead warriors swam up before him; each ghostly figure raising their drinking cup in salutation.

"Valhalla, Valhalla, I will soon be with you," he mouthed before laying very still.

He looked up into the blue sky and saw two ravens flying overhead, their beating wings blocking out the summer sun. He closed his eyes and the last thing he heard was their harsh 'caw-cawing' and the distant beat of their wings as they flew north.

Chapter 39: Robert's Other Reckoning

Robert Fitzroy felt neither triumph nor joy after defeating his brother; the only emotion was one of complete despair. His recent return from his pilgrimage to the Holy Land had fulfilled him completely, knowing that he had done his duty for the Duchy in the eyes of God. Since his return Robert's world had crumbled beneath his feet. His church had been built on sand, he thought, on the ride back to Mortain and it had all been his fault. He knew that Eleanor had never loved him and that their arranged marriage, like many others, was only a mechanism for strengthening the family's blood lines and accruing wealth. To that end it had been successful. He was a man of great influence and importance - but the cost, he admitted to himself, was a high one. He had loved Hari and once, at least, he had received the respect and unconditional support of the mother of his children. Before leaving he met with the Duke to tell him of the outcome of his confrontation with his brother. William struggled to contain his delight at the demise of Harald Fitzroy but commiserated with Robert's loss, while encouraging him to conclude the rest of his 'family business' before returning to full duties.

It was with a heavy heart that the Lord of Mortain stood before the gates of his castle. The journey from Rouen had been rapid on the dry, flat roads heading west and he pushed his escort of ten horsemen hard. He had been tempted to journey alone but, despite the relative peace, the roads were still not completely safe. Robert brooded in silence throughout the five-day ride; his sense of desperation at the outcome of his actions had now been replaced by high dudgeon. He was determined that Eleanor should be punished accordingly and had decided not to publicly shame his wife for her adultery, but her freedom would be curtailed, at least for the moment. She had committed a serious offence in the eyes of God, not to mention causing great unrest by her actions and needed to be punished. Robert was the Chancellor of the Duchy of Normandie, a position of the highest rank which demanded respect. How could he command the respect of the people if he could not even keep his wife in order at home, he asked himself?

He led his men through the castle gates as dusk was settling and without waiting for a servant to take him up, he marched through the great hall and up to the family *solar* at the top of the keep. He found Eleanor at work in her chamber, pouring over a large, heavily bound ledger. She looked up from her desk as he pushed unceremoniously through the door. The look of fear on her face was quickly replaced by one of anger and she stood up to face him.

"You have returned, Robert. Is there something you have forgotten?" she said defiantly.

"I have forgotten nothing, Lady," he said, "but you seem to have forgotten your marriage vows."

He kept his anger in check and strode over to where she stood and watched her expression change. There was silence between them as she grasped the situation. Eleanor quickly determined that there was little point in denial, and her combative spirit came to the fore.

"Let me remind you, sir that you deserted me long before I countenanced lying with another man. You abandoned me long ago to pursue your own destiny and it should come as no surprise to understand that I found solace elsewhere," she spat.

"But with my brother? Have you no shame?" he said, trying hard to restrain from shouting.

"It might pain you to hear this, but you should listen. Your brother was the only one who came to our aid when you took leave of your family. When I was dying Hari saved me. When you were far away, he was in the next room willing me back. Is it any wonder I went to his bed?"

"You have the grace to admit your adultery then?"

"I would deny my feelings for your brother no more than I would poison my children. You should know that I pursued him and if anything, he avoided my advances," she hit back.

"It no longer matters and the conflict between us has been resolved."

"Resolved?" she said quizzically.

"Indeed. He is dead at my hands, as a direct consequence of your wantonness. You must blame yourself."

He watched the colour of his wife's face change as she took in his words. Her eyes widened, and her hands reached up to cover her mouth.

"Now, to business, madam. I will not publicly shame you for your actions for you were once a dutiful wife and a good mother. You have run my estate efficiently and may continue to do so but I insist on changes. I will appoint a new *castellan* and your servants will be replaced. If you object, you will be sent to join your mother at the nunnery in Caen and your children will be taken away. Do I make myself clear?" he said calmly.

Eleanor could not hear any of this; she was still reeling at the news from Rouen. Seeing his wife stagger backwards into a chair, Robert decided not to punish her further and turned and left the room. Eleanor put her head in her hands and felt her shoulders wrack and her chest heave, as she began to sob uncontrollably.

She woke up with a start in the small hours of darkness before dawn. She had fallen asleep at the table, and she felt the imprint of the leather journal which had made a mark on her face. It took a few moments to compose her thoughts before she remembered the details of her brief meeting with Robert and the awful news he brought. The Lady of Mortain was bereft and alone in a bottomless pit of sadness.

She remembered her last few days with Hari spent in the remote farmhouse when he asked her to return to Italy with him. It seemed like a lifetime ago when she agreed to take the children and go. Harald told her to come to Regneville on the day of the next spring equinox where the *Evas Prayer* would be waiting for them in the harbour. They were to leave everything behind them, and he would take them to a new life in Italy. All that was lost now, and she needed to resign herself to staying here, locked in a marriage of convenience for the rest of her days. She lit a candle from the last embers of the dying hearthfire, made her way to bed and sobbed quietly until falling into a troubled sleep.

Eleanor's despair had increased manyfold by the time she awoke for the second time. Light streamed through the window and fell on her face, but she found herself unable to move. Were it not for the fact that her children would miss her at the breakfast table, she would have stayed where she was all day. Normally, Beatrice would have woken her and helped her dress, but today she had not come. Eleanor resolved that today would be spent like any other and rose, washed and dressed before leaving her room. She went straight to the dining room in the *solar* where she received another shock. Instead of her children waiting for her, there was Robert and another man sitting at the table. Determined not to show any weakness she went and sat at her normal place before her husband broke the uncomfortable silence.

"Eleanor, this man is Gabriel, and he will be the new *castellan* here. He has been my trusted friend and comrade for many years, and you can rely on him completely."

The man stood up, nodded curtly and regarded her with piercing, hawk-like eyes that gleamed with a zealot's fervour. Robert dismissed the new *castellan* and waited for him to leave them before continuing.

"Beatrice and her husband are banished. They will be sent away from Mortain; they will not return. Your new maid will be here later today. I will accompany you on all the affairs of the estate from now on until I am familiar with them myself. I have been remiss, leaving you to your own devices for so long and I intend to spend more time here at home with my family. You may inform the children of the changes and I will talk to them myself tonight. Do I make myself clear?"

Although seething with anger Eleanor nodded that she had, indeed, understood.

"Oh, and one more thing," Robert added, "please comport yourself with dignity as the Lady of Mortain. There will be no more training at arms with the men - that part of your life is over. I have no need for a lioness - I need a wife." She looked up at him and her eyes lit up in rage.

"Then you should have taken me as I was and not waited until it was too late. You were a good man once, Robert. Where did he go?" she asked.

He reflected on her question before replying.

"I will pray for us both, Eleanor," he said.

Her new maid duly arrived but she refused to see her. Eleanor went down to the kitchens and instructed one of the servants to find Beatrice and give her a bag of silver which she pressed into the girl's hand. After taking time with her children, Eleanor spent the rest of the day alone in miserable solitude. She retired to her chambers for ten days seeing no-one but her children. Robert took up quarters away from the family's *solar* in the main keep and husband and wife managed to maintain an uncomfortable distance. She resolved to find out where Harald's last resting place was and unsure of who to trust, kept her own counsel. She decided to speak with Rolande of Coutances, who although a close friend of Robert, could at least be relied upon for his discretion and sought him out in the garrison refectory one day.

Eleanor had not spoken to the commander since Robert had returned from his reckoning with Harald, and she beckoned to him after breakfast one morning. After excusing himself from his comrades, they climbed atop the battlements and walked along the walls. He had known her since she was a small girl and Eleanor trusted him implicitly.

"I must know where Harald Fitzroy fell, Rolande, I need to know the place where he died," she confided.

The old knight turned to her and taking both her hands in his, he beamed a huge smile.

"Then there is something you should know, Lady," he said.

Chapter 40: Back From The Dead

Jeanotte looked down at Harald and assessed the injuries. The side of his head was hugely swollen where he had been struck by the hilt of Robert's sword. Lord Harald lay very still, and the once white linen shirt was now soaked in his own blood. The knight knelt down and tore off the shirt and used it to staunch the flow of blood from the knife wound. It was deep, the width of two fingers and on the right side of his chest but after applying pressure for some time the bleeding slowed and stopped. Jeanotte took a flask of brandy and cleaned the wound as best he could. Then he fetched a bag from his saddlebag, a gift from Harald's late wife, and took out a needle and catgut thread. With one hand he held the wound together while stitching it with the other. He stood up and admired his handiwork, then took a bandage and bound it around Harald's skull which after a rudimentary examination he adjudged to be fractured.

"Lady Eva would be proud of me," he said aloud before going in search of wood from the forest with which to make a travois.

It was getting dark by the time he finished, and he transferred Harald's massive frame onto the travois and dragged it back to camp. Their arrival caused great consternation and a monk was summoned from Rouen monastery to come and treat the commander.

He and Jeanotte sat watch that night and by morning Harald opened his eyes and spoke.

"I knew he would not kill me," he said quietly, waking up Jeanotte who was dozing in a chair. "Quick, bring me some wine my mouth feels like it is full of chicken feathers,"

"Lord," shouted Jeanotte excitedly "You are back from the dead."

"I was nowhere near death. I have had a thousand spats with my brother like that and he has never yet come close to sending me to Valhalla," he replied, touching his bandaged head and wincing, "but judging from the size of this headache, he caught me with a lucky blow."

Despite Harald's protestations to the contrary, it was clear that he had received serious injuries. Although they were not enough to kill him, they were sufficient to keep him bedridden for several days, but under the diligent eyes of his carers he made a swift recovery. When he finally got to his feet, orders were given to break up the camp and return home. Jeanotte led the men back to Ambrières and the other castles along the Norman border, while Harald travelled west to Dives, with his friend, Earl Godwinson. The Saxon and his entourage were finally travelling home after Duke William had released him from service.

"When can we expect to see you in England, Hari?" asked Godwinson as their column plodded on toward the coast.

"I will be with you when fate allows me to do so," replied Harald vaguely.

"If your brother does not kill you next time he sees you. He might be luckier the second time."

"Ah, this," said Harald touching the livid, blue and green bruise that covered one side of his face. "It is no more than a family disagreement. Surely you have argued with your siblings before?" he laughed and changed the subject. "Tell me, how does it feel to be a Norman knight in the service of the Bastard?"

"I am honoured, of course, but it was no more than words and politics, was it not?" said the Saxon.

"I am not sure that Duke William takes oath-making so lightly. It is a serious matter here when a knight commits his word," said Harald feigning a stern countenance.

It was the Earl's turn to laugh, and he turned in the saddle to face his friend.

"And when you plighted your troth to my little sister, albeit in her absence, were you also sincere."

"Like I said, brother, I shall be with you when fate allows me to be back in your Wessex heartland," said Harald.

"Then we shall rejoice when that happy day arrives," declared his friend lightheartedly.

Their party arrived at the mouth of the Dives estuary the next day and they embraced fondly and said goodbye. Harald watched and waved as the ship left the harbour, wondering when they would meet again. A sharp pain from his ribs brought him back to the present, reminding him there was much to do before he too boarded his ship and left for Italy.

When he returned to Ambrières, he summoned his captains and informed them that come spring he would be taking his leave of them to head back to the Kingdom in the Sun. He would be delegating the command of his castles and estates to Jeanotte. The captains all agreed this to be a popular choice, the men respected the knight, and his reputation preceded him. Harald told them there would be two hundred men joining him in the spring and he began to prepare the five ships that would join the *Evas Prayer* when she left at Easter. He began to count the day when he would take the helm of his beloved *dromon* and take to the sea with Eleanor at his side.

He thought of her constantly, and since his fight with Robert he had been even more anxious to hear from her. However, what perplexed him most was how their secret came out. Firstly, there was the outrage of the Bishop of Coutances and then came his brother to challenge him by *holmgang*. There had always been suspicion ever since he stayed in Mortain to care for Eleanor, but for Robert to act in such a fashion had meant that the details of their affair had come from someone his brother trusted. That person Harald deduced could only be the Duke. He was not concerned for himself, but it was Eleanor's well-being that he worried about particularly, as his brother had doubtless confronted her by now. All he could do was sit and wait until she sent him a message. Harald had given her the time and place of their departure and all that remained was to pray to the gods that the Norns did not cut their cords again.

He threw himself into planning his exit from the Duchy and hand-picked two hundred men for the trip. The journey south would take over a hundred days and each ship would have to be prepared for the variable conditions of different climates and oceans. As well as the men and their families there would be horses to care for on the long journey and supplies for both would have to be provisioned. He decided against informing the Duke of Normandie of his departure, particularly in light of the tumult his liege-lord had caused. Jeanotte and the men of the borders would still be loyal bannermen in Harald's absence and there was, he felt, nothing to reproach himself for by the manner of his leaving. Robert, he hoped, would one day forgive him for taking Eleanor away, but as she had so often repeated her husband had abandoned her and the children a long time ago. In any case, Harald reasoned, honour had been satisfied during the *holmgang* and their conflict was over.

He had not heard from Eleanor in over forty days, and he was concerned for her. Normally, Beatrice or her husband would have come to him with a message. One of the squires at Ambrières, a reliable and resourceful young man of fifteen named Jonas, came from Mortain. He and his master had been on the campaign to Brittany and the boy had been fearless in his service during the action at Dol. Jonas would be sent home on the pretext of family business and deliver a message to Lady Eleanor. The journey to Mortain was only fifteen leagues and the squire was back in Harald's main hall in four days.

"You saw her? She is well?" asked Harald.

"I did and she is well," said Jonas, "but it was not easy to see her, Lord. She was almost constantly in the company of her servant. She still visits her horses in the stables every day and I hid myself there and waited until she was alone."

"The servant? Was it Beatrice, the red-haired woman?"

"No, Lord it was not her. It seems that when Lord Robert returned, he dismissed all of Lady Eleanor's personal staff in the castle. There is even a new *castellan* - a cruel man named Gabriel. My mother says that he watches her like a hawk, and she is scarcely left alone. He told her you were dead."

"And you repeated the message as I said?"

"Yes Lord, I asked her if she would be ready to leave come the first day of Easter."

"And her reply?"

"She said there is no force on God's earth that will prevent her from being with you."

Harald stepped forward and embraced the boy in a powerful bear-hug that threatened to crush the life out of him. He set the squire back on his feet again

"That is good news Jonas. You have done well but I will need you to return home again soon," said Harald, still smiling broadly.

Chapter 41: The Prison of Mortain

Harald's fleet of five ships were sailed to the seaport of Granville on the far west coast of the peninsula where they were prepared and supplied for the spring voyage. It had once been an old Norse settlement, but these days it was just a small fishing village that would not attract too much attention. He had thought about leaving from his family home of Regneville just up the coast, but there had been too much strife with Robert recently to countenance such an event. The thought of his mother waving farewell to him and his brother's estranged wife, made him chuckle. Everything would have to be done in secret or Eleanor might never escape Robert's close attentions.

It was important that they leave on the day of the Spring Equinox, when the ocean bulged under the power of the moon's gravity and the tides were at their highest. The *Evas Prayer* had a deep draft and was an ocean-going vessel. With a full cargo of horses, men, weapons and supplies, she would be weighed down to the gunwales and would need every bit of assistance to get her out of the shallow waters of that coastline. There was another reason Harald wanted to leave on the pagan feast day of Ēostre. He had been told in a dream that this was the day he would take his charges over the water to a foreign land. The Goddess

Freya visited him one night and told him that his union with Eleanor would be blessed only if they started their journey on this day. Harald had promised her they would leave on this holy day and no other.

He learned from Jonas's visits home that Robert maintained constant vigilance over his family in Mortain. Eleanor was always watched, and the hated new *castellan* dogged her every step. The squire took care not to be over-eager, and when the coast was clear he would slip a note into her hand from Harald. He told her to be steadfast and be ready in the spring. She could endure her confinement, she told the boy, as long as she knew Harald was coming for her.

Robert heard the news that his brother still lived with mixed emotions. From deep within himself he was glad that he had not killed his sibling and he quietly gave thanks to God for Harald's deliverance. His relationship with his wife grew colder as winter drew on, and he wished a thousand times that he had paid her a little more attention when he, at least, had her respect. All he had from her now was barely concealed contempt and he sometimes wondered whether it would have been wiser just to let her go. He prayed often and regularly for his family and remembered the times when his marriage had not just been for show. Their union had given him wealth and power, but it had come at great cost.

Duke William on the other hand was clearly delighted. He had not wished Harald slain and was gratified to learn that the outcome of his mischief-making had not been fatal. Harald had been chastised, Robert had asserted authority over his brother and his wife once more, all was well in the Duchy. He would one day soon rule the wealthy kingdom of England which would be given to him without so much as a hint of rebellion.

Christmas came and went and with it the long, dark months of winter. As the days grew longer and the snow and frost retreated, spring began to spread its tendrils through the Duchy. It was still a good thirty days from Ēostre and Jonus slipped into the stables of Mortain castle to do Harald's bidding. He took up his hiding place and waited for Lady Eleanor to come and visit her horses. This was one of the few times she was left alone, and she would come in to greet her favourite animals and groom them until their coats shone with a deep lustre.

"Madam," he whispered as loudly as he dared.

She looked up and nodded to him before checking that she had not been observed. When she was satisfied, she was alone, she moved quickly into one of the empty stalls to the rear of the stables and the boy dropped down silently, beside her. He spoke without preamble.

"Lady, I am to tell you this," he said quickly. "Lord Harald said your escape will not be without danger. I will meet you with my father at the rear wall of the battlements on the eve of Ēostre . We will take you and the children down the stairs through the sewers, where there is a small postern gate. On the other side you will be met by Lord Harald's men, and they will take you away to safety. There will be a signal, an alarm will be raised for a fire set in the town - as soon as you hear it you must take the children and flee."

She nodded and thanked him for the risk he and his family were taking. Then without warning she flung her arms around him and kissed him.

"You are a very brave young man, Jonas. I am already in your debt," she whispered tearfully.

The squire's cheeks flushed with embarrassment.

"You have always been kind to me and my family, Lady. We will get you out of this place, do not fear."

Then he swung himself back up into the loft and disappeared.

Chapter 42: Escape And Flight

The moon was in full wax and hung suspended like a beautiful yellow orb in the firmament over Mortain, bathing everything it touched in an ethereal, silvery light. Keeping to the shadows Eleanor led her children forward. She was in her hunting clothes - leather trousers, tunic and boots - and around her waist hung a long dagger. Within touching distance, behind their mother, her two boys kept close and the older one, Richard, held his little sister's hand. They crept forward stealthily toward the stairs leading up to the battlements, taking care to keep close to the walls.

She had given them no notice of the plan to flee their home other than a brief order to be dressed, have warm clothes ready and to speak to no one of these requests, not even their father. Eleanor sat on her bed fully clothed waiting for the signal. It felt good to be back in her old clothes again, even if they were a lot tighter on her now. As she waited in the dark, she went over the plan once more, before the silence was broken by the sound of bells ringing. Distant cries of "fire" could be clearly heard. The servants were nowhere to be seen and the scrutiny under which she had been constantly watched seemed to have stopped for the time being. She assumed they had been paid off to clear the way for their escape.

Eleanor left her chamber as quietly as she could and tip-toed along the passageway to her sons' bedroom. They were ready, waiting for her beneath their blankets and without a word they fell in behind her moving toward their sister's room. Turid was woken gently, dressed and placed between the two boys behind their mother. It was approaching midnight and the *solar* was deserted. They stole through it silently and took the stone staircase which descended to the great hall. A pair of wolfhounds were fast asleep in front of the guttering hearthfire and one of them woke. He looked up disinterestedly before dropping off to sleep again.

When they reached the staircase leading to the battlements, she picked up her daughter and started to climb. She was pleased to see they too were also deserted and started walking around the wall's perimeter to get to the rear of the castle. Eleanor looked down over the castle walls to where the sleeping town was starting to wake up. The church was on fire, and she saw a chain of people handing buckets of water to one another to fight the blaze. The conflagration had taken hold of the wooden building and flames were licking through holes in the roof. She smiled to herself, wondering which of Robert's losses he would feel most; his wife or his precious church. They hurried on toward a glowing brazier on top of the back wall, and she sunk into the shadows as she heard footsteps. The figures of two men appeared and the first called to her.

"Lady, it is Jonas," he whispered, stepping into the fire light. "My father, Bertin will take the children and I will lead you down. The place is deserted, they have all gone to fight the fire."

The older man moved forward quickly and picked up Turid in one arm, holding out his free hand for the younger boy to grasp.

When they were ready, Jonas lit a torch from the burning coals of the brazier and put his shoulder to a large door in the back of a recess built into the wall, inching it open. He went through it without hesitation and emerged moments later.

"Follow me, all is clear," he beckoned and turned back to head down the dark spiral staircase.

Richard followed his mother and after them came Bertin, holding tight to the two younger children. They descended into the gloom, one after the other, following the light of the torch until the eye-watering stench of unemptied latrines rose up to meet them.

"Nearly at the bottom now," said the older man gently as Turid wriggled in his arms. When they reached the foot of the stairway, they found themselves in a large chamber in which stood a huge stone container that held the fetid contents of the castle's human waste. Jonas led them gingerly round one side and into a narrow passageway that was damp and slippery underfoot.

"Careful," he warned the others before thrusting his torch forward. "There it is, the door is there."

His father handed Turid to her mother and came forward to join him and they inspected the solid oak door which was secured firmly by two massive iron bolts that ran across it. It had obviously been used recently and was clear of any of the moss that grew around the ingress. The bolts, although old, had no rust but would need some effort to move them. Bertin, removed a large leather bag from his back and retrieved a metal hammer. He wrapped a piece of rag around its head in an attempt to deaden any sound and tapped away at the first bolt. It began to move slowly across the door until it was free of the latch bore that secured it in the doorway. Jonus smiled at his father and clapped him on the back as quietly as his excitement would allow. The second bolt was a little more stubborn but moved eventually, and the two men pushed with their shoulders until the door shifted and swung outward. A welcome rush of cold air blew in as the little party walked out into the open air.

The night was clear, and the full moon lit up their escape route. They were at the top of a steep, boulder-strewn slope leading down to a water-filled moat surrounding the solid rock on which the castle was built. The moat was spanned by a rickety wooden bridge periodically used by local people when they came to empty the latrines. Jonas scanned the area of flat ground beyond the bridge to the wooded area in the distance. He saw movement at the tree line and pointed toward it. Bertin followed his gaze and nodded to where they both saw the horsemen waiting. The younger man found the narrow path leading to the bridge and picked his way carefully down the escarpment. The young boys both stumbled and fell during the descent but urged on by their mother they quickly got to their feet and continued.

It was when Eleanor set her feet on the solid, flat ground on the far side of the bridge that she finally felt a glimmer of hope. The horsemen by the trees left their cover and galloped toward them. She held the hands of both her sons and dragged them forward. With Turid back in his arms Bertin exhorted them all to greater speed. He gave a cry of alarm as he saw another group of horsemen approaching at speed into the space between them and their rescuers.

Jeanotte saw the little band emerge from the bowels of the castle first. He had been waiting patiently for them ever since the alarm had sounded that the church was on fire. A local man had been richly rewarded for setting the blaze and the fire had attracted the desired attention. Jeanotte had been here with a cohort of twelve horsemen since arriving under the cover of darkness. As the fugitives ran across the bridge and onto open ground, he moved out with the spare horses to meet them. Suddenly, he too was alerted to movement on his flank and diverted some of his riders to intercept whoever was heading in their direction. Moments later he heard the clash of steel and looked over to the ensuing melee but could not tell which way the fight was going. He saw several riders split off and head directly toward the little knot of running people and spurred his mount forward in an attempt to reach them first.

Eleanor gasped in horror as she realised what was happening. They had obviously been betrayed and Robert had laid a trap for them. Jonas and Bertin drew their swords and moved to her side to protect their charges.

The older man was the first to die, a lance caught him in the chest. Jonas managed to evade his assailant, but a second horseman knocked him down and finished him on the ground. A third man slipped out of the saddle and caught hold of both of the boys round their necks, hauling them away from their mother.

"You will return to the castle immediately, Lady," shouted Gabriel.

The two boys did not struggle and lay limply in their captor's arms. Eleanor let go of Turid, drew her dagger and advanced toward the man holding her sons. The sight of the Lady of Mortain approaching the *castellan* with murderous intent created enough uncertainty to allow Jeanotte to enter the fray and dispatch one of the other foemen. Eleanor sprang at

Gabriel and slashed him across the face causing him to release the boys who ran toward their sister gathering up the weeping girl.

"Run to me," shouted Jeanotte, "I am your uncle's man, boys. Quickly now."

Richard reacted fast but his younger brother, encumbered with his baby sister in his arms hesitated. William looked first at his mother and then to Jeanotte.

"Run,"called Eleanor, "run to safety." William started to run but he was off-balance and fell to the ground spilling Turid who howled in fear. Before he could get to his feet again Gabriel stood over them. He grinned triumphantly at Eleanor and holding the two children, one in each arm, walked backward toward his own men, dripping blood from a deep facial wound on the heads of his captives.

"You shall return to the castle, Lady," he sneered. "Your husband is on his way and will deal with you and your friends shortly."

The outcome of the nearby melee had been decisive. Jeanotte's men had emerged from the fight intact, unhorsing and killing four of their opponents in the darkness. They re-joined their captain and formed up beside him to face their adversaries. Richard in the meantime had reached the sanctuary of their company and scrambled up onto the back of one of the spare horses.

Each opposing side, now reinforced by their comrades, faced each other from the saddle. Eleanor, once more the Lioness of Mortain stood defiantly between the two groups of horsemen. She held out the dagger in her outstretched hand and never took her eyes off the man holding her son and daughter. She knew Robert would not harm their children and made a desperate decision. In one swift movement she edged back to Jeanotte's line, caught the saddle pommel of one of the other spare horses and swung herself onto the animal's back.

"Be brave, my children," she called to William and Turid. "You know your mother will never desert you."

Then she dug her heels into the animal's flanks and galloped off into the night, with Jeanotte and his men in close attendance. The company did not stop until they crossed Mortain's county lines, and the pace slackened enough for Eleanor to check on her son who clung desperately to his horse's mane. When they realised they were not being pursued they let their animals rest briefly, before resuming their flight and headed toward the coast.

Gabriel ordered his men to stay put until the arrival of Lord Robert, who came soon after his wife's departure. He dismounted and embraced his children before ordering the men back to their barracks. There would be no pursuit, he said, and no need for more blood to be shed this night. He walked his horse back to the castle with William seated behind and Turid in front of him. He took them up to the family *solar* and put them gently to bed.

"Will mama return home soon, father?" asked Turid.

"Soon, my love, she will not leave you alone for long, I promise," Robert assured her. The little girl reached out and wound her arms around his head. Then she kissed him on the cheek and fell asleep.

He went to sit alone before the hearthfire which a servant had built up for him. He was sanguine in his thoughts, despite the events of the evening and closed his eyes in quiet reflection.

"This time will pass, and I will count my blessings again," he thought, "the time for bitterness has gone and I must learn to forgive. I cannot change God's will, and neither can Hari."

Robert felt at peace with the world for the first time in a long while and closing his eyes he fell asleep in the chair.

Chapter 43: Evas Prayer Sets Sail

Harald Fitzroy stood on the cliffs overlooking the harbour in Granville. Below him his little fleet was finalising preparations to leave on the high tide. It was still early morning and they had almost half a day to complete the loading of the last vessel. In all, two hundred men, thirty-five women and three hundred horses were making the journey south. The clamour to join Harald had been loud when he announced his intentions and he had to refuse many men. The women were married to some of his men, and they all knew of the hardships of the long journey to southern Italy. They would be safe from all but the largest pirate fleets, but disease, shipwreck and storms were ever-present perils.

Harald looked down the road one more time. He felt sure that some misfortune had befallen Eleanor and she would not come. He looked back to his fleet before looking down the road yet again and then he saw them. He watched the group of horsemen in the far distance approach. As they grew closer, he quickly counted fifteen riders in all and before long he could discern Jeanotte and Eleanor riding together at their head. The column drew to a halt in front of him and Harald, smiling broadly, clapped his hands together applauding the success of the mission. He reached up to Eleanor and helped her dismount the large bay stallion she rode and wrapped his arms around her in a warm embrace. He saw Richard on the horse behind her and waved to him

"Where are the other children?" he asked her. "I do not see William or Turid?"

It was when he looked into Eleanor's wan and tear-streaked face that he felt the Norns snipping away at the chords that bound their fate together.

"Their father still has them," she said quietly, "we could not get them all away."

She turned and smiled at her son astride his horse, and then to the horsemen and thanked them all for their service.

"It was our duty, Lady. We are loyal bannermen to the Fitzroys wherever they might be. Let me take the boy and find him something to eat," said Jeanotte and led the rest of the horsemen away.

She turned back to Harald who was struggling to remain calm.

"Eleanor, I shall retrieve them myself. Robert shall not win this battle," he said angrily.

"No, you will not," she said stridently. "I have been the cause of too much bloodshed already and I will not be the reason for the destruction of the Fitzroy clan. They are my family too."

"You are not coming with me, are you?" said Hari, more as a statement than a question.

She shook her head, and he began to feel his world crumbling.

"Wait, before you say more," she said putting her finger to his lips. "You must promise to obey me for the sake of our child."

Harald's mouth dropped open as she took his hand and put it on her swollen abdomen.

"Do you promise?"

She waited for him to nod before she continued.

"This child growing in my belly is ours and come the summer you will be his father. I would gladly go with you today, but I cannot leave without all my children. Robert will not harm them, but I will not leave them alone."

Harald tried and failed to hide his bitter disappointment.

"You will return to Mortain?" he finally asked.

"I will, but when your brother discovers I am carrying your child, he might not treat me quite so generously. You must take Richard and treat him as your own son. This will be my safeguard and no harm will come to me while Robert's first-born is with you. But you must leave with him today on the high tide. You must both be gone far from the Duchy. Do you understand?"

He did not reply and desperately tried to fathom what he had just been told, but Eleanor was relentless and would brook no argument. Realising that further questions were useless he promised to do all that she asked. A servant brought some food and drink for Eleanor, and he lay his cloak out on the ground for her to rest on. When she had eaten, she lay down and with Harald's arm around her, she pressed herself into his chest and slept.

She woke to the sound of the gulls squawking overhead, wheeling high above her on the sea-breezes. The bright spring sun was now high in the sky and she raised herself up in spite of her great weariness.

"Is it time for you to leave?" asked Eleanor quietly.

Harald nodded.

"I will come for you when the gods allow it," he said.

"And I shall count the days that we are apart. But until then remember that you have my most precious possession in your care. I charge you with keeping him safe until you come back for me. He is your blood; he is a Fitzroy, and you will learn to be his father."

She moved her face towards his and kissed him tenderly on the mouth, before turning her head away as the tears welled up inside her. They waited for Richard to return, and Eleanor hugged and kissed her son goodbye.

"You must go with your uncle, Richard. Do not weep, for our time apart will be brief and I will see your face every night in my dreams," she said. "Go now. I will watch you leave from here."

The boy did as he was told, and with Harald's arm around his shoulder they walked down the cliff-steps to the *Evas Prayer*. They boarded the huge ship and stood on the deck watching the men make their final preparations.

"Have you ever steered a mighty ship like this before, Richard?" asked his uncle.

The boy shook his head, unsure of himself in the noise and bustle around him.

"Well, it is about time we made a seaman out of you. Did you know your great-grandfather was a mighty Norse warrior who sailed many oceans?"

Richard shook his head again.

"I will have plenty of time to tell you, his story. Now come, take the tiller with me and we shall start our great adventure together."

When all was ready the ship pushed off from the jetty, the oars were lowered and two banks of rowers drove her powerfully into open water followed closely by the other four vessels. The oars were shipped and the great sail bearing the image of Odin's ravens was unfurled. Harald turned *Evas Prayer* across the wind and she planed lightly over the flat water like a hawk gliding on the thermals.

He looked to the top of the cliffs and saw Eleanor waving. When he looked up again, moments later - she was gone.

to be continued..................

Glossary

Aett: Clan or tribe
Castellan: Keeper of the castle
Chelandia: Byzantium ship for transporting horses
Cog: Wide bodied cargo ship
Conrois: A tight group of Norman calvary. (Plural: conroi)
Consanguinity: The crime of two cousins marrying
Courser: Hunting horse
Danske Tong: Widespread and generally understood language (Norse)
Destrier: War horse (stallion)
Dromon: Byzantium war ship
Frey & Freya: Ancient Norse god and goddess of love, fertility, battle, and death
Gambeson: Padded leather jerkin
Gonfanon: Heraldic flag or banner
Hauberk: Long chain-mail tunic worn by Norman warriors
Hobelars: Light mounted infantry
Holmgang: Duel between two opponents, often to the death
Huscarl: Saxon household bodyguard (often of norse origin)
Keep: Fortified tower and place of last refuge in a castle which also served as living quarters for the noble family
Midgard: the name by which the gods called Earth

Mangol: A large catapult
Njord: An ancient Norse god
None: Noon
Palfrey: Fine riding horse
Puer: Page boy
Rouncey: An ordinary, all-purpose horse
Seneschal: Steward
Serjeant: A professional soldier drawn from the lower classes.
Sigel: Banners
Skalds: Norse poets and story tellers
Solar: The Lord and Lady's family quarters
Sumpter: Horse used for carrying wares
Thor: Norse god of war
Trebuchet: Siege weapon
Vé: A holy spring (Norse)
Zirid: Muslim dynasty that ruled in parts of North Africa and Spain

Characters

Argyrus: Byzantine prince and general
Alberada: Wife to the Guiscard
Aldred: Head farmer of Regneville
Aubin: Robert's squire
Bishop Mauger: Bishop of Rouen, Duke William's Uncle
Bjorn Halfdanson: Jarl and Count of Regneville, Grandfather to Robert, Harald, Floki and Siegrid Fitzroy, Wandering Warrior of Haugesund
Cnut: Son of the King of Denmark and successor to the English throne after the defeat of the Saxon, King Aethelred
Duke William: The 'Bastard', ruler of Normandie
Eleanor Werlenc: Lady of Mortain, wife of Robert Fitzroy, mother to Richard, William and Turid
Eva: Wife of Harald Fitzroy
Floki Fitzroy: Captain of the Riders of Regneville
Gabriel: Robert Fitzroy's trusted man
Guiscard: Rob or Robert de Hautville, one of twelve sons of Tancred of Hauteville
Guiscard, the (Cunning): Son of Tancred de Hauteville and brother to eleven warriors
Harald Fitzroy: Marchis of Ambrières, Prince of Capua, brother of Robert and Floki, The 'Papal Shield'
Harold Godwinson: Powerful Saxon Earl and King Edwards emissary

Hild: Wife of Torstein the Warrior Skald
Kjartan: First captain of the Riders of Regneville
Lanfranc of Pavin: Robert Fitzroy's mentor and archbishop of Caen
Mathilda: Duchess of Normandie and wife of Duke William
Oddo: town priest of Regneville
Olaf Trygvasson: King of Norway who was killed at the Battle of Svolde
Robert Fitzroy: Lord of Mortain, Chancellor of the Duchy of Normandie
Rolande of Coutances: Captain of Mortain, friend and confidante of Robert Fitzroy
Rolande of Coutances: Captain to the Lords of Mortain
Rolf: Count of Pirou
Rouallon: Lord of Dol
Serlo; One of Tancred's twelve sons and captain of the Riders of Regneville
Sigrid: Daughter of Bjorn and Turid
Tancred: Count of Hauteville
Torstein Rolloson: Grandfather to Robert, Harald, Floki and Siegrid Fitzroy, Wandering Warrior of Haugesund
Turid: Wife of Jarl Bjorn and matriarch of the Fitzroy clan

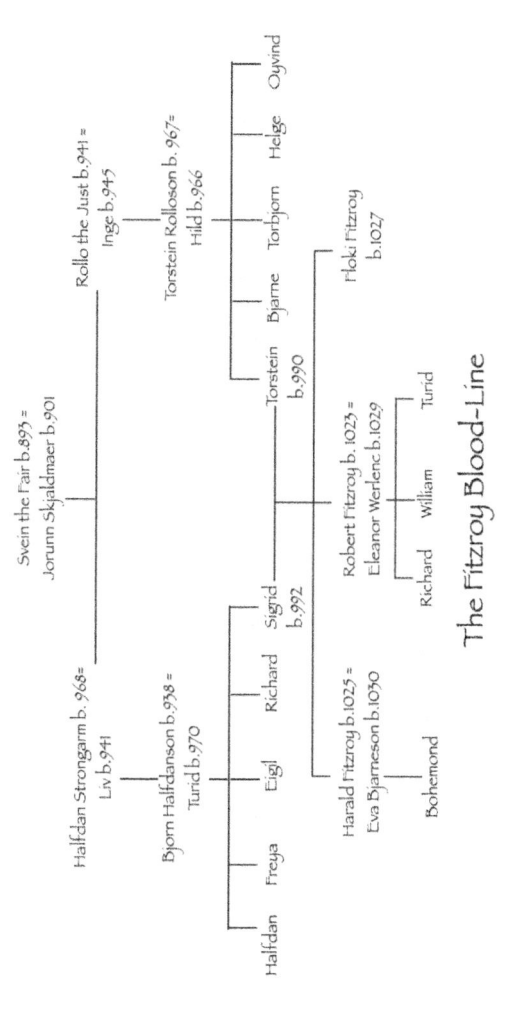

The Fitzroy Blood-Line

```
Svein the Fair b.893 = Jorunn Skjaldmaer b.901
                │
    ┌───────────┴────────────┐
Halfdan Strongarm b.968 =    Rollo the Just b.941 =
    Liv b.941                    Inge b.945
    │                            │
Bjorn Halfdanson b.938 =     Torstein Rolloson b.967 =
    Turid b.970                  Hild b.966
    │                            │
 ┌──┬──────┬──────┬───────┐   ┌──────┬─────────┬──────┬──────┐
Halfdan Freya Eigl Richard Sigrid Torstein Bjarne Torbjorn Helge Oyvind
                          b.992  b.990
                            │
         ┌──────────────────┴──────────────────┐
Harald Fitzroy b.1023 =              Robert Fitzroy b.1025 =        Floki Fitzroy
    Eva Bjarneson b.1030                 Eleanor Werlenc b.1029         b.1027
    │                                    │
Bohemond                         ┌───────┼───────┐
                              Richard  William  Turid
```

Printed in Great Britain
by Amazon